Negative Peace
David S. Florig

David S. Florig

Book cover design by David S. Florig

Ocean Park, Maine

Library of Congress Control Number: 2025922527

ISBN: 979-8-9885545-6-1 (Paperback)

ISBN: 979-8-9885545-7-8 (Hardback)

BISAC:

FIC037000 FICTION/Political

FIC019000 FICTION/Literary

FIC014000 FICTION/Historical/General

Printed in the United States of America

10 9 8 7 6 5 4 3 2 1

www.davidflorig.com

To my wife, Nancy, who, for the fourth time now, has cheerfully endured the writing and editing of a book.

Acknowledgements

I am extremely grateful to my faithful advance readers, Scotte and Paul Mason, who offer insight, wisdom, and encouragement, usually during and after some Thai food. They often see what I don't.

Preface

I'm tired of the wars and fighting. During my lifetime, somewhere in the neighborhood of 40,000,000 people have died in wars. *Forty million people.* The number grows larger every day. Every one of them was a living, breathing, human being with family and friends. As this story was being written, two major wars were raging.

Negative Peace explores one man's attempt to stop it. The story takes him from his hometown of Bucksport, Maine, to the curling club in Belfast Maine, to the White House. Along the way, he learns about Negative Peace and Positive Peace. Negative Peace, he concludes, will have to do.

The sport of curling plays a small, yet significant role in *Negative Peace*. Curling is certainly a niche sport, known primarily from being featured on television every four years during the Winter Olympics. Most people are wholly unfamiliar with the sport, or know it only as a curiosity. For those people, I suggest reading the Appendix first, which provides a primer on the game's long history, how it is played, the equipment that it is played with, and the ice surface that it is played on.

A little understanding of the game and its history dating back more than five centuries to the frozen lochs, rivers, and ponds of Scotland will help provide context to the story. Fortunately, an in-depth knowledge of the game is completely unnecessary to enjoying the story in its own right.

Negative Peace contains elements of historical fiction, particularly some presidential and Maine history, which is woven into the tapestry of the story. For the most part, I think that I've gotten it right, or at least come close. If I haven't, you have my email.

David S. Florig
Ocean Park, Maine.

Chapter 1
Trust

"The best way to find out if you can trust somebody is to trust them." – Ernest Hemingway

"Can we trust them, Bao?" he asked in Mandarin, almost whispering. He was asking himself as much as he was asking her. He didn't turn to look at her when he asked, he simply stared straight ahead. The question had kept him awake most of the night – *Can we trust them*? Chinese President Yu Song and his wife were standing on the balcony of the Blair House in Washington, D.C., outside of their bedroom, on the final morning of their state visit. It was May. The spring air enveloped them.

President Yu had witnessed sunrises on every continent other than Antarctica. Everywhere, they were the same. The rising sun triggered something primal in him. Re-birth? Hope? Second chances? Creation, maybe? He held a cup of steaming Sumatran coffee in his right hand, the hand that was missing the tip of its pinkie. Steam wisping from the coffee hovered in the sticky, humid spring air. The aroma mingled with that of azaleas and rich, damp soil and mulch from the awakening gardens below.

He was facing east, watching the sun rise, as it morphed from red, to orange, to yellow. President Yu had been standing there since well-before the sun inched its way over the horizon. He was still in his silk pajamas. At

6:32 a.m., Washington was quiet, but rousing. Important people were in the planes droning above, heading off to important places to discuss important things with important people. The coffee wasn't helping President Yu answer the question which had troubled him all night, depriving him of sleep. His instincts told him that he could trust the new American president. Experience counselled that he could not.

President Yu's gaze shifted a few times, across the lawn of the White House to the North Portico. It was involuntary. He somehow expected that he might see President Sheehan. He did not. President Yu suddenly sneezed, then sneezed again, hard enough that he splashed coffee onto his bare feet.

"Are you alright?" Bao asked.

"Pollen. The pollen is awful," Song said. "I have a tickle in my throat. My eyes itch. My nose itches." Pollen rules springtime in Washington.

"Do you need your medicine?" Bao asked. She always asked and always got the same answer. He was a stubborn child when it came to his medicine. Said it made him jumpy.

"No, I'm fine. Let's go back inside," he answered. President Yu took one more glance at the White House. It really was a beautiful building, especially by the dawn's early light. Bao noticed him staring at it. She guessed what he was thinking.

"It was built by slaves, you know," Bao said. She had studied before their arrival in America.

Four months later, the American president of less than a year was asking the same question. "Can we trust them, Steph?" Joshua and Stephanie Sheehan, the first Mainers to occupy the White House, were side-by-each on the balcony adjoining their bedroom at the Diaoyutai State Guesthouse in Beijing. The state visit to China was winding down. The Secret Service was watching them from somewhere, probably multiple somewheres. It always was.

Stephanie took hold of his hand. The dry, crisp September air embraced them. It smelled of flowers and of leaves, of lotuses and willows, of the nearby ponds. President Yu had restricted driving and manufacturing in the week before the state visit to alleviate Beijing's nasty air quality. It helped a little. The autumn morning smelled delicious.

A flock of azure-winged magpies cackled and chattered below, energized by the return of the sun. The sparrows cheeped as they pecked the grass for seeds. Joshua took a deep, intentional breath and held it. The sun, yellow and bright, had risen completely over the horizon.

Their coffee, brewed from Yunnan Province beans, tasted nuttier, more chocolatey, than the coffee back home in America. They drank slowly, savoring the unfamiliar flavor and aroma. "Aren't the gardens amazing?" Stephanie asked. She didn't have an answer for the question she knew was troubling him. She asked about the gardens to break the silence, to draw him out. He was thinking about something altogether different.

"I'm sorry, what?" Joshua asked.

"The gardens. Aren't they awesome?"

"They're beautiful," Joshua said.

"They're 800 years old, you know," Stephanie said. She had studied before their arrival in China.

J oshua rose long before the sun that morning in Beijing. He had been standing outside, looking at the few stars bright enough to be visible. His thoughts transported him back to Bucksport, Maine, to home, to a simpler time when he didn't have to worry about this kind of thing. To when what he did or said didn't change history. To one particular night long ago with Stephanie. He didn't choose the memory, it chose him.

It was December, it must have been the fourteenth or fifteenth, when they were still newlyweds. He remembered taking Stephanie to nearby Fort

Knox, where there was little light, in the middle of the night. It was frigid, maybe fifteen or twenty degrees, but the heavens were clear and dark and glorious. The waning crescent moon kept the sky dark. They were lifelong Mainers, so it didn't really seem *that* cold. Joshua took her to Fort Knox to watch the Geminid meteor shower. All week, he had tracked the forecast to see whether the meteors would be visible. The weather cooperated. Sharing a thermos of coffee, they settled into folding chairs and looked up. It took time for their eyes to adjust to the night sky.

"Where do I look?" Stephanie asked. "Just anywhere?"

"Look for Gemini," Joshua answered. "The meteors will look like they're coming out of Gemini. It's how they got their name."

"I don't know Gemini," Stephanie said. It surprised him.

"You're kidding. Really? Gemini's your birth sign and you don't know where it is?" He assumed that everyone knew their constellations, especially the Zodiac.

"Sorry. I know Orion. I know the Big Dipper and the Little Dipper. I don't know Gemini, though. Mrs. Cochran made us learn the constellations in fourth grade science, but I only remember those three," Stephanie said. "I can name all of the planets in order, though," she announced proudly. "Mercury, Venus, Earth, Mars, Jupiter, Saturn, Uranus, Neptune, Plu . . ." She stopped mid-syllable. "Oooo! Did you see that one!" She grabbed his arm and pointed. "Quick! Make a wish!" As quickly as it flashed across the sky, it vanished. *"Star light, star bright, first star I see tonight, I wish I may, I wish I might, have this wish I wish tonight,"* she recited.

"I missed it," Joshua said. "You almost got your planets right."

"Almost?" Stephanie repeated the list slowly, thinking, counting the nine on her gloved fingers. "Mercury, Venus, Earth, Mars, Jupiter, Saturn, Uranus, Neptune, Pluto. That's it."

"Pluto just got demoted on a technicality. It's not considered a planet anymore. To be a planet, it has to have a clear orbital path. Pluto doesn't. Now it's just a dwarf," Joshua said. "I'll give you credit this time. What did you wish for?"

"You know I can't tell you that. Then it won't come true."

A big meteor shot through the night, lasting a full four or five seconds before flaming out, briefly illuminating their faces the soft yellow of candlelight. "Did you know that meteors are only the size of a grain of sand or a pea? They're tiny," Joshua said. He was enjoying leading the astronomy lesson. The night sky fascinated him. It always had. Stephanie made for a good student.

"Really? It seems like they're big," Stephanie said. They continued their watch. Meteor-watching requires patience and lots of staring.

"They're farther away than they seem, too. Fifty, sixty, a hundred miles," Joshua said.

"No way. I would have guessed a mile or two. They look so close. How do you know all this stuff, anyway? I know they don't teach it in architectural school."

"My father used to bring me here to watch the meteors and learn the constellations. He bought me a telescope when I was ten," Joshua said. Two smaller white meteors raced side-by-side. "Did you see those? I never saw two at once."

"That was awesome!" Stephanie said. "I must be good luck."

"You must be. There's something about the universe that I've never really been able to understand, Steph. I just can't wrap my head around it," Joshua began. "Everything is moving. All the time. Some of the stars are moving away, some are moving closer. Some are moving left, some are moving right. Thousands, tens of thousands of miles an hour. The sun's moving, the earth's moving. But the constellations, the whole sky, looks exactly the same as it's looked for thousands of years. The first people saw exactly what we see. Things never seem to change. How can that be? If it's always changing, why doesn't it ever change?"

"Now that I think about it, it doesn't make much sense, does it?" Stephanie answered. "We probably won't figure it out tonight. Show me where

Gemini is, then let's go home, Copernicus. A warm, cozy bed sounds pretty inviting."

Gemini is, then let's go home, Copernicus. A warm, cozy bed sounds pretty inviting."

Chapter 2

Bucksport, Maine 04416

"I know at last what I want to be when I grow up. When I grow up, I want to be a little boy." – Joseph Heller, Something Happened (1974)

Any excuse to see Miss Jacobson was a good one. Carly Jacobson was the new librarian at the Bucksport Middle School. She replaced Gladys Ledbetter, a mean, surly, thick-necked woman who didn't like kids all that much, especially boys. "You kids settle down!" and "That's enough!" were her favorite admonitions.

Carly Jacobson, on the other hand – Wow! She was fresh out of college, only ten or twelve years older than Joshua and his fifth grade classmates, the boys guessed. Joshua was certain that Miss Jacobson could have been a model in one of his mother's women's magazines. Miss Jacobson favored skirts and dresses that stopped above the knee and heels that accentuated her already statuesque presence. A marvelous contrast to Ledbetter's khakis and black, clumpy shoes.

Miss Jacobson's long, shiny hair always hung loose, and Joshua noticed how often she brushed it away from her face. If she glided by or got close enough, he would catch a fleeting whiff of something that smelled very good. Today, Joshua was in the school library to work on a report.

"Hi, Joshua," Miss Jacobson said. It thrilled him that she knew his name. "Can I help you with something?" Miss Jacobson always wanted to help, unlike old Leadbottom, who was constantly on high alert for gum-chewing or other library malfeasance. He made himself as tall as he could, but it didn't help much. Her hand on his shoulder distracted and flustered him. It took a moment for Joshua to recover his composure.

"I have to do a report about Jonathan Buck and his grave," Joshua finally said, softly. "Do you have any books about him?"

"I'm sure we do," Miss Jacobson said. "Bucksport was named after him, you know. Follow me." She needn't ask twice. She turned and walked as gracefully as a sprite, Joshua studying every breathtaking step as he followed. She stopped at a wall of books and reached for three, Joshua transfixed by every movement.

"These should help," Miss Jacobson said, handing the books to Joshua. "Are you going to use them here or would you like to take them out?"

"I'll look at them here. I can stay for a little while." He would stay all day if he could.

"OK. Make yourself at home and let me know if you need anything else. I'm here to help."

"Thank you," Joshua said, finding a seat with a good view of the circulation desk. He began flipping through the books, occasionally peeking up, very discreetly, he thought, to see what Miss Jacobson might be doing. Rather than check books out, Joshua elected to do all of his research for this project in the library.

Two weeks after Miss Jacobson got him started, his presentation was ready. Joshua strode confidently to the front of the classroom. He wasn't the least bit nervous. He knew that his presentation would be good. He rather liked public speaking, although he didn't know then that it was called that.

"Colonel Jonathan Buck was the founder of Bucksport," he began. "It used to be called Buckstown before they changed the name to Bucksport in 1817. Jonathan Buck was a Justice of the Peace. Like a judge. He was a very important man. He sentenced a woman to death for being a witch. Some people say she was hung – I mean hanged." Miss Jacobson told him that people were hanged, pictures were hung. "Before she was hanged, the witch put a curse on Colonel Buck – an evil curse. Miss Jacobson helped me find a newspaper story about what happened." He liked saying her name. Some of his friends looked at each other. They had taken to teasing him about his crush. Joshua read the account from the *Haverhill Gazette*, struggling with a few of the words, even though he had practiced them. He used his most dramatic voice.

Buck was a severe and Puritannical judge who once ordered the execution of a woman accused of witchcraft. The woman went to her death cursing Buck, who stood unmoved. At the moment of her death she allegedly shouted this prophecy:

'Jonathan Buck, listen to these words, the last my tongue will utter. It is the spirit of the one and only true living God which bids me speak them to you. You will die soon. Over your grave they will erect a stone, that all may know where your bones are crumbling into dust. But listen, upon that stone the imprint of my foot will appear, and for all time, long after you and your accursed race has vanished from this earth, will the people from far and near know that you murdered a woman.'

Joshua placed his pencil drawing of Buck's grave on an easel. He had spent several hours in the library at one of the big tables working on it. It showed the ten-foot granite obelisk with its stain resembling a leg or boot below the word "Buck." Miss Jacobson had complimented Joshua's drawing. "You're very talented," she told him. *She thinks I'm talented*!

"This is the witch's leg," Joshua said, pointing at the stain. "People have tried to scrub it off, but it always comes back. They can't make it go away." The fifth-graders thought it was spooky. Some giggled.

"Some people say the witch vowed that she would dance on his grave." Joshua set his second drawing on the easel, showing a witch in a black robe and pointed black hat dancing on the grave. He modeled her after the Wicked Witch of the West from *The Wizard of Oz*. "If you think I'm lying, you can go to Buck Cemetery and see for yourselves . . . If you dare!" Joshua concluded.

Joshua's tale was true, as far as it went, but there are more preposterous versions of the story. One tale is that rather than being hanged, the woman was burned alive. Both were proper and time-tested means of doing away with witches. As the fire consumed her, one of the woman's legs rolled out of the fire and settled at Colonel Buck's feet. Another expands on that version and claims that one of the woman's children picked up the blackened leg and hit Buck with it. Yet another alleges that the woman was pregnant with Buck's child, and that the witchcraft ruse was concocted by the good colonel to do away with that inconvenient little problem. In none of the stories does the woman have a name. Never mind that there are no records of anyone being executed for practicing witchcraft in Maine, or that a Justice of the Peace had no authority to order an execution. A good haunting tale is a good haunting tale. Nearly every day, tourists stop at the monument to marvel at, and take pictures of, the mysterious stain. It really *does* look like a foot.

The next school year, Joshua had to prepare a report on the "Red Paint People" of Bucksport. He had never heard of the Red Paint People, but he knew that Miss Jacobson must have. He had grown three inches over the past year, and his voice had gotten a little lower, but he still had to look up at her. She, on the other hand, hadn't changed at all.

"Wow, Joshua, you've grown so much," Miss Jacobson said. *She noticed! She actually noticed!* "What can I help you with today?"

"I have to do a report on the Red Paint People. Do you have any books about them?" Joshua asked.

"Red Paint People? I'm afraid I've never heard of them," Miss Jacobson said. Joshua was surprised. He imagined that Miss Jacobson knew everything. "Are they from Bucksport?"

"I think so," Joshua answered, one belief shattered. Miss Jacobson still looked and smelled amazing.

"I'll see what I can find out," she said. "Come back tomorrow and I'll try to have something for you, OK? I have to go meet my boyfriend for lunch." Did she really say *boyfriend*?

The next day, Joshua returned to the library, slightly less excited about seeing Miss Jacobson. "I only found two books that mention the Red Paint People," she said. "These might be a little difficult for you, but you can ask me if you don't understand something."

Joshua took the books and found his seat with the good view. He began reading and thinking about his report, sneaking the occasional peek at the circulation desk as Miss Jacobson touched up her makeup and headed out. He had trouble picturing what the Red Paint People might have looked like or what they might have worn. These drawings would be trickier than Buck's grave. A week later, he presented his report to the class.

"Four-thousand years ago, before white people came to Bucksport, the Red Paint People lived here. Nobody knows what happened to them or why they left. Nobody knows much about them, except for two things. They were fishermen who went into the ocean in canoes and caught swordfish. They were very good fishermen." Joshua displayed his first drawing of Red Paint People, drawn to look like Native Americans, spearing a gigantic swordfish nearly as large as their canoe.

"The only other thing we know about the Red Paint People is that their graves leaked *blood*," he said. "That's why they're called the Red Paint People."

"Ewww!" his classmates responded in unison. Some squirmed. "Cool!" one of his friends said.

Joshua revealed his second drawing, blood flowing like a lava stream from a grave. "The graves didn't really bleed," Joshua said. "That's just what the farmers said. When the farmers accidentally dug up graves, this red stuff that looked like blood came out. When someone was buried, the Red Paint People put a lot of red stuff in the grave – red hematite and ochre, whatever they are. The farmers were scared and thought that the ground was bleeding. When they found the bones, they knew it was a grave.

"Nobody really knows why they left or where they went. Maybe they caught all of the fish. Some of the graves are on MacDonald Street next to Wilson Hall . . . but don't try to dig them up!" As his classmates clapped, Joshua noticed Miss Jacobson leaning in the doorway, smiling.

Joshua's reports, and Miss Jacobson's help, got him interested in learning more about Bucksport's history. It also gave him a good excuse to spend time in the library. Every new story he learned, he shared with his friends in the lunchroom. They took to calling him "History Man" or "Mister Jacobson," if they wanted to fluster him.

"Did you ever hear about the elephant named 'Charlie?'" he asked one day.

"There's a paper mache elephant named Charlie in the public library," one of his friends said.

"Not that Charlie, the real elephant named Charlie," Joshua said. "More than a hundred years ago there was a circus in Bucksport. Charlie escaped from the circus and roamed around town for a few days."

"Did they catch him?" one asked.

"Yep. A pit bull cornered him and he was captured. Why would an elephant be afraid of a dog he could step on and squash? Maybe elephants aren't really that smart." The story of Charlie inspired one of Joshua's "David Dudd" comic strips that he started drawing in eighth grade.

The next week, Joshua entertained his friends with the story of a notorious unsolved murder in Bucksport, a cold, cold case from the late nineteenth century. On the night of September 17, 1898, fifty-two-year-old Sarah Ware went missing. Sarah Ware worked for local families as a babysitter and housekeeper. On the night she disappeared, Sarah was making her rounds to collect her weekly fees. One of her stops was at the home of William Treworgy. Sarah never returned home that night, and was never seen alive again. Days later, her body was discovered near Miles Lane, in some brush, her head severely beaten, her skull fractured. "When the police were removing the body, Sarah's head fell off!" Joshua announced. His friends liked that part of the story.

William Treworgy, owner of both a quick temper and violent disposition, was arrested after a blood-stained hammer bearing the initials "WT" was discovered. During the investigation, two witnesses told police that Treworgy had paid them to move Ware's body on the night she was murdered, although both recanted that testimony before trial. Somehow, the hammer went missing before the trial, too. With no witnesses and no murder weapon, Treworgy was acquitted. But . . . just in case there might be another trial, Sarah's head was stored in the evidence room at the Hancock County Courthouse for eighty long, lonely years.

When two unsuspecting clerks discovered Sarah's head decades later, arrangements were made for it to be buried, reunited with the rest of her body, in her grave at Oak Hill Cemetery. Except that it wasn't. When Sarah's grave was excavated, there was no body in what was supposed to be poor Sarah's resting place. Her family had apparently surreptitiously moved her headless body to another, unmarked, grave, leaving her head in one grave and the rest of her in another, somewhere. Another of Joshua's comic strip series featured a search for Sarah's grave.

Bucksport also claims its own small place in a tiny corner of pop culture history. *Dark Shadows,* the wildly popular Gothic soap opera from the 1960s, featuring vampire Barnabas Collins, was set in the fictional town of Collinsport, Maine, which was based loosely on Bucksport. Very loosely, since not a single scene was ever shot in Bucksport, nor was Bucksport ever mentioned by name.

Into that quaint, quirky little town of barely 5,000 on the Penobscot River, Joshua Sheehan was born, checking in at seven pounds, ten ounces, and twenty inches. Until becoming Maine's governor and moving to Augusta, it was the only place that he ever lived, other than while away at college. Joshua was raised in Bucksport, went to school in Bucksport, bought a home in Bucksport, opened a business in Bucksport, and got married in Bucksport. If he had any say in it, he would take his eternal rest in Bucksport, preferably on high ground, with a grand view of the Penobscot River.

Charles and Marjorie Sheehan owned a federalist-style home in the heart of town. It was classic, white, and exquisitely cared for inside and out. It was the home where Charles had been raised. The living room was dominated by an enormous stone fireplace, long ago used for heat and cooking.

"Joshua! Your father's making a fire. Do you want to help?" Marjorie would call, usually on a Friday or Saturday evening. Joshua raced down the stairs to take his place on the hearth. Boys like it when their fathers need their help.

"Crumple up some newspaper for me," Charles always said. It was Joshua's job until he got older and was allowed to light the fire, one of life's grandest milestones.

"Now, pass me the box of kindling," Charles said. "These go on top of the newspaper. Here, you try." Joshua carefully arranged sticks atop the newspaper.

Kindling in place, Charles struck the match and reached in. The fire started slowly, then spread to the kindling, hissing, spitting, and crackling as it caught. With the kindling going, Joshua helped Charles add the smaller logs. Charles checked the damper and closed the screen. "Always make sure the damper's open when you make a fire," he said every time. "And always close the screen so that sparks don't fly out." Joshua loved staring at the fire as it grew and radiated. He liked how it made his face feel. Their dog, Jesse, liked to lay on the hearth by the fire, too. Jesse's ears got really hot.

The mantel over the firebox was populated with candles, a silver snuffer, an antique mechanical clock which Marjorie carefully wound with a key each morning, and pictures. There was a black-and-white wedding picture, a family portrait with Joshua sitting on Marjorie's lap, and a portrait of a man Joshua didn't know. The man looked happy. Joshua had seen his picture before, at some friends' houses, restaurants, the library, maybe some other places, too. Joshua knew that he must be important. "That's President Kennedy," his mother explained one time. "He was from New England. People loved him."

Joshua spent his pre-K and kindergarten years at the G. Herbert Jewett School on Bridge Street, before attending Miles Lane School for grades 1-4; Bucksport Middle School, with Miss Jacobson, for grades 5-8; and finally Bucksport High School. Joshua was a fairly typical middle-class Maine boy, if there is such a thing as a "typical" boy. He played sports, Little League baseball and town rec soccer and hockey, mostly. He liked baseball and hockey – soccer, not as much. He preferred playing outdoor hockey with his friends over the highly-structured, adult-dominated youth hockey run by well-meaning, but uniformly over-zealous parents. Saturdays playing pond hockey with only kids around was way, way better, without some public address announcer excitedly bellowing the name of a nine-year-old goal scorer to ruin the fun – *"River Raptors goal scored by number twenty-two, Joshua Sheeeeeeee-han!!!"* – and no fanatical coach perturbed with their puck movement on the power play. Only kids announcing the game as they played. They pretended to be whoever they wanted, usually someone from the Boston Bruins or an older local kid who made it all the way to the University of Maine Black Bears. It was during a pond hockey game that Joshua took the puck that left him with a lifetime scar above his right eyebrow.

In the winter, Joshua's father took him ice fishing, usually at Silver Lake, where they caught perch, an occasional bass, and crappie. Charles showed Joshua how to clean the fish, which Joshua didn't care for all that much. It was gross. At night, his mother pan-fried fresh fish while father and son took their showers to get rid of the bait and fish stench.

Joshua was a good athlete – not great, but good. He was better than most, less talented than some. What he lacked in physical tools, he compensated for with determination and will. He tried harder and played smarter than most other kids, learning to be a good teammate. He also welcomed and thrived under pressure, happy to be the goalie in hockey and the pitcher in baseball. Not everyone was wired to succeed under pressure, but Joshua was.

Joshua also did well in school. He wasn't some kind of prodigy or "gifted" student, just a smart, curious kid who liked learning. None of his teachers or counselors predicted greatness in his future, but they all saw good things.

Arithmetic and math were his favorite subjects, but he also enjoyed art and drawing. In eighth grade, he developed his own comic strip, featuring twelve-year-old David Dudd, which he shared with his friends. At night, after finishing his schoolwork, he worked on that week's strip at the small drafting table his parents had given him. Fridays were release days for the new comic.

David Dudd and his dog, Julius, solved mysteries and rescued people from all kinds of distress in the town of Port Buck. Joshua's friends suggested some harrowing situations in which David Dudd and Julius could come to the rescue. It was invariably hapless adults who needed David Dudd's assistance. He always succeeded in saving the day. After each success, David and Julius shared ice cream from the Lick It Good dairy bar, boy and dog licking from the same cone.

Joshua knew early on that he wanted to be an architect, although he had no real idea what an architect did other than build things. His obsession with Legos was an early indicator, although lots of kids, and a surprising number of adults, are Lego-obsessed. Every birthday and gift-bestowing occasion meant more Legos. Boxes kept them sorted by color and shape. He preferred building his own creations – not the things that came pre-designed and only needed assembling, like Darth Vadar or the Empire State Building – such as stadiums full of Lego people or bridges and skyscrapers. Building the pre-designed things only involved following instructions, not creating anything new. Joshua wanted to create things.

He applied to four colleges – Boston Architectural College, the University of Maine at Augusta, the University of Massachusetts Amherst, and Roger Williams University in Rhode Island. Each of them, except for the University of Maine at Augusta, offered both bachelor's and master's programs in architecture. If the University of Maine had a master's program, it would have been his first choice, because he would be able to stay home in Maine and study. It didn't, so he settled on Boston Architectural College. The University of Massachusetts Amherst rejected his application, and he passed on Roger Williams, preferring Boston over Providence. That, plus the fact that Boston Architectural was closer to home.

As Joshua discovered all along the way, it isn't easy becoming an architect. First, he had to be accepted into a National Architectural Accreditation Board-approved college or university program. Then, he had to graduate, in his case with 140 credits at the undergraduate and 30 credits at the graduate level. Boston Architectural College awarded him his Master of Architecture, *cum laude*. Not *magna cum laude* or *summa cum laude*, but plain old *cum laude*.

After graduation, Joshua accepted a job with Strong and Doddington, a mid-sized architectural firm in Bangor where he had interned for two summers. Internally, employees used the acronym "SAD," although the firm was anything but. It was a fun, fast-paced, challenging place to work and learn.

Strong and Doddington was a general-practice firm, working mostly on smaller projects like homes, small businesses, warehouses, expansions, and remodels. It was great experience for Joshua, gaining exposure to a broad array of projects, and being mentored by accomplished partners who were committed to quality of work, not just quantity of work. Both Kyle Strong and Harry Doddington took time to explain the business aspects of budgeting, billing, and running a firm, impressing on Joshua that quality of work, no matter how exceptional, wouldn't matter a whit without quantity of work. "Gotta pay the bills" was Harry's mantra.

Working at Strong and Doddington enabled Joshua to satisfy the requirement of having 3,500 hours of work under the supervision of a licensed architect before he himself could become licensed. As soon as he completed his required hours, Joshua took the Architect Registration Examination. Until he passed the exam, he couldn't call himself an architect.

The examination itself is time-consuming, comprehensive, and grueling. There are six parts – Practice Management, Project Management, Programming and Analysis, Project Planning and Design, Project Development and Documentation, and Construction Evaluation. While some candidates take up to three years to complete the examination, Joshua finished it in fourteen months. At last, he could announce himself to the world as an honest-to-God architect.

Three years after joining Strong and Doddington, Joshua, newly-armed with his license, struck out on his own, opening a firm in Bucksport, where he still lived. It was a leap of faith. He didn't know if there was enough work in Bucksport to make a successful go of it, but his ties to the community would help. Joshua designed homes, additions, remodels, businesses, and public projects, painstakingly forging a name for himself with hard work, creative, yet practical designs, attention to detail, and growing commitment to sustainability. His projects were consciously designed to reduce their carbon footprint and environmental impact, incorporating sustainable energy elements whenever the client was willing. Solar was popular, but geothermal and wind also increasingly succeeded on smaller scales. As much as he learned at Strong and Doddington, and as much as he valued his time there, Joshua felt that the firm wasn't completely invested in those goals, which was one reason he decided to give it a go on his own. That, and to work in Bucksport. It was slow going, but Joshua steadily built a viable practice.

In addition to getting his firm up and running, often working long hours alone, Joshua volunteered with two local nonprofits. His favorite volunteer job was at the Hancock County Animal Welfare Association on Saturdays, where his main responsibility was walking and exercising the dogs. He loved dogs. All dogs. Cats, he could take or leave. To him, cats seemed far less invested in the owner-pet relationship than dogs.

His parents had adopted a dog – a Collie/Husky mix named Jesse – when Joshua was in kindergarten, and Jesse was with them until Joshua's senior year in high school, when time and age set about their cruel work. Joshua sat on the veterinarian's floor stroking Jesse's head and talking to him during Jesse's final moments as his leg was shaved and the poison injected. All too soon, Jesse took one final, desperate gasp, never exhaled, and went still. Joshua closed Jesse's eyes and rubbed his own. It was then that he understood Agnes Sligh Turnbull's wise, awful words, *"Dogs' lives are too short. Their only fault, really."*

Joshua and his father carried Jesse to the car and gently laid him in the back seat, covering him with a blanket. They buried Jesse and his favorite toys in a place of honor in their back yard, marked by a single granite stone. "Jesse loved you very much, you know," Joshua's father told him.

At the animal shelter, Joshua fell hard for a two-year-old Pit Bull mix, or maybe a Staffordshire Terrier mix, named Lily. What the "mixed" part was, no one could really say. Everyone had an opinion, though. Doggie DNA testing to find out seemed a little excessive to Joshua. Joshua described Lily as, "Mother – Pit Bull. Father – from good neighborhood."

Lily was begging for Joshua to free her from the shelter. She told him with her eyes. She promised to be a good girl if he would only take her home with him, which he did. And she was a good girl, as she had promised. Not "destructive" as her surrender papers so slanderously claimed. Now that he owned a house, Joshua could finally have a dog again. A house can't properly be called a home without a dog.

Joshua took to calling her Lily Munster. Sometimes just Munster. Lily was small for a Pittie, only around thirty pounds. She was an inveterate snuggler, getting as close to Joshua as she could, staring incessantly at him, watching every movement, with the odd, inexplicable habit of pressing her face as hard as she could against his when she wanted something, usually food. Lily was also an indefatigable ball-chaser, happy to chase it for as long as her human would oblige.

Joshua's other volunteer project was with Habitat for Humanity, where he had been volunteering since high school. His mother suggested it when it became obvious that Joshua was serious about architecture. Volunteering with Habitat cemented his desire to become an architect, and he learned so much about construction and plans and blueprints from the older hands, although, as a student, he usually served mainly as a go-fer. After becoming an architect, other volunteers, and even Habitat employees, now sought his counsel when tricky problems arose.

And then, he met Stephanie Gagne.

Chapter 3

Joshua and Stephanie

"What do I know of man's destiny? I could tell you more about radishes." –
Samuel Beckett, Enough (1965)

"Do you like Thai food?" Stephanie Gagne leaned in and asked. They were sitting in the warm room of the Belfast Curling Club after their game.

"Love it," Joshua answered.

"Perfect. You can take me to Fon's Kitchen, then, if you want. It's right downtown," Stephanie offered casually. "The food's amazing. So are the spicy margaritas."

Joshua wasn't anticipating being asked out on a date. Not yet, anyway. "When?" he asked.

"Whenever you'd like. But I wouldn't wait too long, if I were you. You might not get this chance again," she said. She was unabashedly flirting. "Life is full of missed opportunities." Eighteen months later, they were married. No description of Stephanie Gagne could possibly do her justice, at least to Joshua.

Joshua was introduced to curling at the Belfast Curling Club in Belfast, Maine, by his parents when he was eleven years old. The club was a forty-minute drive south from their home in Bucksport, but it was well-worth the trip. Joshua began curling with a few other kids, at his parents' suggestion, in the junior program, where he excelled. He honed his slide and delivery, and quickly became quite good at the game, so good that he usually played with the adults.

The Belfast Curling Club is the only curling club in Maine with its own curling facility and dedicated curling ice. The Belfast club features three sheets of curling ice, locker rooms, a kitchen, a warm room with a bar, and a banquet room. That sounds larger and fancier than it is. The club was built in 1959, on a parcel of land which local curlers flooded in the winter to play the outdoor version of the game, as it had been played for centuries, on frozen lochs, ponds, and rivers, originally in Scotland.

The Belfast Curling Club was founded by Dr. Norman Cobb and some of his Canadian curling buddies from the St. Stephen Curling Club in New Brunswick. Before the club was built, curlers from Belfast crossed the Canadian border to St. Stephen just to curl indoors. The Belfast club stands next to several abandoned, rusting commercial chicken coops, once home to tens of thousands of noisy, stinking chickens, a vestige of bygone days when Belfast, Maine, was the chicken processing capital of the world. Tens of millions of chickens met their ultimate fate in Belfast in the middle of the twentieth century.

Three years after the Belfast Curling Club opened, members decided that they needed a bigger club, so they razed the three-year-old building to make way for a larger one. It now boasts three sheets of some of the best curling ice in New England. Curlers from all over the United States and Canada converge on Belfast to play in its bonspiels – curling tournaments – like the Maine-iac Bonspiel, the Men's Little International Bonspiel, and the Wood Memorial Bonspiel, where matching Hawaiian shirts are the team uniforms of choice.

One of the charming nuances of the club is found in the warm room, where curlers gather to have a drink, eat, and watch matches playing out on the ice below. Most clubs have chairs set up so that people can watch. Belfast, however, has repurposed some old church pews to that end. Each curling club has its own character and idiosyncrasies, and that is one of Belfast's. It was in that warm room that Joshua and Stephanie met and began falling in love.

Joshua played in a few bonspiels around New England each year with his parents before heading off to college in Boston. They were good enough to win a few, including the Golden Handle Bonspiel in Connecticut and the Mudspiel in New Hampshire. While attending college, Joshua rarely got to play, only when he came home for Thanksgiving, winter break, or spring break. By the time that he came home for the summer, the club was closed for the season, and wouldn't re-open until after he returned to school in the fall. He missed everything about playing, the comradery most of all. After graduation, back living and working in Maine, he resumed playing a couple of times a week. That's when he met Stephanie.

Joshua was well aware, of course, of the unsolved murder of Skye Brodie, which occurred during the Broilerspiel, named in honor of Belfast's chicken-centric past, at the club a few years earlier. Everyone at the club knew about the murder. Bonspielers asked about it – especially the Canadians. Some had their own theories about the case.

Joshua's parents were playing in the Broilerspiel when they learned about Skye's murder. Like everyone who was playing, the police questioned them on the morning that the Canadian woman was reported missing and later found dead. She was murdered in the driveway of an unoccupied Belfast home – no one could ever explain why she was there – by a single blow to the head with a rock. It was an extraordinarily violent crime, no doubt a crime of passion. A club member, Rich Scamman, with whom Skye Brodie enjoyed a casual tryst the night before her murder, was tried for the crime, but he was quickly acquitted. Justice was served, because Rich had nothing to do with it. The murder remains a cold case, Belfast's most notorious, with no serious leads, suspects, or even persons of interest.

Joshua's life changed forever at the curling club when he met Stephanie. There weren't a lot of young adults at the club, but Stephanie and Joshua were two of the few. On a Wednesday night in February, after Stephanie's team had defeated Joshua's, the two teams sat together in the warm room, honoring a curling tradition. Also per tradition, Stephanie, from the winning team, bought her counterpart a drink, a Marshall Wharf Brewing Company oyster stout, as Joshua would forever recall. Every year on their anniversary, he celebrated with that same beer. They struck up a conversation, kindled a connection, and arranged their first date.

As Joshua and Stephanie discovered over pad thai at Fon's Kitchen – hers spicier than his – sitting next to each other in the warm room was not their first meeting. In high school, each had been on the debate team. When Stephanie was a senior and Joshua a junior, they had debated against each other, Joshua for Bucksport High School and Stephanie for Belfast Area High School. Her hometown of Northport was too small to have its own high school. They spent some time over dinner trying to recall the exact wording of the resolution they had debated. They came close to remembering that it was, "*RESOLVED: That the federal government should provide employment for all employable United States citizens living in poverty.*" Stephanie argued the affirmative, Joshua the negative.

"You remember who won the debate, don't you?" Stephanie asked. She was bursting to say it.

"Not really," Joshua answered. "But I have a strong suspicion that *you* might." He was right. She remembered exactly who won.

"I do," Stephanie said. "We won!" She then burst into the Belfast Area High School cheer. "*We've got razzmatazz! Pep, punch, and pizzazz. Hey, you, you've been had! Belfast Lions got razzmatazz! Razzmatazz!*" There was not a hint of self-consciousness about her.

Joshua watched in feigned horror. He did not offer up Bucksport's cheer. A couple of locals gave approving nods on hearing the familiar chant. Adorable probably shouldn't describe a grown woman, but he couldn't think of a better word. Joshua knew then and there.

Stephanie Gagne grew up in Northport, a coastal town of just 1,500 people immediately south of Belfast. Her parents owned a nineteenth-century Victorian cottage on Penobscot Bay, which they spent years restoring. They weren't rich, but they were comfortable. Her father was an editor for *Down East* magazine, her mother a pediatric nurse at MaineHealth. While in nursing school, her mother entered the Miss Maine pageant on a lark, at the wine-inspired urging of her friends. She won the evening gown competition, but only managed to take third runner-up overall. Stephanie inherited a lot of things from her mother's side, although entering pageants was not one of them. She did, however, wear her mother's Miss Maine gown to her senior prom.

Victorian houses have lots of interesting, mysterious places for little girls to explore and play in. They are especially good for finding crannies and hideaways in which to read, undisturbed. Stephanie took full advantage. Rainy days were the best. The chirring of a steady rain on the tiled roof induced a Zen-like state as she lost herself in her books. Her body may have been in a nook in Northport, but her essence was in Avonlea or Misselthwaite or the secret annex at Prinsengracht 263. As an only child, she learned how to entertain herself. Her favorite way was reading. The girls in her books made marvelous surrogates for the sisters she didn't have, telling her stories and leading her on fantastical adventures.

The Gagnes' home was not far from the vacant lot where the doomed Cosgrove Mansion once stood. Cosgrove Mansion was home to Edward Grove, his wife, and their three young boys, Edwin, David, and Geoffrey. On December 14, 1954, Mr. and Mrs. Grove were in Boston for the birth of their fourth child, and had left the boys at home with two caretakers. Wind whistled around the mansion, its shutters, windows, and eaves, muffled by a thick, cold fog. A fire broke out that night, quickly engulfing the wooden structure, claiming the three boys and their caretakers. The wind made the fire's work easy. After the fire, the only things that remained at Cosgrove Mansion were the foundation, two chimneys, and the blackened stone steps leading to the front door. And five charred bodies. Although tragic, the fire would be little-remembered, but for some tourists snapping pictures years later.

When the pictures were developed, the tourists didn't recognize them, nor did they remember taking them. They showed the mansion as it was *before* the fire, not after. Others claim to have done the same thing, taking pictures of the vacant lot, only to find "the house that wasn't there" in the prints. One of the eerie pictures hangs in a Northport diner.

Stephanie knew the story and tried taking pictures of the scene with her phone a couple of times. It didn't work. All of her pictures simply showed an overgrown lot.

"Do you have a camera?" Stephanie asked on one of their early dates.

"I have my phone," Joshua answered.

"I've tried that. I don't think it will work," Stephanie said. "I mean a real camera. One that uses film. The older the better. Like 1950s era."

"My parents have a couple of old cameras. I think they still work," Joshua said. "I can ask."

"Good. Bring them down next time," Stephanie said. "Make sure they have film in them."

"Really? I never would have thought of that," Joshua answered sarcastically. "Thanks, Steph." He had no idea how a film camera worked or how to load film, but he wasn't admitting that to her. His father would show him.

"Just do it. I want to try something," Stephanie said.

The next weekend, Stephanie and Joshua went to the Cosgrove Mansion site. Joshua using one camera, Stephanie the other, they shot two full rolls of film from every angle. Stephanie located a place in town that still developed film. Nothing. Nothing at all. Just a vacant lot. She told Joshua the disappointing news.

Stephanie Gagne was a third-generation Mainer. She definitely wasn't *from away*, a colloquial, pejorative term Mainers tag anyone not born and raised in Maine. Some of the more persnickety old-timers also demand that one's parents must have been born and raised in Maine, too, just to prove their bona fides. Stephanie qualified as a Mainer either way, although her surname hinted at her family's Canadian heritage.

Stephanie's maternal grandparents had made their way to Maine from Canada, settling in Camden, on the mid-coast, where there was good work at good wages. Stephanie's grandfather worked in the Knox Woolen Mill on the Megunticook River, as did fully half of Camden's adult residents at the time. The Knox Woolen Mill mainly produced felt for the E.H. Best Company in Massachusetts. Felt used to line coffins, among other things. When the mill was really cranking in its heyday, suds from the washed wool cascaded down the river to Minot Falls, filling Camden Harbor with soapsuds and turning the surface a frothy, bubbling white.

When Stephanie was a little girl, her grandfather would hold out his hands and ask her to feel them. It was an odd request, for sure. He did it to show her how soft his hands were, odder still. But his hands *were* incredibly soft, a byproduct of decades working with wool. Wool rich in lanolin. Pépère's were not the rough, scarred, callused hands of a shipbuilder or logger or mason.

When Stephanie was thirteen, Pépère was sick, bedridden, dying. Stephanie and her parents visited often, helping Mémé cope with what they each understood was coming soon. Stephanie had taken Pépère's golden retriever, Jacques, home with her months ago, since Pépère could no longer take care of him, and Mémé had more immediate things to attend to. Stephanie always brought Jacques back to see his master and friend when they visited. Pépère usually remembered to have a treat ready for Jacques, until he didn't anymore. Jacques seemed to understand what was happening.

"Pépère, can I feel your hands?" Stephanie asked. It would be the last time. He didn't respond. Working in the mill, and the impending call from the reaper, had left him nearly deaf. She asked again, louder, by his ear. "Pépère, can I feel your hands?"

Her grandfather managed a faint smile, a smile of recognition and understanding, and slowly lifted his hands from under his blanket. Stephanie stroked them. "Still soft," she told him. Pépère nodded.

Stephanie was more athletic than Joshua, although he would dispute that. And she was a better debater, apparently. In high school, she was a captain of the field hockey team. She was fast and aggressive. Belfast High advanced to the semi-finals of the state championship during her senior year. Late in the first half, Stephanie took an errant ball to the nose. Blood flowed fast and heavily from her nostrils, staining the front of her gold uniform, but Stephanie wasn't deterred. She ran to the sideline. "Get me some tissues! Hurry up!"

She stuffed the tissues up her nose and resumed playing, breathing through her mouth. Her coach knew better than to try to pull her out. She looked for Stephanie's parents in the stands. They simply shrugged. Belfast lost the game, and fortunately her nose wasn't broken, but Stephanie arrived at school the next morning with a nasty-looking pair of black eyes, purple, yellow, and swollen. She made no attempt to hide them. They were a badge of honor, and she had earned them.

Like Joshua, Stephanie attended college in Boston, at Simmons University, earning her master's degree in Library and Information Science. Also like Joshua, she immediately returned home to Maine after graduation. Her first job was as assistant director of the Camden Public Library. When the director's position opened up at the Carver Memorial Library in Searsport, Stephanie jumped at the chance. Eventually, after marrying Joshua, she was hired as the director of the Buck Memorial Library in Bucksport, home to Charlie, the paper mache elephant and unofficial town mascot.

Joshua and Stephanie were a couple ever since their dinner at Fon's Kitchen. They did the usual things – movies, restaurants, a few concerts, trivia nights, rock-scrabbling on the coast. They put together their own team at the curling club. The point was to be together.

"Have you ever been to MoMo's?" Joshua asked one Sunday morning.

"Nope," Stephanie said. "I've heard of it, but I've never been."

"Get in the car. We're going to Momo's," Joshua announced. "You're in for a treat." They headed up Route One toward Ellsworth. Half an hour later, they pulled into the driveway, which had five cars squeezed in at varying angles.

"This is it?" she asked. "It looks like somebody's house."

"This is it," Joshua said.

"Why's it called MoMo's?" Stephanie asked.

"Short for 'Motor Mouth.' Apparently, the owner's pretty chatty." They walked into what used to be the house's garage. Its walls were lined with glass-doored refrigerators, packed with dozens of flavors of cheesecake slices. They were greeted by the sweet, thick bouquet of vanilla, baked sugar, and cream cheese. The aromas of sin.

"What'll it be?" Joshua asked. He had already decided on a pumpkin and a chocolate for himself.

"Guess," Stephanie said.

"Raspberry, of course," Joshua answered. Stephanie removed one from the refrigerator.

"How do we pay?" she asked.

"Entirely on the honor system. We just drop the money in the box and go on our merry way."

Once a year, they took the elevator to the top of the Penobscot Narrows Observatory just outside of Bucksport, the tallest public bridge observatory in the world, at 420 feet. The observatory sits atop the west tower of the Penobscot Narrows Bridge, spanning, naturally, the Penobscot River, connecting Prospect to Verona Island. On a perfectly clear day, the 360-degree view is majestic, offering up views of Mount Katahdin, Maine's highest, a hundred miles to the north; Camden Hills, forty miles south, past Belfast and Northport; and the Appalachian Trail to the west. Osprey and eagles soared over the river, scouting for an unfortunate fish swimming too close to the surface. A pair of osprey, mates for life, maintain a nest on the bridge and return to it every spring.

Not every adventure ended perfectly. Being Maine, many places were open or closed on the whim of the owner. At a bookstore in Lincolnville, they encountered a sign in the window reading, "Closed. Back around 12ish." At a brewery in Liberty, a sign read, "Closed. Gone fishing." At an antique store in Unity, "Closed. Back Wednesday, maybe."

Stephanie and Joshua made a long weekend of it in Lubec, Maine. At one time, Lubec was home to more than twenty sardine canneries and thirty herring smokehouses, all gone now. A few hollowed-out shells still stand as ghostly sentries, reminders of Lubec's booming past. Lubec has never fully recovered from the loss of the canneries and the "Lubec sardine ladies" who cut and packed the fish. All of the women who proudly wore the crown as Maine Sardine Queen are gone, too.

They heard from some locals at the Lubec Brewing Company that the clams in Lubec were not to be missed. Joshua, in particular, had been dreaming of them. He had a faraway look all day. They sat down to dinner in a picnic-table-seating seafood joint on the water. The windows were open. The place smelled of salt water, fish, and cooking oil. The waitress, a veteran server long on efficiency and short on small talk, stood over them.

"What can I get you?" she asked. Stephanie opted for scallops. Baked, not fried.

"I'd like the fried clam dinner," Joshua said, his avarice palpable. "Tartar sauce, please. And an Allagash White."

"I'm sorry, honey, we're all out of clams," the server announced.

She didn't sound all that bothered, but Joshua was crushed. It couldn't be. He grimly regrouped and ordered fish 'n' chips. On another day, fish 'n' chips would have been a perfectly fine choice. Today, it was a most dispiriting consolation.

As Joshua took his first forlorn bite, a man in hip waders walked by the table, carrying two heavy metal pails. He ducked into the kitchen. Anticipation swept over the room. Not two minutes later, the server exited the kitchen. "We have clams!" she announced. Some patrons clapped. Not Joshua.

"Of course they do," Joshua mumbled as he forked a piece of fish.

"Gotta be in the right place at the right time, babe," Stephanie said. "If you hadn't been in such a hurry to get here . . ."

While vacationing in Lubec, they visited West Quoddy Head Light, a two-hundred-year-old lighthouse painted in a red and white "candy stripe" pattern, the only lighthouse daymarked that way in the United States. At the lighthouse, for a few minutes, Stephanie and Joshua were the two easternmost people on the United States mainland. They were also standing closer to Africa than anyone on the mainland, only 3,154 miles away. Joshua shot a video. "Can you see Africa, Steph?" he asked. She looked southeastward through binoculars. She was not the least bit shy about being on camera.

"No," Stephanie answered. "Too foggy. Maybe when it burns off. And I think Nova Scotia's in the way." She looked into the camera and ambled directly toward it, slow and easy, like she was narrating a documentary. "Let me tell you the sad, tragic story of Joshua Sheehan and his quest for clams," she said. Joshua hit the red "stop" button. It was simply too soon to joke about such things.

Canada was directly across the Quoddy Narrows, an inlet of Passamaquoddy Bay. In fact, while at West Quoddy Head Light, they were so close that Joshua's phone automatically switched to international, thinking that he was in Canada.

Joshua and Stephanie took a day trip from Lubec to Campobello Island, across the Franklin Delano Roosevelt Memorial Bridge, a short, two-lane bridge connecting the United States and Canada. The Customs officer checked their passports, asked a few innocuous questions, determined that they were just harmless tourists, and wished them a nice visit. The bridge is so-named because the Roosevelts owned a "cottage" on the island, a cottage with thirty-four rooms, featuring eighteen bedrooms and six baths. Only the monied class would call a mansion a cottage. They *so* identified with the common folk.

The first stop was Roosevelt Campobello International Park, where Roosevelt Cottage still stands. When the owner of the cottage passed away in 1908, Sara Delano Roosevelt purchased it as a belated wedding present for Franklin and Eleanor. If you're going to be late with a wedding present, you need to make it a good one. It was at Roosevelt Cottage that FDR first displayed symptoms of polio, at the age of thirty-nine. Joshua and Stephanie stopped on the immaculately manicured front lawn for a quick game of croquet before embarking on the tour.

After touring Roosevelt Cottage, Joshua and Stephanie drove eight miles to the northern tip of Campobello Island to visit Head Harbor Light Station, also known as East Quoddy Lighthouse. Their visit had to be planned and timed perfectly, because getting to the lighthouse is entirely dependent on the rapidly-changing tides in the Bay of Fundy, which rise and fall at five feet per hour.

Head Harbor Light Station stands perched on a tiny islet, accessible only to those adventurous enough to attempt to reach it on foot. Doing so means following a footpath down to the rocky cliff at the end of Campobello and climbing down a steep, rusting ladder built into the cliff, to the wet, rocky, treacherously slippery floor of the Bay of Fundy, fully exposed at low tide.

While Stephanie and Joshua waited on the ebbing tide to expose the floor of the bay, they watched scores of seabirds, and several eagles, go about their daily hunting. When the eagles were successful, they flew directly overhead, back to their nests, a confused fish writhing in their talons. They also saw seals, their heads rising out of the water to catch a breath of air, dolphins, and even what they thought might be a minke whale chasing a school of herring.

"I have a confession to make, Steph. I might as well get it out now," Joshua said as they sat and waited on the receding tide.

"Oh? I don't like the sound of that. Tell me," Stephanie said. "Are you having an affair?" She knew that he wasn't. He wouldn't dare.

"No. It's not that. It's just that you should know . . . You're not the first librarian in my life."

"Really? Who is she?" Stephanie dropped her chin and stared at him over her sunglasses.

"She was my middle school librarian. Carly Jacobson. My first true love. I don't know if I'll ever get over her." Thank God he's just playing, Stephanie thought. It would be a long ride home if he was confessing to something nefarious.

"Listen, Buster, you better get over her, and fast, or I know another librarian you'll have to get over."

When the tide finally went out enough for them to walk across the floor of the bay to Head Harbor Light Station's islet, Joshua asked, "You ready?"

"Sure, but you go first," she answered. "Nervous?" She sensed that he was. It was out of character for him.

"Of course not," he lied. "Let's do it."

Stephanie and Joshua tentatively descended the ladder, Joshua first. As they had been warned, the walk across was tricky, the rocks wet, slimy, and slippery. Joshua took a pratfall, like a cartoon character on a banana peel. Stephanie gasped.

"Are you alright?" she asked. Assured that he was, she started laughing. Hysterically. "Can you do that again? I want to take a video. Do that again!" she said. They finally made it across, their shoes wet and muddy, like the back of Joshua's pants. They climbed the stairs up onto the islet and walked lazily to the lighthouse, swatting at swarms of no-see-ums.

After circling the tower and mugging for selfies, they sat on one of the benches, the cool, salty sea breeze in their faces. The quiet was interrupted only by the scores of screaming, squawking seagulls. They wouldn't be able to linger for long, lest the tide come back in and leave them stranded for twelve hours. Joshua had something he needed to do before they left. Quietly, while Stephanie had her eyes closed and her head tilted back to catch the sun, Joshua got down on one knee in front of her.

"Steph," he said. She heard that Joshua's voice was no longer coming from beside her, but from in front. She opened her eyes. "Will you marry me?"

S tephanie and Joshua's wedding was small and intimate. Four parents, some extended family, and twenty-five friends. No siblings. Neither Stephanie nor Joshua had any. No lavish rehearsal dinner, no gowns and tuxedos, no extravagant destination bachelor and bachelorette parties. Just a simple ceremony in Joshua's backyard, officiated by a friend of Stephanie's parents. Stephanie decided to inject some humor into the ceremony.

"Stephanie, do you take Joshua to be your husband?" the officiant asked.

"I do," Stephanie answered, straight-faced. The officiant turned to Joshua.

"Joshua, do you take Stephanie to be your wife?"

"He does," Stephanie answered. The guests roared their approval.

A New England lobster and clambake followed, then S'mores and juicy IPAs around the fire pit. Lily Munster did an outstanding turn as ring bearer, earning her favorite treat, a crunchy, delicious, dehydrated chicken leg.

The curling club insisted on doing something for them, so it hosted a Sunday morning wedding breakfast the next day, which included three toasts – one, the traditional champagne wedding toast; the second, a toast with the Marshall Wharf oyster stout which Stephanie had bought for Joshua when they first met; and, third, the traditional Drambuie curling toast, a staple at bonspiels in tribute to curling's Scottish roots. When the breakfast was done, the members had one more surprise for the newlyweds – a high-stakes draw to the button, each player throwing one stone, with whoever landed closest to the button the winner. The club announced that the winner would be honored with a crown denoting them "Head of the Household." Emily Carlton, Stephanie's long-time friend, made the cardboard crown, adorning it with cheap, plastic, faux diamonds. The newlyweds played along.

"You can go first, Mrs. Sheehan," Joshua said, bowing and gesturing.

"Oh, no, Mr. Sheehan. I insist. You go first and show me how it's done." Stephanie knew damn well how it was done.

"As you wish," Joshua said. "Pay close attention, now." He knew that everyone in the room was rooting for Stephanie, not because they didn't like him, but just because.

Joshua stepped into the hack and squatted down. He drew himself back and pushed out, as he had done thousands of times before. Just before reaching the near hog line, he released the handle with an in-turn. The stone meandered down the ice, a soft, rumbling sound in its wake. He knew immediately that it was a good shot and tracked it as it began to curl toward the button. Twenty-some seconds after he released it, it came to rest fully within the four-foot ring. It was an outstanding shot. He looked up at Stephanie and shrugged. He half-heartedly tried not to smile.

"Your turn, if you want to bother," he said.

"Oh, why not?" she said. "Nothing to lose." She stepped into the hack and prepared to deliver the stone. Her competitive instinct kicked in.

"You've got this, Steph," her friend and maid-of-honor Emily Carlton encouraged. The others whooped and roared, then went silent as Stephanie prepared for her shot.

She pushed out of the hack, went into her graceful slide, and gave the handle an out-turn. The stone crossed the far hog-line, entered the house, and curled through the twelve-foot ring, then the eight-foot, then the four-foot ring, until it came to a stop just touching the button. Joshua was not at all surprised. The crowd erupted. Stephanie stood and walked over to Joshua. "Just lucky, I guess," she said. Stephanie bowed down as Emily placed the crown on her head.

She lorded it over Joshua for the rest of their marriage. When they disagreed on some decision, Stephanie took care to remind him, "I'm the head of the household, remember?"

It was during one of Joshua's firm's public works projects that he first appeared on the Bucksport Town Council's radar. The council was impressed not only with Joshua's professional acumen and the quality of his work, but also with his obvious love for the town and for Maine. They talked about him and poked around a little to see what more they could learn. They heard nothing but good things, personally and professionally. They decided that they would go ahead and make the ask.

Chapter 4

Moms for Freedom

"Mothers may still want their favorite sons to grow up to be president, but, according to a famous Gallup poll of some years ago, they don't want them to become politicians in the process." – John F. Kennedy, February 19, 1957

"Good morning, Mr. Sheehan. My name is Kevin Ford. I'm on the town council." Joshua was hunched over his drafting table when he took the call.

"Morning, Kevin. But please, call me Joshua. Mr. Sheehan's my father."

"Great. Joshua it is," Ford began. "Listen, I'm wondering if there might be a time when Glenn Williams and I could stop by to chat for a few minutes. It won't take long. You know Glenn, don't you? He's on council, too."

"No, I'm afraid I don't," Joshua said. "But sure, how about tomorrow around one? I'm tied up most of today."

"Perfect. Tomorrow at one it is," Ford said. "Say hello to Stephanie for me." How does he know Stephanie, Joshua wondered.

Joshua only knew Kevin Ford tangentially. The call was a surprise. Joshua assumed that the council had some building project to discuss. Better yet, maybe it was inviting bids, which would have been even more welcome news. Government projects paid pretty well, although not necessarily promptly. He had done some work for the town before.

Joshua had no political ambitions. None whatsoever. He had none of the carefully cultivated, ambitious politician gifts, either. He wasn't a back-slapper or a glad-hander. He didn't have a joke or story always at the ready, just in case he was asked to offer some off-the-cuff remarks. He had no driving desire or impulse for power. He hadn't perfected an on-demand smile. He hadn't even had his teeth whitened. He wasn't registered with any particular political party. He never donated a single dollar to a candidate or campaign. So it came as a complete surprise when he was approached about becoming the next mayor of Bucksport.

What Joshua Sheehan did have, politics aside, was a certain way about him, an authenticity. His manner projected confidence and humility, of taking his work seriously, but himself, less so. It was a way of interacting with people that felt real, genuine, uncontrived. He had a greater capacity for listening than for talking. He was capable of both sympathy and empathy. No, no one was ever going to peg Joshua Sheehan as a politician.

And yet, he also had a steel about him. He was no pushover, no one's fool, and was more than willing to stand for his beliefs. He could hear you out, acknowledge your argument and point-of-view, and then tell you exactly how and why he saw things differently. You could disagree with Joshua Sheehan, maybe even dislike him, but it was hard not to respect him.

Bucksport doesn't elect its mayor directly. Instead, it elects a seven-person town council, which in turn elects one of its members as mayor at its first meeting of the new year. Being a town councilor in Bucksport isn't even a full-time job. Councilors get paid forty dollars for each meeting that they attend, except for the mayor, who pulls down a princely fifty. Not many do it for the money.

The next afternoon, Kevin Ford and Glenn Williams arrived at Joshua's office at precisely one o'clock. They had heard that he was a stickler about punctuality. To Joshua's disappointment, the councilors weren't there to discuss any building projects. There would be no bids to submit. Rather, they wanted to recruit him to run for council, and to possibly become the next mayor. They didn't care or ask about his political views, or his political party, for that matter. That wasn't what interested them in Joshua Sheehan.

"Why me?" Joshua asked. "Don't get me wrong, but are you sure you've got the right guy? I've never even attended a council meeting. Zoning board, yes, but not council."

Ford chuckled. "Yes, you're the guy we're looking for. You are Joshua Sheehan, right? Charles and Marjorie's son? Bucksport High? Born and raised here?"

"Guilty," Joshua said. They had done some homework, Joshua noted.

"Let's cut right to the chase, shall we, Joshua? I'll tell you why we'd like you to consider running," Ford said. "We're looking for someone who knows the town inside and out, someone who has a history here, who knows the rhythm and pulse. Someone committed to Bucksport. Someone who isn't political, doesn't have an agenda. We feel like you might be that guy. There are going to be two openings on the council next year. We'd love to see you fill one of them.

"Listen, Joshua. I'm obviously not in a position to promise anything, but I think you'd be elected and would be a great choice for mayor. Glenn and I aren't the only ones who think so," Ford added.

At first, Joshua was adamant that he had no interest. He had a business to run and nonprofits that he volunteered with. He liked his life as it was. And he disliked politics. Politicians, more precisely. Ford and Williams listened to, and acknowledged, his objections. That didn't mean that they gave up. They appealed to his love for his hometown.

"Let me ask you something, Joshua," Ford said. "You set up shop here in Bucksport. Why? Why not somewhere bigger, higher-income, faster-growing, with the chance for more work?" Ford asked. It was an easy question.

"It's my home, Kevin. Stephanie and I are happy here. I want to see it grow and thrive. We both do," Joshua answered.

"That's exactly what we thought," Ford nodded. "And that's exactly why we're here and it's exactly why we hope you'll consider doing this." Ford and Williams noticed a hesitancy.

"I'm not saying yes or no. I have to talk about it with Stephanie, obviously. I have no idea what she'll say. But honestly, my inclination is to say no," Joshua said. He had heard enough and was ready to get back to work. *Gotta pay the bills* as Harry Doddington used to counsel.

"Fair enough. Talk to Stephanie and let us know what you decide," Ford responded. "Stephanie's the town librarian, right?" Ford knew the answer. Joshua nodded. "We've heard a lot of good things about her."

"They're all true, but don't tell her I said that," Joshua said. "When do you need an answer?"

"How about next week?" Ford proposed. He sensed that Joshua needed some time to think things through. If Ford had needed an answer on the spot, it would have been no.

"OK," Joshua said. "I'll let you know by Wednesday, if that works for you."

"Fair enough," Ford said. "We hope it's a yes. Bucksport could use someone like you. If you have any questions, just ask. You have my number." With that, Ford and Williams stood and excused themselves. It was hardly the meeting Joshua had anticipated. He hadn't woken up that morning thinking, "Boy, I'd really like to run for mayor." From his office, Joshua saw Ford and Williams talking in the parking lot. Unfortunately, he couldn't hear them.

"What do you think?" Ford asked.

"Seems like a decent enough guy. I like him. Doesn't seem all that interested, though," Williams answered.

"No, but who knows?" Ford said. "Maybe he just needs a couple days. You never know." He opened the car door. "See ya, Glenn. Say hi to Beth for me."

"I had a meeting with Kevin Ford and Glenn Williams today," Joshua told Stephanie after they sat down for dinner. "You know them, don't you?"

"I know who they are. Town councilors, right? I don't know either one personally. I think Glenn might have called the library once to ask something about our budget," Stephanie answered. Even if Stephanie didn't actually know someone in Bucksport, she probably at least knew who they were. As the town's librarian, she met and talked with lots of people. She heard, and overheard, lots of town talk, too. People talk much louder in libraries than they used to. They used to whisper, or at least tried to talk softly enough not to get shushed, but those days have passed. Nobody thinks twice about having long, loud public discussions. Their business is everybody's business. Speakerphone conversations for all to enjoy are increasingly popular.

"What did they want? Are they building something?" Stephanie asked.

"I wish, but no. They want me to run for council in November and maybe be elected mayor," he answered. "It came as a bit of a surprise."

Stephanie looked at him, pausing for a few seconds, before asking, "What did they *really* want?" She knew it couldn't be *that*. How could anyone possibly think that Joshua Sheehan would have any interest in running for office?

"They really asked me to run for council. They seemed pretty serious about it," Joshua answered.

"Are you sure you aren't being pranked?" she asked. "Joshua Sheehan for mayor?"

"Pretty sure. Maybe, but I don't think so. I hadn't thought about that."

"Why you?" Stephanie asked. "Don't get me wrong, I think you'd be great, but why you? You're not really the political type. Hard to picture you kissing babies and shilling for votes."

"That's exactly what I asked them, 'Why me?' It's funny, but they didn't ask me a single thing about politics. They didn't even ask what party I belong to, or who I voted for for president, or even whether I like wind and solar. They probably saw my hybrid in the lot, though. That might have been a clue." He had wondered, after Ford and Williams left, why they hadn't asked any questions about his political or social leanings. Not one.

"They said that they were looking for somebody who loves Bucksport and who wants to see it do better. Someone with roots here, who understands the place, sees the potential. They're looking for a real townie, I guess. A lifer," Joshua explained.

"Well, you certainly are that," Stephanie said, smirking. "What did you tell them? Are you going to do it?"

"I told them that I'd talk to you and let them know next week," Joshua said. "We have some time to think about it. No rush. I did tell them that my inclination was to say thanks, but no thanks." Stephanie took a sip of wine. She already knew her answer. When her instincts told her something, she had learned to listen. When she didn't, she usually came to regret it.

"Tell them you'll do it. Call them tomorrow and tell them you'll do it," Stephanie said. Joshua was surprised. Shocked, actually. He had expected a fast and hard no, and he wouldn't have argued. "And while you're at it, tell them that I need a raise."

"I might have to recuse myself from that vote," Joshua said. Just like that, the decision was made.

T he municipal election was held on November 6th. To the surprise of some, particularly Joshua, he was the top vote-getter, garnering 1,654 votes. No other candidate topped 1,500 – not Kevin Ford, not Glenn Williams, not any of the sitting councilors. The only person who wasn't the least bit surprised was Stephanie, who sensed early on that Joshua would be elected. At the library, she interacted with a lot of people, most of whom were anxious to tell her how they were going to vote. Most were not shy about telling her some of the changes they would like to see around town, and she made note.

At the newly-elected council's first meeting, after being sworn into office – *"I solemnly swear that I will support the Constitution and will obey the laws of the United States and of the State of Maine; that I will, in all respects, observe the provisions of the Charter and ordinances of the Town of Bucksport and will faithfully discharge the duties of the office of Town Council"* – the first order of business was selecting a mayor. The council unanimously elected Joshua, as Ford and Williams predicted. The only mild surprise was that the vote was unanimous. Not all votes were. Ten extra dollars per meeting wasn't worth being at the tip of the spear when the property tax rate went up or the roads weren't plowed, and the size of Joshua's electoral victory made the decision easy. Stephanie took to calling him "Mr. Mayor" or "Your Honor," especially when she was annoyed, but sometimes just for fun. "Time to mow the lawn, *Your Honor* . . . Pick up some dog food on your way home, *Mr. Mayor* . . ."

Joshua recognized that Bucksport needed changing. The population was stagnant, the same size as it was thirty years earlier. It was an older population, too. Attracting younger, college-educated people to come to Bucksport, or to stay, was an ongoing challenge. There had to be jobs, opportunities, amenities, places to meet and gather, affordable housing, and things to do. There should probably be a Starbucks, even. The closest one was up in Bangor, and even the most ardent fan wasn't making that drive for a cup of coffee.

One of the first things the council did under Joshua's leadership was to poll residents about what would make Bucksport a more attractive place to live, work, and raise families. They fielded dozens of suggestions, some good, some bad, and some just asinine and mean-spirited. Trolling was still popular. The council chose some of the best, realistic suggestions as priorities – EV charging stations, a brewery, a farm-to-table restaurant, river cruises, a year-round concert venue. Led by Joshua, council set about trying to make some of those things happen, knowing that not all of them were achievable. They slowly started to make progress.

Joshua secured a grant from the state to install five high-speed EV charging stations. He had no idea how to write a grant application, but Stephanie did, and she guided him through it. She was constantly applying for grant funding for the library and knew the process. The trend toward electric vehicles wasn't going to reverse itself, despite the best efforts of climate deniers, but the lack of convenient access to charging stations remained a sticking point. Mainers wanted them, Bucksporters were asking for them, and Mayor Sheehan secured them. Electric cars became an increasingly common sight around town. The charging stations were almost always full. Joshua wrote a grant for five more. A small solar farm in town was also on the horizon.

Maine has more than 160 breweries, more per capita than any other state, but Bucksport didn't have one. Joshua and Stephanie enjoyed craft beer – *Maine* craft beer. They kept a log of their favorites – *Dinner, Oh-J, The Thirsty Botanist, Hipster Apocalypse, Nikita, Gunner's Daughter, Epiphany, Swish, Gigantic Dad Pants, Sexy Chaos.* Joshua knew that many breweries had become community centers, even for places much smaller than Bucksport, hosting trivia nights, author talks, open mic nights, food trucks, fundraisers, and animal adoptions. The residents of Bucksport wanted one of their own.

Working with the Maine Brewers Guild, Joshua convinced some adventurous brewers to give it a try in Bucksport, and offered them a viable venue and tax incentives, which were his only available carrots. Bucksport finally got its own brewery, Bucks ME Brewing. For the grand opening, Joshua and Stephanie were invited to drink the first pour. They also won the first trivia contest by correctly answering the question, "What is the only letter in the English language that is never silent?" Bucks ME Brewing became a favorite spot, even for some who didn't care much for craft beer. The letter "V," Stephanie divined, is never silent.

Joshua was no Starbucks fan, but he knew lots of people who were. He didn't particularly care for their coffee. It always seemed a little burnt. Their hot chocolate was good, though. Nor did he care for the long lines, complicated ordering and fulfillment process, high prices, sizes (tall, grande, and venti), or the fact that he had to give them his name just to get a large – *venti!* - cup of dark roast to go. Waiting patiently was not one of Joshua's strongest attributes, either in traffic or in line, and when he did occasionally go to Starbucks, he invariably found himself behind someone ordering an "iced triple blonde espresso, two pumps white mocha, three pumps cinnamon dolce, oat milk, double extra caramel drizzle." Those poor baristas, he thought.

Putting his personal prejudices aside, Joshua negotiated with Starbucks about opening a franchise in Bucksport. It didn't really fit with their business model – the pedestrian and vehicular traffic was too low, the median age in the town was too high, income was too low – so they balked. Joshua jokingly offered to change the town's name to Starbucksport, which the company's marketing department really liked. Finally, Joshua and the council offered enough perks and a prime location for the coffee chain to agree to give it a try. It became a popular addition to town, although Joshua generally stuck with brewing up a pot of dark roast in his office each morning.

Attracting someone to open a farm-to-table restaurant was more challenging than luring Starbucks. For one thing, restaurants require double, triple, or quadruple the footprint. The restaurant business also boasts far more failures than successes, the capital investment is enormous, profit margins are razor-thin, and attracting and retaining workers is an endless chore. Some studies claim that half of all restaurants fail within the first year and that eighty percent don't survive for even five years.

On the other hand, there were more than 400 farms in Hancock County alone, with thousands more around the state. Maine was a leader in organic farming, boasting the second highest number of organic farms per capita in the country. Organic dining was increasingly popular, especially among younger adults. Farm-to-table dining was on-trend, and local ingredients were plentiful – meat, poultry, root vegetables, fruits, even oysters are farmed in Maine. Two of the women who cooked and worked at the Lost Kitchen in Freedom were willing to give it a try in Bucksport.

Joshua, again with Stephanie's guidance, worked with the women to develop a business plan and to cobble together a patchwork of state and county grants, small business loans, crowdfunding, and investors to get the restaurant up and running. Joshua worked on the architectural plans pro bono and helped tend bar at the grand opening, while Stephanie bussed tables. It brought her back to her college days, painfully reminding her of how tired her feet were after an eight-hour shift. Not long after it opened, you couldn't get a table on Friday or Saturday night without making a reservation days in advance.

While tending bar on opening night, a middle-aged couple sat down. Joshua noticed them immediately when they walked in. "What can I get you folks?" Joshua asked.

"A spicy margarita please, with salt," the woman said.

"A New England IPA for me," the man added.

"Coming right up," Joshua said.

The woman's voice, her face, even her walk, reminded Joshua of something, but he couldn't place it just yet. Whatever it was, it brought a smile. As he readied the drinks, he kept glancing up at her reflection in the mirror behind the bar. She didn't seem to notice, chatting with her companion, her husband, most likely. Joshua had noted the wedding ring. He set their drinks down in front of them.

"Excuse me, but do we know each other?" Joshua asked. The woman looked up. She was still beautiful, but twenty years had added some fine lines and character. Her hair was shorter, too.

"I don't think so," she said, after a brief look. She was wrong.

"Miss Jacobson?" Joshua was a twelve-year-old boy with a crush again.

"I used to be," she said. "It's Mrs. Parsells now. This is my husband, Nate." Nate didn't look that pleased.

"Joshua. Joshua Sheehan. I went to Bucksport Middle School. You helped me with my reports on Jonathan Buck and the Red Paint People." He blurted the words out, dying for her to remember.

She didn't seem to, at least at first. Her face betrayed that. She had helped hundreds, if not thousands, of kids in the library. Then it clicked.

"Oh, yes. Joshua Sheehan. Of course." He couldn't tell whether she was faking or not. She wasn't. "You used to spend quite a bit of time in the library, as I recall," she said through a mischievous little grin. Busted, he thought, blushing. "I understand that you're the mayor now." She *did* remember him!

"I am. Tonight, I'm just the bartender, though."

"Well, you make a darn good margarita," she said. Miss Jacobson sipped her drink.

"Thanks," Joshua said. "So, what have you been doing . . ." Nate put his hand on Miss Jacobson's shoulder.

"Our table's ready, Carly," Nate said. They stood and took their drinks.

"Excuse me, We have to go. It was nice to see you again, Joshua," Miss Jacobson said, then turned and walked away. He remembered that walk fondly. Joshua never saw her again.

It was during Joshua's fourth term as mayor that Moms for Freedom came calling. Three of them showed up at his firm on a Monday morning, unannounced, TV news crew in tow, ready for action. They insisted on meeting with the mayor right then and there. It was urgent, they claimed. Joshua heard the commotion in the lobby and emerged from his office. Someone's perfume ambushed his olfactory. He sneezed. "Excuse me," he said, before sneezing again.

"God bless you," the three women offered in unison.

"Is there something that I can help you with?" Joshua blinked, eyes burning.

"There most certainly is," Mom for Freedom Number One answered. "We would like you to address what is going on in our schools. We have grave concerns about the welfare of our children." At least they weren't frivolous concerns, Joshua thought. Who isn't concerned about children?

Joshua had heard that the MFers were poking around and that they would be armed with their list of books which must – *must* – be removed from classrooms and school libraries immediately, before more irreversible damage was done. He had no tolerance for their mission, their tactics, or their choices of fragrance. Barging into his office certainly wasn't the best approach. "I can give you five minutes. If we still have anything to talk about after that, we'll have to schedule something. Step into the conference room," he said, gesturing. "But please, leave your phones with the receptionist."

"Why do we have to do that?" MFer Number One asked. She always had her phone at the ready for these showdowns, fully charged, usually with the voice recorder turned on to capture the drama.

"Please, just leave them out here," Joshua answered. "And the camera can wait outside," he added, nodding towards the news crew. The news crew was fine with it. MFer Number One was not. She didn't care for the mayor's ill-mannered reception.

Joshua and the three MFers sat. He wished that the windows in the conference room could open. "Now, what exactly is it that I can help you with today?" Joshua asked, deferentially, rubbing his eyes.

Once again, it was Number One who spoke up. "Joshua . . ." she began. There was no mistaking that Number One was the alpha.

Joshua interrupted. "Since you're here on what seems like official town business, you can call me 'Mister Mayor,'" Joshua instructed. He wasn't going to cede any ground, even though he detested being called "Mister Mayor." He didn't even care for "Mister Sheehan." Regardless, there was going to be a hierarchy to the meeting, and he would be at the apex.

Number One was offended, but trudged on. "Very well, *Mister Mayor*," she began, her words steeped in sarcasm. Joshua didn't appreciate the tone, but at least Number One understood who was dictating the ground rules. The mayor's deplorable behavior had her on her heels. She tried to get back on script.

"It has come to our attention that some very inappropriate and highly offensive books are being used in our classrooms and are available in our school libraries. We want you to . . . ." Joshua interrupted her again. He was in charge, and was making sure that they all knew it.

"Forgive me, I'm so sorry," he began, "but I didn't get your names." One by one, beginning, as always, with Number One, the women introduced themselves. Joshua jotted down the names. "And what part of town do each of you live in?" Joshua asked. "You said 'our schools,' so I assume that you all live here in Bucksport, correct?"

MFers Number Two and Number Three nodded. Number One noticeably did not. Joshua remembered where he had seen Number Two before. She had come to a council meeting to rail against opening a brewery in town. Something about a den of iniquity and lascivious behavior.

"So, where do *you* live?" Joshua asked, looking at Number One.

Reluctantly, the alpha replied, "Bangor."

"Bangor. That's a fair ways away from Bucksport. You understand that our school district only encompasses Bucksport, Orland, Prospect, and Verona Island, don't you?" Joshua asked.

"Of course I know that," Number One huffed. She wasn't stupid. "However, I'm very worried about the children. The indoctrination. The grooming."

"I'm sure that you are, just as we all are," Joshua said. "As mayor, what I'm most interested in is the concerns of Bucksport residents. I am less concerned about the opinions of outsiders. What I'm going to do at this point is ask you to step outside while I discuss this with our residents." Number One was appalled at the abysmal treatment.

"Do you mean that you won't even discuss this with me? You're kicking me out of my own meeting?" Number One snapped. She wasn't used to being summarily dismissed. She was an important woman with important wrongs to right.

"First of all, this isn't *your* meeting. Second, yes, I'm asking that you wait outside while I discuss this with the two people who live here. I'm very interested in hearing their concerns. It won't take long." Joshua stood and opened the door. He waited as Number One theatrically collected her things and left. Her every motion brought a powerful whiff.

"Now," Joshua asked the remaining two, "what can I help you with?"

Without their leader, the two remaining Moms for Freedom were tentative, unsure what to do, where to begin. They expected their leader to be their voice. They were only there for support. Number Two finally began to clumsily talk about their concerns and demands about some "highly inappropriate" books poisoning the schools and the unsuspecting children.

"Let me stop you there, Ms. . . . ." Joshua looked down at his notes for her name. " . . . Ms. Clark. As you may or may not know, the Bucksport Town Council is not in any way, shape, or form in charge of running our schools or setting the curriculum. Regional School Unit 25 has that responsibility." Joshua was correct. Council's only role was in funding the school district's budget.

Outside of the conference room window, Joshua saw Number One in the parking lot, talking to the news crew. She was animated, and apparently agitated. The reporter looked bored and anxious to move on to a more interesting story. There might be a fire or a water main break somewhere. He was never going to make anchor covering this crap. He listened and pretended to take some notes. Mercifully, his phone rang. "I have to take this," he said, turning away. Number One wouldn't make the evening news, not even the extended early edition.

"Perhaps I can help point you in the right direction and save us all some time," Joshua offered. "The proper procedure, as I understand it, Ms. Clark, is for you to address your concerns directly with the person you have the issue with. If it is a classroom book that you are worried about, you should contact the teacher. If it is a library book, contact the librarian. I believe that RSU 25 has forms you can fill out to initiate the process."

Number Two was not enamored at the prospect of filling out forms. "We just thought that it might be quicker to . . ."

Joshua interrupted. "How quickly you might want something done isn't really relevant to the process. If you have a complaint and want it resolved, my suggestion is that you go through the proper channels. RSU 25 will move as quickly as possible. Now, I have to get back to work. Thank you for letting me know your concerns." With that, Joshua ushered the women out. As they left, Joshua added, "And just as a heads-up, I believe that the school district will want you to have read the books in question before discussing the issue with you. You have read the books that you're concerned about, right?" The women's faces revealed the answer. Joshua didn't know whether what he said was true or not. He just wanted to make a point. Finally, he advised them, "Next time, please make an appointment. Thank you for coming by."

Back in his office, Joshua leaned back in his chair, clasped his fingers together behind his head, and thought, "God help them if they try this on Stephanie." He thought about calling to warn her that the MFers might be on their way, but decided against it. Stephanie could handle herself. Joshua never found out which books the MFers were concerned about, or why, but he was certain that he had lost two votes.

Most of the residents liked what was happening in town. Things were looking up. They elected Joshua to the council three more times, and the council unanimously elected him mayor each time. It might have continued for years, but Augusta came calling.

Chapter 5
James G. Blaine House

> *My Captain does not answer, his lips are pale and still,*
> *My father does not feel my arm, he has no pulse nor will,*
> *The ship is anchor'd safe and sound, its voyage closed and done,*
> *From fearful trip the victor ship comes in with object won;*
> *Exult O shores, and ring O bells!*
> *But I with mournful tread,*
> *Walk the deck my Captain lies,*
> *Fallen cold and dead.*
> *Walt Whitman – O Captain! My Captain! (1865)*

Just three weeks into his first term as governor, Joshua got the phone call from his mother. The call that everyone knows will come one day. Charles, Joshua's father, had suffered a stroke. A big one. The doctors didn't think he was going to make it.

"How long, Mom? How long? Did the doctors say?" Joshua asked.

"I don't know. They won't tell me. A couple of hours, a couple of days," Mom answered. "I don't know. I'm so confused. They won't tell me anything." Her voice trembled. Joshua heard her fear.

"Who's with you, Mom?"

"Nobody. I'm by myself. I rode in the ambulance."

"Tell the doctor to call me. Tell him the governor wants to talk to him. I'll get there as fast as I can. Find the doctor and tell him to call me. I love you, Mom. I'm on my way," Joshua said. He raced to the residence in the Blaine House to find Stephanie.

"It's my dad. He had a stroke. Let's go! We have to get there fast."

Joshua and Stephanie scrambled to a motorcade and sped toward Bucksport, sirens screaming, lights flashing, when Joshua got another call from Mom. He listened, dropped his head and said, "OK, Mom. I'll be there soon. Find someplace to sit down. I'm on my way," and lowered the phone. Turning to Stephanie, he shook his head. She took his hand in hers. Joshua knuckled on the glass between the front and back seats. The state trooper opened it. "You can slow down," Joshua said.

The next four days were a blur. Funeral arrangements, writing an obituary, tending to Mom, carrying on the business of government, postponing the address to the legislature. The ordeal, which no one is ever quite prepared for, ended with Charles' burial in Oak Hill Cemetery, almost within eyesight of his home. There, he would take his rest and wait for Mom. Being governor, it turns out, doesn't come with immunity. The pale rider has scant regard for station.

Joshua had never considered a cemetery plot or his own funeral. Now, he did. Maybe it was a generational thing, but his parents had purchased their side-by-sides early-on in their marriage, as soon as they could afford to. It may have been symbolic or romantic, a gesture of lifetime commitment. Perhaps it was simply practical and an act of parental kindness, saving Joshua from the chore. Joshua couldn't remember anyone his age announcing, "Hey, guess what I did today? Bought me and the missus two great burial plots. Fantastic view. Got a real good deal, too. Buy one, get one."

His father's burial got Joshua thinking. "Where do you want to be buried, Steph?" The casket had been lowered, the mourners were gone. Joshua and Stephanie stood together, hillside, next to Charles' grave, facing the Penobscot River. Stephanie had never considered the question, either.

"I don't know. I've never really thought about it, I guess. Not to be morbid or anything, but I don't think I'll really care much by that point," she said.

"How about right here? Right where we're standing. As good a place as any, no?" Joshua said. Stephanie took it in. It was peaceful, out of the way. And it was home.

"Not bad. Nice view, not too crowded. Good place for a mayor," she said. She looked at him. "You want that on your headstone? Mayor Joshua F. Sheehan?"

"I think I'll go with Governor. *Governor Joshua F. Sheehan – Devoted and Faithful Husband of Stephanie Gagne Sheehan.*"

She nestled her head on Joshua's shoulder. "That works for me," she said. "I like it."

"G overnor?" Stephanie asked. "Of the whole state?" Being recruited to run for mayor was one thing. This was different.

"Yes, of the whole state," he answered. "They don't have different governors for different parts."

"Well, I'll be damned. When, exactly, did you turn into a politician? If I had known . . ."

The party had been following Joshua's accomplishments as mayor. Younger people were beginning to move to Bucksport and were staying, starting families. School enrollment was up. There were good jobs and things to do. Students were performing better. The average age was inching downward and incomes were creeping up. The town had a newfound spring to its step.

The party thought that Joshua might be able to accomplish some of those things statewide. It also concluded that he was electable, which was its number one criterion in selecting a candidate. If the candidate couldn't win, after all, what was the point? They told Joshua that he was their top choice to run for governor, and that he could win.

Joshua got a fire going in their backyard pit. He had designed and built it himself, a pentagonal stone wall to contain the fire, skirted in bluestone slabs. It was where they habitually retreated to talk. Lots of decisions were made while staring into the fire. The hissing, crackling, and glow calmed their minds and grounded them. Stephanie poured two Bucks ME beers and brought them out.

"What's the worst that could happen if you run?" Stephanie asked.

"I win," was Joshua's immediate response. "Being mayor didn't really change anything for us, except add a few things to the calendar. Governor would be different. I'd have to close the firm, which, in case you haven't noticed, is doing pretty well. You'd have to quit the library, unless you'd be staying here while I trudge off to Augusta." It was dusk, and a cauldron of bats were feeding overhead.

"Of course not," Stephanie said. "But I would miss my library."

"We'd have to leave Bucksport, at least for a few years. We'd have to live in the governor's house in Augusta. None of that sounds very appealing now that I say it out loud. Our lives would never be the same."

"On the other hand," Stephanie said, "this is a chance to really do something for the state, maybe help make life a little better, a little easier for folks. You're doing it here. Not many people get that chance, or the chance comes and they're too scared to grab it. You're not scared, are you?" Joshua ignored the question.

"So, you want me to do it? You actually want me to do it? Is that what you're saying?" Joshua asked.

"I didn't say that. But if you did, we'd always be able to come back. Besides, Augusta isn't horrible."

Joshua and Stephanie genuinely agonized over the decision. Almost every evening, they bandied about a new set of pros and cons, a new set of what-ifs. It wasn't a public agonizing put on for show, to get people to beg them to run. They just didn't know if they wanted to, particularly Joshua. Politics at this level is a nasty, nasty business. Joshua, and even Stephanie, would come under fire. Lies and rumors about them, carefully planted and amplified, would test them. Some people, even some people they knew as friends, might even believe that they were true.

One night, just before turning out the light, Stephanie finally said, "Joshua, let's do it. You're the right person. I think that Maine could use you right now."

"Are you sure, Steph? Are you absolutely sure? If we say yes, you know that our lives change forever?" Joshua asked.

Stephanie knew all of that, but she accepted it. "I'm sure, Joshua. You need to do it."

"Unless I lost, of course. Then things would go back to normal," Joshua said.

"The thing is, babe, you won't lose."

The campaign slogged on, month after month after month, Joshua traveling the state nearly every day. If there is a state where retail politics matter, it's Maine. You have to actually meet people, talk with them, look them in the eye. They need to size you up, take your measure. Joshua settled on *You CAN Get There from Here* as his campaign slogan, playing off of the famous Mainer response to a lost tourist desperate for directions. He incorporated it into his talks on the trail, over-accentuating the Maine accent, turning "there" and "here" into two-syllable words missing their "r." People loved it, even those from away.

Joshua attended more church and firehouse "Bean Suppahs" than he cared to count. Forty-four of them. By election night, he hoped to never see a baked bean again. Before the campaign began, he had loved baked beans. Now, even the smell was wicked offensive.

He shook hands with voters in what seemed like every diner in the state. He choked down a lot of really bad coffee, too. There were no huge rallies. The campaign was rooted in living rooms and church halls, coffee shops and libraries. It was personal, intimate and conversational, even. Usually, Joshua spoke with groups of just five or six people, occasionally as many as twenty or twenty-five.

Joshua listened to people far more than he talked at them, and they noticed. His opponent preferred the opposite approach. Joshua didn't cut people off when they spoke, even when they disagreed. He didn't talk over them. He waited until they were finished. They sensed that he was actually interested in hearing their concerns rather than rattling off his own. Voters did not get that sense from the other candidate. Joshua even took notes at most events.

It helped immensely that voters really liked Stephanie, who was also on the campaign trail. She radiated warmth and empathy. Neither she nor Joshua ever said anything negative about Joshua's opponent, even when goaded to. Joshua and Stephanie made it clear that they didn't want the PACs that supported them doing it, either. For the most part, the PACs complied.

While Joshua didn't have the usual political skills – practiced authenticity, carefully calculated style – he had others. The greatest was setting a tone. It came naturally. He was good at de-escalation, at turning down the temperature, tamping the vitriol. He didn't trade in insults or belittling. It was refreshing; startling, in fact. It wasn't how politics were played in America.

Joshua's opponent, on the other hand, had no qualms about bomb-throwing. He revelled in it. The Honorable Winston T. Kelly, United States Representative from Maine's Second Congressional District, denigrated Joshua's experience as merely that of a part-time, small-town mayor, a rube, by not-so-subtle implication. Joshua Sheehan was not an Ivy Leaguer or an important and deserving man like a seasoned United States congressman. Winston T. Kelly somehow forgot that most Mainers were from small towns and were proud of it. He had spent far, far too much time in Washington.

"A part-time mayor? For governor? Do you really want to hitch your wagon to a part-time mayor? I certainly don't. You need someone who has walked the halls of Congress, who has conversed with presidents, grappled with the important issues of the day, not someone whose biggest concerns were a few potholes that needed a-fixin' and orderin' enough salt for the winter." The congressman thought that dropping his g's was clever. Voters found it condescending and obnoxious. "No. You need experience at the highest level. I, alone, bring that experience, not Mayor Sheehan."

Surely, Mainers needed a wise, accomplished man like Winston T. Kelly to blaze the way forward and let them know what it was that they truly needed. Voters overwhelmingly felt otherwise. Fixing the potholes and salting the roads was exactly what they wanted.

What Joshua understood even before taking office was that Maine needed some changes. Making them would be the challenge. Mainers can be a stubborn, ornery lot. They are proud of it. Change is not always welcomed with overwhelming enthusiasm in *Vacationland*. Mainers are gradualists, too. When changes do come, they come incrementally, so as not to upset the apple cart . . . or the lobster boat, or the knuckleboom log loader.

At the time Joshua was elected, Maine had the oldest population in the country by a large margin. The median age was over forty-five, forty-six for women. Thirty-five states had a median age under forty. Maine ranked thirty-ninth in household income. Educational achievement lagged. Fewer than forty percent of adults had college degrees. The economy was overly-dependent on seafood harvesting, agriculture, logging, healthcare, and tourism, not the seductive kinds of industries terribly attractive to young talent in the twenty-first century.

In the interval between his election and inauguration, Joshua met with each of the fifteen department commissioners who would comprise his cabinet.

Governor-elect Sheehan had been briefed on each of them. The common practice was for commissioners to offer their resignations when a new governor took office, especially if the new governor hailed from the other political party. The new governor would routinely accept the resignations and appoint new commissioners, invariably from his own party. Joshua believed this practice led to a lurching back-and-forth kind of governing, with every new administration ushering in a whole new set of priorities and initiatives. It also meant that a lot of people had to learn important jobs on the fly. Why not keep those who were doing a good job and wanted to continue serving?

In the end, Joshua asked three of the incumbent commissioners to stay on during his administration. They were not from his party, but they were competent, experienced, and well-intentioned public servants. The party wasn't happy about it. The party had a laundry list of loyal party folks itching to join the governor's cabinet. There were donors and allies expecting their rewards. The party relished as much control and power as it could get its partisan hands on, and allowing the opposition to share even a fraction of it was unthinkable to those who viewed politics as a deathsport. Joshua felt otherwise, and he was in charge now.

The voters who paid attention to state politics favored Joshua's view. It wasn't full-blown bipartisanship – that was still a bridge way too far – but it seemed like it just might be a start.

James G. Blaine, three-time candidate for the Republican presidential nomination in the late 1800s, purchased a home at State and Capitol Streets in Augusta, which would come to be known as the Blaine House. He bought it in 1862 as a gift for his wife; a very nice gift. After the Blaines' passing, their heirs gifted the Blaine House to the State of Maine, provided that it serve as the governor's official residence, and it has been used that way ever since.

Newly-elected Governor Joshua Sheehan and Stephanie moved in immediately after his inauguration.

Joshua set about the hard business of governing. He surrounded himself with the best people he could find and devoted his attention to Mainers' needs, rather than to making the party happy. His goals were similar to the ones he had for Bucksport, but on a much grander scale. It was a balancing act, trying to attract and keep talented young people while preserving a way of life. Slowly, incrementally, change began to come.

Joshua didn't care for living in the Blaine House, or for living in Augusta, for that matter. Neither did Stephanie. Joshua much preferred small-town life in Bucksport, the only life he ever knew. Stephanie missed her library far more than she had anticipated. The Blaine House was simply too big, too formal. And it was too busy. No matter, it came with being governor, so he and Stephanie made the best of it. Fortunately, it was only an hour from the curling club, so they at least got to see their friends and play once in a while.

Stephanie made literacy and libraries her cause as Maine's first lady. She loved a challenge, and set her goal at visiting every one of Maine's 257 public libraries within four years. It was a logistical nightmare, but Stephanie and her scheduling secretary somehow pulled it off, appearing in every public library from Kittery to Fort Kent.

She read stories to children, always about Maine – *Miss Rumphius, One Morning in Maine, The Circus Ship, Little Loon*, and, of course, *Blueberries for Sal*. Stephanie was a natural with children, even though she would never have any of her own. She talked to them about her life as first lady, about reading and books, and about curling. She even brought a curling stone made from sixty-million-year-old granite for the kids to touch. "Dinosaurs might have walked on this granite!" she would say, although that was a slight exaggeration. She posed for pictures. She gave each child a book. She had fun.

"Time to fire up the grill," was Stephanie's usual Saturday night suggestion, even when Joshua was governor. One of the things that they had agreed on in an attempt to mimic a semblance of their life in Bucksport was that Joshua, once a week every week, would cook supper on the outdoor grill at the Blaine House. The Blaine House came furnished with a very nice grill, a Blackstone four-burner, far better than Joshua's aging two-burner Weber back home.

Joshua grilling up supper was a constant throughout their marriage. Burgers, sausage, bourbon barrel-aged maple syrup encrusted salmon, blistered shishito peppers, anything within Joshua's limited culinary ability. He could never get trickier things like lamb chops or duck breast quite right. Rendering the duck fat and crisping the skin befuddled him. Either he didn't render enough fat or the skin was burnt. "Delicious, but a little overdone," was Stephanie's frequent assessment. It was his great failing as a chef. Although the Blaine House had its own chef, having Joshua do some cooking for the two of them felt right.

Joshua also brought his raised cedar garden bed to Augusta. He didn't have to, he chose to. There was staff to tend to that sort of thing. Nonetheless, Joshua insisted on working the garden bed himself, which contained the only things he actually tried to grow on his own. The staff had free run of the rest of the gardens.

"What do you want in the garden this year?" Joshua asked each spring.

"Cilantro, dill, basil, and shishitos, for sure," Stephanie said. "Jalapeños, too. Why don't we try some Carolina reapers this year?"

"Because they'll set my head on fire, for one thing," Joshua said. "I'll grow some for you, though, if you want." She did.

Another big change for Joshua and Stephanie was the utter loss of privacy. The Blaine House was constantly full of people, populated by staffers, legislators, maintenance workers, kitchen staff, the press, people taking the tour. The tourists occasionally came across the governor tending to his little garden, much to their delight. They all wanted pictures of the governor planting, pruning, clipping, or aerating. There was also a constant Maine State Police presence, mostly from the Executive Protection Unit, Maine's equivalent of the United States Secret Service. Neither the governor nor Stephanie could go anywhere without a protective detail. It took a lot of getting used to, but it came with the job. Private moments were hard to come by, and they were precious.

Chapter 6
The Fire Pit

"Now, if I, whose name is Peace, am the . . . guardian of every blessing which either heaven or earth can bestow; if without me nothing is flourishing, nothing safe, nothing pure or holy, nothing pleasant to mortals, or grateful to the Supreme Being; if, on the contrary, war is one vast ocean, rushing on mankind, of all the united plagues and pestilences in nature; if, at its deadly approach every blossom of happiness is instantly blasted . . . and every thing that was sweet by nature is turned into bitterness; if war is so unhallowed that it becomes the deadliest bane of piety and religion; if there is nothing more calamitous to mortals, and more detestable to heaven, I ask how, in the name of God, can I believe those beings to be rational creatures; how can I believe them to be otherwise than stark mad; who, with such a waste of treasure, with so ardent a zeal, with so great an effort . . . endeavor to drive me away from them, and purchase endless misery and mischief at a price so high?" – Desiderius Erasmus, The Complaint of Peace (1521)

President Joshua F. Sheehan's overarching agenda was short and remarkably concise. He was going to bring peace, once and forevermore, to the world. He wasn't sure how he was going to do it quite yet, but he had the genesis of an idea. It was admittedly a bit ambitious, grandiose even, but why not? His predecessors came to the office with bold, ambitious plans, too. Perhaps not quite like this one, but ambitious in their own ways. A few even succeeded. Joshua Sheehan nearly would, too.

Joshua was the first Mainer elected president, but he was not the first to try. While others had harbored deep ambitions and aspirations, Joshua did not. In fact, he believed that anyone who sought the office should be summarily disqualified from holding it because of an overly-aggrandized sense of self. Anyone who believed that they *should* be president probably *shouldn't* be. That kind of person, that cumbersome an ego, would be dangerous. Joshua wasn't an entirely accidental president, but he was a decidedly unexpected one. It was largely because he didn't reek of ambition and self-grandeur that he won. He didn't make the election all about himself. People were exhausted by the vanity and the fighting and just craved competence and calm.

Unlike all of the other candidates who were certain that they were hewn from sturdy presidential timber, Joshua had to be recruited and convinced to run. His accomplishments and bipartisan popularity in Maine, as well as his work as chair of the National Governors Association, caught the party's lustful eye.

The country was simply sick of the bickering, grandstanding, and name-calling that had been going on seemingly forever, accomplishing little, other than feeding on itself. The people wanted a worker, not an attention-monger; an adult, not a petulant child; they wanted competence, not ineptitude; they were longing for someone – *anyone, please* – with the capacity to listen, learn, and lead. The party thought that Joshua just might be that person, and the American people resoundingly agreed.

"Why me?" Joshua asked when the party first approached him about a presidential run.

"Because you can win, Governor. You can be the next president of the United States," was the party's standard answer. They thought the words and their implications would prove intoxicating, a siren song. They were wrong. Those words were terrifying. Merely being electable didn't seem to him like a compelling reason for anyone to be president.

"You're not serious? Why you?" Stephanie asked when Joshua told her he was being courted for a presidential bid. "For God's sake, I thought I married an architect and I wound up with a goddamn politician." She feigned indignity, but there was no malice or venom.

"I'm dead serious. They want me to run for president," Joshua said. He felt silly even saying the words.

"Who's going to vote for you?" Stephanie asked. "I'm sorry, that sounds awful. I don't mean it like that. I mean, a small town guy from a small, out-of-the-way state. Has anybody from Maine ever been elected president?" She couldn't think of anyone off the top of her head. It was autumn in Bucksport, and Joshua and Stephanie had retreated from Augusta for the weekend to think.

They sat by their fire pit, where they usually huddled for serious discussion, the sweet smell of burning pine thick in the air, glowing embers drifting upward, then going dark. Most of their important decisions were made while staring into a fire. It focused their concentration and centered them.

"No, no one has. Funny you should ask, though. I've done some research. A surprising number of Mainers have given it a try," Joshua said. "Remember when we went to Mount Hope Cemetery in Bangor and saw Hanibal Hamlin's grave? He was Lincoln's vice president during the civil war. Helped write the Emancipation Proclamation. He had quite the résumé, too. Congressman, senator, governor. Lincoln dropped him in favor of Andrew Johnson for his re-election. Even then, vice presidents were picked mainly to help win elections. If Hamlin had stayed, he would have become the first Mainer to be president after Lincoln's assassination."

"Didn't somebody say that being vice president wasn't worth a bucket of spit?" Stephanie asked.

"A *warm* bucket of spit, more precisely. John Nance Gardner, FDR's vice president, supposedly said that," Joshua answered. "But that didn't discourage a bunch of Mainers from running for VP. Every last one of them lost, though. Except Hamlin." Joshua stood and placed another log on the fire.

"That doesn't sound very encouraging," Stephanie said. The wind changed and they moved their chairs away from the smoke.

"Arthur Sewall ran with William Jennings Bryan in 1896. He was rich, a shipbuilder, with basically no political experience. The only office he ever held was councilman in Bath. The fact that he believed in 'stolen' elections, imperialism, and high tariffs probably didn't help. He and Bryan lost in a landslide to McKinley. They didn't even carry Maine. And Edmund Muskie, of course, was Humphrey's running mate in 1968. They lost to Nixon and Agnew, but at least Muskie helped them carry Maine."

"You *have* been thinking about this, haven't you? You've done your homework. So far, you're not giving me very much hope, though," Stephanie said.

"It gets worse. What do you know about James G. Blaine?" Joshua asked.

"Not too much, except that we live in his house," Stephanie answered.

"Blaine really, really wanted to be president. He had the credentials, too. Much better than mine. Speaker of the United States House for six years, senator, secretary of state. He tried to win the Republican nomination three times. He finally got it in 1884. It didn't matter, though. He lost to Grover Cleveland."

"Is that it?" Stephanie asked. "Just a long list of losers?"

"Oh, no. Not by a long shot. There were more. Muskie tried to win the Democratic presidential nomination in 1972. A lot of people thought that he would get it, too, including Nixon, so Nixon's team cooked up some fake scandal using a forged letter, accusing Muskie of bigotry and of calling French

Canadians 'Canucks.' Muskie held a news conference to deny it, but apparently started crying. That was it for him. Americans didn't want a president who cried."

"You should be OK, then," Stephanie said. "I don't think I've ever seen you cry."

"Yeah, I'm probably safe there," Joshua said. "Have you ever heard of Benjamin Calvin Bubar?"

"I don't think so, but the name sounds kind of familiar," Stephanie said. "Who is he?"

"*Was* he," Joshua said. "Youngest person ever elected to the Maine House of Representatives. Twenty-one years old when he took his seat. He couldn't even vote for himself, since he was only twenty years old on election day. Anyway, he was a United Baptist minister, just like his father, who also happened to be a regular speaker at Ku Klux Klan rallies in Maine."

"I didn't know that the Klan was in Maine," Stephanie said.

"Neither did I, but apparently it was. Anti-Catholic, mainly. Bubar, Sr. wrote a book called *The Devil Let Loose in Maine*, about the apocalyptic problem of alcohol use in the state." Joshua took a sip of beer. Stephanie did likewise.

"That's where I've seen that name! We had that book in the library. Scary cover, as I recall. I think it showed the Devil rising out of a liquor bottle like a genie. Horns, fangs, red eyes," Stephanie said.

"Never read it. Doesn't sound like my genre," Joshua said. "Anyway, Bubar, Jr. ran for president on the Prohibition Party ticket in 1976. Got fifteen-thousand votes out of eighty-million. He ran again in 1980 and only got seven-thousand votes. Seems like the country just wasn't ready for a return to prohibition."

"Good thing," Stephanie said. She took another purposeful sip.

"His sister ran for vice president in '96, also as a prohibitionist. Sounds like a really fun family. Got twelve-hundred votes," Joshua said. "The Bubars were trending downward."

"That's it?" Stephanie asked. "That's all the Mainers who ran?"

"There was one more. My favorite. Margaret Chase Smith," Joshua said. He pulled out his phone and read the notes he had taken about her.

"Margaret Chase Smith contracted the presidential bug in 1964. She was a Republican from Skowhegan. Very conservative. She was elected to the United States House of Representatives in 1940 and served in the House until 1949, when she began the first of her four terms as a United States senator. By the time that she retired in 1973, she was both the longest-serving woman senator and the longest-serving Republican senator in history.

"Margaret Chase Smith also gave one of the most significant speeches in American political history, the 'Declaration of Conscience' speech on June 1, 1950, on the floor of the United States Senate. Without mentioning the infamous Senator Joseph McCarthy by name, it was clearly about him." Joshua had read and studied the speech. He was struck by how little things had changed, even generations later. It took spine for her to deliver it, more spine than any of her ninety-five male colleagues could muster:

I speak as briefly as possible because too much harm has already been done with irresponsible words of bitterness and selfish political opportunism. I speak as briefly as possible because the issue is too great to be obscured by eloquence . . . I speak as a Republican. I speak as a woman. I speak as a United States Senator. I speak as an American . . .

I think that it is high time for the United States Senate . . . to do some soul-searching . . . on the manner in which we are performing our duty . . . I think that it is high time that we remembered that we have sworn to uphold and defend the Constitution . . .

As a woman, I wonder how the mothers, wives, sisters, and daughters feel about the way in which members of their families have been politically mangled in the Senate debate ... I am not proud of the way in which the Senate has been made a publicity platform for irresponsible sensationalism ... I don't like the way the Senate has been made a rendezvous for vilification ...

It is with these thoughts that I have drafted what I call a 'Declaration of Conscience.' The declaration reads as follows:

We are Republicans. But we are Americans first. It is as Americans that we express our concern with the growing confusion that threatens the security and stability of our country ... Certain elements of the Republican Party have materially added to this confusion in the hopes of riding the Republican party to victory ...

It is high time that we stopped thinking politically ... and started thinking patriotically as Americans about national security based on individual freedom. It is high time that we all stopped being tools and victims of totalitarian techniques – techniques that ... will surely end what we have come to cherish as the American way of life.

"Margaret Chase Smith announced her candidacy for the 1964 Republican nomination," Joshua continued. "She didn't fare well. Her best showing came in the Illinois primary, where she got just a quarter of the vote. Despite her underwhelming performance, she nevertheless refused to drop out of the race and became the first woman to have her name placed into nomination by one of the two major parties."

Joshua left out some other politicians with presidential ambitions and tangential ties to Maine. None could remotely be considered a true Mainer. Nelson Rockefeller, who sought the Republican nomination in 1960, 1964, and 1968, and who also served as Gerald Ford's vice president, was born in Bar Harbor and spent a few summers at his parents' summer home in Seal Harbor. Despite being born in Maine, no one would possibly consider Nelson Rockefeller a Mainer.

George H.W. Bush owned a summer home on Walker's Point in Kennebunkport. He visited the home frequently as a child, and purchased it from his uncle's estate in 1977. During his presidency, Walker's Point served as the "summer White House." His son, George W. Bush, spent lots of time at Walker's Point both before, during, and after his presidency. Although the Bushes can't properly be considered Mainers, they come a lot closer than Nelson Rockefeller ever dreamed of.

Joshua balked at the party's overtures, just like he had done when he was being recruited to run for mayor of Bucksport and then governor of Maine.

"So, what do you want to do?" Stephanie asked. It was getting late. The fire was all but out.

"What do you think we should do?" Joshua responded.

"Oh, no, you don't," Stephanie demurred. "I asked you first."

Chapter 7
Running for President

"Democracy is based on the conviction that there are extraordinary possibilities in ordinary people." – Harry Emerson Fosdick

The presidential primaries were fiercely contested early on, with representatives of the many factions within the party eager to jump into the fray. Sixteen of them, in all. Most had been plotting their moves for years, attending all the right events and granting all the right interviews. You couldn't swing a cat by its tail in Iowa or New Hampshire without hitting a would-be president during the year leading up to the caucuses and primary. Pollsters, consultants, and operatives were swimming in cash. Some accepted crypto.

Many of the hopefuls had written heartfelt books paying tribute to their remarkable hometowns, loving parents, dedicated teachers, and humble, all-American upbringings. A couple of them actually wrote the book themselves, with lots of AI input. Each candidate was more fervently patriotic than the other. Their websites, uniformly adorned in red, white, and blue, touted their many accomplishments and years of selfless, dedicated public service. Fewer than half of them survived Iowa, fewer still, New Hampshire. Joshua didn't represent any particular faction, nor did he think to write a book, which, in the end, made him the sensible choice.

Iowa and New Hampshire were perfect for Joshua. States where small gatherings in living rooms and libraries and churches dominate. Where sitting down with voters matters and civility still carries weight. It was a lot like campaigning in Maine. Joshua and Stephanie were comfortable in those settings and the voters noticed. *"Are You Sheehan What I'm Sheehan?"* yard signs populated lawns, sprouting up like crocuses as soon as the snow melted. Some of the other candidates may have attracted larger crowds, but size doesn't always matter.

By late-April, it was clear that Joshua would capture the nomination. The other candidates, some enthusiastically, some grudgingly, abandoned their campaigns and fell in line behind him. If they played their hands right, there might be plum jobs awaiting them in a Sheehan administration. Better yet, he might lose the general election and they could give it another shot in four years.

The party convention in Denver was a tightly-orchestrated affair, a four-day television production designed to prove to the world how wonderful the party was and what wondrous things awaited Americans if they were only wise enough to hand it the power. Joshua stayed away from the convention until the final night, when he would deliver his acceptance speech. It helped build the drama. Television cameras were perched around the Blaine House in Augusta to capture his movements. That wasn't the reason that he stayed away. He simply hated the silliness of political conventions. Almost everything repugnant about politics is on vivid display at conventions. Staying ensconced in Maine was far more enjoyable, even if it was in the Blaine House. Joshua sat alone in the garden most evenings, fine-tuning his speech.

Stephanie, on the other hand, spent the entire week in Colorado, even making a stop at the Denver Curling Club for a game. She missed playing, so any chance to get out onto the ice was welcome. Stephanie was Joshua's greatest asset. She could chat easily with almost anyone, about almost anything, a gift from her mother. She enjoyed meeting people more than Joshua did. Stephanie spent most of her time on the floor of the convention, talking casually with the delegates and posing for pictures. She drew the line at donning any of the ridiculous hats. By the time the convention was gavelled closed, she had charmed nearly every one of the delegates.

J oshua trusted his instincts. He didn't rely much on polls or focus groups, but he did pay some attention to them. Stephanie was his most trusted advisor, not his pollsters and red-eyed data-crunchers. Her instincts were even better than his.

With the nomination settled, the main focus of the party, and Joshua, too, turned to choosing a running mate. A lot of time and energy is spent on finding someone to fill what John Adams called "the most insignificant office that ever the invention of man contrived." And Adams would know, being the first to hold the office. Joshua wanted someone who shared his vision, his values. He favored a leader, someone bold and unafraid to get out front and advocate for something, to believe in something. Not a firebrand, not an arsonist, but an influencer, if you will. He had some specific people in mind. Vetting uncovered few vulnerabilities in any of them.

Joshua settled on his friend, Governor Elijah Turner of New Jersey, a popular governor six years his junior. Joshua and Elijah had worked together at the National Governors Association and became close, as did Stephanie and Sandra. The Turners vacationed with Joshua and Stephanie in Maine a couple of times and marvelled at the slower beat of life, and, compared to New Jersey, the seemingly traffic-less roads. If New Jersey is like a frat party, Maine is like a christening. Joshua and Elijah never talked politics, never debated policy, while vacationing. Instead, they ate lobster, slurped Damariscotta oysters, scavenged for beach glass, and explored the mid-coast. They sat atop Cadillac Mountain in Acadia at five o'clock to watch the sunrise. Joshua told the party elders that he wanted Elijah Turner on his ticket.

The party heads hated the idea. Yes, Elijah Turner was popular, charismatic, and a rising star. Television cameras loved him, as did interviewers.

He had a bright future, too. For present purposes, though, Elijah Turner simply wouldn't do.

First of all, he was a governor. Joshua needed someone with federal government experience, who knew their way around Capitol Hill and the acronym bureaucracy. Second, Governor Turner was from the Northeast and the ticket needed geographic balance. Someone from the Midwest or South, maybe even the West, who would help with the electoral map. Third, a Sheehan/Turner ticket would look too young, too inexperienced, too risky. Someone with a full head of gray hair would strike the perfect aesthetic balance. Besides, Elijah Turner was short, only five-foot-eight. His vice presidential opponent was six-foot-two. Party data suggested that the taller candidate usually wins. No sense taking unnecessary chances.

The party came armed with its own list. Elijah Turner was not on it. Electability topped their criteria, followed closely by party loyalty. The party saw little utility in a vice president beyond the campaign trail and electoral map. Which demographics could the nominee help win? That was the party's focus. They bombarded Joshua with polling data, focus group results, and election simulations. The senior senator from Wisconsin, sixty-one-year-old Edward Todd Anderson, was their choice. He checked exactly the right boxes.

Senator Edward Todd Anderson – he insisted on using all three names – was a cautious man, a slow-moving man, a man living in fear of taking a misstep. Behind his back, colleagues, especially friends, called him "ETA," for his habitual lateness. A common question around the Senate was, "Do we have an ETA on ETA?" Senator Anderson was also a party favorite. His vote could always be counted on. It could also be counted on to be one of the final votes cast.

During Anderson's fourteen years in the Senate, he had introduced exactly one bill, something innocuous, something that passed with ninety votes. After consulting the polls, though, he was usually happy to co-sponsor some other senator's bill, provided that it was popular and a lock to pass. As long as his constituents liked it, he could brag about being a sponsor. Senator

Anderson steadfastly avoided the crucible of the political talk shows, where some aggressive reporter might try to pin him down on something before he was quite ready to take a public stance.

The party arranged a meeting. Senator Anderson kept them waiting, but not for too long. It did not make a great first impression on the habitually on-time Joshua. Oddly enough, once Anderson entered the room, the first thing that Joshua noticed was the senator's hair, thick and silvery-white, very short. Not a hint of receding or thinning. Not a single hair out of place. Edward Todd Anderson, Joshua would come to learn, got a haircut every week, usually on Tuesday, on the taxpayers' dime in the Senate's barbershop. His sideburns were high and razor-straight, his eyebrows perfectly trimmed.

Joshua was surprisingly impressed by Senator Anderson, once he arrived. He knew the issues inside and out. He agreed with Joshua on most of them, although he favored taking a less aggressive, more gradual approach to implementing them. The senator was polite, mannered, and spoke in measured words. He was someone that Joshua could work with, but not the one he preferred to work with.

"Can I tell you something that I've learned during my many years in the United States Senate, governor?" Anderson asked.

"Of course," Joshua answered.

"I've learned that the early bird catches the worm, but the second mouse gets the cheese."

Stephanie was unconvinced. "Stick to your guns. Trust your instincts," she argued. "Are you going to start off by being their puppet? If you want Elijah, tell them you want Elijah. This should be your decision, not theirs."

"I do want him, but it's not quite that simple, Steph. There are lots of things to consider."

Joshua caved to the party pressure. They had proven themselves right so far. It was against his nature and against Stephanie's advice, which he rarely discounted. His gut told him Elijah Turner. Usually rock-solid in his decision-making, this time he wavered. It's only the vice presidency, anyway, he rationalized. He could find something far more useful for Elijah than being squirreled away in the Executive Office Building. Senator Edward Todd Anderson joined the ticket.

The general election was tougher than the primaries had been. People play dirtiest when the stakes are highest. Joshua's opponent, United States Representative Henry "Hank" Stockton, was a crude, noxious fellow who niggled his way through politics. His specialties were grievance and grudges, which he relished airing. It gained him a noisy, rambunctious social media following, many of whom struggled with grammar and punctuation.

Representative Stockton, a fierce and public Virginia patriot, never ventured out without being adorned in at least three places with Old Glory – an American flag lapel pin, pocket square, and cufflinks. He also maintained an impressive collection of imported American flag ties. No politician was going to out-flag the Honorable Henry Stockton.

Hank Stockton, and more particularly his super PACs, let loose to do their mischief, ran thousands of ads on television, radio, social media, and even in increasingly irrelevant print, warning that Joshua Sheehan was a wild-eyed, crazed ideologue coming for whatever they held dearest – their kids, their money, their church, their guns. The narration was always by a gravelly-voiced baritone designed to scare the bejesus out of voters and make them lock their windows and doors. Stockton used the worst pictures of Joshua that he could find, photoshopping and AI-ing them, and set them loose across America with their dire warnings.

The ads didn't hit home. Voters simply didn't see Joshua Sheehan that way. He seemed rational, reasonable, thoughtful, and most importantly, likeable. Hank Stockton was none of those things. After years of unpredictable, erratic, nasty, mercurial, and even unstable behavior, voters pined for normal. And Joshua Sheehan seemed to them, if nothing else, normal.

All along the campaign trail, Joshua stopped in curling clubs whenever one was nearby and open. During the summer, most weren't. Arrangements were made in advance to play games with some of the local club members. If Stephanie was with him on the trail, she played, too. Joshua always invited Stephanie to tell the story of their meeting.

"Joshua and I met after a league game at the Belfast Curling Club in Maine. My team had just beaten Joshua's team, rather handily I might add. I felt a little bit sorry for him." She looked at Joshua, smiling. He shook his head. "I must give him credit, though. He tried really hard, bless his heart. While we were broomstacking after the game, I asked him out. I thought he was kinda cute. Actually, he still is, don't you think?" Joshua suggested that she leave out that line, but Stephanie liked it. "On our first date, we went to a Thai restaurant and discovered that we had actually met before, when we were on debate teams from neighboring high schools. I won that match, too." Crowds always cheered wildly. Joshua dutifully played her foil.

Even curlers who were not inclined to vote for Joshua jumped at the chance to play with the man and woman who might be the next President and First Lady of the United States. The warm rooms were always crammed to capacity with serious curlers and the simply curious. The national sense was that this was a stupefyingly regular couple.

Joshua's election was secured by the presidential debates. Before the first debate, polls showed the candidates in a dead heat. When it was over, Joshua held a commanding lead. Hank Stockton pontificated in carefully-crafted sound bites and dog-whistles and barely-disguised innuendo. He was relentless in trying to bait Joshua into argument, talking loudly, incessantly interrupting, and doing lots of finger-pointing. Stockton was infuriated that Joshua ignored his antics. Joshua, on the other hand, tried to listen and answer questions. If he was asked a yes or no question, he sometimes actually answered yes or no, surprising the moderators, who were conditioned to expect ninety seconds of pre-scripted gibberish.

At the first debate, the moderator asked, "My next question is directed to Representative Stockton. In the past, the federal government has provided grant funding to farmers to install windmills or solar panels on portions of their farmland as renewable energy sources. That grant funding has been paused indefinitely by the current administration. Are you in favor of making those grants available again during a Stockton administration?"

"Finally, a question about American energy from the lamestream media. America has always led the world in energy production. There is no reason why we can't continue that dominance. The coal miners, the oilmen, the refinery workers, those people are America's backbone, the people that built this great country. The elitist Joshua Sheehan disdains those great patriots. We must reclaim our rightful place as the world's largest energy producer. We should be granting new permits to open up more lands to drilling. *Drill, baby, drill*, I always say. We should re-open shuttered mines and harvest more beautiful American coal. *Dig, baby, dig*! Bring gas prices down. Bring home heating costs down. Sure, we should be open to new technologies, but we must first re-commit ourselves to tried-and-true ones. By the way, did you know that there is enough oil under the United States to meet demand for the next 100 years? I would focus my administration's . . ." Hank would have bleated on and on all night had his time not expired and his microphone not been cut.

"Representative Stockton, your time is up. Same question for you, Governor Sheehan. Would you make federal grants available for farmers to use a portion of their farmland for wind and solar electricity generation?" the moderator asked.

"Yes, I would," Joshua replied. The room sat silently waiting for him to continue. He didn't. He had answered the question.

It was a radical approach to presidential debating. Hank, an experienced and practiced politician, would never be so naive as to actually answer a question. Most times, his answers bore little relation to the questions. Voters felt, even if they didn't agree with Joshua on everything, that he was different, serious, not a panderer. His likeability polling outpaced his opponent's by twenty-five points, climbing after each debate. Policy and politics aside, likeability matters. Who wants to spend four years with someone they can barely stand?

President-elect Sheehan made two unconventional moves immediately after the election. On election night, after all of the networks had declared him the winner, he waited for a call from Representative Stockton conceding the election and offering congratulations. Joshua should have known better. The call never came. Instead, Stockton took to the stage at his headquarters to rant and bay at the moon, veins and eyes bulging, sweat overrunning his ruddy, angry face. He was in such a hurry that he forgot to wear his American flag pocket square. It might be the last time the country was treated to hearing him, and he was taking full advantage.

As soon as Stockton started, Joshua raced down to his own stage at his headquarters in Augusta to deliver his victory remarks. He knew that all of the networks would immediately cut away from the loser's screed to broadcast the winner's speech. As he left his suite, the networks unceremoniously cut away from Hank mid-sentence. They confined him to a small box in the corner of the screen, muted. "We understand that the president-elect is making his way to the stage," the anchor announced. "There he is, he just entered the hall with his wife, soon-to-be first lady, Stephanie. He's approaching the podium. Let's listen to president-elect Sheehan." The rest of Hank's speech never hit the air.

To raucous cheers, President-elect Sheehan began by thanking his campaign staff, volunteers, and supporters for their selfless, hard work. He thanked Stephanie most profusely. When he did, the crowd went crazy. He even summoned the grace to congratulate Representative Stockton for a well-run, thoughtful campaign, somehow managing a straight face. Then, he did something extraordinary.

Joshua asked the crowd to be silent, to not cheer or clap or interrupt what he was about to say until he was finished. The sharp crack of a balloon popping offstage made supporters, and even the Secret Service, flinch. Joshua looked directly into the television cameras and began:

I want to take a few moments to address the American people. First and foremost, I want to thank you for your support throughout this long campaign. I hope to prove myself worthy of the high honor you have bestowed on me.

I know that almost half of you are disappointed by the result tonight. That is the blessing and curse of our democracy. But regardless of who you may have voted for, my promise to you – especially to those who chose not to vote for me – is that I will try my best to make this country an even better one for all of us. To enhance opportunities for all of us. To provide a measure of financial security to everyone. To make good, rewarding jobs available to those that want them. To care for those who can't care for themselves. To realize the dream of justice and liberty for all. To help everyone feel safe and welcome. Perhaps, even, to bring a measure of peace around the world. It will not be easy, nor will it happen quickly.

We are a country of good, decent, kind people. Generous people. People who value work and education and family. We live a shared belief in fairness and opportunity. I imagine a country where one person's gain need not be another's loss. Where one person's success need not mean another person's failure. We want to live the American dream together, knowing that there really is more that binds us together than could ever tear us apart. Today, let us pledge together to become a more perfect union. We, the people, can shape that more perfect union. We can embark on that journey together.

Not all of this will happen today, or tomorrow, or maybe even in a thousand tomorrows. We will never become perfect. After all, we are people burdened with flaws, with shortcomings. We will fall short of perfection, but we can always become more perfect. The work will not be completed in our lifetimes, even. But let us take that first small step. And tomorrow, take the next one. And the day after, the next one, and then another. When one of us stumbles, let another take their hand. When one of us weakens, let another be their strength. We can do this. We will do this. We will not be guided by fear, but by courage. Our reward awaits us if we begin now. Thank you.

The crowd erupted. In that room, and in homes around the country, for a moment, at least, the impossible only seemed improbable.

The second thing that the president-elect did in the days immediately after the election was also different. His campaign coffers had millions of dollars which hadn't been needed. He could have hoarded the money, saved it for the next battle, but he didn't. Instead, he bought television ads in every state, whether they cast their electoral votes for him or not, and took to the air to ask everyone for their help. The ads weren't slickly produced, no dramatic music or star-spangled banners waving in the breeze, just fifteen or thirty seconds of Joshua talking calmly to the camera. In some, Stephanie stood beside him. The ads ran most heavily in places where he had done the poorest. Voters, even those who did not support him, were conditioned to politicians vanishing like vapor as soon as the polls closed, not to emerge until the next election, and they appreciated the gracious gesture. Maybe this guy *is* different, they hoped. Perhaps we should give him a chance.

Chapter 8
The Tour

The first thing that President-elect Sheehan did after the election was to request that a curling rink be built at the White House. Two sheets would do just fine, he calculated. No need to go overboard. It wasn't *really* the first thing that he did – there were plenty of other obligatory, annoying tasks to attend to first – phone calls to donors and handshakes and fending off people angling for appointments and such, but it was *one of* the first things. It was a far-from-ordinary, expensive request, but when you win thirty-nine states' electoral votes and 55.4% of the popular vote, people are motivated to listen. Besides, lots of presidents had added their own idiosyncratic touches to the White House, inside and out. Truman had the whole thing gutted and rebuilt, for God's sake. Trump bulldozed the entire East Wing.

The White House grounds are a patchwork of swimming pools, putting greens, horseshoe pits, tennis courts, jogging tracks, and basketball courts on the outside, and bowling alleys, game rooms, music rooms, and movie theaters inside. It was almost expected that each new president would want to add something to call their own. The request for a curling rink was perhaps a little more idiosyncratic and problematic logistically, but not too much more than some of the others. The request was more readily received when the president-elect promised that no government money – only private funds – would be spent on the project. Raising the money would only take a few quick phone calls. A few million or so for a popular, landslide winner would be easy pickings. The big donors would be offended if they weren't asked to pony up.

Not everyone thought that installing a curling rink at the White House was a great idea. Some critics had practical, considered reasons; others simply knee-jerked opposition to anything and everything that the new president proposed. Opposition pundits flocked to social media, television, talk radio, podcasts, and op-eds to lambaste the idea. They called the new president an unserious man, though none of them had ever thrown a curling stone or set foot in a curling club. None of them knew the difference between a hog and a biter, anyway, so how seriously should they be taken? The "Spirit of Curling" would be foreign to them. Regardless, they felt honor-bound to air their complaints and further fortify their brands. Words like "frivolous," "wasteful," "stupid," and "self-indulgent" were bandied about casually. One cable commentator was fired for calling the president "retarded."

Joshua Sheehan didn't care about the outside noise, nor did he engage with the noisemakers. Some tried to position the curling rink as a threat to national security, although their reasoning was, politely stated, questionable; bluntly stated, ludicrous. If they only knew why he was building it, perhaps they might see things differently. That was something they would eventually come to learn.

The president didn't feed the drama machine. The resistance had its agenda and he had his. They could have their clicks and likes, maybe even rustle up a few new followers – the president-elect got votes that actually mattered. Tens of millions of them.

Presidents, as they came and went, left behind their personal marks at the White House. Many were athletic or recreational, something to provide a few precious moments of respite from the relentless barrage of information and questions, as well as the constant, awful weight of the office. The largest such project, before Joshua's curling rink, was Franklin D. Roosevelt's heated indoor swimming pool. If an indoor pool could be managed, a couple of curling sheets could be squeezed in somewhere. A curling rink would cost quite a bit more, but would spare the public dime, just like FDR's pool had.

On November 10th, the president-elect arrived at the White House to meet with the outgoing president. Tradition dictates that the departing president invite his successor for a visit, one courtesy still largely surviving in American politics.

"Good morning, Governor. Welcome to the White House," the lame duck said by way of greeting. "Congratulations on the election."

"Good morning, Mr. President. Thank you," Joshua said. "It's an honor to be here." The president seemed distracted. Maybe some national security matter needed his attention. More likely, he was thinking about his double bogey on eighteen the day before.

The sitting president hadn't bothered to run for re-election. He opted to let someone else take the fall. He was wildly unpopular, personally, mostly, but also politically, and was counting the hours until his escape from Washington. When historians considered his place among American presidents, he would fall much closer to James Buchanan and Andrew Johnson than to Abraham Lincoln and George Washington. After fifteen minutes of strained chit-chat, Joshua headed out for a tour of the White House complex with the Administrator of the General Services Administration, Isaac Raven. As part of the tour, Joshua had specifically asked to see all of the athletic facilities.

Isaac Raven was a fabulous docent, with lots of insider stories to share. They started at what was once FDR's indoor pool, in the West Terrace, between the White House and the West Wing. It no longer resembled a swimming pool. Joshua noticed that Raven unconsciously dipped his head whenever he passed through a doorway. Joshua guessed six-five, maybe six-six. Magnetic reading glasses hung around Raven's preternaturally long neck, with its pointed, prominently protruding Adam's apple.

"FDR had this installed in 1933, smack dab in the middle of the Great Depression. It opened less than three months after he took office. The *New York Post* raised the money. Twelve grand. Can you imagine a newspaper raising money for a president today?" Raven began.

"Times are a little different, I guess," Joshua answered. "Newpapers can barely pay their own bills these days."

"Roosevelt used the pool as therapy for his polio," Raven said. "He went to great lengths to hide his condition from the public. It was easier back then. No reporters and cameras everywhere. The press release at the time boasted that swimming kept him 'in perfect physical condition,' even though he spent most of his time in a wheelchair. He ordered the Secret Service to confiscate and destroy any pictures taken of him in his chair, you know."

"I didn't know the Secret Service could do that. Makes you long for the old days, doesn't it?" Joshua said.

"Sometimes it does," Raven answered.

"After Roosevelt died, Harry Truman would take a swim with his glasses on. I think he did it just to entertain his staff and the occasional guest. I understand they found it quite funny," Raven related.

"I would think so," Joshua said.

Raven continued, "Eisenhower didn't use the pool much, if at all. He preferred golf and his putting green. We'll get to that a little later. President Kennedy is a different story. He swam a lot to ease his back pain, which tormented him ever since his college football days at Harvard and his World War II heroics. JFK took a lot of meds for his pain, too – codeine, Demerol, methadone. It's amazing that he could even function, but that's another story. Kennedy invited Jackie to swim with him sometimes, although I understand that he also invited some women *not* named Jackie on others, if you know what

I mean." The two men smiled. "He had the walls painted in a panorama of a Virgin Islands harbor so that he felt like he was swimming in the Caribbean."

Raven sensed that Joshua was enjoying the stories, so he continued. "At least they all wore bathing suits, as far as I know," Raven announced. "Lyndon Johnson, on the other hand, preferred swimming naked." That was news to Joshua. "The story goes that during LBJ's first month as president, right after what happened in Dallas, he summoned the Reverend Billy Graham to the White House. Billy Graham never turned down a presidential invitation. He knew every president from Truman to Trump. It became his calling card. 'Pastor to the presidents.' Rubbing elbows with presidents was good for Billy Graham's brand and the Billy Graham Crusades, and hobnobbing with Billy Graham was good presidential politics.

"Well," Raven continued, "Billy Graham arrives at the White House with his friend, Grady Wilson, another evangelist, in tow. After they finished praying and talking, Johnson suggested that they take a swim right here in this pool. It hadn't dawned on the preachers to pack bathing suits, and Johnson didn't offer them any, so they joined him for some good old-fashioned Texas-style skinny-dipping." Raven paused, wondering whether to add the next detail. He decided to go ahead. "Johnson was said to be rather – how should I put this – 'gifted.' And proud of it. Named the thing 'Jumbo.' We have plenty of pictures of Truman swimming with his glasses on. LBJ thought it best not to invite any photographers," Raven added. "That scene has been lost to history."

"Probably for the best," Joshua offered. He tried not to picture it.

"Probably," Raven agreed.

"Nixon closed the pool, although he insisted that it not be demolished, just in case. He was a bit paranoid, from what I understand," Raven concluded. FDR's abandoned pool now lies beneath the press center, housing most of the infrastructure for the press room.

The next stop was the outdoor pool. The men donned their coats as they made their way outside. Joshua immediately noticed that Raven's puffer jacket came from L.L.Bean.

"Have you ever been to Maine, Isaac? I see you're wearing a Bean coat," Joshua said.

"Yes, sir, quite a few times. My wife insists on a trip to L.L.Bean every couple of years. We always come home with a trunkful of stuff. On one trip, I had a lobster roll for lunch on four straight days."

"You say that like it's a bad thing, Isaac. Butter or mayo?"

"Butter, sir."

"Good man," Joshua said. "The proper way to eat a lobster roll." The two men arrived at the outdoor pool.

"After Nixon resigned, Gerald Ford had this pool installed," Raven began. They were standing on the South Lawn, next to the fifty-foot-long pool, closed and covered for the season. "Kinda funny, because Nixon had just closed the indoor one. But Ford was a good athlete and loved swimming. All-American football player, you know. He hated being away from his home in Virginia with its heated pool, so he had this one installed. Ford said that fifteen minutes in a swimming pool was worth two martinis. And he enjoyed his martinis." Raven paused. "A shame about Betty, though. As things turned out, Ford wouldn't need the pool for long, since he lost the election the next year," Raven continued. "You know what the most ironic part is?" he asked.

"What's that?" Joshua asked.

"Ford probably could have used this pool for four more years if he hadn't pardoned Nixon," Raven answered.

They made their way to the tennis court on the South Lawn. "Teddy Roosevelt installed the original tennis court behind the West Wing. Taft replaced it with this one in 1910. Obama decided that it would be better as a basketball court, so he had the hoops installed and the lines painted for basketball," Raven began.

"Obama liked his hoops," Joshua said. "I hear he was pretty good."

"Fanatical, too. And a world-class trash-talker, from what I understand. Probably why he preferred basketball to tennis. Much more amenable to chatter," Raven said. "He played with Kevin Durant, Scottie

Pippen, LeBron James, Chris Paul, Derrick Rose, Joakim Noah, Maya Moore, Alonzo Mourning, and Magic Johnson, off the top of my head, right here on this court. Probably some others, too. Like a White House all-star game." Pointing to a tennis pavilion, Raven said, "That was added during Trump's first term. It was really Melania's project. She broke ground wearing a pair of snakeskin stilettos from some fancy designer. I heard they cost a thousand dollars. All my shoes together didn't cost that much." Joshua snuck a peek at Raven's shoes. They had seen better days.

"Does that surprise you?" Joshua asked.

"Not really," Raven answered. "Just seems like tennis shoes might have been a more reasonable footwear choice. Do you play, sir? Tennis? Basketball?"

"I've played, but not for a long time," Joshua said. "Stephanie and I are curlers."

"Yes, so I've heard," Raven said. "Will you be able to find a place to play in Washington, sir?"

"We hope so," Joshua answered. "I suspect that I won't have a lot of free time, though."

It was getting colder outside. Winter hadn't officially arrived in Washington, but the weather wasn't paying attention to the calendar. They made their way back inside, to the basement. Joshua had heard rumors that there was a bowling alley in the White House, but he didn't know whether they were true. They were. He found himself standing at the one-lane alley.

"Nixon installed this in '73. He was a serious bowler. Spent hours and hours alone down here. He was pretty good, too, from what I understand," Raven began. "This isn't the first bowling alley in the White House, though. Truman got one as a gift from some friends in the '40s."

"You mean like the old man in *A Christmas Story* when he thought he won a bowling alley?" Joshua asked. Raven didn't get the reference, so he continued with his story.

"It was an odd gift, because Truman wasn't really a bowler. Poker was Truman's game. Had chips made with the presidential seal on 'em. They're at his presidential library. Anyway, I'm told he rolled a seven with the first ball," Raven explained.

"Did he convert the spare?" Joshua asked. If anyone knew, it would probably be Raven.

"No one seems to know. A very good question, though. I've never really tried to find out. Maybe you can dispatch some poor intern to look into it for you. You'll be surprised what interns can find out," Raven answered. "Anyway, they took Truman's bowling alley apart piece by piece and reassembled it in the Old Executive Office Building next door. They still use it over there." Like Gerald Ford and his swimming pool, Nixon wouldn't get to use his bowling alley for very long. Watergate saw to that.

Sufficiently warmed, they continued their tour outside. The wind had picked up. The roar of leaf blowers mixed with the rustling of the trees. They stood just south of what was left of the Kennedy rose garden, next to a putting green.

"Clinton had this built," Raven began. "He wanted a sand trap next to it, but the Secret Service would have none of it. They were sure that Clinton would skull one of his blasts from the trap and damage the White House. It's bulletproof, so I'm not really sure how much damage a golf ball would do. Are you a golfer, sir?"

"No," Joshua answered. "I never cared much for golf. A good way to ruin a nice walk. Maybe the vice president can use it. I understand he likes the game."

"I don't care much for it, either," Raven said, then continued with the story of the putting green. "Bush 43 used it a lot. He had this dog named Barney – Scottish Terrier – that would get the balls out of the cup and drop them at Bush's feet."

"Our dog's not that well-trained," Joshua said. "And I'm not sure he's that smart."

"Will your dog be coming with you in January?" Raven asked.

"Oh, yeah. Where Stephanie goes, Baxter goes." Raven frowned.

"What's the matter?" Joshua asked. "You're not a dog person?"

"Quite the contrary. We have two chocolate labs," Raven answered. "It's just that the Secret Service has had some rather unpleasant experiences with dogs. One of Biden's bit agents a couple dozen times. Staffers were scared to death of the thing. Called it 'Cujo.'"

"They won't have that problem with Baxter. He's a lover, not a fighter. The only thing he's ever bitten is food."

"The Secret Service will be relieved to hear that," Raven said. Getting back to the putting green, Raven continued, "Obama and Biden would come out here for some private discussions. Obama was hyper-competitive, and I think some small wagers were involved. I never knew Trump to use it. He said that the greens at his golf courses are much, much better."

"Of course they are," Joshua said.

As they were about to move on to the horseshoe pit, Raven said, "This isn't the original putting green. Ike had one made on the South Lawn. His had a sand trap. Nixon took the green and the trap out. No swimming or golfing on Nixon's watch. just bowling." Both men chuckled. "Bush 41 had it reinstalled and Clinton finally moved it here."

They made their way to the South Lawn and the horseshoe pit. "This is Bush 41's contribution. A regulation-size horseshoe pit. Bush insisted on using blue clay instead of sand."

"Why's that?" Joshua asked.

"Beats me, but that's what he wanted and that's what he got," Raven answered. "Anyway, they had this big grand opening party, 150 guests. He even arranged tournaments and leagues with a horseshoe commissioner. He entertained Queen Elizabeth II here with a few tosses. Yeltsin, too. I think he tried to get the queen to give it a try, but she demurred. Probably would have gotten her white gloves dirty. She did give him a pair of silver-plated horseshoes, though."

"I thought presidents couldn't accept gifts from foreigners," Joshua said.

"Paperwork. Do the paperwork and you'll be fine," Raven advised. "Would you like to toss a few?"

"No, thanks," Joshua said. "Maybe some other time."

On their way back inside, they stopped on the South Lawn driveway. "Clinton used to have a jogging track here. A full quarter-mile made from crushed tires," Raven said.

"I remember Clinton being a runner. I didn't know they built a track for him," Joshua replied.

"He used to go out into the streets some mornings," Raven explained. "The Secret Service hated it. The commuters hated it more. It made traffic a mess. So they built him a track. He used it a couple of times, but didn't like it. Too spongy, he said."

Raven gestured toward the White House. "Let's head back inside. That's it for the athletic facilities. There is one more thing that I can show you, though. It's in the new East Wing, off of Trump's ballroom." They made their way to the East Wing and arrived at a movie theater.

"Before Trump bulldozed the old East Wing and the East Portico, there was a movie theater in the portico. FDR converted a cloakroom into the movie theater. It could seat forty people," Raven began. "Roosevelt learned that even the president has to have a movie night sometimes. I hope that you and the first lady get away now and then. I've been with the GSA for a long time, and I've seen presidents age right before my eyes. Don't let that happen to you."

"Good advice, Isaac," Joshua said. "I'll see to it. Maybe we'll have you over for the holidays to watch *A Christmas Story*. I can't believe you haven't seen it."

"Thank you, sir. I'd enjoy that. My kids keep telling me to watch it," Raven said.

"The old theater used to be just some chairs and a screen. Bush 41 outfitted it in movie theater red for a more authentic experience. There used to be a popcorn machine in the old one. I have no idea what they did with it. Now, we have this. As you can see, the red seats have been replaced with gold ones. They say that Jimmy Carter watched 500 movies while he was president. I don't imagine you'll watch that many," Raven said.

"I don't think I've seen 500 movies in my life," Joshua said. "So I doubt it."

"I believe it's time to get you back upstairs. They're probably waiting for you," Raven said.

"I doubt that the president is," Joshua said. "He seemed annoyed that I actually showed up today."

Raven chuckled. "Don't take it personally. He's been like that for a year or so. Seems like all he wants to do is get the hell out of here. Most of his staff feel the same way."

As they headed back toward the Oval Office, Raven said, "There are a couple of other small things. There's a pool table on the third floor. There've been pool tables here since John Quincy Adams. There's also a music room up there. Hillary set it up so that Bill could play his saxophone without bothering everyone. Do you play an instrument, sir?"

"No. Not very musical, I'm afraid."

"Too bad. We have some wonderful old grand pianos in storage," Raven said.

The president-elect stopped before reaching the Oval. "Thanks for the tour, Isaac. Fascinating stuff."

"It was my pleasure, sir," Raven replied.

"You should write a book about all of this," Joshua said. "Or at least do a podcast."

"Maybe," Raven said. "Once I retire."

"Will you be staying on come January?" Joshua asked.

"That is entirely your decision, sir. The administrator serves at the pleasure of the president," Raven answered. "If you would like me to stay on, it would be an honor to serve."

"Good," Joshua said. "I'd like you to." That decision had been reached five minutes into the tour.

"Thank you, sir. It will be a privilege," Raven said.

"Let me ask you one more thing, Isaac. Do you think we could fit a curling rink in somewhere?" Joshua asked.

"I'm sorry, sir. I don't know what building a curling rink entails," Raven answered.

Joshua laughed. "Not many people do. We'd need a piece of land, flat, maybe two-hundred feet by sixty feet, water, 600 amps, 480 volts."

Raven thought for a moment. "I know a spot that might work," he said.

Chapter 9

Studying

"Treaties, you see, are like girls and roses: they last while they last." – Charles de Gaulle, 1963

For the president-elect, there was the domestic agenda and the international agenda. On the domestic side, President-elect Sheehan was most interested in addressing the climate crisis, which prior administrations had kicked down the road or been openly hostile to dealing with. He had made some progress on the problem in Maine, building EV charging stations, along with solar and wind farms. For politicians, avoiding dealing with long-term problems is easy. The longest-term they ever think about is the period leading up to the next election, which is why most congresspersons spend half of every working day fundraising.

Joshua was also interested domestically in income inequality and job creation, particularly in the trades. As an architect, he experienced first-hand how difficult it was to find skilled tradespeople. He was, however, astute enough to realize that he was not an expert in those things, so he appointed people who were, and let them do their jobs. It was the way he governed, setting goals and objectives and letting competent people go about executing on them. He didn't need to have his fingers in everything. He governed that way in Maine, and it worked for him. It also freed him, as president, to focus most of his attention on international affairs, particularly on China. Almost exclusively on China. If he were going to succeed in bringing about global peace, which he fully intended to do, it would require China's cooperation.

Between his election and inauguration, Joshua spent a lot of time studying history and the three major multi-national treaties of the twentieth century – the League of Nations Covenant, the United Nations Charter, and the NATO Treaty. Each of them brought the promise of peace, but never the reality of peace. Joshua needed to know what caused each to fail and whether it was even worth trying again.

In early December, during the transition, the president-elect invited three experts in twentieth-century history and international affairs to meet with him in Portland. There was already slushy, mucky snow on the ground and sidewalks. His transition team identified three experts – Shawn Michaelson, Dennis Murphy, and Jill Mendoza. Joshua had studied their résumés. They gathered in a hotel suite overlooking the bustling waterfront. Commercial Street smelled of diesel, seaweed, and fish.

"First of all, thank you very much for coming to Maine on such short notice. I hope to learn a lot from you today," Joshua began.

"As you know, I want to discuss the League of Nations, the United Nations, and NATO. What was good about them, bad about them, whether they have been successful or not. What we can learn from them." Over Speckled Ax coffee and Cookie Jar pastries, they began with the oldest – the League of Nations, established in 1919 at the end of World War I. Jill Mendoza directed the discussion.

"The ultimate goal of the League was to bring about a permanent world peace. World War I had just ended. More than sixteen million people were dead. President Woodrow Wilson proposed the idea of a world assembly in his 'Fourteen Points' address to Congress," Jill said. "I've taken the liberty of bringing copies of the League of Nations Covenant for you.

"Just for some quick historical background, Wilson's proposal for a world body was not anything new. Three hundred years earlier, Emeric Cruce had proposed a permanent world council to resolve disputes between countries and an executive council comprised of more powerful countries in *The New Cyneas*. Hugo Grotius proposed a council comprised of Christian European countries two years later. Neither went anywhere," she said. "Finding a path to peace has proven elusive." Jill was completely unphased talking to the man who would soon be president.

Shawn Michaelson and Dennis Murphy were anxious to get involved and get the president-elect's ear. "The League of Nations established an assembly of its forty-two members. The assembly was empowered to address 'any matter affecting the peace of the world,'" Michaelson began. "No small task, sir."

Shawn Michaelson could be pegged as an academic on sight. On this day, he sported a tan Harris tweed jacket on top of a brown crew neck sweater over a light blue collared shirt. His hair settled where it pleased, refusing the urgings of a comb or brush. His belly draped ever-so-slightly over his belt. The faculty dining room's menu was fabulous. He also knew as much about twentieth-century American history as anyone.

"The League revolved around the pivotal pillar of mutual disarmament, positing that a reduction of arms around the world would mean a greater likelihood of peace. Fewer weapons, fewer and smaller wars, the reasoning went," Dennis Murphy added. Murphy, the former United States Ambassador to the United Nations and to NATO, knew his way around treaties and international affairs.

"It's probably worthwhile at this point to take a look at the Covenant itself," Jill said. "The two foundational provisions are the Preamble and Article 8." They read them:

THE HIGH CONTRACTING PARTIES, In order to promote international co-operation and to achieve international peace and security by the acceptance of obligations not to resort to war, by the prescription of open, just and honourable relations between nations, by the Firm establishment of the understanding of international law as the actual rule of conduct among Governments, and by the maintenance of justice, and a scrupulous respect for all treaty obligations . . . Agree to this Covenant of the League of Nations.

Article 8: The Members of the League recognise that the maintenance of peace requires the reduction of national armaments to the lowest point consistent with national safety and the enforcement by common action of international obligations. The Council . . . shall formulate plans for such reduction for the consideration and action of the several Governments . . . After these plans shall have been adopted by the several Governments, the limits of armaments therein fixed shall not be exceeded without the concurrence of the Council . . . The Members of the League undertake to interchange full and frank information as to the scale of their armaments, their military, naval and air programmes and the condition of such of their industries as are adaptable to war-like purposes.

When they finished reading, Joshua asked, "Why did the League of Nations fail?"

"In my view, the Article 8 provision that every member disclose the kinds and quantities of weapons in its arsenal, as well as the full scope of its military capabilities, doomed it from the start," Jill Mendoza began. "Countries went to great lengths to keep those things secret, just like they do today. No one saw any benefit in being completely candid with that information, including the United States, had it joined. The League was reliant on every country being honest and on every other country trusting them. Trust in international relations is, and always has been, in short supply." Michaelson and Murphy nodded.

"OK," Joshua said. "What else besides full disclosure and trust?"

"The League of Nations council could dictate what kinds and quantities of arms each member could stockpile," Michaelson offered. "That was destined to fail. Every sovereign nation, to this day, wants to make those decisions for itself. Looking back, it's surprising that anyone agreed to those terms in the first place. Can you imagine a country allowing some world council to tell it how it could arm itself?"

"Definitely not. Any others?" Joshua asked.

"I would add that the United States' refusal to join destined the League to fail," Murphy added. "Without the United States, the League was without the world's greatest superpower, militarily and economically. Along with that, our enemies weren't going to limit their capabilities while we were left on our own to amass whatever arms we pleased."

"Would the League have succeeded if the United States had joined?" Joshua asked.

"No, I don't believe so. The other problems we talked about would have applied to the United States, as well. We weren't going to be dictated to," Jill answered. "Congress refused to ratify the Covenant. Republicans in the Senate had a deep distrust of President Wilson. He won the Nobel Peace Prize for proposing the League. Even that didn't persuade us to join." Joshua couldn't take his eyes off of Jill when she spoke. He flashed back to the middle school library with Miss Jacobson.

"What about strengths? The League certainly had noble goals. Did it get anything right?" Joshua asked.

"In my opinion, it did, sir," Jill began. "Its core tenet was that an act of war against one member was deemed an act of war against all members. It foreshadowed NATO's Article 5. In theory, it created a powerful mutual defense alliance."

"It also provided for joint economic and diplomatic sanctions against an aggressor. The League imposed relatively minor sanctions against Italy before World War II, but those weren't a sufficient deterrent to prevent the war," Michaelson added. "While sanctions can be an effective tool in discouraging bad actors, they must be strong enough to act as a meaningful deterrent."

With its core provisions destined to fail, within twenty-five years of the League's founding, World War II was raging. Germany, Italy, and Japan had all been members of the League, but withdrew in the 1930s. The Soviet Union was expelled in 1939. When the Axis powers became aggressors at the beginning of the war, the League found itself impotent, unwilling and unable to effectively respond without the United States. The League formally dissolved in 1946, although it had been dead for some time. It was replaced by the United Nations.

While the League of Nations and the United Nations were different, in many ways they were alike. Both sought to foster an increasingly-elusive world peace through an assembly of all member nations and a council of larger, more powerful ones. The United Nations did not go so far as to propose disarmament.

"Let's talk about the United Nations, then," Joshua said. Just as she had done with the League of Nations discussion, Jill Mendoza began the analysis.

"World War II left more than seventy million people dead. An almost incomprehensible number. Nearly one of every thirty people in the world. There was a hunger for some way to bring about and maintain peace. There had been two world wars within the span of twenty-five years. Between the Preamble and Articles 1 and 2, the United Nations Charter uses the words 'peace' or 'peaceful' eleven times. I've brought copies for you." She passed around the Charter.

WE THE PEOPLES OF THE UNITED NATIONS DETERMINED to save succeeding generations from the scourge of war, which twice in our lifetime has brought untold sorrow to mankind, and to reaffirm faith in fundamental human rights, in the dignity and worth of the human person, in the equal rights of men and women and of nations large and small . . .

AND FOR THESE ENDS to practice tolerance and live together in peace with one another . . . and to unite our strength to maintain international peace and security, and to ensure . . . that armed force shall not be used, save in the common interest . . .

Article 1: The Purposes of the United Nations are: (1) To maintain international peace and security, and to that end: to take effective collective measures for the prevention and removal of threats to the peace, and for the suppression of acts of aggression or other breaches of the peace, and to bring about by peaceful means . . . adjustment or settlement of international disputes or situations which might lead to a breach of the peace; (2) To develop friendly relations among nations based on respect for the principle of equal rights and self-determination of peoples, and to take other appropriate measures to strengthen universal peace; (3) To achieve international co-operation in . . . promoting and encouraging respect for human rights and for fundamental freedoms for all without distinction as to race, sex, language, or religion . . .

Article 2: The Organization . . . shall act in accordance with the following Principles: (1) The Organization is based on the principle of the sovereign equality of all its Members . . . (2) All Members shall settle their international disputes by peaceful means in such a manner that international peace and security, and justice, are not endangered . . . (4) All Members shall refrain in their international relations from the threat or use of force against the territorial integrity or political independence of any state . . . (7) Nothing contained in the present Charter shall authorize the United Nations to intervene in matters which are essentially within the domestic jurisdiction of any state . . .

They finished reading. "Let's try the same exercise for the United Nations. What are its weaknesses?" Joshua asked.

Jill Mendoza went first. "The greatest weakness is that there is no enforcement mechanism for preventing threats to the peace or for suppressing acts of aggression. It doesn't establish an army or military force to deter or respond to bad acts or bad actors. Time and again, we've seen it powerless to act. Ambassador Murphy probably can speak to that better than I can. Just off the top of my head, we've had Korea, Vietnam, the Six-Day War, the Yom Kippur War, Algeria, the Afghan War, Iran-Iraq, the Persian Gulf War, the Iraq War, Bosnia and Kosovo, the Russia-Ukraine War, Israel-Hamas, India-Pakistan, Israel-Iran. I'm sure I'm missing some. All of those conflicts happened *after* the creation of the United Nations. The UN couldn't prevent any of them."

"That's a pretty depressing list," Joshua said. "Other weaknesses?"

"There is no explicit mutual defense agreement," Murphy offered. "Almost everything in the Charter is couched in aspirational, not concrete, terms. It speaks of 'effective collective measures' and 'suppression of acts of aggression' and 'adjustments of international disputes.' That intentional vagueness renders it largely feckless when simmering hostilities break out into wars. The UN is left to issue warnings and rebukes, perhaps impose sanctions, and to try to aid in recovery once the war is over." Murphy had sat through days-long debates over the precise, picayune language to be used in condemning conflicts. It was universally watered-down in the end.

"There's also the problem of the Security Council," Michaelson added. "Any permanent member, whether it be the United States, the UK, France, China, or Russia can block any significant action with one vote. A unilateral veto to taking any action. One-hundred-and-ninety countries might be in favor of something and one can block it. It's a very undemocratic structure. It also vests the five permanent members of the Security Council with extraordinary control over the whole body."

"OK," Joshua said. "What about the UN works well?"

"Quite a few things, actually. For one, just about every country in the world is a member," Jill began. "There is a collective benefit to having everyone in the same room, hearing the same thing. It is the largest international body ever assembled. Most members at least feel like they have a chance to be heard."

"The UN is also well-positioned to respond to disasters – earthquakes, floods, tsunamis, famines, those kinds of things – and to provide humanitarian aid," Murphy added. "There is a good infrastructure in place to respond quickly and to get aid where it is needed. It has been very effective in responding to disasters and mobilizing relief."

"It also has some very useful programs not directly related to maintaining peace. It's pretty good at promoting health and nutrition, economic development, and education. The United States' commitment to those programs has been significantly compromised in recent years, unfortunately so, in my view. It also advocates for human rights, although it is mostly limited to words and public pressure," Michaelson added.

"The Paris Climate Accords provide a perfect example of that," Murphy said. "Other than public and social pressure on the signatories, the Climate Accords provide no enforcement mechanism whatsoever to compel compliance. No sanctions, no fines. Compliance is entirely subject to the whim of whoever controls the reins of government at any given time. We've seen that play out quite vividly here at home. First, we're in, then we're out. Then we're in again, then out again."

"I can assure you, Dennis, that I take the climate threat very seriously. I intend for us to be the world leader in addressing it," Joshua said.

"I'm heartened to hear that, sir. If there is anything I can do, I am at your service," Murphy said.

"There is one more thing about the UN that I believe is a positive," Jill Mendoza added. "The charter explicitly states that the UN will not intervene in the domestic affairs of any member. No one wants some international body involving itself in its own purely internal affairs."

"Thank you. This is all extremely helpful. If there's nothing more about the UN, let's move on to NATO," Joshua said. Jill provided the primer.

"The NATO treaty was adopted in 1949, three years after the UN was formed. There were twelve initial members. Now, it's grown to thirty-two, democracies, more or less. The United States, Canada, and Western Europe, all aligned against a common enemy – Russia. Several share a border with Russia, Finland's being the longest. Even the United States shares a maritime border with Russia in the Bering Sea. NATO is a very different organization than the League of Nations or the UN. An explicitly military alliance, as set forth in Article 5. Nothing more, nothing less." She presented copies of the NATO treaty to everyone. "As you read, notice how often it uses the words 'peace' or 'peaceful.' Notice, too, that those words are not defined."

> *The Parties to this Treaty reaffirm . . . their desire to live in peace with all peoples and all governments. They are determined to safeguard the freedom, common heritage and civilisation of their peoples, founded on the principles of democracy, individual liberty and the rule of law. They seek to promote stability and well-being in the North Atlantic area. They are resolved to unite their efforts for collective defence and for the preservation of peace and security*
>
> *. . .*

Article 1: The Parties undertake . . . to settle any international dispute in which they may be involved by peaceful means in such a manner that international peace and security and justice are not endangered, and to refrain in their international relations from the threat or use of force . . .

Article 2: The Parties will contribute toward the further development of peaceful and friendly international relations by strengthening their free institutions . . .

Article 5: The Parties agree that an armed attack against one or more of them in Europe or North America shall be considered an attack against them all and consequently they agree that, if such an armed attack occurs, each of them, in exercise of the right of individual or collective self-defence . . . will assist the Party or Parties so attacked by taking . . . such action as it deems necessary, including the use of armed force, to restore and maintain the security of the North Atlantic area . . .

When they finished, Dennis Murphy spoke up. "It's important to note that NATO has been successful in preventing any attacks on its members over nearly eight decades. Historically, that's an extraordinarily long time for none of the thirty-two members to come under attack from somebody. In that sense, NATO has accomplished exactly what it set out to do. So successful that Article 5 has only been invoked once, on September 12, 2001, following the terrorist attacks in the United States. NATO members fulfilled their Article 5 responsibilities in defense of the United States."

"Thank you, Dennis," Joshua said, then asked, "So, tell me about the NATO treaty's weaknesses." By now, it was assumed that Jill Mendoza would start, which she did.

"To me, the main flaw is that it sets up an 'us against them' paradigm. Democracies versus communism and authoritarianism, the West pitted against the Soviet Union, originally, now Russia. It was primarily designed to protect central and western Europe against the looming Soviet threat during the Cold War."

"Another potential weakness is the question of whether every member would be willing to come to the military aid of another if circumstances arose. Sure, everyone jumped in after 9/11, but that was coming to the defense of NATO's most powerful member. If they didn't come to the defense of the United States, they risked us not coming to theirs. It's an open question whether everyone would do the same if a smaller member were attacked," Shawn Michaelson said. "For example, we're not sure how all of the NATO members would respond if Russia were to attack, say, Latvia or Estonia."

"What about strengths?" Joshua asked. "What about NATO works?"

"That's a pretty easy one, sir," Jill began. "It's the Article 5 agreement that an attack on one is an attack on all and that every member will come to the armed defense of the country under attack. Putting nuclear capabilities to the side, collectively, the NATO countries constitute the most powerful military alliance in history. The combined military power of the NATO countries, counting active duty military personnel, aircraft, warships, and weaponry, is easily two, three, four times that of Russia. Russia understands that very, very well. It's why they do everything they can to undermine the alliance. I am also convinced it's the only reason they've never attacked any NATO country. It no doubt has been a powerful deterrent.

"There is one other important treaty which we haven't discussed – the Inter-American Treaty of Reciprocal Assistance, usually referred to as the Rio

Treaty. It was adopted after World War II and is basically NATO for North and South America. The United States is the only country signatory to both. It is rarely discussed, but contains the same 'an attack against one is an attack against all' language and the pledge to come to each other's defense. It's a much shakier alliance than NATO, mainly due to the lack of the one common enemy that unites NATO," Jill offered.

Joshua was particularly enamored with Jill Mendoza. She had served in the State Department or Defense Department for more than fifteen years, with a PhD in International Relations from Princeton. She was confident in her knowledge and direct and thoughtful in discussion. She was a leader, and the others willingly deferred to her. Joshua had noticed her legs, too.

When the meeting adjourned, Joshua asked Jill to stay behind. "Thank you for meeting with me, Jill. I enjoyed hearing your insights," he said.

"It was my pleasure, sir. Thank you for including me," she said.

"You're welcome, but let's stop with the 'sir' stuff, please," Joshua said. "Joshua will do, at least in private."

"OK, sir . . . I mean Joshua. Sorry, it's a habit," Jill said. Joshua had never been called "sir" as often as he had been during the month since the election. Virtually everyone he met began or ended a sentence with the word. He invited a select few to address him by name. Jill Mendoza was now one of them.

"Let me ask you something, Jill," Joshua began. "Do you think that peace is actually possible? Could it ever happen?" She thought that he might ask something different.

Jill stood and walked toward the window. She didn't make a sound as she glided across the carpet. She cradled her chin between her thumb and forefinger and stared out over Casco Bay. Joshua was drawn to her silhouette, slender, defined, against the rambunctious December sky. From behind, she could easily be mistaken for Stephanie. Joshua rose and walked quietly toward her. Suddenly, she turned to find him in front of her. They were barely three feet from each other.

"I try to be an optimist, Joshua, and I'd like to think that it is. It would take the right person, the right moment, the right idea, luck, fate, karma, whatever you want to call it, but, yes, I believe that it is."

"In our lifetimes?" Joshua asked.

"Maybe," Jill answered. "I have two daughters. They lost their father to war. I want to believe it. I need to believe it."

"I'd like to, too," Joshua said. "Thank you again, Jill. There's a driver waiting for you downstairs. Have a safe trip home. Let's stay in touch." He showed her to the door and watched from the window until she emerged from the lobby and slid into the back seat of her limo.

T wo weeks later, the president-elect nominated Jill Mendoza to be his Secretary of State. The vetting revealed more of her story. *Magna cum laude* Bachelor's degree in United States History from Williams, all-conference tennis player, PhD from Princeton, Fulbright Scholar, four years teaching at Cornell. Spotless academic credentials. Department of Defense. Department of State. Widowed four years ago by a suicide bomb.

President-elect Sheehan understood the value in the collective defense treaty, and appreciated its deterrent effect. He concluded that NATO offered a model with the greatest chance of bringing about worldwide peace, although it would be a peace based purely on raw, overwhelming collective military power. "Negative peace," it was called; simply the absence of fighting. The nobler goal of positive peace based on respect for, and acceptance of, the inherent rights and dignity of all people, rather than fear, seemed impossible. You have to walk before you can run, Joshua reasoned.

The term "negative peace," the absence of war or conflict, carries such uninspiring connotations. "Positive peace" would be so much better, a peace based on social justice, inclusion, and nonviolent conflict resolution. Joshua recognized that negative peace is far from perfect. It has everything to do with stopping the shooting, not addressing the cause of the shooting. He agreed with Martin Luther King, Jr., who, in his 1963 letter from a Birmingham jail, criticized those who were "more devoted to 'order' than to justice, who [prefer] a negative peace . . . to a positive peace, which is the presence of justice." Joshua didn't prefer a negative peace – quite the contrary. Regardless, he concluded, negative peace wouldn't be such a terrible place to start. Positive peace would just have to wait.

Chapter 10
The White House Curling Rink

"If you build it, he will come." – Field of Dreams (1989)

Construction began on the White House curling rink five weeks before President-elect Sheehan even took office. Isaac Raven muscled the project through the red tape and bureaucracy of the United States Commission of Fine Arts, the National Capital Planning Commission, the National Park Service, and the Environmental Protection Agency, all of which demanded their say in the planning and approval. Groundbreaking commenced on the afternoon of December 14th, after the Electoral College votes were cast and recorded. To be safe, groundbreaking could have waited until Congress certified the votes on January 6th, but that wasn't going to present a problem this time around. No one seriously disputed that Sheehan had won. Even the Honorable Henry Stockton couldn't bring himself to claim that the election had somehow been stolen.

Groundbreaking took place without fanfare, without Stephanie pretending to work a shovel in stilettos. She and Joshua were ensconced in Maine, Joshua buried in the logistics and progress of the transition. If it weren't for the nor'easter moving in, Stephanie and Joshua probably would have been heading outside to Fort Knox to watch the Geminid meteor shower rather than sitting together in front of the fireplace.

Making a big production of the groundbreaking would have wasted valuable hours. Joshua was in a hurry to get it built, and the outgoing one-term president had long ago lost all interest in politics or in what his successor might be building or planning. As long as the construction didn't interfere with his sleep, he didn't care.

The sitting president was no longer spending much time at the White House anyway, preferring long weekends at his compound down south, where it was warmer, now that winter was rolling in to the capital. At first, the president would leave Washington on Friday evening, then it became Friday afternoon, until he settled on leaving on Thursday after dinner. He would return on Sunday night at first, then Monday morning, and finally on Monday night, after a much-deserved round of golf. By November, he was spending more time at home than in Washington. He no longer had to answer to the voters, who didn't much mind or notice his extended absences. His cabinet and staff had been polishing and circulating their résumés for months.

The only significant presidential duty which the lame-duck president was attending to during his final few weeks at the wheel was doling out pardons and commutations. It was the new presidential fetish, bestowing "get out of jail free" cards on sketchy allies and supporters. As recently as George H.W. Bush's one term, the president granted only seventy-seven pardons and commutations. By the time that Barack Obama was done, he had issued nearly 2,000. Joe Biden went on a rampage, more than doubling that number to 4,300. Donald Trump pardoned 1,500 on a single day. The outgoing president, doling out pardons like Halloween candy, would easily reach five figures, as long as his signing hand didn't cramp up. If it did, the autopen would do his pardoning for him.

As it turns out, things in Washington can move quickly when the commander in chief wants something done and doesn't need a congressional appropriation to do it. But, before anything happens in Washington, tribute must first be paid to the acronym gods, and they are omnipresent. For example, construction and building operations at the White House complex are supervised by the White House Office of Administration (OA), which includes the OCOS, FSMD, GSA, FMB, CMB, PSB, and COOP. President-elect Sheehan delegated the navigation of that acronym-rich sea to his beleaguered friend and chief of staff, Sam Pelletier.

The Department of Homeland Security even maintains an official compilation of department acronyms titled *"The DHS Acronyms, Abbreviations, and Terms List."* Homeland Security, Joshua learned, has even come up with DAAT as the acronym for the list of acronyms. During his first week in office, Joshua instructed everyone in the White House that they were not to speak to him in acronyms, but in actual words.

"No more acronyms!" Joshua instructed. He considered putting it in an Executive Order, but the Office of White House Counsel advised against it. "I'm always two sentences behind trying to de-code the acronyms," Joshua said. Offenders were required to put a dollar into the Too Many Acronyms (TMA) jar on the Resolute Desk, next to the M&M dispenser. It was a sweet irony, since M&M is an acronym for Mars and Murrie. The TMA jar filled up quickly as staffers and bureaucrats struggled to comply. "That'll be a dollar," Joshua said in reprimanding offenders. The only permissible exceptions to the no acronyms rule were the FBI and the CIA.

B uilding even a small curling rink and making perfect ice is neither cheap nor easy. It requires at least a quarter-acre of land for two curling sheets and a modest warm room. Then, there must be space for the chiller plant, which makes the ice. Temperature control systems, dehumidification systems, water purification systems, insulation, and lighting have to be installed. It's like building a small hockey arena. Building it is only the beginning, though. Once a curling rink is built, someone has to actually tend to it, making the ice and repeatedly pebbling and scraping to make it playable. Given his professional background, President-elect Sheehan appreciated how complex a project it was. Resisting his instinct to meddle, he kept his distance as construction progressed.

Fortunately, there are companies that specialize in building curling rinks. Not surprisingly, they were all willing to move building one for the President of the United States to the top of their project lists. Their other clients would just have to wait. The OCOS – rather, the Office of the Chief of Operation Services – hired the company personally selected by Joshua to build the rink.

Normally, it takes upwards of a year or more to build a curling rink, even a small one like President Sheehan's. For this project, though, everything was accelerated. Operation "Git 'er Done," Isaac Raven dubbed the project. The environmental impact statement was approved within a few days, after a cursory review. Political appointees, hoping to keep their jobs in a new administration, were happy to exert their influence to expedite things. No eight-week lag times waiting for deliveries, no days off for the contractor or subcontractors, plenty of overtime for the workers. The White House grounds, largely dormant in the winter, were alive with a cacophony of backhoes, bulldozers, cement mixers, nail guns, and the beep-beep-beep of trucks backing up.

Joshua's critics, still stinging from their electoral humiliation, went berserk. It was an egregious waste of time and money, and the construction desecrated the sacred White House grounds. Having a curling rink served no purpose other than feeding Joshua Sheehan's ego. The construction moved forward regardless. The critics had no idea why he was building it. It had nothing to do with ego.

Within three months of taking office, President Sheehan had his curling rink. On the inside, it looked like any other, with a few exceptions. There were the usual scoreboards on the far wall; racks for hanging brooms; and two sets of brand new Ailsa Craig curling stones, adorned with red, white, or blue handles, a gift from the Scottish government. The rink had a small warm room and bar for watching games, like almost every curling club. President Sheehan ordered that the bar only stock Maine beer, the best in the country, as any Mainer will proudly attest. He would personally curate the beer list. There was always at least one beer from Bucks ME Brewing on tap, an homage to Bucksport. In the center of the sheet, the presidential seal was visible through the ice. At the entrance, a sign warned, *"No Business or Politics on the Ice! – by Order of the President of the United States."* Joshua thought that one up himself.

On a side wall, the "Spirit of Curling" was displayed, reading:

While the main object of the game of curling is to determine the relative skill of the players, the Spirit of Curling demands good sportsmanship, kindly feeling and honourable conduct.

Stephanie threw the first stone in the new curling rink, without fanfare, as Joshua watched. The official White House photographer captured the moment. The photo was not shared with the media, but a framed print was placed on the credenza behind the Resolute Desk. Stephanie was a very good curler, having played for years back in Belfast. She was actually a slightly better curler than her husband. She still had her cardboard crown to prove it.

"So, how's the ice, Steph?" Joshua asked.

"Good. A little frosty, but good," she answered, adding, "But not as good as Belfast's."

"Pretty much everything's better in Maine than in D.C., if you ask me," Joshua said. "That's off the record, of course." They stayed and threw stones for an hour, Joshua playing hookey from his job, adjusting to the ice, learning its nuances, playing a game against each other. It quickly became part of their routine, a chance to get away from the suffocating weight of responsibility and power.

On Sunday nights, when they were both in town, Stephanie and Joshua would head to the rink at seven-thirty to play a game. It was their time. Date night. The stakes were monumental. The loser would deliver coffee in bed to the winner on Monday morning. More often than not, Stephanie was the beneficiary. Joshua made it clear to his staff that, in the absence of a true national emergency, he and Stephanie were not to be disturbed while curling. His staff tried its best to comply, but there were occasional transgressions. For those few hours, Joshua and Stephanie were able to forget, for the most part, that they were the President and First Lady of the United States.

Even with their Sunday night curling dates, adjusting to life in the White House was infinitely more challenging than adjusting to life in the Blaine House. If activity at the Blaine House was busy, activity in the White House was frenetic. The West Wing was a 24/7 machine, running on coffee, Red Bull, and sometimes, something a tad stronger. Joshua and Stephanie were so far removed from the easy pace of Bucksport, or of Augusta, for that matter, that it really did seem like they had wandered into a different world. The only peace and quiet they could find was in the residence and in the curling rink on Sunday nights, as long as the president's staff remembered not to pester him with inconsequential matters. Even First Canine Baxter needed time to adjust to the new sights and smells and sounds.

It was Stephanie who made the discovery. "Come here, Joshua," she said one Saturday night. "I have something to show you. Grab a sweatshirt." A Secret Service agent led the way.

"Where are we going?" Joshua asked. They were headed to the third floor, above the residence, which was vacant. Joshua had only been there once, on one of his first days in office.

"You'll see," Stephanie said. "Have a little patience."

The agent opened a heavy, creaking door leading to yet more stairs. "Watch your step, please," the agent said. The trio climbed the metal stairs to another door, where the agent entered the access code. The door opened and the Washington night sky burst forth before them.

"Wow. I had no idea we were allowed up here," Joshua said. He slowly turned, gazing out on the Washington Monument, the Capitol dome, planes leaving and arriving at Reagan National. Only a few stars were visible in the light-polluted sky. The Secret Service snipers were around somewhere, out of view, lost in the shadows.

"You're the President of the United States, Joshua. Where, exactly, do you think you're not allowed to go?"

"Right this way, please," the agent gestured. Joshua saw the Adirondack chairs beside the fire table, which already had a low flame burning. An ice bucket held two Maine beers – *Mr. Grumpypants* for him, *Gigantic Dad Pants* for her.

"Happy birthday, Mr. President," Stephanie said. "Surprise!"

"It's not my birthday – not until Tuesday," Joshua said.

"Don't be such a fart. It's close enough. Besides, you don't like spending a romantic Saturday night on the White House roof with your bride?"

"Of course. Can't think of anything better," Joshua said, settling into one of the Adirondacks. "But if it's gonna be a presidential birthday party, you have to do it up right. Like Marilyn Monroe to JFK."

"I *knew* you were going to say that!" Stephanie said. "I *knew* it! I *knew* it! I *knew* it!" She scanned the roof to see how far away the Secret Service was. She reached one hand into the pouch of her hoodie and pulled out a platinum blond wig. She put it on and began singing oh-so-slowly, in an exaggerated, breathy voice.

"Happy birthday to you. Happy birthday to you. Happy birthday, Mister Pres-i-dent," she purred. She inched closer, wiggling as she sang. "Happy birthday to you."

"Very, very nice. Well done. Thank you, babe. I'm sure the Secret Service enjoyed that. If you don't mind my saying, you look fabulous as a blond, you know. You should really consider it. The press would go nuts. You could start a whole new fashion craze. Now, have a seat. But keep the wig on." When Stephanie was settled in and had recovered from her performance, Joshua asked, "Where did all this stuff come from? Adirondacks, fire table."

"Isaac Raven. I swear the man can find anything, including wigs. They must have a warehouse around here somewhere."

"So it seems," Joshua said. It was the most relaxed that he had felt in months. He wondered whether any of his predecessors had cracked open a beer on the White House roof. Obama, if he had to guess.

"Remind me where Gemini is," Stephanie said, rubbing her hands together over the fire. "It's been so long, I've forgotten."

Joshua surveyed the Washington sky. "Not from here. There's way too much light and way too much pollution. I can only see five or six stars, much less constellations. Remind me to show you again, if we ever make it back to Maine."

If it took a little getting used to having the Executive Protection Unit around constantly as governor, it took a lot of getting used to having round-the-clock Secret Service protection. Neither the president nor the first lady were ever out of earshot, and rarely out of eyesight, of at least one Special Agent, usually several. Every movement, every trip, every venturing outside, was coordinated with the Secret Service. A few lucky agents had no doubt witnessed Stephanie's *Happy Birthday* performance and would have a story to tell. "I can't go to the john without those guys knowing where I am and how long I'm taking," Joshua joked. They never fully got used to it, but they knew that it was, sadly, necessary. And they were grateful for the men and women who risked their lives protecting them.

Even as president, Joshua maintained his weekly grilling responsibilities, national, international, and political crises permitting. It had worked for them in Augusta, bringing a welcome slice of domestic life from Bucksport to the Blaine House, so why not try the same thing at the White House? It also provided great amusement for the staff, watching the President of the United States scurrying back and forth to the grill, trying not to overcook things. Once a month, he shucked Damariscotta River oysters, usually Pemaquids or Moondancers, for appetizers, a skill he had mastered on an oyster farm tour as governor. His staff pilfered some money from the nearly-overflowing Too Many Acronyms jar to buy him a chef's hat and a "Griller in Chief" apron, which he dutifully sported.

Stephanie felt the loneliness of Washington and of living in the White House more acutely than Joshua did. While Joshua was constantly surrounded by people, Stephanie had fewer responsibilities and not nearly the entourage. Sure, she gave a few speeches and attended some social events, but that was being with strangers, not being with friends. She came up with an idea that she hoped might boost her spirits.

During a Sunday night curling date, she asked, "What do you think about having a little bonspiel here at the White House? I was thinking that we could invite a few teams from Belfast to come down. I miss our friends."

"I know you do, Steph. I do, too. I don't see why not. It would be fun. They'd get a kick out of curling at the White House," Joshua answered. "Do you have any particular idea who you might invite?"

"I thought we'd leave that up to the club. However they want to decide is fine by me. Maybe a lottery, maybe a playdown. They'll figure it out," she answered.

"Have you thought about a bonspiel name? You can't have one without a name, you know." Bonspiels always have a name reflecting something about the location or time of year.

"I've been trying to think of one, but I'm not having any luck. Can you think of one?" she asked. "I've thought of the WhiteHouseSpiel, the FirstLadySpiel, the SheehanSpiel, but I'm not crazy about any of them."

"This isn't my strong suit. I'm not really too creative that way. But I'll try to think of something," Joshua answered.

After another hour of playing, Stephanie and Joshua headed back to the White House. This time, Joshua had earned Monday morning coffee in bed. "I've got it!" Stephanie burst. "The FLOTUSpiel!"

"I like it. I think you've got it. The FLOTUSpiel it is," Joshua said.

The next morning, after dutifully presenting Joshua with his coffee, Stephanie called her friend, Emily Carlton, now the president of the Belfast Curling Club, to extend the invitation. Emily Carlton would not be described as athletic-looking, being short and stout, but she was one of the best curlers in the club. She was also the most organized person Stephanie knew. Whose kitchen doesn't have a junk drawer? Stephanie had considered asking Emily to come to Washington as her chief of staff, but Emily would never have abandoned her beloved Belfast for that long.

Stephanie and Emily had curled together on an all-women's team at the club. It was Emily who was sitting next to Stephanie in the warm room when Stephanie invited Joshua to Fon's Kitchen for their first date. "Go ahead, ask him," Emily had whispered. "Or else I will."

Eight teams of four could play in the FLOTUSpiel from Friday night through Sunday morning, Stephanie told Emily. The club could pick which members to send. "Make sure that one of the teams only has three on it so that I can play," Stephanie added. "You should be one of them. I've missed playing with you."

"Will do. I've missed playing with you, too. I'm pretty sure we won't have any trouble finding teams," Emily said. "Bye, Steph. Love you. I'll keep you posted."

Eight weeks later, the FLOTUSpiel was in full swing. It wasn't only a curling event, though. Stephanie wanted her guests to get the full White House experience, so that when teams weren't curling, they were bowling on Nixon's bowling alley, playing horseshoes on Bush's pit, or putting on the putting green. A complicated scoring system based on the curling, bowling, horseshoes, and putting results would determine the winners of the inaugural FLOTUSpiel.

On Saturday night, the guests filled the movie theater to watch the Beatles' *Help!* With the popcorn machine at work, it smelled like an honest-go-God, melted butter, movie theater. Each guest received a box of Goobers, Whoppers, and Good & Plenty. Thanks to the White House janitorial service, the floor wasn't even sticky.

Stephanie chose *Help!* because of the brief scene with John, Paul, George, and Ringo curling outdoors in Austria. In the scene, a villain hands George a curling stone with a smoking bomb inside. After George throws the stone, he realizes that it's a bomb and yells to his mates, "A thingy! A fiendish thingy!" The band escapes just before the bomb explodes and leaves a gaping hole in the ice, out of which a scuba diver emerges.

The audience howled at the sight of the Fab Four curling, with John, inexplicably, sweeping *behind* the stone. The entire weekend was like an extended kid's birthday party, the adults giggling and laughing as they scrambled from one event to another, wildly over-stimulated.

Stephanie wanted everything at the FLOTUSpiel to be as casual and unpretentious as possible. These were her curling friends, not some stuffy diplomatic delegation. There would be no fancy White House sit-down dinner or fine china. Instead, she opted for taco night in the warm room on Friday and pizza in the residence before the movie on Saturday. While her guests wanted to know everything about being first lady and about life in the White House,

Stephanie preferred to catch up on what was happening at the curling club and what was going on in Belfast.

Joshua largely stayed away, although he attended movie night and doled out popcorn and candy, and he dropped by the warm room a couple of times. Baxter, too, made the rounds. This was Stephanie's time, and Joshua didn't want to detract from it. Besides, he had a state visit to prepare for. On Sunday, he presented the winner's trophy, a small replica of the White House, which would find a home in the club's trophy case back in Belfast.

The FLOTUSpiel did wonders for Stephanie. Her mood lightened. It felt a little more like home. She decided that the FLOTUSpiel would be an annual event.

Chapter 11
A Curling Cabinet

In what was mocked as frivolous, even dangerous to the national interest in some quarters, President Sheehan required that his Secretary of State and Secretary of Defense learn to curl and that they, in turn, require their senior staff to learn as well. It was a prerequisite for the job, which was made clear during the appointment, vetting, and confirmation process. Why that was so, only President Sheehan knew.

During the confirmation hearings, some senators used their entire allotted time questioning the nominees about curling, when they should have been asking about, say, qualifications, experience, and policy priorities. For President Sheehan, it was a disqualifier if a potential nominee wouldn't commit to learning the game. Every short-listed candidate readily agreed to the demand. A few, eager to get a leg up on their competition, quietly arranged to take to the ice at the Potomac Curling Club to learn to play even before being short-listed. Maybe, they hoped, knowing how to curl would catapult them to the top of the list.

On a Sunday morning in early May, Secretary of State Jill Mendoza and her three highest-ranking subordinates, along with the Secretary of Defense and his three highest-ranking subordinates, met President Sheehan in the curling rink for their introduction to the *Roarin' Game*. For the occasion, President Sheehan had secured curling shoes and a curling broom for each. If they were going to become curlers, they would need the proper equipment. Finding out their shoe sizes was a snap. Six-and-a-half for Jill, 10EEE for Defense. Background checks and vetting produce a wealth of personal information. First, Joshua gave them a quick overview of the game's history.

"Curling was invented over five-hundred years ago in Scotland, when some folks – men, no doubt – apparently decided that it would be fun to throw large, heavy stones across the ice on frozen lochs and ponds. At first, there were no real rules, people just trying to get the stones closest to a mark. Over the centuries, rules were standardized into what is now the Olympic sport of curling, with all of this equipment and indoor ice-making capability," the president explained. "Although it seems fairly simple, I think that you will quickly discover that it can be quite a challenge." The Secretary of Defense, a veteran of Marine special operations, was always up for a challenge, especially one where he wasn't being shot at.

They all knew most of the history already. It helps to learn everything you can about your boss and what your boss likes, and they had been briefed by their staff on the history and rules of the game. Every possible advantage helps.

President Sheehan invited two United States Olympic curlers, medalists, one from the men's team, one from the women's, to serve as instructors. "Wear your medals, please," Joshua asked. "People will want to see them, including me." If the secretaries were going to become at least adequate curlers, why not start with a lesson from some of the best players in the world? Despite their advanced degrees from the most elite schools and their impeccable credentials, the sight of Olympic medals grabbed the attention and respect of the students. They wanted to touch them. After the preliminaries, the Olympians began their lesson with a discussion about safety on the ice.

"Always pay attention to your surroundings," they began. "During a game, there will be sixteen stones and eight people on the ice, and you don't want to be tripping on one of them or bumping into them. We don't need any of you in the hospital. A war just might break out because you're laid up." The students laughed.

The Olympians proceeded through the meticulous step-by-step process of showing each pupil how to approach the hack, how to properly step into the hack, how to use the stabilizer for balance, how to grip the stone, how to push out from the hack, how to slide, how to turn the stone's handle to make it curl, and how to sweep. A couple of the students tipped over while pushing from the hack, like toppled chess kings. Others wobbled like Weebles, but didn't fall.

Not everyone was in optimum condition for the rigors of sweeping. Jill Mendoza had no problem with it. She was in terrific shape. Every day for her started before dawn with forty-five minutes on the elliptical. Neither did the Secretary of Defense, a former member of the elite Marine Raider Regiment and competitive triathloner.

Throughout the entire course of the two-hour lesson, the secretaries and undersecretaries were smiling and laughing, occasionally at their aptitude, but far more often at their ineptitude. An outside observer would have been hard-pressed to know where each person placed on an organizational chart at the Pentagon or the Department of State. On the ice, everyone is equal, the curling adage says, and it contains at least a nugget of truth. Lessons about strategy and tactics would come later. For today, the basics were more than sufficient.

Like almost everyone trying the game for the first time, the secretaries and undersecretaries struggled mightily with delivering the stones. Sometimes, the stones didn't even travel halfway down the ice, much less cross the hog line. Other times, the stones sailed clear through the target area, known as "the house." Every once in a while, though, someone managed to get a stone to settle somewhere in the house, an event sparking celebration and immense admiration for whoever threw it. By the time the lesson ended, the newbies were tired, but enjoying the game and the challenge of making the stones do what they were intended to do.

President Sheehan, now joined by the first lady, welcomed the new curlers and their instructors into the warm room as they stepped off the ice. They all sat around a table. Some ordered a drink from the bar, even though it was barely noon. Even the president and first lady allowed themselves a beer. The secretaries, not easily impressed by credentials and titles, were in awe of the Olympic medalists. They asked lots of questions about the game itself, and about what they had just been taught, but what they really wanted to know was what it was like to play in the Olympics. What kid, or adult for that matter, hasn't dreamed of that?

"What was your favorite part about being in the Olympics?" someone asked.

"The opening ceremonies. The parade of nations. Walking alongside some of the greatest athletes in the world – skiers, ski jumpers, figure skaters, speed skaters, snowboarders, wearing the USA colors."

"How long did you have to train?" Jill asked.

The Olympians smiled at each other. "About twenty years," Tiffany Patterson said. "I started playing when I was eight and competing seriously at twelve. Then I started playing in Juniors, then Regionals, then Nationals, and Worlds. We finally qualified for the Olympics."

"Can I touch your medals?" an undersecretary asked. It had only been a matter of time before someone worked up the nerve to ask. The Olympians removed their medals and passed them around. The students handled them like Fabergé eggs.

"Are you going back to the Olympics?"

"Maybe. We have to qualify. They don't make it easy. Just because you went once doesn't guarantee that you're going back. Perhaps you might put in a good word for us, Mr. President?" Tiffany said.

"I doubt the Olympic Committee would look kindly on that, I'm afraid," Joshua said. "You'll just have to go out and earn it, which I know you will."

For those few moments in the warm room, the President and First Lady of the United States were just two of the folks sitting around talking about curling and fawning over the Olympians. The president's plan was unfolding.

What the two secretaries didn't yet know was "Why?" Why did the president want them to learn to curl? Why had he invited Olympians to teach them? Why were State and Defense the chosen departments? The answers would come in due time. For now, they could only wonder.

President Sheehan didn't add the curling rink to the White House just so that he and his cabinet and advisors would have a place to play. He already had the swimming pool, putting green, tennis court, basketball court, bowling alley, pool table, and horseshoe pit for that. No, he had a specific and considered plan for how the curling rink would be used. He just hadn't told anyone what it was yet. Why give anyone extra time to concoct their opposition?

P resident Sheehan scheduled a meeting with the Secretary of State and the Secretary of Defense in the Oval Office the following morning. Neither one had seen an agenda. They did see, however, that there was now a curling stone on the credenza behind the Resolute Desk, a present from the president's friends in Belfast after the election. The president welcomed the secretaries into his office. "So, how did you enjoy your introduction to curling yesterday?" he asked.

Both State and Defense smiled. "It was so much fun," Secretary of State Mendoza answered. "It was a lot more challenging than I imagined. I think I got one stone in the house the whole day. My legs are a little sore."

"We'd love to do it again sometime if we get the chance," the Secretary of Defense added.

"Good. I'm glad to hear that," the President answered. "You will get that chance, I promise. In fact, you'll have quite a few opportunities." President Sheehan began to unveil another small part of his plan. Just a small part.

"I want you to identify sixteen people in each of your departments, including yourselves and the folks who played yesterday, to learn the game. Not desk jockeys, not policy wonks, but high-level people who will be traveling and meeting people. I want them to be people who will be working all parts of the globe – Western Europe, Eastern Europe, Africa, Asia, South America, the Middle East, Central America. I want people who can deal with democracies, monarchies, dictators, autocrats, and theocracies. A really well-rounded group who take our foreign policy and foreign relations seriously. Do you think that you can find me those kinds of people?"

The secretaries thought for a moment and jotted notes. "Yes, sir," Jill said, as did the Secretary of Defense. They were already thinking of who they might choose. More than that, they were wondering why.

"Good. I'd like your lists by noon on Thursday," the president said. "And I'd like eight from each department to be here on Sunday at 9:00 a.m. and the other eight from each department to be here at 11:30. Can you see to that?" The secretaries made more notes.

"Yes, sir, Mr. President," Jill answered. "Of course, Mr. President," Defense echoed.

"Mr. President, I'm thinking about my Undersecretary for Policy. He's in a wheelchair. I assume that I'll have to exclude him?" Defense asked.

"A very good question. Not at all. He can curl right from his chair. Adaptive curling is popular and growing. He'll fit right in. Same for people who might not be able to crouch down. They can play standing up. It's called stick curling. A little bit like shuffleboard. Don't exclude anyone just because of physical limitations. If they're otherwise a good choice, include them. Is there anything else? If not, I'll see you on Sunday," the president said, rising from his chair.

"One thing, Mr. President, if I may," Secretary Mendoza said. "Should we tell them why they're being asked to do this? I'm sure they're going to ask. The people yesterday were asking." Neither secretary had any clue what the president was planning. Jill hoped that she might find out this way.

"Just tell them we all need a little R&R sometimes. Good for morale." It was not the answer the secretary was fishing for. Joshua asked Jill to stay behind, as was becoming his custom. The president showed the Secretary of Defense to the door. "Thank you for coming. I look forward to seeing everyone on Sunday morning. And keep up the good work." The door to the Oval closed, leaving Joshua and Jill alone in the Oval.

"How are the plans for the China state visit coming along?" Joshua asked.

"Good. We're finalizing the agendas, working with the first lady on the state dinner, everything's in good shape, pending your final approval," Jill said. "I expect to have everything finalized and on your desk by tomorrow."

"Sounds good. Could you do one more thing for me, Jill? It's very important."

"Of course."

"I want to know everything there is to know about President Yu. Everything. Favorite food, hobbies, education, friends, worldview, religion, pets – everything. Not just résumé stuff. I want to know how he thinks, how he processes, who he listens to, how he makes decisions. Do you have that kind of intel?"

"We do, sir . . . Joshua." Old habits die hard. "How soon?"

"Friday. We can sit down and talk about President Yu on Friday."

"D on't look back. Something may be gaining on you," Satchel Paige famously warned.

Washington, D.C. is teeming with lawyers, lobbyists, congresspeople, diplomats, special envoys, ambassadors, secretaries, undersecretaries, assistant secretaries, deputy secretaries, journalists, all kinds of successful, educated, accomplished people. The Ivy League is grossly overrepresented. Washington is also full of petty, jealous people, most of whom also fall into one of the prior groups. Even at the highest stations, insecurity runs rampant. Almost everybody in town is looking over their shoulder, sensing footsteps, paranoid.

Word that the top people at State and Defense were being invited to the White House to learn the president's favorite game left other members of the cabinet nervous. "Some" is an understatement. Of the fifteen department heads in the cabinet, except the secretaries of State and Defense, all were envious of the special treatment. Why were they the only ones chosen to learn to curl? Even at cabinet meetings, the Secretary of State always sat next to the president to the right, the Secretary of Defense to the left. The most important seats. The ones from which they could whisper to the president. Proximity is power, and the Secretary of State and the Secretary of Defense had it at cabinet meetings and now on the ice. Especially Secretary Mendoza. She was clearly the one who had the president's ear.

On Thursday, Sam Pelletier delivered the names of the thirty-two State and Defense representatives submitted by the secretaries. Along with the names, the chief of staff attached a curriculum vitae and headshot for each. President Sheehan took a few minutes to study them. Most of the names meant little or nothing to him, but their collective credentials were impressive. Almost all had better résumés than the president himself, a fact which did not go unnoticed. His master's degree in architecture from Boston Architectural College paled in comparison. He had no objections to anyone on the list. The secretaries had chosen well.

By nine o'clock on Sunday morning, the sixteen chosen ones from State and Defense were assembled in the warm room of the curling rink. Coffee and pastries were spread out on a table in front of the bar, along with paper plates and napkins bearing the White House insignia. The president was there to greet them, as were four volunteers from the Potomac Curling Club, who would serve as instructors. At 9:00 a.m. sharp, the president addressed the first group.

"Thank you all for coming out this morning on such short notice. I think you're going to have fun. In fact, I *order* you to have fun. You're probably not exactly sure why you're here, but don't worry about that right now. It will become apparent in due time. For today, though, I would simply like for you to pay close attention to your instructors, be very careful out on the ice, and, most importantly, enjoy yourselves. And pay special attention to these words," he said, pointing to the sign reading, "*No Business or Politics on the Ice! – by Order of the President of the United States.*"

"It is one rule which must never be broken," the president explained. "Out on the ice, the game is all that matters." For fun, he had them raise their right hands and repeat the words aloud. It eased the nervousness.

Partly by nature, partly because of ambition, the attendees were extraordinarily competitive people. To get to where they were, they had worked longer, harder, and smarter than others. They had made sacrifices and compromises. To get to where they aspired to be, they would continue that way, especially with the president watching. They were going to learn to do this, and learn to do it well. Who knew what reward might be in store for those who excelled?

Everyone stepped onto the ice for the beginning of their lesson, except for the Undersecretary of Defense for Policy, who wheeled himself onto the ice. After watching for a few minutes, President Sheehan made his way back to the Oval Office to meet with Chief of Staff Sam Pelletier and review the week's agenda. Sam Pelletier had come with Joshua from Augusta, where he had served in the same role. He brought his Maine accent with him. Sam knew exactly how the president liked things done and he made certain that they were done that way. He controlled access to the president and countenanced absolutely no drama in the West Wing.

The sixteen students were split into four groups, each group taking its place with an instructor in one corner, at one of the hacks. Some were natural athletes, some not as much. For the next two hours, the instructors introduced them to the basics of the game, just as the Olympians had tutored Jill Mendoza and the Secretary of Defense. By the time the lesson was over, the students were tired, and a little sore, having used muscles they hadn't used in quite that way before. The best part was that they all seemed to enjoy playing.

As the nine o'clock group stepped off the ice, they were greeted by their colleagues in the eleven-thirty group, who had already gathered in the warm room. None dared be late. They had been warned that the president was a noodge about punctuality. The latter group took notice of how excited the first group seemed to be and of how they all were chattering and laughing. That was encouraging. At eleven-thirty on the nose, the president was back and addressed the second group just as he had the first, made them raise their right hands to recite the words on the sign, and sent them off to the ice.

President Sheehan had once again scheduled a Monday meeting in the Oval Office with the Secretary of State and the Secretary of Defense. There were a few international issues to address – nothing particularly worrisome or urgent, but things worth keeping an eye on. The secretaries assured the president that they had a good handle on each and were working the diplomatic and military channels. There were also the plans for the upcoming state visit from China to fine tune, now that Joshua knew more about President Yu Song.

With all of that business taken care of, President Sheehan moved on. "Let's talk about curling," he began. "Now that we have thirty-two brand new curlers at State and Defense, it's time to get some experience actually playing. I want each of you to make four teams of four players each from your department. You can organize them however you want. Send your rosters to Kelly in the chief of staff's office. Kelly will make a schedule for each team to play one game a week. We'll have instructors there to help." He paused. "You know how Bush 41 had a horseshoe league? We're going to start a White House curling league." Neither secretary knew anything about Old Man Bush's horseshoe league. They made mental notes to look into it.

The secretaries nodded their understanding. Not everyone was going to be thrilled about adding something new to their calendars, but it came with their ambitions and career choices. Most, however, would gladly do it. After all, it was coming directly from the President of the United States, and they had been personally selected for the honor by their secretary. As the secretaries had surmised, everyone was curious to know why they were doing this. "I wish I could tell you," was the usual answer. It would have to suffice.

League play began the following week. Scheduling and re-scheduling consumed a few hours of Kelly's time each week. It was the life of a twenty-four-year-old West Wing intern. Hastily arranged meetings and crises, large and small, wreaked havoc with the schedule and had to be dealt with. Finding a couple of hours each week when everyone on a team was available was a logistical nightmare, but Kelly made it happen, even if games had to be arranged for eight-o'clock at night or on weekends. Conflicts created by official duties were acceptable excuses, those of a personal nature were not. People would just have to miss the Nationals or Capitals game, even if they had great seats. Kelly was good at her job.

Many of the curlers' colleagues in the federal bureaucracy were jealous. Why couldn't they play, too? President Sheehan didn't want them left out, he just needed to prioritize State and Defense. Once State and Defense were up and running with their leagues, the president invited each of the other cabinet members to learn the game along with a few of their staff, as well. Some politely passed on the invitation, which was fine with the president.

When word began spreading through each department, the jockeying to be selected began. An invitation to curl at the White House became the most prized ticket in town. It was the lawyers at the Department of Justice who maneuvered the hardest to be chosen. There were sharp elbows. Knowing how to curl might prove especially helpful to the Secretary of Agriculture when he made his rounds through the curling hotbed of the upper midwest. It was more exciting than staring at soybeans and cattle or quibbling over the wording on food labels.

Kelly's job as curling scheduler eventually required more hours than she had to devote to the task. The chief of staff's office is the busiest in the West Wing, and Kelly's personal life was basically non-existent. She could catch up on her sleep in a year or two, maybe even go out on a date, after she left the White House.

More than one hundred people had to be enrolled in learn-to-curl classes, volunteer instructors from the Potomac Curling Club had to be scheduled and cleared, and leagues had to be formed and booked. Kelly deftly handed off all of her curling-related duties to an unsuspecting, eager, and extremely ambitious twenty-three-year-old, who was thrilled to work on the president's pet project. "I'm in charge of the president's curling schedule!" she proudly announced to her parents, who wondered whether two-hundred grand for a degree in international relations from Georgetown was proving to be worth it.

Naturally, word that the President of the United States' cabinet – the departments of State and Defense in particular – were taking to curling spread through the international diplomatic community, just as President Sheehan had hoped. As it did, a few other countries began asking their diplomats to learn the game. There was no real reason for it other than the fact that the United States diplomats were doing it, and it's always wise to be prepared. For a few, particularly Canadians and Scandinavians, it wasn't much of an ask, since many of them had played the game before. "Curling" searches were trending online. Curling club membership around the world was spiking. Rumors circulated that the President of the United States was planning a curling summit at the White House.

Despite its niche status within the pantheon of sports, curling is played, to a greater or lesser degree, almost everywhere. Most popular in Canada, Sweden, Switzerland, and Scotland, the sport has spread to some surprising places. There are curling clubs all throughout Europe, but also in Afghanistan, Australia, Brazil, China, the Dominican Republic, Guyana, India, Israel, Jamaica, Japan, Kenya, Kuwait, Mongolia, New Zealand, Nigeria, Pakistan, Puerto Rico, Qatar, Russia, Saudi Arabia, and Thailand. When one thinks of the Caribbean, the Middle East, or Southeast Asia, winter sports do not jump immediately to mind.

As United States diplomats made their stops around the world for contentious talks and high-stakes negotiations, those who had learned to play at President Sheehan's request arranged for games with their diplomatic counterparts who were also learning to play. It was a small thing, really, but it was a human thing. For a couple of hours, they were able to set aside some of what stood between them, relax, and have fun – a rare thing in the environment in which they toiled.

Everywhere they played, signs warning against discussing business or politics on the ice were prominently displayed. The press had fun with it, too. Sometimes, it made for a more interesting story than whatever issues were being negotiated. Some of the United States diplomats reported that relations were less tense and more cooperative after a little time time spent together on the ice. Progress was actually being made. Another piece of the president's plan was falling into place.

What Joshua wanted was for the world to try something new, to learn something together, to share an experience. Going through something together, even something as silly and inconsequential as learning how to slide some stones down the ice, brought people closer, provided a commonality. The studies around friendly competition clearly demonstrated that it fosters respect and kinship among and between the competitors. Station matters little, the peasant can take on the king, the pauper best the baron. People with seemingly nothing in common, neither language nor color nor religion nor history, can learn about each other by the simple act of playing a game. The oddest thing was that it was working.

Chapter 12

Yu Song

"I don't like that man. I must get to know him better." – Abraham Lincoln

"Tell me everything we know about Yu Song, Jill," Joshua began. It was as open-ended a question as he could think of to begin his education. The state visit from China was only a week away. Jill set her coffee down. Joshua noticed her fresh manicure and that her apple red nail polish perfectly matched her shoes.

"He's a complicated man, Joshua," Jill began. "Tell me more about what you really want to know."

"Why not start with the basics. Give me his résumé," Joshua said.

"He studied economics at Tsinghua University in Hangzhou. Top of his class at one of the great global universities. He rose quickly through the ranks of the Chinese Communist Party. His father was a very senior intelligence officer who groomed his son for a future within the party. He is both respected and feared, which is not necessarily the case with all world leaders. He is not the least bit afraid to use his position and power to shape his vision and to squelch dissent. Human rights are a decidedly low priority. Criticizing China's human rights record will not be received well. In fact, criticizing anything about China's internal affairs will not be. His decisions are seldom challenged and are never ignored. For now, he is in complete control of China's government. Our assessment is that he will remain so for the foreseeable future.

"His wife's name is Bao. They've been married for twenty-nine years. One son, one daughter. Four grandchildren. Bao studied music at Shanghai Conservatory. She is also a dog-lover. They currently have three, but have had as many as five or six."

"OK," Joshua said. "Good to know about the dogs. Answer me this. How would I go about trying to convince him to do something? What approach would work?" Although Joshua had known Jill Mendoza for only six months, he trusted and relied on her for straight, uncompromised information more than he did anyone else in his administration.

"I'm not sure that you could convince him, quite frankly. He makes his decisions based solely on what he thinks is best for China. Your opinion on the subject won't matter much to him," Jill answered.

"What does he think is best for China? What does he want China to be? How does he see its role in the world?"

"That is becoming increasingly clear. His actions tell us exactly how he sees its role. His primary interest is in making China the greatest economic power in the world. Since Yu took office, China's percentage of global GDP has risen dramatically and continues to grow. Right now, it is about two-thirds the size of ours. By far the second-largest economy in the world. Twenty years ago, it was maybe half our size. He wants China to be number one.

"President Yu has poured huge sums into manufacturing plants, infrastructure, data centers, technology, energy generation, and artificial intelligence," Jill continued. "The United States has contributed substantially to China's growth by outsourcing much of its technology and even its military supply chain to China. His overarching agenda is fueling China's economic growth. He does not hesitate to steal intellectual property and violate patents."

"Is he cautious, or is he tolerant of risk?" Joshua asked.

"I don't think that I would couch it in those terms," Jill said. "I would say instead that he is willing to consider and try new things that he thinks will be beneficial to his country. He has that luxury because of his firm grip on power. Early on after he became president, there was an uprising within the party to oust him. The leaders of that movement – those who are still alive – now find themselves ensconced at Qincheng Prison. No one has been foolish enough to challenge him since.

"Rather than continue along a path of simply manufacturing and exporting cheap consumer goods, Yu has funneled enormous resources into making sophisticated, hi-tech products for the future – batteries, solar panels, communications equipment, satellites, microchips, computers, those kinds of things. He has also invested heavily in their space program. Obviously, they succeeded in getting to the moon, a source of great pride to his country. If he believes that a new program or initiative will help his country in the long-term, he is willing to try it. He plays a long game, not focusing simply on immediate or short-term outcomes. He is in a good position in that regard, unlike Americans who tend to only focus on the short-term because of politics and elections," Jill explained.

"Does he trust us? Does he believe that the United States will keep its word?" Joshua asked.

"Yu is a pragmatic and practical man, to the extreme. The only thing that he truly trusts is action, not words. He has seen us reach agreements, only to see them, if not broken, at least skirted. Our shared history is not defined by a high degree of trust, in both directions. He doesn't know you, Joshua. You're a blank canvas to him. Perhaps that is to your advantage. He will want you to prove that you are trustworthy."

"What about global stability? China has spent a lot of resources supporting some pretty bad actors around the globe – North Korea, Syria, Myanmar, Hezbollah. Why is Yu supporting instability around the world? Destabilizing markets doesn't seem like it is in his economic interest," Joshua asked.

"That's a very good question, and one which he appears to be rethinking. President Yu seems to be backing away from fomenting instability.

That might be for a number of reasons. First of all, he has probably calculated that chaos and unstable markets are not good for the Chinese economy. They need trading partners to buy their goods. The more things they make, the more buyers they have to find. They need to exploit as many markets as they possibly can. More stable markets mean a greater ability to sell their manufacturing output. They also make for greater predictability, which helps with long-term planning. Selling weapons and military hardware helps, because they are expensive and always in demand, but it isn't enough. Besides, China has seen some of its people killed in incidents around the world. Yu can't like that," Jill said.

"The inverse is equally important. China is very dependent on imports, especially energy – oil, gas, coal. Their economy demands enormous supplies of energy, especially as they invest in massive AI data centers, which require huge amounts of energy, and turmoil in the Middle East, Russia, and even the United States, threatens the supply. They also rely on imports of raw materials needed in the technology sector, like copper. A significant portion of those come from Africa, which is not noted for political stability. China also depends on food and agricultural imports to feed its people. They simply can't do it by themselves. They have four times the population that we do living in an area the same size as ours. They need wheat and corn and soybeans and meat from all over the world."

"Go on," Joshua said. "Don't let me stop you."

"We have also detected a decrease in China's military expenditures, at least as a percentage of its GDP, over the past five years. It is a very small decrease, almost imperceptible, but a decrease nonetheless. President Yu is trying to find ways to pay for all of his investment in infrastructure to support its continued economic growth. Military spending is a drag on that.

"Another change that we have noted is more of a change in tone as opposed to an official change in policy. There has been less talk of annexing Taiwan over the past several years than at any time since 1949. There has also been a very noticeable reduction in naval exercises menacing Taiwan. President

Yu doesn't appear to have abandoned the idea, just deprioritized it. Finally, spreading communism across the globe is a very low priority. In short, we don't believe his goal is military or political or ideological dominance. It's economic dominance."

"Who does he listen to? Who advises him?" Joshua asked.

"He has an extremely small group of advisors. People who have been with him for years. Just four or five that he seems to trust and rely on. In the end, he makes his decisions and they fall in line. That's officially. Unofficially, his wife, Bao, may be his closest advisor. Much like you and Stephanie," Jill said.

"Smart man," Joshua replied.

"Bao is a very interesting person. Not at all what you might expect of a Chinese president's wife. She is not constrained by formality. She is her own person, not simply an appendage or ornament. She has a personality and shows it, sometimes to President Yu's discomfort. In colloquial terms, she might be considered something of a hippie. But we know that Yu listens to her. They're a team, like you and Stephanie."

"So, if I were to make a proposal to him, the best way would be to do it directly, not go through intermediaries?"

"That would be my advice, if it were something you felt was that important. He understands and respects directness. Our assessment is that President Yu subscribes to the "Great Man" theory of history. Do you know about Great Man theory?" Jill asked.

"I'm afraid that I don't. I don't remember hearing about that in architectural school. Tell me about it." Joshua felt pitifully undereducated sitting next to Jill.

"Great Man theory posits that some people, almost always men, I might add, are born with certain traits and characteristics that make them great leaders. Leaders, in other words, are born, not made. One of the theory's early proponents said that the history of the world is the biography of great men. Think Abraham Lincoln, Gandhi, Martin Luther King, Jr., George Washington, Churchill, Jesus. The theory is no longer in vogue, replaced by a more nuanced analysis of how people become great leaders – environment, opportunity, societal evolution, chance, even. But given what we know about President Yu, he seems to subscribe to the theory and believes that he himself is one of those great men. He displays many of the characteristics of the prototypical great man – a firm grip on power, seeing himself as the best person to make important decisions, decisiveness, trusting his instincts above all else."

"You're saying that he has an enormous ego? Does that mean that flattery would work on him?"

"Quite the opposite, surprisingly," Jill began. "He would interpret that as weakness, a lack of confidence in either yourself or your ideas. Why would you resort to flattery if your argument had merit? Besides, Yu's sense of self and ego are fully-formed. They don't depend on what you or I or anyone else thinks of him."

"OK, no flattery. How about personally. What does he like?"

"Peanut butter," Jill offered. "He's absolutely crazy about peanut butter." The fact that the State Department knew that small detail about President Yu left Joshua wondering how much the Chinese knew about *him*.

"Really? Smooth or chunky?"

"Our intel is pretty good," Jill said, "but not quite that good. I don't know. We just know that he likes peanut butter. I can probably find out for you, if you really want to know."

"Thanks, but that won't be necessary. What else? What else does he like?"

"Sports, for one thing. He was on crew at university and is an accomplished skier, a very good athlete. Two entirely different skill sets. Rowing requires extraordinary teamwork, trust, and cooperation. Skiing is an individual discipline. Man against mountain. He is very proud of China's national sports programs and funds them at very high levels. China has some of the best training facilities in the world to prepare its athletes for the world stage. Performing well in international competition demonstrates to the world

Chinese athletes' strength and discipline. That is important to him and to his people. They're becoming very good at curling, you know," Jill said.

"Yes, I'm aware," Joshua replied. "I've seen them play."

"Do you want to tell me what this is all about, Joshua? I might be able to help, you know."

"I wish that I could, Jill, but I can't. For now, I have to do this alone."

Chapter 13
China

"As you enter positions of trust and power, dream a little before you think." – Toni Morrison, The Source of Self-Regard: Selected Essays, Speeches, and Meditations (2019)

China was the cornerstone of President Sheehan's plan. The one indispensable part of his plan. Without China's agreement, his dream of bringing about world peace would be only that – a dream. Even with China's agreement, the odds of success remained long.

The hardest part of President Sheehan's plan would be persuading President Yu that it was in China's own interest to enter into an alliance of any kind with the United States, much less a military one. The next hardest would be proving to China that the United States could be trusted. Maybe vice versa. President Sheehan concluded that there was no point in wasting time trying to tell China what was in its own best interest. President Yu would make that decision for himself. Jill Mendoza made that abundantly clear.

There was an almost complete lack of trust between the two great powers, fostered, and stoked by many, over decades. China was a convenient boogeyman for the United States, and politicians relished in exploiting it. Joshua's predecessor certainly had. Trade deficit? Blame China. National debt? Blame China. Job loss? Blame China. President Sheehan was determined to change that. For his plan to have any chance, he calculated, he would have to build some kind of personal relationship with the Chinese president. They didn't need to become best friends, but they would have to come to trust each other. That's why President Sheehan invited him to the White House for a state visit.

"You're going curling. With the president of China. During a state visit?" Stephanie said when Joshua told her. Hearing it aloud, it did sound rather preposterous. "Why don't you tell me what this is really about, Joshua? You've had something that you haven't told me on your mind for a long time. It's about time you let me in on it."

"You're going to think I'm crazy, Steph, but I've thought long and hard about this," Joshua said. "Since right after the election."

"I already think you're crazy, so why don't you just try me," Stephanie offered. "Get it out, for God's sake."

"OK, but don't laugh at me," Joshua said. "I'm nervous enough about this already. Scared, really."

"Just tell me, babe. Maybe I can help."

"Alright. Here goes," Joshua began. "China and the United States account for around forty percent of the world's output of goods and services. We are, by far, the two biggest economies in the world. No one else comes close." He was stalling, worried that even Stephanie would think it was stupid. "We are also the two most powerful militaries in the world. We spend nine hundred billion dollars on our military every year. China spends maybe five hundred billion. Nobody really knows. They keep secrets a lot better than we do."

"That's fascinating, but you're not telling me anything. Why curling? Why a state visit? What is it that you're avoiding telling me? Just say it," Stephanie said.

"I want President Yu and I to bring about world peace. I have this idea," he said. That got Stephanie's full attention. "It goes like this . . . " Joshua spelled out the details, including what Jill Mendoza had advised about President Yu and Bao. Stephanie didn't say a word, trying to take it in. Joshua broke the silence. "I thought that curling together might help us connect with each other, start to trust each other, I guess."

President Yu arrived with his delegation in May. It was the first state visit hosted by the Sheehan White House. Usually, a new president's first invitation would be to a long-time ally, not an adversary.

The curling ice in the White House rink was in splendid condition. The ice technician worked overtime to get it just right. President Sheehan had specifically asked that the Chinese delegation include two of the Chinese Olympic curlers. The most promising path to forging a relationship, President Sheehan calculated, was on the ice, teaching President Yu the game, throwing curling stones together. It was just a hunch, maybe a silly one, but he followed it. He had suggested to President Yu that they spend some time together curling. Joshua offered to teach him.

President Yu surprisingly agreed to the suggestion. Joshua took that to mean that President Yu was open to trying something new. A new sign had been installed at the entrance to the rink, written in Chinese, echoing the one in English, advising, "*No Business or Politics on the Ice! – by Order of the President of the United States.*"

What President Sheehan didn't know was just how extensively President Yu had prepared for his White House visit. In addition to the routine preparations on trade, economic, security, and tech issues facing the two great powers, President Yu prepared to do some curling with the United States president. President Yu and his senior staff were taught and coached at the National Aquatics Center in Beijing, where the curling competition took place during the 2022 Winter Olympics. The Center, known as the "Water Cube," was nicknamed the "Ice Cube" when reconfigured for curling. The Chinese delegation spent some serious time in the Ice Cube prepping for their trip to America.

Over the course of a few months, President Yu, under the tutelage of the best Chinese instructors, made himself into a passable player. His athletic background helped. He was tutored not just on rules and mechanics, but also on strategy. If he were going to meet an experienced curler like President Sheehan on the ice, he wasn't going to embarrass himself or China. He was confident that President Sheehan would be both surprised and impressed. Yu's delegation might even be able to win.

The diplomatic visit included breakout talks on trade, tariffs, cybersecurity, AI, and the rivals' increasing, grudging dependence on each other in the global marketplace, the kinds of issues over which they constantly butted heads. Usually, the talks were a zero-sum game. Not a lot of progress was being made.

The state dinner was held in the State Dining Room of the White House, with 130 guests, in addition to the two presidents and their wives. Much of the planning for a state dinner is traditionally done by the first lady, with lots of help from her own staff, the Department of State, the Chief of Protocol of the United States, the White House Social Secretary, the Graphics and Calligraphy Office, and the White House Chief Floral Designer. It is no easy chore, and there is no room for faux pas.

State visits are tightly choreographed affairs with a certain decorum required. Seating is expected to be just so, the music classic, and toasts offered at the proper times by the right people. First Lady Stephanie Sheehan worked tirelessly to get things right, observing all of the requisite protocols and etiquette. Secretary of State Mendoza helped guide her through all of it. Joshua insisted on adding a few unique touches of his own.

Traditionally, a top United States chef is invited to plan and prepare the meal. It is one of the highest honors a chef can receive. For this dinner, Stephanie invited Cecily Moncrieg, founder and chef at the Kitchen on the Lake in Greenville, Maine, to prepare the meal. The Kitchen on the Lake was the only three-star Michelin restaurant in New England, and one of only fifteen in the country. Stephanie and Joshua had shared a candlelight dinner there on their fifteenth anniversary, when he was governor. Cecily Moncrieg knew how to cook. Although reluctant to spend time away from the Kitchen on the Lake, Cecily accepted the invitation. It was a difficult one to turn down, particularly because it was for the two most powerful people in the world, one of whom happened to be a Mainer. There was a surprising twist to this state dinner, though, one proposed by Joshua.

President Sheehan asked President Yu if his delegation could include a Chinese chef, who would share responsibility for preparing the meal. President Yu accepted the offer. It was different, but it was interesting and creative, a generous gesture of goodwill and respect. Perhaps President Sheehan was someone he would be able to work with, someone unlike his dour predecessor. Someone he might even come to like, Yu thought. He resolved to keep an open mind.

Stephanie was the star of the reception and dinner in her first appearance on the world stage. She was beautiful, classy, and effortlessly charming; but better yet, she was warm and approachable. The best part was, none of it was the least bit contrived. Maybe it was the Mainer in her, maybe it was the small-town upbringing, maybe it was the fact that she hadn't spent years planning and scheming for all of this. Whatever it was, people liked it. Most of the guests were more interested in Stephanie than they were in Joshua. Her gown became an internet sensation. Even the most discerning fashion critic was hard-pressed to find fault, either with her dress or her bearing. Nearly everyone wanted their picture taken with her, more, even, than wanted a picture with the president.

Stephanie and President Yu's wife, Bao, genuinely enjoyed each other's company. It helped that Secretary Mendoza had briefed Stephanie on Bao. Like Stephanie, Bao was unencumbered by pretension. Their bond began to take root when the Chinese delegation first arrived and Joshua and Stephanie greeted President Yu and Bao at the North Portico. The first ladies already knew a surprising amount about each other.

One of a first lady's duties during a state visit is giving a tour of the White House to the spouse of the foreign head of state, a tradition designed to keep the ladies occupied while the men got down to their important business. Stephanie and Bao, along with their interpreters, set out on the tour. They were accompanied by Baxter, the Sheehans' rescue dog, which was an historic first for a White House tour. It was not by accident. Baxter had a job to do. Having done their homework, Stephanie and Joshua knew that Bao adored dogs, and she immediately bonded with Baxter. Dogs know instinctively which people truly like them.

Stephanie and Bao walked the halls, their heels' staccato clacking amplified by the marble and plaster. Baxter led the way. They stopped occasionally as Stephanie showed Bao some of the portraits and artifacts, describing each's significance. It was slow and, frankly, a little dull, as the interpreters translated the details. Bao was gracious, but obviously more interested in Baxter than she was in the tour.

"Can we sit for a minute, please?" Bao asked. "My feet are sore and a little swollen from the long flight."

"Of course. Mine are aching, too," Stephanie said. "Where I come from, there isn't much reason to wear such high heels. Here, let's sit." They were in the Blue Room, a small, oval reception room. "One of our presidents – Grover Cleveland – got married in this room," Stephanie said, still in tour mode. Baxter flopped down with a grunt at Bao's feet.

Bao pulled out her phone, a slight breach of etiquette. She sensed that Stephanie wouldn't mind. Bao opened the phone and called up pictures of her three dogs and showed them to Stephanie.

"Oh, my God! They're so cute! What are their names?" Stephanie asked.

Bao was happy to relate their names and breeds. She even knew each of their birthdays. The first ladies forgot about their tour and the boring paintings, furniture, and pottery in favor of discussing their dogs. Stephanie showed pictures of Baxter in various poses and videos of him performing his limited set of tricks. The dogs were far more interesting than some old water pitcher allegedly used by Abigail Adams in 1800. Baxter knew that they were talking about him and nosed in.

"Unless you want to see the rest of the White House, I'd suggest that we go upstairs for some tea," Stephanie said.

"Yes. Tea would be wonderful," Bao replied through the interpreter.

Stephanie's staff knew exactly what kind of tea, imported from China, that Bao preferred, and they called ahead so that it would be ready. As the first ladies entered the residence, Bao immediately noticed the piano, a Steinway Model D Grand, serial number 300,000, freshly polished and tuned. The piano was a gift from the Steinway family to Franklin D. Roosevelt in 1938. It had only found its way into the residence that morning, courtesy of Isaac Raven.

Gesturing to the piano, Bao asked, "May I?" Joshua and Stephanie knew that Bao was an accomplished pianist, and the piano wasn't there by happenstance. Stephanie had suggested that Raven prepare the piano for Bao's arrival.

"Of course," Stephanie answered. "Go right ahead."

Bao sat and adjusted the bench, feeling for the pedals. Before she began, she asked, "Do you and the president play?"

"I play a little bit, but not very well," Stephanie answered. "Joshua, absolutely not. I don't think he could play a kazoo. His singing is even worse." *Kazoo* baffled the interpreters.

"Just like my husband," Bao smiled. "I forbid him to sing in the house." She made a God-awful screeching sound like you might hear in the deep woods during fox mating season. Or during a particularly grizzly murder.

Bao began playing Chopin's *Nocturne No. 13 in C Minor, Op. 48 No. 1*, flawlessly, elegantly. Stephanie sat and listened, mesmerized. She knew that Bao could play, but not like *that*. When Bao finished the piece, Stephanie could only say, "Wow. That was beautiful. Where did you learn to play like that?" Stephanie knew the answer, but she asked anyway. Bao played along.

"I studied at the Shanghai Conservatory for two years. It was very demanding. You know that already, Stephanie. You don't have to pretend," Bao said. Stephanie was startled by her bluntness. "I'm a little rusty, I'm afraid," Bao said. "I don't play as often as I should." Running her fingers across the mahogany, she added, "This piano is magnificent."

"Van Cliburn and Leonard Bernstein played that piano," Stephanie said. "So did Duke Ellington and Elton John," she added.

"Elton John!" Bao exclaimed. "I love Elton John!" She launched into the opening piano riff from *Bennie and the Jets*. The first ladies started singing, tentatively at first, then with increasing conviction, "*Hey, kids, shake it loose together, the spotlight's hittin' something that's been known to change the weather . . .*" They could barely keep themselves composed. When they got to "*B B B B Bennie and the Jets,*" they burst into laughter.

"Our teachers got very angry when we played pop music," Bao said. "'*Laji*' they called it. Rubbish. They warned us that we would develop bad habits if we played it. We had to wait until the teachers left. Then we would sneak into a studio and play. We were very bad girls."

Bao decided to try another one and began playing *Don't Go Breaking My Heart*. They alternated singing the lines, just like Elton John and Kiki Dee. Bao started:

"*Don't go breaking my heart.*"

"*I couldn't if I tried,*" Stephanie vamped.

Bao could vamp, too. "*Oh, honey, if I get restless.*"

"*Baby, you're not that kind.*"

They struggled to make it through the song without cracking up. If their husbands could only see them. When they had recovered, Bao gestured to the bench. "Come sit with me, Stephanie."

Stephanie settled onto the bench. Bao smiled and slid over. "Play something," she said. Stephanie thought for a second and started playing *Heart and Soul*. It was the only thing she knew by heart. No pianist, good, bad, or in between, virtuoso or hack, can resist joining in and making the piece a duet, and Bao did exactly that, adding a bass line. They were having so much more fun than the men could possibly be having, arguing about tariffs and semiconductors and soybeans.

The morning after the state dinner was the one Joshua had been waiting for, with both dread and hope. Today was the day when he would present his proposal to President Yu. While other members of the delegations wore their expensive suits and sat around long, dark tables trying desperately to hash out some agreements – tedious, contentious, negotiations – President Sheehan, Secretary of State Mendoza, the Secretary of Defense, and the United States Ambassador to China, along with President Yu and three of his top deputies, gathered in the warm room of the curling rink. President Sheehan was ready to give the Chinese their first curling lesson.

The eight leaders spoke through interpreters, even though the Chinese spoke and understood English well. "Are you ready for your curling lesson, Mr. President?" Joshua began. A grin worked its way across President Yu's face, and his dark, coffee-colored eyes livened. It was a mischievous look, the look of a child with a secret dying to be let out. Until this moment, the Chinese president had been inscrutable.

"There is no need for a lesson, Mr. President," Yu began. "We have been learning and practicing in preparation for the visit. I assumed that you would prefer to play a game, not teach a lesson."

President Sheehan was surprised, although he probably shouldn't have been. He was pleased, too, that Yu had taken an interest in the game, even if it was only for this one occasion. The Chinese were always extraordinarily prepared for meetings, usually far more so than their adversaries.

"Well, then, Mr. President, if that is the case, shall we head out onto the ice?" President Sheehan proposed. He pointed to the sign, written in Chinese, forbidding discussing business or politics on the ice. President Yu smiled. A nice touch, he thought.

"By order of the President of the United States," Joshua pointed out. He was testing the contours of their nascent relationship.

"We understand, although I am not accustomed to taking orders from an American president," Yu joked. He just might come to like this new president. He didn't care for President Sheehan's predecessor, a stuffy, humorless, duplicitous bore.

Before the game started, the players shook hands and wished each other, "Good Curling," a longstanding curling custom which the Chinese had also learned. The two presidents served as their teams' skips, or captains, and took their places near each other on the ice, their respective interpreters standing some distance behind, off of the ice, out of the way. Jill Mendoza served as Joshua's vice skip. President Sheehan and President Yu called the shots for their underlings a-hundred-and-fifty feet away, who played surprisingly well for being new to the game. It isn't difficult to play the game. It is extremely difficult to play it well. Both teams having been taught and coached by Olympians didn't hurt.

President Sheehan, who had been curling for most of his life, was a better player than President Yu. However, the other Chinese players were better than their American counterparts, at least on this day. By the time the game ended nearly two hours later, the Chinese were on top, 9-7. After the teams shook hands and headed off the ice, President Yu leaned in and whispered to his interpreter, "Tell the president that perhaps his secretaries should practice a little more." The interpreter relayed the message. Both men laughed.

"I think you're right," Joshua said, putting his hand on Yu's shoulder. "I will certainly see to it."

President Sheehan asked everyone to leave the room, except for the interpreters. The Central Guard Bureau agents looked to President Yu for approval. He nodded. Joshua wanted to reveal his proposal to President Yu and no one else. The six other curlers left, heading off to don their serious-person clothes and join the talks slogging on in the White House. They would have much preferred to keep curling, or at least sit and have a beer with the presidents. Joshua went to the bar and drew two beers – *Gunner's Daughter*, a peanut butter stout from Mast Landing Brewing Company in Maine. Why leave anything to chance?

"Mr. President," Joshua began, setting the beers down, "I have a proposal for you. No one else knows or has heard anything about it." President Yu looked Joshua in the eyes, a quizzical look on his face. This wasn't how the business of state was conducted. These kinds of things were floated at lower levels and percolated up the chain, accompanied by studies and data and memos. He hoped that President Sheehan wasn't trying to ambush him. President Yu took a sip of *Gunner's Daughter*. The unmistakable aroma of peanut butter hit his nose before he tasted it.

"This is quite good, Mr. President," President Yu said. "Different, sweet, but very good. It tastes like peanut butter. You know that I have a weakness for peanut butter, of course. Your intelligence officers have done good work."

"Yes, they're pretty good at what they do," Joshua acknowledged. "*Gunner's Daughter* is my favorite. I thought that you might like it. But please, you can call me Joshua in the curling rink," President Yu reciprocated. "Inside, they'll expect us to be more formal, I'm afraid," Joshua continued. "Would you like to hear my proposal?"

"Of course," Yu answered. "I have learned that there is rarely any harm in listening. People talk far too much and listen far too little."

"Thank you," Joshua began. "I know that you've never heard anything like this. But trust me, I am very, very serious. I believe that what I propose would be very beneficial to your great country and to mine. To the world, in fact." Joshua had President Yu's complete attention.

"I want us to bring lasting peace to the world, Song. And the only way for that to happen is if you and I agree to make it happen. We are the *only* ones who can make it happen. You and I," Joshua began. He hoped that Jill

Mendoza and her Great Man theory about Yu Song was correct. He could see the skepticism already forming on Yu's face and sensed the questions already being formulated. "You have two children, don't you?"

"Yes. One son and one daughter. Shan and Lian," Yu said. "Grandchildren, too."

"And don't you wish for a better world for them? A peaceful world, without war?"

"Of course. Everyone wants that for their children."

"Then let me explain my thinking," Joshua continued. President Yu made no effort to stop him. He sipped his *Gunner's Daughter* and listened.

"You know how NATO works, Song. Thirty-two countries allied with a pledge of mutual protection if one of them is attacked. NATO has proven itself to be very effective in preventing Russia from waging an attack on any NATO countries for nearly eighty years. Russia would love to, but knows that it cannot. And you understand that the reason for that is that Russia knows that the combined power of the NATO countries is far greater than its own.

"What if our two countries were to enter into a similar agreement and invite the rest of the world to join us? An attack against China is an attack against the United States. An attack against the United States is an attack against China. The same thing for anyone else who wants to join." President Yu's interpreter hoped that he got the translation right. President Sheehan waited for Yu's response. To his surprise, President Yu did not immediately reject the idea. In fact, he said nothing for a long time.

J ust as Stephanie was Joshua's most trusted advisor, Bao was President Yu's. That night, in the residence at the Blair House, President Yu asked Bao, "What do you think of the president and first lady?"

"They seem like very nice people. And I adore Stephanie. She is so genuine, so natural and warm. There is no pretense about her. We could be friends under the right circumstances," Bao offered.

"Do you trust them?" Song asked. Bao considered the question.

"I have no reason not to. Until they prove otherwise, yes, I would say that I trust them. Why are you asking?" Bao asked.

"The president made a proposal to me today. Only to me. A very unusual proposal . . ."

Chapter 14
The Agreement

"The Great Peace towards which people of good will throughout the centuries have inclined their hearts, of which seers and poets for countless generations have expressed their vision, and for which from age to age the sacred scriptures of mankind have constantly held the promise, is now at long last within the reach of the nations. For the first time in history it is possible for everyone to view the entire planet, with all its myriad diversified peoples, in one perspective. World peace is not only possible but inevitable." – The Promise of World Peace, Bahá'í Faith Universal House of Justice, 1985

President Yu didn't tell anyone except Bao about President Sheehan's proposal during the remainder of the state visit, or even on the flight home. He was intrigued, but he also needed time to think. It was so unusual, but it also carried some real promise. He thought about his children and his grandchildren. Mostly, he wondered whether he could trust the American president.

The Chinese economy was doing well, but not as well as President Yu would have liked. Devoting enormous amounts of money and human resources to its military remained a drain. President Yu was also growing increasingly weary of arming regimes engaged in terrorism and their vain and pointless military excursions. Supporting chaos and disruption was getting old. And it was terribly expensive. He was tired of constantly choosing sides in battles that were of little consequence to him. The return on investment was *jiaos* on the *yuan* – pennies on the dollar. President Yu increasingly believed that it just wasn't worth the cost. A more stable and predictable global marketplace was best for China. He needed reliable supply chains and predictable markets. A disincentive for countries to destabilize those things might prove itself to be of great benefit.

No one in the United States, other than Stephanie, and now Secretary of State Jill Mendoza, knew what President Sheehan had proposed to China. Stephanie enthusiastically approved of the idea. Jill embraced it, too. If there were any possibility of peace, shouldn't it at least be given a chance, negative peace or not? If word of President Sheehan's proposal leaked, though, opponents would do everything they could to sabotage the idea, and it would be dead before President Yu even had time to consider it.

T wo weeks after arriving home from the United States, President Yu extended an invitation for President Sheehan to come to China for a reciprocal state visit in September. President Yu extended the invitation personally, not through the usual diplomatic channels. It was a short time frame in which to plan a state visit, but President Sheehan jumped at the invitation without consulting either his chief of staff or his calendar. There were lots of people who could work out the logistics, even on a short turnaround. That was their job. The anti-Sheehan politicos sounded the reactionary alarm that the president was "cozying up with the Chinese."

"Be sure to bring your curling shoes. I will arrange time to play a game or two," President Yu offered when extending the invitation. "My rink has been practicing hard."

"I will, Mr. President," Joshua said. "My secretaries have begun practicing more diligently as well, as you suggested. I look forward to avenging our loss."

"We shall see about that," Yu answered. "I am glad to hear that your secretaries have been practicing." Joshua chuckled. The leaders were comfortable enough with each other to exchange friendly barbs. It was another small, promising step.

"One more thing," Yu added. Was the answer he had been waiting for finally at hand, Joshua wondered. "Bao would like it if you brought Baxter along with you. She is very fond of him." President Yu said nothing about Joshua's proposal; didn't offer the slightest hint.

"I think that can be arranged. Baxter's never been on Air Force One," Joshua answered. "Goodbye, Mr. President. Give my regards to Bao." With that, the conversation ended, leaving President Sheehan completely in the dark about what Yu might be thinking.

T he American delegation, including Baxter, arrived to great fanfare in Beijing. There was far more public ceremony than there had been in Washington, featuring marching bands, a military parade, acrobats, aerial displays, and fireworks. Baxter hated the fireworks. After the elaborate welcoming festivities, most of the delegation was consigned to the usual mind-numbing, mostly-unproductive, meetings.

The state dinner was even more extravagant than the one staged in Washington a few months earlier. Once again, Stephanie was the most photographed person in the room. Everyone wanted their picture taken with her. Her Christmas-red mermaid gown again set the internet on fire. "Stephanie Sheehan gown" became the most-searched term in the world after the pictures were released. She had checked with Bao weeks earlier to make sure that their gowns wouldn't clash.

"Excuse me, please," Bao said as she rose from her seat after the meal. "I am wanted on the stage." The men at her table stood. Bao made her way slowly up the steps to the stage and stood behind the microphone. President Yu had only reluctantly agreed to this.

"Good evening, ladies and gentlemen, Mr. President. We have a very special surprise for you tonight." She waited as the interpreter repeated the message. "I would like to invite the First Lady of the United States to come and join me." Stephanie looked at Joshua. He shrugged. Clearly, he had no idea what was in store. As Stephanie rose, the room burst into steady, crescendoing applause. She made her way to the stage and joined Bao.

"Now, would you please help me welcome, all the way from London, England . . . Sir Elton John!" Bao announced. Stephanie's eyes widened. She covered her mouth with her hands. Sir Elton took the stage and stood between the first ladies. In her heels, Stephanie was easily the tallest. When the crowd settled, Elton gestured toward the piano.

Stephanie looked at Bao. "No!?" she mouthed. Bao mischievously nodded yes. The trio walked to the piano. Elton theatrically motioned for Bao to sit to his left, then Stephanie to his right, closest to the audience.

"Ready?" Elton said, looking at Stephanie. She furiously shook her head no. The audience howled. "Come on, now. I know that you've practiced."

Sir Elton launched into the opening riff of *Bennie and the Jets*. Stephanie noticed how short and stubby his fingers were for a pianist. "*Hey, kids, shake it loose together, the spotlight's hittin' something that's been known to change the weather. We'll kill the fatted calf tonight . . .*" He stopped mid-lyric. He lowered his head and shook it slowly.

"Ladies, ladies," he said. "The people can't hear you. Always give the audience what it wants. They want to hear you sing!" The audience cheered wildly. "Let's try again, shall we? With conviction this time."

Bao and Stephanie rose to the occasion, even encouraging the crowd to join in. They received a thunderous ovation. Stephanie began to stand to return to her table. Sir Elton took her hand and stopped her. "Would you like to hear one more?" he asked the audience. Of course, they did, and they let the performers know it. Stephanie sat back down. Elton launched into *Don't Go Breaking My Heart.*

"*Don't go breaking my heart,*" he sang, looking directly at Stephanie.

"*I couldn't if I tried,*" Stephanie and Bao answered, more confident now.

"*Oh, honey, if I get restless,*" Elton sang.

Stephanie and Bao leaned their heads toward Elton, fully engaged, making goo-goo eyes. "*Baby, you're not that kind,*" they sang.

They managed to get through the song, fumbling over some of the lyrics, but no one cared. To rapturous applause, the three rose, held hands, and bowed to the audience.

Jill Mendoza leaned over to Joshua. "You don't know what a lucky man you are," she told him.

"Oh, no, Jill. You're wrong. I know. Believe me, I know. And if I somehow forgot, she'd be sure to remind me."

As President Sheehan had done during the Chinese visit to the United States, President Yu blocked out time for a curling match at the Ice Cube. It was the morning after the state dinner. President Yu had still said nothing about Joshua's proposal. Not a clue. Before they stepped onto the ice, the same eight players as before, President Yu pointed to two newly-installed signs, in English and Chinese, advising against discussing business or politics on the ice. "By order of the President of the People's Republic of China," he pointed out. Touché.

"I'm not accustomed to taking orders from a Chinese president," Joshua said.

While the curlers were gathering in the Ice Cube, Stephanie and Bao were sitting down to tea in the Chinese president's residence in Zhongnanhai.

Baxter and Bao's three dogs were with them. The adrenaline high of their performance the night before had mostly subsided, replaced with the gentler one of caffeine.

"I suppose the curling match is beginning," Bao said.

"Yes. Joshua is hoping to win this time," Stephanie answered.

For a moment, Bao didn't say anything, wondering whether she *should* say anything. She wasn't sure what Stephanie knew. Finally, she asked, "Do you know about the proposal your husband made to Song?" Stephanie was uncertain about how much to reveal, how to answer. She settled on the truth.

"Yes. Yes, I do. I guess you do, too."

"I do. It is a brave and bold idea."

"And?" Stephanie asked.

"I told Song that he should agree to it, that it is a good thing," Bao said. "What did you tell your husband?"

"I told him that if there was even a small chance to bring about peace, I would not forgive him if he didn't at least try," Stephanie said. "What is Song going to do?"

"He is going to tell your husband that he accepts the proposal. Today. After they are finished playing. Song loves our children and grandchildren very much." There was long, relaxed silence.

"Do you have pictures?" Stephanie finally asked. "Of your grandchildren?" Bao had lots of them.

After their rematch, which China again won, the two teams adjourned to the warm room in the Ice Cube. As President Sheehan had done in Washington, President Yu asked everyone other than the interpreters to leave. President Yu went to the bar and poured two Ye Brewing Company beers, *The Velvet Underground* stouts. Yu knew that President Sheehan was partial to stouts. Chinese intelligence was every bit as good as America's. He proposed a "Good Curling" toast. Their glasses clinked.

As President Yu lowered his glass, Joshua noticed that Yu was missing the tip and fingernail of his right pinkie. "May I ask what happened to your finger, Song?" Joshua asked. He wasn't sure if it was appropriate, but it was personal. Jill Mendoza's briefing hadn't included this detail about Yu's finger. Yu smiled.

"I was a young boy. Twelve years old," Song said. "One of the chores which my father assigned to me was mowing our lawn. Let me advise you to never reach under a lawnmower when it's running. Be sure to shut it down first."

"Sounds like very wise advice," Joshua said.

President Yu looked directly at President Sheehan. One final chance to size up the American president. Joshua knew that the moment was at hand. He braced himself. "Joshua, I have decided to accept your proposal," he announced. "I have taken the initiative to write an agreement." Joshua was stunned. He had never truly believed that China would accept.

President Yu withdrew a folded sheet of paper from his vest pocket and handed it to Joshua. "I call it *CurTO. The Curling Treaty*. I prepared it myself. If the bureaucrats wrote it, it would be twenty pages long and indecipherable. I believe in brevity and clarity," he said. He handed it to Joshua.

Joshua began reading. Although it borrowed liberally from the League of Nations, United Nations, and NATO documents, there was none of the aspirational and prosaic language about "fundamental human rights," "the dignity and worth of the human person," "equal rights of men and women," "practicing tolerance," "fundamental freedoms," and "individual liberty." All noble things, things that Joshua believed in, but this was neither the time nor the place for that fight. Besides, President Yu had little interest in those matters. This was a military pact, plain and simple. No need to muddy it up.

> *THE PARTIES, in order to promote international peace and stability, Agree to combine their efforts to accomplish these goals and to maintain international peace and security. The Parties agree to unite their efforts for their individual and collective defense.*

THE PURPOSES of this Treaty are to maintain international peace and security; to take swift and effective collective measures for the suppression of acts of aggression by any nation against any member nation hereof; and to unite our actions in furtherance of these common goals.

THE PRINCIPLES of this Treaty are recognition of the sovereign right of all Members to their individual territorial integrity; that each Member shall refrain from the use of force against the territorial integrity of any other Member; shall hold international borders inviolate; that each Member will provide cooperation and assistance in any action taken under this Treaty to respond to acts of aggression against another Member; and that nothing herein shall authorize any Member to intervene in any matter exclusively within the domestic jurisdiction of any other Member.

In order to achieve the objectives of this Treaty, each Member will maintain and develop its individual and collective capacity to resist an armed attack against itself or any other Member. The Members will immediately consult with each other whenever the territorial integrity of any Member is breached by force.

The Members agree that an armed attack against one or more of them shall be deemed an attack against all Members and agree that, if such armed attack occurs, each of them will assist the Member or Members so attacked by taking forthwith, in concert with the other Members, such action as deemed necessary, including the use of armed force, to restore and maintain the territorial integrity of the Member so attacked. Such actions shall be terminated when the territorial integrity of the Member so attacked is restored.

International borders are agreed to be those on record with the Secretariat of the United Nations as of the date of a prospective Member's entry into this Treaty. No prospective Member shall be admitted to this Treaty prior to the submission of such territorial borders to the Secretariat, and the Secretariat's approval thereof. No territorial border shall be changed or adjusted without the approval of three-fourths of the Members of the Treaty and the approval thereof by the Secretariat of the United Nations.

Joshua finished reading and looked up. "This is perfect, Song. It is exactly what I proposed. It says what it needs to say, no more and no less. Your government agrees to this?"

"It does. As you know, I have an easier time persuading them to my way of thinking than American presidents do," President Yu answered. He fully understood his grip on power. He also had a deep and intimate understanding of American politics. He then asked, "The real question is, will you be able to convince your senators to approve this?"

The Chinese president knew that Joshua needed two-thirds of the United States senators to provide their "advice and consent" before the United States could enter into an international treaty. Yu doubted that Joshua would be able to muster up that much support. Getting sixty-seven United States senators to agree on virtually anything was a herculean struggle. In that regard,

Vice President Anderson might provide some value. He knew the Senate and most of the senators. He could be persuasive when he wanted to be. If necessary, he could twist arms.

"I don't know the answer to that, Song. I simply don't know. But I promise you that I will try," Joshua answered. He took a sip of *The Velvet Underground*. "This stout is not bad. Not bad at all. Is it possible that your Ministry of State Security hacked one of our breweries and borrowed the recipe?" Joshua hoped that the jab would be understood for what it was.

"I am not familiar with the activities of our Ministry of State Security," Yu deadpanned. Yes, President Yu got it.

In their suite that night, Joshua told Stephanie that China had once again won their curling match. "You need to get your rink to practice more," Stephanie said. She waited for Joshua to tell her the real news.

"I know. That's what Song told me," Joshua replied.

Joshua then told Stephanie that President Yu had accepted his proposal. "I know," she said. "Bao told me. I think that she may have been the one who convinced him." That was news to Joshua.

"It seems like it was too easy, Steph. I propose a military alliance with China and they just say OK? Just like that? What am I missing?"

"I don't think you're missing anything. I think President Yu wants to do this. For his children and grandchildren. That's what Bao told me, anyway. I think it's as simple as that."

"Can I trust him, Steph? Do you trust him?"

"I think so. You'll never know if you don't give him a chance, will you? I would guess that he's wondering the exact same thing about you right about now." The question kept Joshua awake most of the night, and found him on the balcony of the Diaoyutai State Guesthouse before dawn the next morning.

Stephanie was right. The only way that the two men would find out was to actually go ahead and find out.

Joshua didn't get the final say on agreeing to the treaty. That decision belonged to the United States Senate, unfortunately. The Senate had long ago forfeited its claim to being "the world's greatest deliberative body." The Founding Fathers, leary at the prospect of an overly-powerful executive, decreed that the president "shall have Power, *by and with the Advice and Consent of the Senate*, to make Treaties, provided two-thirds of the Senators present concur," under Article II, Section 2 of the Constitution. Two-thirds is a steep hill.

"Do you think there is any way that I can get sixty-seven senators to vote to ratify it?" he asked Stephanie. It seemed unlikely. He was getting good at congressional vote-counting.

"Well, you have fifty-four from your party that you can probably count on. Ten or twelve from the other side think you're the devil incarnate and wouldn't sign off on a cure for Alzheimer's if it were *you* who stuck it in front of them. Convince the others. And if you can't convince them, then leave them with no other choice," Stephanie counseled. It took a moment for Joshua to grasp what she meant.

"You mean make it a referendum on peace, not a deal with China?" Joshua asked. "Let the people decide?"

"That's exactly what I mean," Stephanie answered. "Let the people do the convincing for you."

Joshua and Stephanie bandied back-and-forth how to go about it. Meeting individually with senators would take forever and would require too much horse-trading. Every recalcitrant senator would want something in return for their vote. Things that Joshua probably couldn't or shouldn't offer. That wouldn't do. It would also give opponents too much time to organize. Finally, Stephanie suggested, "The only way is to let the people do the heavy lifting. They're sick of wars. They're exhausted. They've been fighting them since Vietnam. If not fighting in them, at least paying for others to fight them.

The people like you, Joshua. They believe you. They'll listen to you." Stephanie almost always had a better sense of the mood in America than the president did.

"How, Steph? How do I convince them?" Joshua asked.

"Talk to them. Tell them that peace is possible if they want it badly enough," Stephanie told him. "But you need to do it quickly."

A quick phone call to the chief of staff, and within twenty minutes Jill Mendoza, the United States Ambassador to China, and the Undersecretary for the Bureau of East Asian and Pacific affairs were assembled in the president's suite. The meeting wasn't on anyone's agenda. President Sheehan told them about the proposed treaty which President Yu had agreed to. The ambassador and undersecretary sat stunned. Neither had any inkling about what the president had proposed. Jill was learning that China had agreed to the proposal for the first time.

President Sheehan handed them copies as he explained the terms in broad strokes. Everyone began reading. One-by-one, they finished and looked at the president.

"Thoughts?" Joshua asked.

"Are you serious, sir?" the ambassador asked. He was dumbfounded, but he was more angered that he hadn't been told anything about it before now. "You want a military alliance with China? Seriously?"

"Yes and yes," Joshua answered. The ambassador's tone did not register well with the president.

"China has agreed to this?"

"President Yu wrote it himself," the president said. "His government agrees to it."

"How do you know that they can be trusted to honor it, sir?" the undersecretary asked. The question hung for a moment. Everyone harbored the same nagging question.

"I don't. I believe that they can, but I don't know. I'm certain that they are asking the exact same thing about us. Until we're put to the test, I doubt that we will really know."

Secretary of State Mendoza hadn't spoken. She was the one the president wanted to hear from. Finally, she spoke.

"Mr. President, if China agrees to this, and if other countries join in, it has historic possibilities. Nothing like it has ever been attempted before. Never even been contemplated, to my knowledge. But, honestly, I'm hard-pressed to see a downside. Merely signing doesn't commit us to anything other than having a strong military able to act. We already have that, anyway," Secretary Mendoza said. "If I were a country with hostile intentions toward a neighbor, I would think twice about acting out if I knew that China and the United States were willing and prepared to join forces to shut me down. And the more countries that you and President Yu persuade to join, the greater the deterrent will be. It would be a suicide mission to attack a member. Aside from the politics of securing the Senate's agreement, which is an altogether different matter, I believe that this has a chance of establishing a more peaceful world order."

No one challenged the Secretary, nor did anyone offer agreement, either. The chief of staff addressed the practical, political question. "Sir, even were you to sign this, you still need ratification. Frankly, I can't see enough votes. There's not a lot of pro-China sentiment in Congress right now. You'll be pilloried for climbing into bed with the enemy."

"Then we don't make it pro or anti-China. We make it pro or anti-peace," the president said.

Joshua could tell that neither the ambassador nor the undersecretary were on board. Their pride and egos were wounded. They should have been consulted ahead of time. "Not a word about this to anyone, understood?" the president said. "Not a word. I don't care whether you approve or don't approve, this stays in this room." He waited for their acknowledgement. "Well?"

"Yes, sir," came four replies. Joshua knew that neither Jill nor Sam Pelletier would leak. He wasn't so sure about the ambassador and undersecretary. Joshua would fire the ambassador when the delegation got home. For now, he just needed him to keep his mouth shut. "Keep an eye on these two, Sam," Joshua whispered to his chief of staff.

Joshua adjourned the meeting, but asked the Secretary of State to stay for a moment. Hers was the assurance he needed. "Are you sure, Jill? Are you sure this isn't a fool's errand?"

"Honestly, it very well may be," she answered. "But what if it isn't . . ."

President Sheehan took to television that evening from Beijing to address the American people and the world. Every news outlet agreed to cover it live, even though they had no advance notice of what the president was going to say. The talking heads, the standard collection of on-call bloviators, were summoned to newsrooms to dissect, berate, denounce, praise, or deconstruct whatever the president said. Their various responses would depend less on what he was going to say than on which tribe they shilled for. The words the president spoke were his own, not some speechwriter's:

My fellow Americans. I am addressing you from China this evening with hope and joy in my heart. Chinese president Yu Song and I have reached an historic agreement, one that holds the promise of peace, the promise of an end to the relentless wars constantly engulfing the world, the promise of security and prosperity for us and our children and our children's children. In this moment, we can choose peace over war, over death and destruction. It is a choice which we can make and which we must make.

Our agreement is a simple one. Our two countries have agreed to a mutual defense pact. We invite all other countries – all other countries – to join with us. The agreement is simply this: If any party to this treaty is attacked by force, all other parties will respond with force to stop the attack. The response will be swift, it will be coordinated, and it will be overwhelming. Our collective resolve and might will make it folly for any nation to attack another, regardless of the reason. Any country which attacks another will wish that it had not. Out goal will not be to destroy the aggressor, but to ensure that the aggression stops. Every country has the right to exist and to be secure from attack. We will provide that security together.

I want to be absolutely clear that the internal affairs of any Member country will remain just that. We have no intention or desire to interfere or involve ourselves in those matters. Those are for the people and their governments to decide.

I know that there will be opposition. I know that there will be those who object to entering into an alliance with a perceived enemy. But China and the Chinese people are not our enemy. The violent, tragic deaths of young men and women are the enemy. Even more tragic are the deaths of children and babies, robbed of the chance at life by adults who simply will not stop fighting. Those objections pale in comparison to ending the plague of endless wars which lead to nothing but still more death and still more war. It is time for the wars to end. You, the American people, can make the wars end if that is what you choose.

President Yu and I understand that there will come a time when we are tested. Some nation, somewhere, will seek to do harm to a neighbor. We wish that it were not so, but history counsels that it is. When that happens, the peace-seeking members of this treaty will quickly put an end to that mistake. We will take no joy in it, but neither will we back away from our commitment to peace.

I need the help of all Americans to make this long-elusive dream of peace a reality. We Americans have never been afraid of chasing this dream. We have never backed away from trying to fashion a better world. I am asking you to make your voices heard. Let your leaders know that you want this. That you demand this. Or that you at least want to try, for your children and your grandchildren. To those who will ask 'why?' I will simply answer, 'why not?' Good night. And may the blessings of peace be with you.

As President Sheehan was speaking, so was President Yu. The world needed to hear from both of them, had to understand that they were each committed to this. They didn't coordinate their words, they simply trusted each other to say the right things. To let the world know that they were serious. By the time that President Sheehan finished speaking, the phone lines and inboxes at the White House and in congressional offices were ablaze. Stephanie was right. The people were speaking, and they were with the president.

Chapter 15

Dominoes

"Self-preservation is the first law of nature." – Samuel Butler, The Odyssey of Homer

There are 193 members of the United Nations, virtually every country in the world, from Albania to Zimbabwe. One hundred and ninety-three countries, home to 8,100,000,000 people. Fewer than a quarter of them live in the United States and China. Presidents Yu and Sheehan had their work cut out for them. Not every one of those countries had a compelling interest in maintaining the peace, either. A few of them had no interest at all.

The ground rules were clear. Any country wanting to join CurTO had to agree on its precise borders with its neighbors. CurTO would use borders as reflected in border treaties filed with the Secretariat of the United Nations as of the date that a country agreed to join CurTO. The new United States ambassador and the Chinese ambassador symbolically presented their individual border treaties to the United Nations Secretariat in front of a gaggle of reporters and news cameras. A few borders across the globe remained in dispute. In order to join CurTO and benefit from its promised protections, a signatory would first be required to settle those disputes.

President Sheehan believed that lining up NATO members to join the alliance would be relatively easy, judging by the calls he was receiving, but that could wait. He didn't want to scare President Yu off by immediately getting a host of United States allies to sign on. While trust between the countries was growing – between the presidents, in particular – it still needed nurturing. Joshua wanted President Yu to do some of the heavier lifting and convince more China-friendly countries to join CurTO first. China had the more difficult task – to convince countries that hated the West to enter into a military pact which included the United States. President Yu went to work. He could be gently and gracefully persuasive, or he could be brutally demanding. He also had the full weight of China's economic, technological, and military power behind him, and he did not hesitate to brandish it.

President Yu's first approach was to the Democratic People's Republic of Korea – North Korea. He knew that the Supreme Leader would refuse, but making the ask was important. North Korea was the lone country with which China had a formal mutual defense military alliance in the nature of the NATO treaty. China would be breaking that alliance in favor of CurTO, President Yu told the Supreme Leader. North Korea was furious and absolutely refused. The Supreme Leader would never agree to any treaty that included the United States imperialists. If South Korea joined, matters would be that much worse.

North Korea stomped its feet and blustered mightily, but China had all of the bargaining power. Without China, North Korea might not survive. Although North Korea had a strong military in its own right, it was negligible compared to China's. The United States stayed out of those talks completely. Nothing good could come of its involvement. President Yu was more than capable of handling North Korea, or so Joshua thought.

To exert more pressure on North Korea, China initiated talks to persuade other countries within its sphere of influence to sign on. Smaller countries, simply dwarfed by China and the United States' combined military and economic power, really didn't have much of a choice. Cambodia, Laos, Belarus, and Serbia quickly fell in line and signed on. North Korea began to understand that China was serious. At China's urging – insistence – more countries within its orbit joined CurTO. Once the dominoes started falling, President Yu no longer had to ask. Countries came to him asking for admission.

The United States had an easier time persuading its friends to join, although there was serious resistance from some quarters. The most common objection was that China could not be trusted. President Sheehan and Secretary Mendoza did their best to convince them otherwise. Canada and Great Britain were the first to join, followed by Germany and France. The rest of the NATO countries soon followed. South Korea and Japan, always wary of what an erratic North Korea might do, were eager to accept protection, especially with China on board. Not every country was thrilled to join, but the writing on the wall was clear. Within a year, the collective might of the CurTO members easily dwarfed that of the non-members. If CurTO were serious, which by now almost everyone believed that it was, the holdouts recognized that it made little sense to be on the outside. The downside seemed far less fraught than the upside. Within twenty months, more than one hundred countries had joined the alliance, and the roster was growing.

China's other difficult tasks, besides the still-recalcitrant North Korea, were convincing Russia and Iran to join. Those were the final three significant powers that China had sway over. Russia surprisingly proved to be the easiest of the three to convince. Russia still viewed itself as a dominant world power, although it wasn't quite as fearsome as it believed. Its economy barely ranked among the top ten in the world, and its military, although large and powerful and armed with nukes, would be no match for an alliance of the United States, China, and all the others. It would also be surrounded by CurTO countries and thoroughly isolated. If nothing else, Russia understood brute force. Joining CurTO would mean abandoning its hope of re-assembling the former Soviet bloc, but that dream was now more just a fantasy, anyway.

Iran presented China's biggest challenge, even more so than North Korea. Iran harbored grandiose ambitions to be the dominant power in the region. It was still determined to join the nuclear club. All of its ambitions depended on its neighbors living in fear of what it might do. The Iranians didn't believe that China would choose to side with the United States if Iran exerted its military power against one of its enemies. Iran refused to join CurTO. It would never align itself with Satan. Whether or not Iran joined CurTO didn't matter all that much to the alliance now, because most of Iran's neighbors had. If Iran acted out, it would pay a steep price. If it was afraid to, all the better. That, after all, was what negative peace was about.

Within two years, more than ninety-percent of the world's military and economic power was represented in CutTO. It was working, too. No one had taken military action against a neighbor. Two years without a war breaking out somewhere was impressive. Maybe it was the CurTO alliance that deterred them, maybe it wasn't. It was only negative peace, but it was better than nothing. Presidents Yu and Sheehan had changed the world.

The cessation of border wars had another positive effect. The world economy was improving as countries began to focus a tiny bit less on maintaining armed security and a little bit more on economic development and trade. Some countries were finding new trading partners, even with old enemies. The world was by no means perfect – not even close – but at least there were no hot wars. Sure, there were revolutions and civil wars and coups; religious, ethnic, and racial persecutions; and egregious human rights atrocities; but, as promised, CurTO did not intervene in those. It was not even close to a positive peace. But CurTO, by God, was actually working.

Chapter 16
Teachings From the Bible

"If we pass beyond these matters to a view of American life, as expressed by its laws, its business, its customs, and its society, we find everywhere a clear recognition of the same truth. Among other matters note the following: The form of oath universally prevailing, concluding with an appeal to the Almighty; the custom of opening sessions of all deliberative bodies and most conventions with prayer; the prefatory words of all wills, 'In the name of God, amen;' the laws respecting the observance of the Sabbath, with the general cessation of all secular business, and the closing of courts, legislatures, and other similar public assemblies on that day; the churches and church organizations which abound in every city, town, and hamlet; the multitude of charitable organizations existing everywhere under Christian auspices; the gigantic missionary associations, with general support, and aiming to establish Christian missions in every quarter of the globe. These and many other matters which might be noticed, add a volume of unofficial declarations to the mass of organic utterances that this is a Christian nation." – Supreme Court Justice David Brewer, Church of the Holy Trinity v. United States, 1892

The assigned Scripture for the first Sunday in October, the month leading up to the presidential election, was Matthew 10:34-36: *"Think not that I am come to send peace on earth. I come not to send peace, but a sword. For I am come to set a man against his father and the daughter against her mother, and the daughter in law against her mother in law. And a man's foes shall be they of his own household."* The idea was the brainchild of the Reverend Clifton A. Cutler, III, senior pastor at the Rock of Salvation megachurch outside of Houston, a fifteen-acre complex including a school, swimming pool, gymnasium, broadcast studio, and armed, round-the-clock security. The genesis of the idea had come to him in a vision, from God Almighty, the pastor testified to his faithful. *American Revival Month*, God had christened it. Pastors all across the land, in every state, delivering the same urgent message, just in time, it so happened, for the election. Millions would come to discover Jesus, the warrior king.

The Reverend Cutler not only had his six-thousand member flock at Rock of Salvation, but several million other followers through his books, podcasts, and social media accounts. He was an influencer within his expanding orbit, although he much preferred being considered a prophet. His suits were hand-tailored in London, his shoes Italian calfskin, his teeth bleached, his wrinkles botoxed. He was educated, charismatic, fiercely evangelical, thrice-married, and an unapologetic Christian nationalist. He also subscribed to the prosperity gospel.

The good pastor secured his station, and his immense and growing fortune, by feeding a restless, percolating undercurrent in America. It began long before CurTO and long before anyone ever heard of Joshua Sheehan. Long before Justice David Brewer wrote his opinion in the *Holy Trinity* case, even. It is the divine revelation that America is God's anointed country. It is a belief as old as Manifest Destiny, which justified America's westward expansion and genocide of the indigenous people. In the 21st century, the belief is, if not growing in numbers, at least strengthening in conviction. People like the Reverend Clifton Cutler keep it roiling.

The belief that Christian America is in grave danger of extinction isn't just a feeling, but something far deeper, more imperative. It is a belief, written by God in people's hearts. And it is under relentless assault from everywhere – atheists, globalists, liberals, progressives, Jews, bankers, the United Nations, the World Health Organization, the World Bank, LGBTQIA+, Muslims, Mexicans, illegals, feminists, "others," the media, socialists, communists, CurTO. The barbarians are at the gate. Some have already breached the gate. If something isn't done – and done soon – the barbarians will see to it that America is a Christian nation no more. It is already teetering on a razor's edge. That was Clifton Cutler's message, and he was far from alone in delivering it. Joshua Sheehan had handed them a perfect reason to amplify their warning and mobilize their Christian soldiers.

The Reverend Cutler called on all true and faithful ministers of the Gospel to preach from Matthew 10:34-36 on the first Sunday in October to kick off *American Revival Month*. True, patriotic Christians would all hear the same *Truth* on the same day, unvarnished, straight from the Holy Bible. Like-minded preachers understood what the message must be. The leaders of the Christian Nationalist movement take their direction straight from the Bible – only from the Bible. It is imperative that they find biblical justification for their message, and they do exactly that.

"There it is, my friends," Reverend Cutler said into his headpiece as he strode across the stage. Pulpits were so confining and untheatrical. His congregation wanted to hear a biblical lesson, sure, but they also wanted to be entertained. Clifton Cutler knew that well, and he did not disappoint. Even though he was born and raised in Indiana, attended college in Michigan and then seminary in Pennsylvania, there was the tiniest hint of a practiced southern drawl as he preached. "Jesus's own words. *Think not that I am come to send peace on earth. I come not to send peace, but a sword.*'" The Scripture displayed on the video wall behind him, flanked by two particularly bloody images of a crucified, subtly anglified, Jesus.

"When I was in seminary school, I was brainwashed into believing that Jesus was a meek, mild, gentle little man. That's what the mainstream churches and liberal theologians want us to believe. Even I, myself, believed it once. It keeps us in line and supplicant. Obedient." He surveyed the room until the time was right. "*But it is not true!*" he bellowed. "Here's what I know *is* true, dear friends. I know it is true because I have studied the Gospel. I know it is true through answered prayers. I know it is true because I have been in communion with God." He paused. It had to be the *Truth* if Pastor Cutler had learned it while communing with God. His followers anxiously awaited the *Truth*.

"Jesus was no pansy, and he doesn't want us to be either." Some in the congregation laughed. Many offered "Amen!" or "Praise God!" or "Thank you, Jesus!" Cutler liked his choice of "pansy." It carried so many fascinating implications.

"Jesus, you see, is not a peacemaker. He told us that. *'Think not that I am come to send peace.'* He is a revolutionary. A warrior against evil and against sin. Against corrupt authority and power. Are you going to join Him in the revolution, my friends? I am here today to proclaim to you that *I* am. I join Him because the Holy Bible, the unerring Word of God, commands me to. The First Epistle of Peter 2:21 offers me no other choice but to follow. *'For even hereunto were ye called because Christ also suffered for us, leaving us an example, that ye should follow his steps.'*" Right on cue, the technical crew put the verse on-screen in a menacing, gothic font.

"Do not be fooled, my friends. Satan himself doesn't want you to hear the *Truth*. But here is the *Truth*." The Reverend Cutler walked to the front of the stage and leaned toward the sea of believers yearning to learn the *Truth*. He whispered, "The enemy is upon us. The enemy is in the house." He straightened himself and continued, his voice rising. "It will be *'the man against his father, the daughter against her mother,'* Jesus tells us. Are you ready? Are you ready to expel the enemy from your home?"

"Yes!" the congregation answered.

"Are you ready to face down the enemy?"

"Yes!" they cried louder.

"Are you ready to lay down your life for Him?"

"Yes! Yes! Yes!" The believers were on their feet. Some raised their outstretched palms toward heaven. The Reverend Clifton Cutler understood the psychology of crowds.

For the second Sunday in October, Reverend Cutler chose Luke 12:49-51 as the national topic Scripture: "*I am come to send fire on earth, and what will I, if it be already kindled? But I have a baptism to be baptized with, and how am I straitened until it is accomplished? Suppose ye that I am come to give peace on earth? I tell you, Nay; but rather division.*" Pastors inclined toward reclaiming a Christian nation all across the country preached from the passage. *American Revival Month* was a hit.

"If Jesus did not come to bring peace, what then *did* He come for?" Reverend Cutler asked rhetorically as his sermon wound down. "He has told us, and we must listen. He came to establish His kingdom on earth. '*I am come to send fire on earth,*' He told us. Are you ready for the fire?"

"Yes!"

"Are you ready for His kingdom?"

"Yes!"

"Are you ready to go forth with Jesus into battle?"

"Yes!"

"Are you ready to claim America as *His* America?"

"Yes!" The faithful were in a frenzy. It was electric at the Rock of Salvation.

Precisely on cue, the church band launched into the introduction of *The Battle Hymn of the Republic,* complete with snare drum and trumpets. The choir, seventy-eight strong, rose in perfect, practiced, military precision.

Mine eyes have seen the glory of the coming of the Lord:
He is trampling out the vintage where the grapes of wrath are stored;
He hath loosed the fateful lightning of His terrible swift sword:
His truth is marching on.
Glory, glory, hallelujah!
Glory, glory, hallelujah!
Glory, glory, hallelujah!
His truth is marching on.

The Scripture for the third Sunday of *American Revival Month* would heighten the fervor. John 2:13-15. *"And the Jew's passover was at hand, and Jesus went up to Jerusalem. And found in the temple those who sold oxen and sheep and doves, and the changers of money sitting: And when he had made a scourge of small cords, he drove them all out of the temple and the sheep, and the oxen; and poured out the changers' money, and overthrew the tables."*

"Yes, my friends, you might be surprised that our Lord and Savior Jesus Christ resorted to the whip. Why, you might ask? To drive out the blasphemers. To glorify His Father. To reclaim His Father's temple. To establish His rule. If Jesus Christ cleansed His Father's temple of the ungodly and the heathens with a whip, how can we, as His disciples, do any less? We have been baptized to follow Him, to obey, to walk as He walked. We are called to teach *His* ways, to call forth *His* kingdom and acknowledge *His* rule and dominion over all things.

"Remember the words from the Gospel of Matthew, Chapter 28, verses 18-20. Our great calling." Reverend Cutler had long ago committed the words to memory. *"And Jesus came and spoke to them, saying, 'All power is given unto me in heaven and in earth. Go ye therefore, and teach all nations, baptizing them in the name of the Father, and of the Son, and of the Holy Ghost. Teaching them to observe all things whatsoever I have commanded you; and, lo, I am with you always, even unto the end of the world.'"* The Great Commission, as it has come to be known, justifies a host of things. It justifies evangelism at home and sending missionaries abroad. It is the imperative for establishing a Christian nation and world.

"Jesus did it with a whip, my friends. It was all He needed to drive out the unholy, those who were an abomination. 'But how, Pastor? How can a whip serve me today against the powerful forces of evil and darkness bent on my destruction?' you ask me. 'Surely, they will strike me down.' But be not afraid, my children. Jesus has told us how. For today, what we are called upon to do is to commit ourselves to standing with Him. Will you stand up with Jesus?" The congregation answered by springing to their feet and joining in hymn.

Stand up, stand up for Jesus! ye soldiers of the cross;
Lift high His royal banner, it must not suffer loss:
From vict'ry unto vict'ry, His army shall He lead,
Till every foe is vanquished, and Christ is Lord indeed.

Pastor Cutler saved the crowning Scripture for the final October Sunday. The *coup de grâce.* The call to arms found in Luke 22:36. "*Then said he unto them, But now, he that hath a purse, let him take it, and likewise his scrip; and he that hath no sword, let him sell his garment, and buy one.*" Sell your clothes and buy a sword! If that isn't Jesus's call to arms, what is?

"We must be prepared to take up the sword for Christ!" Pastor Cutler exhorted. He didn't really mean the sword, and his flock understood. Most of them had long ago fortified themselves for the impending battle. They did not confine themselves to whips and swords. They knew better than that. On any given Sunday at the Rock of Salvation church, at least someone in virtually every row had a gun in their purse or holstered beneath their jacket. It was God's army fully at the ready to answer His call.

The Christian warriors were prepared for the conflict to come. They were ready to defend themselves and the Christian way of life. But how? Prayerfully, of course. That was a given. Violently, if need be. Jesus had made it clear that the sword was imperative. The question was no longer whether, but when, and how, they would be called upon to join the battle for Christ's sake.

The video wall came to life with Luke 11:21, this time in an ironic, ominous "Lucifer" typeface. Pastor Cutler had selected it personally. "*When a strong man armed keepeth his palace, his goods are in peace.*" The leap from swords to weapons much, much more powerful is an easy one. Biblical literalism could be relaxed a little for present purposes.

"Will you sell your coat for Jesus?" Pastor Cutler asked.

"Yes!" his flock answered.

"Will you protect your treasure?"

"Yes!"

"Will you raise your swords to defend His kingdom?"

"Yes!"

The Rock of Salvation organist brought the massive pipe organ to life. It had cost nearly a million dollars. The choir rose, followed by the amped-up congregation. The video wall scrolled the lyrics. Hymnals were so old-fashioned.

Onward, Christian soldiers, marching as to war,
With the cross of Jesus going on before!
Christ, the royal Master, leads against the foe;
Forward into battle, see his banner go!
Onward, Christian soldiers, marching as to war,
With the cross of Jesus going on before!

The true believers in Christian Nationalism are particularly fond of Luke 22:36. Its leaders are even more so. Not only does it provide them with exactly the message they are looking for, it can also be exploited for recruitment, public relations, and, crucially, fundraising purposes. Spreading the Gospel doesn't pay for itself. Some hawk tee shirts picturing an AR-15, reading, "*And Jesus said, if you don't have an AR-15, sell your coat and buy one. Luke 22:36.*" It is a bit of creative re-writing of the Gospel, especially for the literalists, but it certainly is catchy.

Others sell gun cabinets inscribed with Luke 11:21. Posters and tee shirts depict Jesus brandishing all kinds of weaponry, from handguns to Uzis to assault rifles. "*If Jesus had a gun, he'd still be alive today*" is a top seller. Again, catchy, but not likely, since He would be 2,000 years old, and, if Jesus did have a gun, the Roman soldiers would have had bigger and better ones. It is also blasphemously unsound theologically, since true Christians believe that He *is* still alive. Jesus's admonition, "*If thou wilt be perfect, go and sell that thou hast, and give to the poor, and thou shalt have treasure in heaven"* is not part of the merchandise catalogue. It is insanely tone-deaf and off-message.

The painting of Jesus gently cradling a lamb, some version of which hangs in virtually every Protestant Sunday School in the country, is the basis for a knock-off depicting him cradling an AR-15. Sometimes, he is draped in an American flag. The believers even offer signs to hang on your front door, reading, *"WARNING: This Home is Protected by Sweet Jesus & a Gun. If You Came Here Uninvited, You Might Meet Both of Them."* Signs reading, *"Be not forgetful to entertain strangers, for thereby some have entertained angels unawares. – Hebrews 13:2"* are not available.

For those who need something a bit glitzier, something fancier to wear on that special occasion, or maybe to church on Easter Sunday, they can buy a gold pin showing Jesus crucified on a cross of assault rifles. Many of the items are available at pastorcliftoncutler.com. October sales were brisk.

Not all Christians take the nationalist warrior view of Jesus. Not the majority, even. Most subscribe to the *Sermon on the Mount* version of Jesus. *"Blessed are the peacemakers, for they shall be called the children of God."* *"But I say unto you, That ye resist not evil: but whosoever shall smite thee on thy right cheek, turn to him the other also."* There is scriptural justification for almost anything if you look hard enough. Slavery comes to mind:

> *As for the male and female slaves whom you may have, it is from the nations around you that you may acquire male and female slaves. You may also acquire them from among the aliens residing with you and from their families who are with you who have been born in your land; they may be your property. You may keep them as a possession for your children after you, for them to inherit as property.* Leviticus 25:44-46.

Urge slaves to be submissive to their masters in everything, to be pleasing, not talking back, not stealing, but showing complete and perfect fidelity, so that in everything they may be an ornament to the teaching of God our Savior. Titus 2:9-10.

The lessons of Christian Nationalism are espoused in the open sometimes, in podcasts and from pulpits, but more often they are found in darker, hidden places. The more violent and apocalyptic, the deeper they are buried, encrypted, out of the light. True believers know exactly where to find them, and they listen.

Among the most popular documents shared among Christian Nationalists and signed onto by many churches and theologians is *The Statement on Christian Nationalism & the Gospel.* The Reverend Clifton Cutler himself had signed it long ago. It didn't go far enough for his liking, but it was a start. A long, comprehensive manifesto, one section reads:

Article X: "WE AFFIRM that nations possess an inviolable right to establish justice and safeguard the peace and prosperity of their own citizens. We affirm that implementing Christian Nationalism in each nation will include the punishment of each nation's great evils and promote each nation's thriving. We affirm that the specific, short-term priorities of Christian Nationalism in the context of the United States are to call our nation, in her laws, formally to acknowledge the Lordship of Christ, to declare solemn days of humility and repentance, to abolish abortion, to abolish pornography, to define marriage as the covenant union of a biological male and a biological female,

> *to de-weaponize the federal and state bureaucracies which*
> *target Christians for censorship and persecution, to secure our*
> *borders and defend against foreign invaders, to recapture our*
> *national sovereignty from godless, global entities who present a*
> *grave threat to civilization like the United Nations, the World*
> *Health Organization, the World Economic Forum . . .*

Their message is simple and urgent – government is the enemy, and it is coming for Christians, to censor and persecute them. As one Second Amendment enthusiast puts it, "The [Second Amendment] is about freedom, and it's about securing a God-given right that every man and woman has to protect themselves and their families. Not only against bad guys, *but also against bad guys with badges.*"

Seizing on that belief, a prominent Southern Baptist Convention pastor wrote that, "[H]uman history and the present day are full of examples of governments that refuse to let Christians worship freely and instead wield the sword against otherwise peaceful citizens. We would be foolish to assume that can't happen in America. Owning guns is a life insurance policy against a dark future that looks more like China than Texas." Better be prepared, because the government is coming for you and yours. Soon. If you listen, you can hear the ominous, clomping footsteps drawing closer. The Reverend Cutler made certain that the faithful heard them.

"They're coming for us," he warned. "You can hear them coming."

The belief that Christians are commanded to "recapture" America's "national sovereignty from godless, global entities . . . like the United Nations, the World Health Organization, [and] the World Economic Forum" holds great appeal within the circle. The words themselves are carefully chosen to elicit a primal response, a survival response – "target," "invaders," "recapture," "grave threat," "dark future." Had CurTO existed when *The Statement on Christian Nationalism & the Gospel* was written, it would have been at the top of the list of godless, global entities. Joshua Sheehan had deployed it to target the Holy Land.

The claim that the government "wields the sword" against Christians has taken root as well. The relentless messaging that government is the enemy, that the government wants to destroy Christianity and must be stopped, has a rapt and receptive audience. Repetition works, even if it is a lie. If something is heard often enough, it becomes true. The "Illusory Truth Effect."

The Christian Nationalist movement has a home among a significant segment of the population. A segment of the population which, at its core, is scared. Scared that the country is changing, becoming browner. Scared that "illegals" are storming our borders. Scared that churches are losing their hold over the common morality. Scared that gays and lesbians are indoctrinating their children. Scared that Jews control the world's banks. Scared that every young woman would happily have an abortion. Maybe several. Most of all, scared that white Protestants are losing their stranglehold on power, and at last they have been ordained to do something about it.

At the Body of Christ megachurch in southeastern Ohio, a young man, dressed casually, but neatly, took in all four lessons of *American Revival Month*. He had heard about it online. He wasn't a regular at Body of Christ; in fact, the first Sunday in October was the first time he had been inside. He was raised a Baptist, but lost interest as a teenager. It was all so abstract, unengaging. He was looking for a purpose, a meaning, a cause he could truly believe in, and he was finally discovering it.

Chapter 17

A Test

"Cowardice asks the question, 'Is it safe?' Expediency asks the question, 'Is it politic?' Vanity asks the question, 'Is it popular?' But conscience asks the question, 'Is it right?' And there are times when you must take a stand that is neither safe nor politic nor popular, but you must do it because it is right." – Martin Luther King, Jr., May, 1967

North Korea was the first country to test CurTO's resolve, although it may not have done so intentionally. No one knew for certain, but it didn't matter. North Korea had long been testing several missile systems, designed to enhance its nuclear weapons program, often over the Sea of Japan. It was menacing and provocative, which was precisely the Supreme Leader's intent, particularly towards South Korea and Japan. North Korea had some successes, but more failures, in its program, with missiles exploding on the launchpad or in mid-flight – "unscheduled disassembly," they called it – or veering wildly off course. North Korea remained a holdout from CurTO, still vowing never to enter into any treaty which included the United States or South Korea.

During one of its tests, a ballistic missile crashed onto the Japanese island of Hokkaido, killing five people, two of them children. At first, North Korea denied that the missile was one of its own, but that was easily disproved. The United States Indo-Pacific Command, NORAD, South Korea, China, and Japan had all tracked the missile. North Korea then claimed that it was simply an unfortunate accident caused by a negligent programmer, who had been appropriately dealt with, the Supreme Leader promised.

Whether intentional or accidental, it was a mistake which would test the CurTO alliance and reveal its commitment and resolve, as well as its might, both to its members and the remaining holdouts – but only if China honored the treaty. President Sheehan had warned that there would come a day when CurTO would be tested, and that day arrived when the North Korean missile claimed the Japanese family. The future of the alliance was squarely in China's hands. President Yu had a decision to make. Quickly.

President Yu and the Central Military Commission convened within the hour.

"What do we know?" Yu demanded. He was seething at the Supreme Leader for being so reckless.

"The missile was launched from Wonsan. Satellite surveillance has confirmed its origin. It landed on Hokkaido and detonated. Initial intelligence indicates that at least five people were killed, two of them children," General Liu recited.

"Was it intentional?" Yu asked.

"The Supreme Leader assured us that it was an accident . . . after he denied that it was their missile," the general answered.

"The Supreme Leader is a liar. And a fool," Yu said. "Do we have assets capable of responding?"

"Yes, sir. They are in position at Yishuntun Airbase and are awaiting your order."

"And the Americans? What do they say?" Yu asked.

"They have the same intelligence that we have. Where the launch originated. Where it landed. Casualties."

"Are they prepared to strike?"

"They are, sir. Provided that you are. Japan, South Korea, India, and Australia are prepared to provide support." The war room fell silent, except for the men's anxious breathing. It smelled distinctly of nervous men.

"Get me the Supreme Leader on the phone," Yu snapped. "Now!"

CurTO responded decisively to North Korea's mistake. Within two hours, three of North Korea's offensive military installations were neutralized. The facility which had launched the missile was gone, as were two other launch sites. It was a limited response, commensurate with North Korea's actions, designed to eliminate the threat and protect the attacked member, not destroy the other country. It sent an unequivocal message to the world.

The Supreme Leader made a second mistake that day, an inhumane one. This one was intentional. CurTO did its best to minimize the human cost, assiduously avoiding civilians, and even military personnel, as best it could. President Yu demanded that the Supreme Leader evacuate the targets minutes before CurTO arrived, but he didn't. He simply did not believe that China would do such a thing, but it was China and the United States who led the assault. There were significant casualties. When the counting was done, fourteen North Koreans were dead.

The Supreme Leader's instinct told him to strike back, to retaliate. But against whom? President Yu had instructed him to do nothing – *absolutely nothing* – retaliatory. An intentional act against a CurTO country would likely mean the wholesale destruction of the Supreme Leader's military arsenal and the end of his regime, if not his life. President Yu had personally assured the Supreme Leader of that. "If you order retaliation, it will be the last order you give," President Yu had warned. The Supreme Leader understood that he had no choice but to stand down.

If there had been doubts about China's commitment to the treaty, or its willingness to strike, they were put to rest for the world to see. Yes,

President Yu could be trusted. The unanswered question was whether the Western powers would do the same to one of their own. When it was over, President Sheehan called President Yu.

"Mr. President," Joshua began. "You showed great leadership and honor by what you did today. I, and the rest of the world, are grateful. I am sorry that you were thrust into that position."

"Thank you, Mr. President," Yu said. President Yu was obviously shaken by what he had done. Joshua felt his friend's torment. "It is a sad day for us, Joshua. North Korea is a friend. The Supreme Leader is a friend. Or was one before today. Now, I don't know. It is not easy hurting a friend."

"No," Joshua said. "It never is."

"I don't know whether what I did today was right or not, honorable or not, strong or weak," Song said, to himself and to Joshua. "Those who write the history books will make that determination, I suppose." Joshua had never heard Song unsure, doubting his decision or judgment.

"History may just record that you saved the world today, Song," Joshua offered.

"Perhaps. Perhaps not. We will find out in due time," Song said. "My hope for you, Mr. President, is that you are never faced with the same decision."

"I hope so, too, Song. I hope so, too. Take care, my friend."

Joshua, too, was shaken by the events. Not by the fact that CurTO had done what the treaty required, but by something more basic, more human. It was the first time that he had had people killed, whether he meant to or not. Presidents take office knowing that they will one day make decisions that cost lives. They carry that awful burden every day. Joshua had now made such a decision. When it inevitably happens, it changes them. How can it not? Some age quickly and visibly before our eyes. All of them, Joshua Sheehan included, learned to find some way to rationalize what they had done. *More people were saved than were killed. We had no choice. We were defending ourselves.*

For the moment, though, staring out over the South Lawn, what Joshua could not shake was the vision of young men – charred, dismembered, some unrecognizable, blood-soaked young men – their eyes frozen open, seeing nothing, their remains being zipped into bags by their comrades. They were North Koreans, which impersonalized them a bit, but they were sons and fathers and husbands, too. What were their names, he wondered? Who was going to tell their families?

It was August. The sweltering heat in Washington had broken, at least temporarily. The humidity was down from unbearable to merely miserable. Joshua and Stephanie had returned to the White House after the party convention in Austin, where Joshua and Vice President Anderson were unanimously nominated for a second term. A week in Maine awaited them before Joshua would hit the campaign trail in earnest.

The United States economy was crackling, inflation had cooled, there was no daily drama within the administration, political rhetoric had cooled for the moment, and CurTO's handling of North Korea was widely praised. Joshua was the most admired and respected man in the world. Stephanie was the most admired woman. The United States had climbed from the twenty-fourth happiest country, according to the World Happiness Report, to fifteenth. The polls gave Joshua and Vice President Anderson a Reaganesque lead in their re-election bid.

Israel remained the most problematic CurTO holdout, even three years later, at least from Joshua's point-of-view. He had spent hours, as had Secretary Mendoza and the United States Ambassador to Israel, pleading with the prime minister to sign on. Just as North Korea had vowed to never enter into a treaty with the United States or South Korea, Israel vowed never to enter into one with its enemies, which surrounded it. Enemies sworn to its destruction. Despite the pleading and pressuring, Israel refused to join CurTO.

The hard-line members of Israel's governing coalition knew that the United States would never dare to strike it.

Israel garnered intelligence that a terrorist cell in southern Lebanon was planning an imminent attack inside Israel. The Mossad was certain of it. Aerial surveillance confirmed unusual, increased activity a few kilometers from the Israel-Lebanon border. Satellite images and covert human assets confirmed a rapid build-up of medium-range artillery.

Taking the offensive, rather than waiting to be hit, Israel launched a drone strike just before dawn which destroyed the site and killed a dozen suspected Lebanese terrorists. Although Israel had not joined CurTO, Lebanon, at China's urging, had, and immediately demanded that CurTO take action against Israel, exactly as it had done against North Korea. Perhaps Lebanon had deliberately provoked Israel's attack to test the United States, perhaps not. It didn't matter.

Within thirty minutes of Israel's action, Secretary of State Mendoza, the Director of National Intelligence, the Secretary of Defense, the Chairman of the Joint Chiefs of Staff, and a team of analysts were in the Oval Office, briefing President Sheehan and Vice President Anderson on what had happened. The president was seething. He called Israeli Prime Minister Kaleb Avraham. He wasted no time with pleasantries.

"What the fuck, Kaleb?" the president barked. The language and tone jarred the Oval. They hadn't heard the president use that word, nor had any of them seen him so angry.

"Good morning, Mr. President," the Prime Minister answered calmly. He knew the call would be coming. He also knew how to manage American presidents. He had been doing it for years. Presidents would occasionally chastise him, but always they came around to supporting him. Offering little nuggets of intel from Mossad usually smoothed the road.

"Why? Why in God's name would you do this?" the president demanded.

"As you surely know, Mr. President, Lebanon was preparing to strike us. We shared that intelligence with your government. You certainly saw it. Your satellites no doubt confirmed it. We took the initiative to eliminate the threat. It was not a difficult operation. The IDF performed flawlessly. Our action was quite successful. The matter is concluded," Prime Minister Avraham answered.

"No. No it's not," the president snapped. "Everyone is waiting to see what we're going to do, Kaleb. Lebanon is demanding justice."

"Let them wait, then. They have no standing to demand anything. They are terrorists. Like I said, we consider the matter resolved."

"And what exactly do you expect me to do?" Sheehan demanded. Prime Minister Avraham was silent for a moment, as if he were contemplating his answer. This was going better than he had hoped.

"I don't expect you to do anything, my friend. As I said, we consider the matter to be resolved. Give my best to your beautiful wife. Goodbye, Mr. President." Kaleb Avraham's arrogance was remarkable.

President Sheehan had considered what he might do if Israel did something this impulsive, but never truly believed that it would. If CurTO were going to survive, the United States would have to participate in military action against its good friend and ally. Prime Minister Avraham had recklessly and, worse yet, intentionally, put the United States, the alliance, and President Sheehan, in an awful, unprecedented spot. If the United States participated, something which had seemed inconceivable before this moment, the domestic fallout would be seismic. On the other hand, if the United States failed to respond to Israel's action it would prove that the United States could never be trusted and would ring the death knell for CurTO while it was still in its infancy. President Yu was watching. The whole world was waiting.

"Is the Situation Room ready?" the president asked.

"Yes, sir," Chief of Staff Sam Pelletier answered.

"Let's go," the president said. They raced to the basement.

The Defense Department had been working its channels. "What's the status?" the president asked.

"We have assets ready to deploy from Syria, Saudi Arabia, and the Mediterranean. Turkey and Egypt are on standby. We have identified where the Israeli strike originated from. We know where Israel maintains other assets with offensive capabilities near the Lebanon border. China has provided excellent satellite imagery," the Secretary answered. "Everything is in place and awaiting your order." The room went still. Everyone was staring at the president.

"What do you think, Jill?" the president asked Secretary of State Mendoza. Hers was the voice he trusted above the others. He needed to hear it.

"Mr. President," she said. "If you want to see this through, you cannot blink now. It will never be put back together if you break it now. You must be quick and you must be decisive."

"Perhaps we should give it a little more time," the vice president interjected. Vice President Anderson's counsel had not been solicited, nor did it carry the weight of Secretary Mendoza's. "Let things simmer down." That was his routine advice. "There is also the election to consider. Striking Israel will be widely unpopular. It will likely mean the end of your presidency. Maybe after the election something can be worked out diplomatically."

"You can't be indecisive, Mr. President. If you want the alliance to survive, there is only one option," Jill said. "If you hesitate, the world will doubt your commitment. No one will trust you. Your word will mean nothing. Our word will mean nothing."

President Sheehan knew what he had to do. The only way to prove his fidelity to maintaining world peace, albeit still negative peace, was to punish Israel for its aggression. And so he did. "Give the order," he directed General Thomas.

"Are you sure, sir?" the vice president asked. General Thomas looked up at the vice president, then the president.

"Give the order *now*," the president commanded. "And get me the Prime Minister back on the phone."

The president spoke into the speakerphone. "Kaleb, listen to me. Don't argue, just listen. You don't have much time. The alliance is coming for your launch site and for two others on the Lebanese border. Get your people out of the way now. Now! We don't want casualties. Do it. And for God's sake, don't do anything else stupid today."

"But Mr. President . . ." the Prime Minister began.

"No, Kaleb. We're not debating this. Just get your goddamn personnel out of the way." Joshua ended the call.

The United States led the response, just as China had led the response against North Korea. It was the same targeted, limited assault that CurTO had unleashed on North Korea, designed to neutralize the threat of it happening again, not to cripple Israel. Not a word was spoken in the Situation Room as one, then two, then three Israeli targets were hit. There were audible gasps each time the screen lit up. The president and his team watched it all in real time. Jill was trembling, thinking of how her husband had been killed. The Secretary of Defense fielded the news.

"It's over, Mr. President. All targets have been successfully neutralized. No alliance casualties. All assets are returning to base," the Secretary reported. The last bit, at least, was good news. Unlike other times in the Situation Room, there were no handshakes or congratulations. It was not a time for celebration. There was bad news on the way.

Israel was furious at the betrayal. Israelis died in the assault. Prime Minister Avraham had not evacuated the sites. Casualties, he calculated, would strengthen his case and fuel the outrage. He ordered the release of photos of the dead Israeli soldiers, not their official army headshots, but personal photos of them with their families, smiling, cradling babies.

The reaction at home in the United States was immediate and unrelenting. How could the United States commit an act of war against its most reliable friend and ally in the region? The American Jewish community was enraged. Evangelicals were equally angry. Israel was given to Jews by God, and when Christ returns, he will return to Israel. Jesus lived and was crucified in the Holy Land. Joshua Sheehan had sided with the atheists and the godless, with the globalists and the heretics. He had desecrated the Holy Land with his bombs. Impeachment was one option. Being tried for treason and hanged was a better one. There was speculation that the Antichrist had arrived in the person of Joshua Sheehan. The Reverend Clifton Cutler began hatching his plan for *American Revival Month*.

Joshua's approval ratings, personally and politically, cratered overnight. The press conference the next day didn't help. Joshua knew that he couldn't send his press secretary or Secretary of State out to face the music, he had to do it himself. The briefing room above FDR's swimming pool was filled beyond capacity. Air was difficult to come by.

It was simply too early. He hadn't slept the night of the attack. For a second time, his decision had resulted in people dying, although they wouldn't have if Kaleb Avraham had just listened to him. He stressed that there were no alliance casualties, that the strike had been limited in scope, that Israel knew what the repercussions of its reckless action would be. He offered condolences to the families of the fallen Israeli soldiers. None of it helped his case. He was defensive, hesitant, overly-cautious with his words. Joshua Sheehan did not appear authentic, parsing words and equivocating. Authenticity used to be what people liked about him.

The presidential election was less than three months away. What was once a foregone conclusion was now anything but certain. As much as his standing had skyrocketed following the retaliation against North Korea, it plummeted after the Israel action. Most of the friends and allies who had supported him so vocally and vehemently after North Korea were nowhere to be found. Others were found all over the place, railing against his betrayal. This was different, they argued. North Korea was evil. Israel was good.

Even some of the president's staunchest supporters developed weak knees, although they did manage to quell the impeachment and treason talk in Congress. Vice President Anderson was instrumental in that, even though the president had ignored his counsel before the strike. Anderson was a loyal party soldier. President Sheehan took to the airwaves and the campaign trail to try to regain his standing. Wherever he went, he was met with protests, but he now believed in CurTO more than ever. He made his case to the American people.

The CurTO response to Israel caused a harsh, unpleasant reality to set in for the remaining CurTO holdouts. The alliance was serious and it was lethal. Most importantly, it was united. It responded immediately, strategically, and with overwhelming force. The holdouts were isolated, and now understood that any attack on anyone, anywhere, would have catastrophic consequences. They were ready to come to the table with pens in hand. Even the most ambitious of regimes became rightfully cautious about exercising any imperialistic or expansionist impulses, or even about settling old grudges.

Two days after the Israel affair, Joshua sat down with Secretary Mendoza. She saw how troubled he was. "Is it worth it, Jill? Is negative peace worth it? Shouldn't we be working toward positive peace? All we're doing with CurTO is keeping people in line through fear," Joshua offered.

"Positive peace would be wonderful, Joshua. A world without prejudice, judgment, violence. It's what we all want to see. Ask yourself, though, does that even seem possible to you? Nothing in human history suggests that it is," Jill said. "You've accomplished something, Joshua. You've stopped the fighting. It's not perfect, but it's a start."

Stephanie watched her husband age in the days after the Israel strike. The transformation stunned her, scared her. His hair, peppered with only a few grays beforehand, was now full of them. If they weren't yet a majority, they were a strong plurality. She used to have fun plucking out the occasional gray strand, but that was no longer feasible. His brow had newly-acquired creases which were deepening by the day. His washed-out pallor alarmed her.

"We need to get away," Stephanie said. "Let's go home for a few days. Get away from here. You can't sleep, you hardly eat. You look, pardon my French, like *la merde*."

"I can't just up and leave, Steph. I'm in the middle of a campaign. It'll look like I'm running away."

"I don't care what it looks like," she answered. "You really need to get out of here. *We* need to get out of here. I'm scared, Joshua. This place is suffocating you. You did the right thing, but it's eating you alive."

She was right, and Joshua knew it. "I'll see what I can do. What day is it?" he asked. He had genuinely lost track. He finally remembered that it was Tuesday. "Let me check the calendar and see what I can do. My opponent's going to have fun with this."

"Soon, Joshua. I'm not kidding. We need to do it soon. Let him have his fun," Stephanie said. "I'd rather be married to a one-term president than be a widow." Joshua understood that it was not a mere suggestion. By Friday afternoon, they were arriving in Bucksport. As the motorcade crossed the Penobscot Narrows Bridge, Joshua looked down at Fort Knox. "Remember watching the meteors, Steph?" She smiled at the memory. "Feels like a long, long time ago, doesn't it?"

"It was," she answered, taking his hand. "I miss it every single day. I'm still upset that Pluto's not a planet anymore. Let's sit outside tonight and see if I can find Gemini." Baxter enjoyed being back home, too. For the first time in weeks, Joshua could breathe.

T he time away did wonders for them both. They only took a skeleton crew with them, the Secret Service detail, Chief of Staff Sam Pelletier, who was thrilled to be home in Maine smelling the pine and digging clams, and a few people from the chief of staff's office. Joshua and Stephanie stayed in during the day and spent evenings sitting outside around the fire pit with a few friends from the curling club. Joshua cleaned and fired-up the grill. They wondered why the hell they had ever left Bucksport.

When Joshua returned to the campaign the next week, he was re-energized. He owned his decision about Israel. He told the truth as he saw it. Yes, he would do it again. On election night, the people sent him back to the White House. Barely. *American Revival Month* had very, very nearly succeeded in taking him down.

Chapter 18

The Secret Service

"Show me a hero, and I'll write you a tragedy." – F. Scott Fitzgerald, Notebook E (1945)

Jackson Carter applied to the United States Secret Service at the beginning of his senior year of college, the day he turned twenty-one. His dream, for as long as he could recall, was to work in law enforcement, just like his father, Steven, a decorated North Carolina State Trooper. Trooper Carter had killed a man once, a bad man. It was in self-defense, but it haunted him nonetheless. It was never spoken of.

Jackson was thrilled to learn that his initial application passed muster with the Department of Homeland Security. His academic and athletic credentials were impressive. That was only his first small step toward becoming a Secret Service Special Agent. Before being approved to even take the entrance exam, Jackson had to pass a background check, which was a breeze. He had never been cited for a broken taillight or gotten a speeding ticket, much less anything serious or worrisome. In short, he was a straight-laced, intelligent, unfailingly-polite, church-going young man who simply wanted to serve his country.

Along with passing his initial background check, the Secret Service had an extensive checklist of requirements for Jackson to meet before he could be hired. Some were simple, others more difficult. In addition to being a United States citizen, an applicant must be twenty-one years of age and have a driver's license. They also must have uncorrected vision better than 20/100 and corrected vision of 20/20 or better; must pass a hearing test; have no visible body markings, including tattoos or brands; must pass the Applicant Physical Abilities Test; qualify for a Top Secret security clearance; undergo a drug screening; be registered with the Selective Service; and submit to a security interview and polygraph test. If he failed just one, Jackson Carter would never join the Secret Service. He sailed through them all.

The Applicant Physical Abilities Test is a test of strength, stamina, and agility, all essential for Secret Service protective duty. Candidates must perform as many push-ups as they can in one minute, as many sit-ups as they can in one minute, achieve a passing time in a mile-and-a-half run, and complete the Illinois Agility Run, a test of anaerobic capacity and agility. Passing the test is not easy, although it was for Jackson. He had played Division 1 lacrosse as a defenseman at the University of North Carolina, and the year-round training regimen for elite college lacrosse was far more grueling than training for this test. Jackson probably could have passed without bothering to train. That wasn't Jackson. He trained hard and passed easily.

"I did it, Dad! I passed! I'm going to take the exam!" Jackson told his father when he got the news.

"Congratulations, son. I knew you would," Steven said. "Why don't you and LeAnn come over for dinner tonight to celebrate? Your mother's making some Nashville fried chicken, fresh from the Pollard's farm. The chicken was squawking just a few hours ago." Jackson's mother was not nearly as excited, but was equally proud.

"Sounds good, Dad. We'll be here at six."

The final hurdle before Jackson could be hired was the Special Agent Entrance Exam. If he passed, he could finally begin his training, which is what Jackson Carter did. It wasn't easy being away from LeAnn, his wife, for the three months of training, but they both knew that it was coming one day. They had gotten married shortly after Jackson graduated from college. LeAnn knew the Secret Service career path. She stayed behind in Black Mountain, North Carolina when Joshua shipped off for training.

Secret Service training means thirteen weeks at the Federal Law Enforcement Training Center in Glynco, Georgia, with 750 hours of classroom and field instruction in marksmanship, use-of-force and control techniques, emergency medical training, financial crimes detection, event and site protection, interviewing, surveillance, money laundering, and water survival, among a myriad of other topics. Firearm and marksmanship training was a breeze for Jackson. The rest of it was new and challenging.

Jackson had been shooting and hunting with his father for more than half his life. Weekends often meant a couple of hours at the shooting range. Jackson knew how to handle a gun. He had been game-hunting since he was twelve. At sixteen, he bagged a 350-pound black bear with a single pass-through shot. His father grilled bear steaks that weekend. They were delicious, slightly fatty, and surprisingly sweet.

"The bear probably ate berries and fruit, mainly," Jackson's father explained. "That's why it's a little bit sweet."

Jackson's first assignment after training was at the Secret Service field office in Memphis, one of 130 Secret Service offices scattered around the country. Every new agent begins their career in a field office. Jackson and LeAnn were thrilled by the Memphis assignment in a state bordering their home. It could have been San Francisco or Detroit or Milwaukee, someplace utterly foreign to them. Jackson had no say in where he was sent. They were lucky. Jackson and LeAnn were at home with the culture in Tennessee, the environment familiar and comfortable.

Field office agents do not protect government officials, which is what everyone immediately associates with the Secret Service. That comes years later. Rather, the majority of new agents' time is spent doing investigative work, largely into financial crimes like counterfeiting, credit card fraud, and identity theft. Most of the work is office work, pouring over complicated financial transactions and conducting interviews. The Watergate-era catchphrase "follow the money" was universally the best advice. A little bit of surveillance was mixed in, too, to break the monotony. Jackson Carter excelled and received the highest marks from his supervisors. He was going to make a name for himself within the Service, they thought.

After two years in the Memphis office, Special Agent Carter was reassigned to a larger office in Chicago. It was a culture shock. Neither Jackson nor LeAnn had ever lived outside of the South. The Chicago weather was the least of it, although that, too, took getting used to. They found the people to be less polite, more aloof and abrupt than people at home or in Tennessee. Some were downright rude, even. LeAnn and Jackson felt the condescension when people took note of their accents. Nonetheless, they made the best of it, finding a church that they felt comfortable in and making a few friends, and they began talking seriously about starting a family. It was more than just talk. By the time that Carter's three-year stint in Chicago was winding down, they had welcomed a son, Lucas, and a second child, a girl, was anxious to leave the womb.

The day that Jackson had been hoping for finally, finally arrived. The Special Agent in Charge in Chicago, a long-time veteran of the service, Michael Pellegrino, summoned Carter to his office. "Have a seat, Jackson," Pellegrino said. "First of all, I must say that your work here has been exemplary. In Memphis, too." Pellegrino was a caricature, almost. Who sports a crew cut these days? His shirt sleeves struggled to contain his biceps. He spoke in a baritone, more loudly than necessary. *Semper Fi* was tattooed on his left calf. Pellegrino preferred his bourbon neat, his coffee black, and his women young.

Jackson was nervous. Starting a conversation with flattery was a time-tested way of softening bad news. Jackson himself resorted to it on occasion. It usually worked. "Thank you, sir," he answered.

Pellegrino got right to it. He wasn't one to waste words. "Jackson, you're being reassigned and I think you'll like this one. It's finally time for you to do what you signed on to do. You're being transferred to Washington – Protective Operations – and you'll receive your training instructions and protective assignment once you get there. They specifically asked for you, and I gave them my highest recommendation. Congratulations, Jackson. You earned this."

"Thank you, sir. I'm honored. When do I leave?" Jackson asked. He immediately regretted sounding so anxious. He enjoyed working under Michael Pellegrino.

"Two weeks. Headquarters will be sending you a complete itinerary this afternoon, along with some housing suggestions for you and LeAnn. For now, just start wrapping up your work and loop Agent Robinson in. She'll be assuming most of your duties."

"Thank you again, sir. I've enjoyed working under your leadership," Jackson said. The two men stood and shook hands. Both had learned the value of a firm handshake. It revealed confidence and authority. Pelligrino sized-up all of his new agents at their first handshake.

"You're very welcome," Pellegrino said. "I know that you won't let me down."

"Absolutely not, sir. I promise I won't," Jackson said.

Back at his desk, Jackson immediately called LeAnn. "I've got great news, hon. We're leaving Chicago. I'm being transferred to Washington. To Protective Operations. We have to be there in two weeks. I'll know more details this afternoon."

"That's awesome, babe," LeAnn said. "It's what you've always wanted. We've always wanted. Congratulations. I'm really, really proud of you. I guess I better start packing up. Two weeks isn't much time." She was happy for him, but she was terrified. LeAnn understood exactly what Protective Operations meant.

Two weeks later, Jackson, LeAnn, and Lucas arrived in Washington and spent the weekend moving into one of the rented condos suggested by headquarters. LeAnn picked it out. It was larger and nicer than their apartments in either Memphis or Chicago. Lucas could finally have his own bedroom.

At nine o'clock Monday morning, Jackson was sitting in the office of the Assistant Director of Protective Operations, James Ogletree. The credenza was crammed with pictures of Ogletree with presidents, vice presidents, senators, ambassadors, and even with family. James Ogletree made Michael Pellegrino seem like a chatterbox. "Congratulations, Agent Carter, and welcome to Protective Operations. You come highly recommended." Ogletree had said the same thing to hundreds of eager agents over the years.

"It's my honor, sir. I'm looking forward to the challenge," Carter answered.

"Good," Ogletree said. "I can assure you that it *will* be a challenge. The first thing we need to do is get you trained. This is a different beast than sitting behind a desk trying to figure out who's been scamming old ladies out of their Social Security checks." It was Ogletree's standard line. "You need to get yourself down to Georgia on Wednesday to start. All of your travel and housing arrangements have been taken care of." Assistant Director Ogletree handed a packet of material to Carter. "Familiarize yourself with all of this. If you have any questions, let me know. Otherwise, enjoy your training. Try to get some rest, too. The training is intense." That was it. No small-talk, no "how was your move" or "are you settled in yet." Welcome to Washington.

Carter found his way to his cubicle two floors below, which three days ago had been home to some other agent. Standard government desk, standard government chair, drawer full of cheap, capless Bics, a few of which worked, a jammed stapler. The only thing that passed for decoration was a promotional calendar from some local insurance broker taped to the glass partition. He settled down with a cardboard cup of federal office building coffee and opened the packet Ogletree had given him. He had hoped that headquarters would have better coffee than Memphis and Chicago. It did not. It was on par with gas station coffee, made no more palatable by powdered creamer.

The information packet included a welcome message from the Director, printed below his official Department of Homeland Security headshot; living and transportation details; a detailed schedule for the eleven days of training; and a curriculum outline. It seemed impossible to cover every item – introduction to Protective Service Operations (PSO), organization of a protective detail, PSO team meetings, aircraft countermeasures, case studies, PSO formations, motorcade formations and movements, protective countermeasures and surveillance, route surveys, cover and evacuation, protective intelligence, attacks on the protectee, the PSO lab, firearms safety and regulations, live firearm engagement techniques, motorcade tactics, advanced vehicle handling, advanced technical driving, vehicle ambush countermeasures, tactical medical first aid – in less than three weeks. He wondered how he could possibly absorb and process all of it.

Jackson called LeAnn to break the news that he would be leaving for Georgia in two days. "I guess we knew this was coming," he said to her.

"I suppose," LeAnn answered. "Just not so soon. We've barely been here for three days. We still haven't unpacked everything. How long will you be gone?"

"Three weeks," Jackson said. "I'll get to as much as I can before I leave. You want some more bad news?"

"Not really," LeAnn said.

"The coffee here stinks. See you tonight," Jackson said. "I'll pick up dinner somewhere. Maybe somebody around here knows a good barbeque place. Do you think there's any good barbeque in Washington?"

"Maybe. Probably not as good as Memphis, though. Get extra hot sauce, please," LeAnn said. Her second pregnancy came with an incessant craving for spicy food. Her first demanded salty food, especially pickles.

Once again, LeAnn was left to fend for herself while Jackson shipped off for more training. This time, though, she had an eighteen-month-old boy to take care of. In Georgia, Jackson's class had fifteen other young Special Agents, all happy to be done with their field office assignments and champing at the bit to be where the serious action was – protecting the most important people in the United States.

A ssistant Director Ogletree was right. The training was intense. Mentally exhausting every day and physically exhausting some days. The most challenging, physically, was learning to drive and maneuver the various armored cars and SUVs used in a presidential motorcade.

Learning to drive "the Beast" was altogether unlike driving anything else on wheels. The Beast, given the codename "Stagecoach" by the Secret Service, is the president's SUV. It is a rolling fortress. The Beast weighs ten tons, more than three Chevy Suburbans. Its shell is eight inches thick, its windows five. Bullets would bounce off the Beast like ping-pong balls. Lee Harvey Oswald's shots would have had as much effect on it as snowballs. The Beast is no sports car, either, so massive that it takes fifteen seconds to go from zero to sixty and musters just four miles per gallon. It is neither a getaway car nor eco-friendly.

"Holy shit," Special Agent Dwayne Robinson said. "This is like driving an iceberg." Jackson rode shotgun as Robinson maneuvered the Beast around the training course. The training model of the Beast is the size and weight of the real thing, without the James Bondish features. The real thing can disperse an oil slick, just like Bond's Aston Martin DB5 in *Goldfinger*, to send chasing cars spinning out of control. It can disperse tear gas and a smoke screen, too. It runs on run-flat tires the size of bus tires. Whoever christened it "the Beast" wasn't kidding.

The training course had a multitude of twists and bumps and sharp turns. "Jesus Christ!" Robinson screamed as a barrel rolled onto the road in front of them. He swerved violently to the left, then back to the right, fishtailing. "What the fuck!"

Jackson never swore. He never heard his parents swear, either. One time, he heard his father call somebody "a pain in the ass," and that surprised him. He didn't care for the language common to his fellow agents, particularly when they took the Lord's name in vain, but he had gotten used to it. Playing college lacrosse had acclimated him to a stunning and wildly creative array of obscenities.

The trainees' heart rates were up after the driving and tactical maneuvering exercises. They returned to the classroom to learn more about the Beast's features and controls. It could be hermetically sealed, they discovered, in case of a chemical or biological attack. The door handles could deliver 120 incapacitating volts to a potential intruder. There is integrated night vision technology. It is loaded with an arsenal of serious weaponry. A small refrigerator stocks blood for the president.

Back in his room each night, Jackson talked with LeAnn for half an hour or so. She sounded tired, but assured him that she was managing fine. Her mother would be coming for a few days to help out, which Jackson thought was a great idea. When the calls were over, Jackson immediately began reviewing the day's lessons and preparing for the next day. He wasn't interested in going out for a beer or two with the guys, which they did most nights. He didn't drink – never had – and wanted to master the material. Before turning in, he spent a few minutes with his Bible, a routine he had followed since high school.

The eleven days of training flew by for Jackson. For LeAnn, they crept by slowly. She was in a new city, in a new home, with aching feet, a sore back, a toddler, an enormous tummy, and no friends around. Thank God her mother had visited.

At the training center in Georgia, as with almost everything he tackled, Jackson excelled, and his superiors took notice.

"Anyone stand out to you?" Assistant Director James Ogletree asked during a call with the training supervisor.

"There are several, sir. It's a very good class. If I had to name one, though, it would be Jackson Carter."

Chapter 19

The Detail

"It is easy to be brave from a safe distance." – Aesop

Joshua's biggest regret was selecting Edward Todd Anderson to be his vice president. He had wanted someone more energetic, with more personality, more conviction on his ticket and in his administration, New Jersey Governor Elijah Turner in particular. Energy and personality were not Edward Todd Anderson's calling cards. Against his judgment, and Stephanie's, Joshua had given in to the party pressure and chosen Senator Anderson to "balance the ticket." Someone from the midwest, someone with experience in Congress. And then, he kept him on the ticket for his re-election run. Dumping him would have been bad politics.

Joshua didn't dislike Anderson. He relied on him to schmooze with senators and make the congressional rounds promoting the president's agenda. Anderson excelled at it, too. He had been especially helpful in quieting the impeachment talk in Congress after the Israel affair. All in all, he was an asset. But Joshua and the vice president just never developed much of a personal relationship. They were political bedfellows, not friends. Joshua relied far more on his cabinet and Stephanie to inform his policies and decisions.

As a senator, Anderson hated being on the wrong side of an issue, and especially of a vote, which would be recorded and preserved for all eternity.

Even more, he despised public criticism. Bold, forward-thinking was not his stock-in-trade. As vice president, his most odious duty was casting tie-breaking votes in the Senate with everyone watching. Regardless, he was well-regarded within the party and was a reliable vote when needed. Not a useful idiot – far from it – but a useful tool.

Vice President Anderson was helpful to President Sheehan in important ways. He knew everyone on Capitol Hill and was friendly with most. He knew how Congress worked and who could get things done. He knew what each member would accept in trade when he needed to offer a carrot, and what they feared if he had to wield a stick. He also knew the federal agencies intimately and who to call to move things along. That experience and knowledge was deployed in service to the president when needed.

It is not uncommon for presidents and vice presidents to have a distant relationship. FDR and Garner, Eisenhower and Nixon, Kennedy and Johnson, Nixon and Agnew, none of those relationships were warm and fuzzy. When Eisenhower was asked about Vice President Nixon's contributions to Ike's presidency, he answered, "Give me a week and I'll think of one." The arrangement didn't bother either Joshua or Anderson. President Sheehan didn't give the vice president much to do, not knowing whether, or when, he might get around to it. That suited ETA just fine.

Even as vice president, Anderson constantly ran late. His nickname "ETA" stood the test of time. President Sheehan, on the other hand, was habitually on time. It is a habit not often found in presidents, but it was one which Joshua had cultivated over his lifetime. Keeping people waiting, wasting their time, was rude and disrespectful. Sure, it was a power move, being the last to arrive and having the meeting delayed, but President Sheehan didn't play that game. He didn't live by the old saw, "A president is never late." An 8:00 a.m. meeting started at 8:00 a.m. Chief of Staff Sam Pelletier eventually stopped announcing that the vice president was "a little delayed" after a few months. It was assumed that he would be.

The vice president didn't feel constrained by schedules. He arrived at his pleasure, even for cabinet meetings and presidential daily briefings on national security issues. President Sheehan started his meetings whether ETA was there or not. "Sorry for my lateness, but I was unavoidably detained," the vice president would routinely announce upon his arrival.

Special Agent Carter was initially assigned to Vice President Anderson's protective detail. It wasn't the prize he had hoped for, but it was nevertheless a prestigious assignment. Absolutely nothing of note happened during his time guarding the vice president. Nothing much of note *ever* happened with the vice president. Jackson Carter did lots of standing around while the vice president did whatever it was he did before he got going. There were the usual speeches before friendly and not-as-friendly organizations and think tanks, symposia and conventions to attend, visits to Capitol Hill, the occasional funeral that the president didn't feel compelled to attend, and the daily comings and goings to and from the vice president's office in the Executive Office Building and his residence at the Naval Observatory.

Protecting the vice president is not easy, but it is a bit easier than protecting the president, since the vice president's movements and activities are less well-known and publicized than the president's. Besides, if someone wanted to try something crazy and make a name for themself, targeting the vice president wouldn't be the best way to go about it. No vice president has ever been assassinated. Four presidents have. Reagan very nearly made it five. Crowds for Vice President Anderson were smaller and more subdued than for the president. Usually, they were bored or disappointed that they were stuck with the vice president rather than the president.

Regardless, Jackson Carter dedicated himself completely to the task of protecting Vice President Anderson. He studied the venues, maps, and blueprints, looked for vulnerabilities, assessed people and crowds. Any missed threat, any overlooked detail, could mean catastrophe.

"It's an honor to meet you, Mr. President," Jackson said when he was introduced. Joshua noted the firm, confident handshake. They must teach that handshake at Secret Service school, Joshua thought.

"The honor is mine," the president said. "I look forward to working with you. Where are you from, Agent Carter?"

"North Carolina, sir. Black Mountain."

"Beautiful part of the country. Married?"

"Yes, sir. LeAnn."

"Children?"

"Two, sir. Lucas and Emma." There was an unmistakable pride in Jackson's voice when he said his children's names. Joshua preferred agents without children. "Lucas is two-and-a-half, Emma is six months." Particularly agents without very young children.

It was the assignment Jackson had dreamed of since joining the service – the presidential detail. Few people in the world work more closely or have more intimate contact with the President of the United States. It is the highest honor and most challenging assignment a Special Agent can receive, reserved for the very best of the very best. It is also the most stressful and demanding. One mistake, one oversight, one momentary loss of focus might change the course of history. Clint Hill, the Secret Service agent who jumped onto the trunk of JFK's limousine in Dallas after the first shot was fired and who shielded the president and Jackie on the race to Parkland Memorial Hospital, spent the rest of his life convinced that if he had acted just one second sooner, he would have taken the bullet that killed the president.

Jackson Carter had been on the presidential detail for three months when President Sheehan held an outdoor rally in Middletown, Ohio. It was one of dozens the president was holding early in his second term, still rehabilitating his standing after the Israel affair and trying to keep his agenda on track before he became just a lame duck focused more on building his presidential library than on governing.

The Secret Service detests large, outdoor events, but presidents feel like they have to do them. The optics of standing in front of an adoring crowd, sun shining, flags waving, are too enticing to pass up. The advance planning for the rally was extensive and comprehensive, snipers on rooftops, magnetometers at every access point, eight-foot fencing around the entire perimeter, K9 units at the ready.

"Sweeper is two minutes out. All agents in position," commanded the voice in Jackson's earpiece. "Sweeper" was the president's Secret Service codename, in honor of his curling background. Jackson assumed his station at the rear of the platform. For the past hour, he had been studying the crowd, the part closest to the stage. He detected nothing noteworthy, just people excited to see the president. A few balloons popped and people flinched, but Jackson instinctively recognized the difference between a popping balloon and something more sinister. Other agents kept close watch over the boisterous protesters gathered in the back. A couple of undercover officers had joined them.

The Beast, along with a dozen other vehicles comprising Joshua's motorcade, rumbled into the space behind the stage. Special Agent Fayad exited the Beast's passenger side, conducted a quick visual assessment, and opened the president's door. Joshua stepped out and began the tedious process of greeting the mayor and assorted local dignitaries who wanted to meet and have a picture taken with a United States president. Neither Ohio senator was there. Their voters wouldn't countenance them hobnobbing and joking with Joshua Sheehan. Jackson assumed his position behind and to the president's right. On cue, the Middletown High School band started up and Joshua bounded onto the stage, smiling and waving.

Jackson Carter stood a few feet away as the president spoke, Oakley sunglasses on, earpiece in, erect and fully present. Everything in Middletown was executed flawlessly and without incident, until President Sheehan decided to work the rope line.

The Secret Service hates surprises, but it trains for them. Agents especially dislike when presidents go off script. The script in Middletown called for the president to exit the rear of the stage after he finished his speech. Regardless, the president was the president and could do pretty much as he pleased, and President Sheehan wanted to get close to the people, to shake some hands, rebuild his connection. He was still working on that more than a year after CurTO's assault on Israel. The Secret Service knew what to do and went into action.

The agents, in Pavlovian response, fell into formation around the president as he approached the crowd, each assuming their assigned position. Special Agent Carter was behind the president at the rope line, off of his right shoulder, scanning the crowd for anything the slightest bit unusual. A sudden movement, shifty eyes, a noise. And then it happened. A young white male, maybe twenty-five years old, if that, bulled through the front row of people and lunged directly at the president. Not even thinking – there was no time for that – Jackson Carter jumped in front of the president and shoved him back with his left arm. Joshua stumbled, but was caught by another agent.

The serrated knife tore through Jackson's suit coat and crisp, white shirt, slicing deep into his upper arm. It did as much damage on the way out as it did on the way in. The pain was instantaneous and intense, masked only slightly by a huge jolt of adrenaline. Blood gushed into Jackson's shirt and coat and ran down past his starched cuff, onto his hand, and streamed from his fingers onto the ground. While other agents whisked the president off and neutralized the attacker, Jackson was on his knees, pale, already in shock, his left hand clutching at the wound. There was so much blood.

While there was chaos and confusion in the crowd, among the Secret Service and other law enforcement, there was not. Agents shielded the president on all sides and hustled him to the Beast, which raced away, escorted by local cruisers and the Secret Service SUVs, spitting stones and dust behind them. They had rehearsed this. Local officers drove the remaining crowd back from where Jackson was kneeling and hemorrhaging. His face was ashen.

In Washington, LeAnn was sitting on the floor with Lucas, cable news on in the background. Emma had finally fallen asleep for her nap. LeAnn watched the beginning of President Sheehan's speech until the network cut away for commercials and other stories. She always felt better when she saw Jackson.

Lucas suddenly needed her attention. Then, she heard the familiar, *"This is breaking news."* She looked up. The video feed was from Middletown, Ohio. She caught a brief glimpse of Jackson on the ground. She watched with horror, panicked, and tried to call him. There was no answer. She tried again. And again.

The medical team, which had first checked on the president and found him unharmed, ran to where Carter knelt. They stanched the bleeding, quickly tried to sterilize the wound, loaded him into the ambulance, hooked up a blood bag, and raced to the pre-selected hospital, which was on alert in case something happened during the president's visit. The ambulance driver knew the precise route. "Hurry up!" they yelled from the back. "Go! Go! Go!" Jackson lost consciousness.

The cut was deep and jagged, knicking bone. It took surgeons three-and-a-half hours, sixty-seven stitches, and nearly three pints of blood to repair. For forty-five minutes after the breaking news, LeAnn tried to reach someone – anyone – who could tell her what was happening with Jackson. Was he alive? Dead? How would she raise two children alone? Why would anyone do this? No one would tell her anything. She did the only thing she could think of. She dropped to her knees and prayed. The television news could only confirm that a Secret Service agent was wounded and that the assailant was believed to be dead. Only after it became evident that Jackson was going to survive did his team leader call LeAnn to tell her what had happened.

Six weeks later, in an emotional, private ceremony in the Oval Office, with President Sheehan and Stephanie, as well as LeAnn, in attendance, the Secretary of the Department of Homeland Security and the Director of the Secret Service presented Special Agent Jackson Carter with the Secretary's Award for Valor, the highest honor bestowed by the department. Stephanie could not contain her tears, try as she might. Someone had tried to kill her husband. Agent Carter nearly died. LeAnn was nearly widowed. Joshua was more successful in controlling his emotions, but only a little. Jackson Carter had suffered a knifing so that he didn't. Jackson may have saved the president's life.

Jackson Carter returned to work only after months of painful rehabilitation, limited to desk duty. His medal resided in the bottom drawer. He was already itching to return to his protective assignment. Jackson needed to get back to it as soon as possible. LeAnn begged him not to return to the protective detail. He could take a supervisory position, maybe even run a field office or train new agents. No one would begrudge him not wanting to go back. Not after what had happened to him. He was a hero.

"Please, Jackson, please," LeAnn begged him over and over. "No one's gonna blame you. Lucas and Emma need you. I need you."

"I'm sorry, babe, I have to go back. It's my calling," Jackson always answered. He was adamant. He belonged on the president's detail. It was where he was meant to be and where he wanted to be.

While he was on medical leave and rehabilitating, Jackson had plenty of time to reflect on what he had done, why he had done it, and who he had done it for. The "why" part was easy. It was his job, to be a physical barrier between an attacker and the president, no matter who the president might be. That was why. It was reflexive, not even conscious, when he jumped between the president and his attacker. It didn't matter in the least whether Jackson Carter thought that the president was too liberal or too conservative, or too *anything*, for that matter. He was programmed to protect the President of the United States, no matter what. When Jackson Carter had a job to do, he did it.

Jackson read and thought a lot about the young man who stabbed him. He was only twenty-four years old, and now he was dead. By all accounts, he was a pretty normal guy. College degree, entry-level job at a shipping company, a few friends, his own small apartment. Nobody had anything bad to say about him – not co-workers, not family, not teachers, not even an ex-girlfriend. No one imagined anything like this coming. But inside of him, there was rage. The document which the attacker – his name was Nathan Shuster, Jackson learned – posted a few minutes before his death was thoughtful, coherent, and eloquent, even, not the ramblings of some madman. Joshua Sheehan and his godless CurTO allies were trying to destroy America and the Christian way of life, he wrote. Someone had to stop him. Someone had to fight back. Someone had to take Scripture seriously. He had learned that during *American Revival Month*. If God requires a martyr, why not me? Jackson Carter offered a prayer for Nathan's soul.

Immediately after the assassination attempt, Congress set about its essential business of finding someone to blame. It didn't particularly matter who, it just needed to be *someone*. The higher up, the better. Fortunately for Congress, it didn't have to deal with the pesky issue of guns this time. The Secret Service agents on the ground had performed flawlessly, Congress concluded, keeping the attacker away from the president and immediately whisking the president away from danger. Special Agent Jackson Carter, in particular, was singled out for praise. Still, there had to be someone at fault.

Ultimately, Congress settled on Assistant Director of Protective Operations James Ogletree to take the fall. There was no particular reason to choose Ogletree, other than it had to be somebody fairly high up the chain of command. Congress's 212-page report did its best to pin blame squarely on the assistant director. Why weren't there more magnetometers? Who let the president get that close to the crowd? Why aren't there better protocols? How did the knife get past security? And so, after twenty-nine years of faithful and exemplary service, James Ogletree submitted his resignation and cleaned out his office. The congressional gods were appeased, the sacrifice offered, even if Congress never did quite figure out how the would-be assassin managed to get a knife into the event. Ogletree hoped they would have the dignity not to come after his pension.

Chapter 20
A Prize

"This is President Sheehan," Joshua said, taking the phone from his chief of staff.

"Good morning, Mr. President," the voice began. "This is Aksel Larsen, chair of the Norwegian Nobel Committee. It is my high honor and distinct pleasure to inform you that you have been selected by the committee to receive this year's Nobel Peace Prize. I am further pleased to tell you that you will be sharing the prize with President Yu Song from the People's Republic of China. Congratulations, Mr. President, on behalf of the entire Nobel Committee."

It was the first Friday in October. Reaching the President of the United States on the phone is no simple feat, but the Nobel Committee has plenty of experience dealing with world leaders, and is extremely persistent when need be. After being put on hold and transferred half a dozen times, Aksel Larsen was finally put through to the president as the sun rose in Washington.

The Nobel Peace Prize Laureate is always notified on the first Friday in October in precisely the same way. A representative of the committee informs the recipient moments before the public announcement is made. No advance notice, no pre-scheduled call which would tip off the recipient. Just an unexpected call in the middle of the night, the middle of the day, or very early in the morning, depending on the recipient's time zone. Most people fielding the call think that it's a prank, at least at first. Not many people sit clutching their phone on that particular Friday expecting a call from Norway. A few do, but they are invariably disappointed. President Sheehan certainly thought it was a prank.

At the same moment, President Yu was taking the same call from the committee. It interrupted his dinner with Bao. It is even harder to reach the Chinese president than it is to reach the American one. President Yu wasn't someone to play tricks on.

President Sheehan wasn't stunned, exactly, but he was perplexed. He had never entertained the notion of receiving a Nobel Peace Prize. How could he possibly deserve a peace prize for entering into a military alliance and ordering military strikes on North Korea and Israel? People had been killed. It didn't make sense.

"Are you sure?" Joshua asked. Aksel Larsen chuckled. He had heard that exact question many times. Almost every time.

"Oh, yes, Mr. President, the committee is very sure. We will be making our announcement in just a few minutes. We very much look forward to hosting you and President Yu in Oslo in December. We will work on the necessary arrangements with your staff. Congratulations, Mr. President." President Yu's reaction was much like President Sheehan's. Just to confirm that it was real, both men watched the public announcement on television.

At seven o'clock in the morning, the West Wing was usually busy. This morning, it was electric. Staffers gathered in a conference room to watch the announcement from Norway. The sober-faced chair of the Norwegian Nobel Committee solemnly approached the podium in the Grand Hall of the Norwegian Nobel Institute. They take the award extraordinarily seriously. The announcement was made in English, not Aksel Larsen's first language:

Good afternoon, everyone. The Norwegian Nobel Committee has made the decision to award the Peace Prize for this year jointly to the President of the United States, Joshua Sheehan, and to the President of the People's Republic of China, Yu Song. The two men are receiving the prize for their efforts to prevent international wars and to provide security and territorial integrity to all nations, large and small. Their leadership has resulted in a more peaceful and less violent world.

The decision to award the Nobel Peace Prize jointly to President Sheehan and President Yu is securely anchored in Alfred Nobel's will. This year's prize Laureates join a distinguished list of peace prize Laureates that this committee has honored as champions of world peace. The Nobel Peace Prize this year fulfills Alfred Nobel's desire to recognize efforts of the greatest benefit to humankind. Thank you.

Stephanie was upstairs in the residence when her chief of staff delivered the news. She made her way down to the Oval Office. "Joshua, is there anything that you want to tell me?" It was rare for Stephanie to stop in the Oval. She asked the question as if Joshua had lost his wedding ring and was afraid to tell her.

"Not that I can think of," he answered. Now they were just playing.

"Oh, OK. For some reason, I thought there might be. Silly me. I'll head back upstairs, then. Let you get back to work."

"Alright. I'll come up around lunchtime," Joshua said. Stephanie turned to leave. She knew that he couldn't bluff much longer. "Oh, wait a minute," Joshua blurted. "I just remembered. I won the Nobel Peace Prize."

"Really? That's great," Stephanie replied casually. "See you at lunchtime, then." She stopped at the door and turned. "Do you know what the weather's like in Oslo in December?" she asked.

"About the same as Maine, I suppose. Cold and windy," Joshua answered. "I haven't really thought about it."

"That's what I figured, too," Stephanie said. "Oh, before I forget, congratulations, Mr. President."

The Nobel Peace Prize has been awarded nearly every year since 1901, pursuant to the Last Will and Testament of Dr. Alfred Nobel, the inventor of dynamite. Nearly every year, because there have been twenty times when no prize was awarded, most notably during the two world wars, when awarding a peace prize was unthinkable, and in 1948, the year Mahatma Gandhi was assassinated. That year, the Nobel Committee announced that there was "no suitable living candidate."

One often-told tale, maybe true, maybe not, is that Alfred Nobel created the prize after a French newspaper prematurely ran his obituary, in which it did not reflect kindly on his invention and its use as a tool of war. The obituary christened Nobel "the merchant of death" who "became rich by finding ways to kill people faster than ever before." It was not the way that most people, including Dr. Nobel, preferred to be remembered.

Per Nobel's Last Will and Testament, the Peace Prize is awarded to "the person who shall have done the most or the best work for fraternity between nations, for the abolition or reduction of standing armies and for the holding and promotion of peace congresses." The Nobel Committee soon expanded the list to include organizations as well as individuals. Later, it further expanded the criteria to include the candidate's commitment to nonviolent methods; the quality of the candidate as a person and of their sustained contribution to peace; the candidate's work on issues of peace, justice, human dignity, and the integrity of the environment; and the candidate's possession of a worldview and/or global impact as opposed to a purely parochial concern.

Four United States presidents prior to Joshua Sheehan were awarded the Nobel Peace Prize: Theodore Roosevelt won in 1906 for negotiating the Treaty of Portsmouth ending the Russo-Japanese War, Woodrow Wilson in 1919 for his role in establishing the League of Nations, Jimmy Carter in 2002 for his lifetime work to peacefully resolve international conflicts and his human rights advocacy, and Barack Obama in 2009 for his more nebulous efforts to strengthen international diplomacy and cooperation. Former vice president Al Gore won in 2007 for his pioneering environmental work.

Chief of Staff Sam Pelletier entered the Oval Office. "The staff is anxious to see you and congratulate you, sir. Shall I order champagne from the kitchen?"

"It's eight o'clock, Sam. A little early for the staff to be drinking, don't you think?" the president said. His long-time friend looked disappointed. "It is Friday, though. Let's do it at nine."

"As you wish. I'll get someone on it."

For the first time that morning, Joshua was alone. He stood at the window looking out at the garden, wondering, doubting, whether he deserved this. The North Koreans and Israelis who had died because of his order still haunted him. The door opened.

"Congratulations, Joshua. I'm thrilled for you," Secretary Mendoza said after the door closed and she realized that no one else was there. How can anyone look so good so early in the morning, Joshua wondered.

"Thank you, Jill. It was quite a surprise."

"You deserve it Joshua. You really do. You've done something extraordinary," she offered. Jill had been with him for nearly seven years, on the curling ice, in the Situation Room, through North Korea and Israel. He decided to tell her. She deserved to know.

"It wouldn't have happened without you, Jill. Do you remember the first time that we met? In Portland?" he asked.

"Of course."

"I asked if you thought that peace was possible. Do you remember what you said?"

"Not exactly," Jill answered.

"Well, I do. Like it happened yesterday. You said that you wanted to believe it. That you have two daughters. That's when I decided that I would try."

Jill smiled. "I remember now. I said that with the right idea, at the right time, the right person, it just might be possible." She stopped. "I guess the right person finally came along."

The Nobel Peace Prize ceremony is held in Oslo on December 10th each year, the anniversary of Alfred Nobel's death. The Peace Prize is the only one of the Nobel Prizes awarded in Norway, as stipulated by Nobel himself. All of the other prizes – Physics, Chemistry, Physiology, Medicine, Literature, and Economics – are awarded in Stockholm, Sweden. Why the Peace Prize is awarded in Norway, Dr. Nobel did not say. President Sheehan and the first lady arrived in Oslo on December 8th, as did President Yu and Bao.

The Peace Prize Laureate stays in the Nobel Suite at the Grand Hotel in Oslo, an elegant, historic hotel in the heart of the thousand-year-old city. With two Peace Prize Laureates, a second suite was required. President Sheehan insisted that President Yu and Bao take the Nobel Suite, while he and Stephanie would stay in the less prestigious Grand Royal Suite. The two presidents recognized the irony of being awarded the prize for creating the most fearsome military alliance in history. They had joked about it during their call back in October.

"Perhaps the Nobel Committee should rename it the Nobel *Negative Peace* Prize," President Yu suggested.

"That doesn't have quite the same ring to it," Joshua said. "But it would be appropriate. Do you want to suggest that to the committee, or should I?"

"Maybe we should keep it to ourselves. They might not appreciate the humor."

The process for awarding the Nobel Peace Prize is a long, painstaking one, conducted in absolute secrecy. The nomination period closes in January and vetting and shortlisting continue until October, when the announcement is made. It takes that long to sort through the nominations, settle on a short list, and ultimately select the recipient. Not just anyone can nominate someone for the award.

"I don't even know who nominated me," Joshua had said to Jill after the announcement. "The committee won't say. They're very persnickety about their rules. What if I wanted to send a thank you note to whoever it was?"

"Does it matter, Joshua?" she asked. Someday, maybe years from now, she would tell him.

"I suppose not. I'm just curious, I guess. It's good to know who your friends are."

According to the statutes of the Nobel Foundation, a nomination will be considered only if it is submitted by a person who falls within one of the following categories. A self-nomination is never considered, although several had been submitted. A nomination can be made by members of national governments or heads of state; members of The International Court of Justice and The Permanent Court of Arbitration; members of l'Institut de Droit International; members of the International Board of the Women's International League for Peace and Freedom; professors; university rectors and directors; directors of peace research institutes and foreign policy institutes; prior Peace Prize Laureates; members of the board of directors of organizations that have previously won the prize; and current and former members of the Norwegian Nobel Committee.

The five-member Norwegian Nobel Committee vets and selects the recipient. Hundreds of people and organizations are nominated each year. Most receive only brief consideration. In retrospect, many nominations seem ludicrous. Among the more questionable nominations have been Adolf Hitler,

Benito Mussolini, Joseph Stalin, Vladimir Putin, Rush Limbaugh, and even Michael Jackson, none of whom took home the prize. Simply nominating someone, though, is a time-tested way of currying favor.

The Nobel Committee carries out its business in complete secrecy and confidentiality. There are no leaks from the committee. Ever. The committee's rules forbid it from even disclosing the names of nominees or nominators for fifty years. That doesn't preclude nominators from announcing who they have nominated. It is a surefire way to ingratiate yourself – nominate someone for the Nobel Peace Prize and announce it to the world. It only works if the person knows that it was *you* who nominated them.

The formal Peace Prize ceremonies began on December 9th, the day before the official award presentation. On that day, President Sheehan and President Yu held the traditional Laureate press conference at the Norwegian Nobel Institute. They joked, laughed, and bantered throughout like old friends, which they had become. That evening, the "little dinner" would be held. It is a quaint, understated title for a large, very formal affair.

The press conference was relaxed and casual, primarily because of the bond which Joshua and Song shared. They had been on an extraordinary journey together and had earned each other's trust. They related the story of their first curling match at the White House. President Yu embellished the scale of his victory and exaggerated even further his victory at the rematch in China. Joshua jumped in.

"President Yu and I do have one very important announcement to make today. President Yu has graciously allowed me to make the announcement." President Yu had intentionally left the opening for his American friend. He could play either the straight man or funny man with equal aplomb.

"Yesterday, at the Bygdøy Curling Club, I am pleased to announce, my rink easily defeated President Yu's. President Yu has promised to practice more diligently and purposefully in the event that we should meet again on the ice." President Yu, and no one else in the world, understood the reference to Yu's comment after their game at the White House long ago, before the two men set about making history.

The questions at the press conference were mostly lighthearted. "What do you intend to do with the million dollars that come with the prize?" a reporter asked.

"President Yu could use some new curling shoes," Joshua joked. "His are in rather deplorable condition. I would like to get him a new pair."

"Now that you've won the Nobel Peace Prize, what comes next?"

"No one has ever been awarded the prize twice. Perhaps President Sheehan and I could be the first. Establish a dynasty," President Yu answered.

The day before their press conference, the two presidents had indeed met at the Bygdøy Curling Club, a two-sheet club in Oslo, for a game with some locals. It was fitting and symbolic, since curling together had started them down this path. Six club members were chosen for the honor of playing with them. The presidents served as skips for the two rinks. President Sheehan's team did, in fact, win the game, just not as "easily" as Joshua had announced to the world. After President Sheehan's announcement at the press conference, President Yu promised that their next game would have a different result.

Feigning indignity, President Yu challenged Joshua to immediately return to the curling club for a rematch. Joshua declined, citing "scheduling conflicts." "I'm afraid that I have a very busy schedule this week," he said. They were naturals, Joshua and Song, trading jabs, even if in different languages, playing off of each other. The press gobbled it up.

The Peace Prize is formally awarded on December 10th at Oslo City Hall, before more than a thousand invited guests. President Yu accepted the prize first, a gold medal featuring Alfred Nobel's portrait on the front with the Latin inscription, *"Pro pace et fraternitate gentilum"* ("For peace and fraternity among peoples"), along with a diploma, handwritten in Norwegian calligraphy. President Sheehan accepted his award only after the applause for President Yu ended.

More so than the award ceremony, the Nobel Peace Prize Banquet, with 350 guests, held in the ballroom of the Grand Hotel, is the highlight of the Peace Prize ceremonies. A very formal banquet, it is steeped in tradition, etiquette, and history. The banquet is a black tie and evening gown affair, featuring a five-course gourmet meal. The Laureate, or Laureates, are seated at a round table in the center of the hall. Also at the table are their spouses, the members of the Nobel Committee, the Prime Minister of Norway, the President of the Storting, and the King and Queen of Norway. Seating is in an alternating male/female pattern. Bao and Stephanie were disappointed to learn that they would not be seated next to each other. "Elton John better not be here!" Stephanie had joked with Bao.

Even as President Sheehan and President Yu were accepting the prizes in the afternoon, the banquet hall at the Grand Hotel was crackling with activity. Tables were set and spaced at precise locations; the delicate, elegant Nobel place settings were meticulously laid out; glasses were polished and polished again; French vintage wine and champagne were being chilled to perfect temperatures; and the chefs were triple-checking that all of the food was ready to prepare. Nothing – absolutely nothing – could be less than perfect. Every bulb in every chandelier had to be working. The head chef was irritable and querulous. He was to be avoided at all costs.

Those honored to make the speeches and propose the toasts were fine-tuning their remarks and practicing their delivery and timing. There could be no missteps, no fumbling over lines, and absolutely no mispronunciation of names. Not with traditions to honor and certainly not in the presence of the King and Queen and the two most powerful people in the world.

Stephanie, as always, was the person everyone simply had to meet. The First Lady of the United States is often the most admired woman in the world, and Stephanie was no exception. She had topped the list for seven straight years. Her husband may have been awarded the Nobel Peace Prize, but Stephanie was the star of the trip. President Sheehan, during his time in Norway, could only recall JFK's speech in Paris in 1961, when he quipped, "I do not think it altogether inappropriate for me to introduce myself. I am the man who accompanied Jacqueline Kennedy to Paris . . ." President Sheehan was the lucky man who accompanied Stephanie Sheehan to Oslo.

As they were dressing for the reception and banquet, Stephanie said to Joshua, "You know, I can't wait to get back home. I think it's time."

Joshua was surprised. "You're in Oslo and you want to get back to Washington? You don't even like Washington very much." He didn't usually misinterpret what Stephanie meant. They had been together for a long time.

"Not Washington. Maine. I'm ready to get back to Maine. We've been away for so long."

"One more year, Steph. We've only got one more year."

Before the grand banquet, there was one more public event for President Sheehan, Stephanie, President Yu, and Bao. One of the most dramatic and moving events. The one where, in the soft, quiet light of torches and candles, peace seems real and palpable. They would greet the well-wishers after the torchlight parade.

Chapter 21

The Torchlight Parade

But if tomorrow everybody under the sun
Was happy just to live as one
No borders or battles to be won.

But if tomorrow everybody was your friend
Happiness would never end
Lord, don't you wish it was true?
John Fogerty, Don't You Wish It Was True? (2007)

Back on the job, Jackson Carter was on President Sheehan's detail during his trip to Norway. Jackson had been on the president's detail for three years, including the last two, after recovering from the stabbing. Jackson and the rest of the Secret Service advance team arrived forty-eight hours ahead of the president and first lady, although planning and preparation had been underway since the trip was announced two months earlier. Maps and blueprints were secured and studied for every location where the president would be appearing or passing by, even the Bygdøy Curling Club. Hospitals were placed on stand-by. The Secret Service knew every square inch of Oslo City Hall and the Grand Hotel. Every point of ingress and egress was noted. Emergency evacuation routes were planned.

Preparations were undertaken in conjunction with the Central Guard Bureau, the Secret Service's Chinese counterpart. The Secret Service and the Central Guard Bureau had coordinated whenever President Sheehan and President Yu were in the same place, and they worked seamlessly together, despite the language barrier. Eye movements, hand signals, and head gestures worked just fine. Tonight, they were preparing for the parade and banquet.

After the award ceremony, in the early evening before the banquet, the traditional torchlight procession was underway in the streets of Oslo, where it would culminate outside of the Grand Hotel, home to the Nobel Laureates. It was a beautiful, comforting sight, torches flickering, creating a warm, yellowish glow. The winter sun had set hours ago. Flecks of dry snow drifted lazily down. It was a reverent and somber affair.

The Laureates themselves weren't in the parade, but rather would appear on the balcony of the Nobel Suite to recognize and salute the well-wishers when they gathered below. It is a time for hope, infused with the sense that true peace, lasting peace, might actually be possible. Perhaps even positive peace some day. Every year, for at least those few passing moments in the ancient streets of Oslo, the promise of peace feels imminent, tangible.

President Yu and President Sheehan, along with Bao and Stephanie, stepped out onto the balcony, radiant and beaming. Stephanie's eyes widened when she saw the crowd.

"Oh my God, it's so beautiful," Stephanie said, awestruck by the sea of light below.

Special Agent Carter assumed his assigned position to President Sheehan's left, as he had done hundreds of times before. The crowd roared its welcome. Joshua and Song shook hands. Stephanie and Joshua shared a kiss. Bao and Song did the same. Cellphones and television cameras were everywhere.

Jackson Carter pulled his Glock 19 from its holster on his hip and emptied the chamber into the back of Joshua's head, behind his left ear. It exited through the president's right eyebrow, below the scar he had gotten playing pond hockey back in Bucksport. The report echoed through the street. Blood and contents of Joshua's skull splattered everywhere, most visibly on Stephanie, who was waving to the crowd with her right hand, her left hand holding her husband's. She was glowing. Unfortunately, she had chosen a yellow gown. Joshua's knees buckled and he collapsed to his right, onto Stephanie. She instinctively tried to catch him. It happened so fast, so incomprehensibly, so loudly, that no one had time to process what was happening. Everyone on the balcony simply recoiled. Or froze.

Jackson Carter couldn't fail. He had no choice other than to fulfill his mission. He had to be certain, and quickly fired another round at the crumpling president's chest. Someone bumped him from behind as he did, and he missed the president. Stephanie wasn't so lucky. The bullet ripped through her left ribcage and tore through her left ventricle. She collapsed to the floor. Stephanie and Joshua lay splayed, touching, bleeding out, Joshua from his head, Stephanie from her chest, their blood pooling, mingling, on the balcony floor.

Joshua was already gone. There was no doubt about that to anyone who saw what happened or who was unfortunate enough to look down at him. His eyes were open, but fixed on nothing. Stephanie, on the other hand, was alive. She gasped and spasmed on the floor as if she were touching a charged wire.

Special Agent Carter didn't live to take a third shot. Within seconds, he was down, damp, red, fleshy matter strewn all around him. His friend and colleague, Special Agent Marcus Love, saw to that. Jackson Carter knew that this was how it would end, and he had come to peace with it. But he had done what God ordained him to do. Joshua Sheehan, the infidel, the heretic, was gone.

I t was the Secret Service's worst nightmare. One of its own. Someone on the inside. There was almost no way to prevent it. It was one thing that they hadn't prepared for. Identifying and stopping a lone wolf was nearly impossible, especially if the wolf had close, intimate access.

The Secret Service practiced and trained for hundreds of different scenarios involving the assassination of a president. It was chaos, but it was manageable. Everyone had a job to do. President Yu, Bao, and the Central Guard Bureau had vanished from the balcony almost instantly. President Sheehan was triaged on the scene by the president's doctor and his team, but there was no point, really. The doctor knew that right away. He looked up and shook his head no. Nonetheless, he feverishly attended to Joshua. Stephanie, on the other hand, might have a chance. She had faint traces of a pulse and respiration.

The president and first lady were carried through the hotel, blood dripping behind them, and loaded into the waiting ambulance, which screeched away. A trauma team was ready and waiting at the hospital, but their services wouldn't be needed for long. Joshua and Stephanie were dead on arrival. The official pronouncement was not made until they were in the hospital and all of the requisite resuscitation protocols had been satisfied. Officially, the president died seven minutes before the first lady. Unofficially, he was gone before they carried him off the balcony. The speed and urgency directed to Joshua and Stephanie were not directed to Special Agent Jackson Carter, whose body still lay on the bloody floor of the Nobel Suite balcony.

Even before the president and first lady arrived at the hospital, social media was ablaze with cellphone videos of the assassination. Everyone wanted to be the first to post. Most were poor quality, showing almost nothing, taken from far away, in the dark. A few showed the event with clarity and in nauseating detail. Those got the most hits, some people reflexively hitting the "Like" button. Other than the grainy Zapruder 8 mm film capturing President Kennedy's assassination, it was the first time that the assassination of a United States president was caught on camera.

Television cameras captured the event in much more graphic detail. The networks agonized for a short time over whether to air it. They almost all made the decision to go ahead. If they didn't, their competitors surely would. It was history, they rationalized. The people deserved to see it. The anchors prefaced each showing with, "*We must warn you, many viewers will find this video disturbing.*"

The Secret Service had two immediate needs – to get President Sheehan and First Lady Stephanie's bodies home to the United States and to determine whether the threat extended beyond Jackson Carter. Who could they trust? Not trust? Who else was involved? They would have to bring Jackson Carter's body home, too, but that was far less urgent. There was no way that Special Agent Jackson Carter was flying home on Air Force One.

The Twenty-Fifth Amendment to the United States Constitution, adopted after President Kennedy's assassination, is clear. In the event of a president's death, the vice president ascends to the presidency. "*In case of the removal of the President from office or of his death or resignation, the Vice President shall become President.*" Within minutes of receiving official confirmation of President Sheehan's death, Vice President Edward Todd Anderson was whisked out of the Executive Office Building and rushed to the Oval Office. The first order of business was being sworn in as the new president. He could not perform any presidential duties before taking the oath. It was a technicality, but a necessary one. The second order of business was to address the American people and the world.

Associate Justice Elizabeth Haddon, appointed to the United States Supreme Court by President Sheehan just nine months earlier, was summoned to the White House to administer the oath of office to Vice President Anderson. Any Justice would do, and she was the first one who answered the phone. She didn't have time to change out of her sneakers or even grab her robe. A White House intern found a Bible. Through her tears, trembling, Justice

Haddon recited the oath from memory, and Vice President Anderson repeated it.

"I, Edward Todd Anderson . . ."

"*I, Edward Todd Anderson . . .*"

". . . do solemnly swear . . ."

"*. . . do solemnly swear . . .*"

". . . that I will faithfully execute the office of President of the United States . . ."

"*. . . that I will faithfully execute the office of President of the United States . . .*"

". . . and will, to the best of my ability . . ."

"*. . . and will, to the best of my ability . . .*"

". . . preserve, protect, and defend the Constitution of the United States."

"*. . . preserve, protect, and defend the Constitution of the United States.*"

The words, "So help me, God," are not part of the prescribed presidential oath, but now-President Anderson added them anyway. Television networks cut away from Oslo to broadcast the swearing-in. The country, and the world, had to see that someone was in charge of the United States government. There were no handshakes or congratulations as the new president was hustled to the Situation Room, where cabinet members were assembling. Things were happening faster than ETA preferred.

Back in the Oval Office, President Anderson settled in behind the Resolute Desk for the first time. He fiddled with the chair's height and lumbar support. President Sheehan had been dead for less than an hour. There was chaos and frenetic action everywhere. Orders were being yelled, questions shouted, sobbing, running. A television camera stared silent and grim at the president. There had been no time to craft and refine an address from scratch, so aides pilfered LBJ's remarks from November 22, 1963 and his address to Congress five days later. They cobbled pieces of the two together, made some edits, and presented it to President Anderson. He made a few quick changes of his own with a red pen, his hand shaking from adrenalin, shock, and, most of all, fear. The light atop the camera turned red and President Anderson delivered his address to the nation and the world:

Good evening. Let me begin by saying that I would give everything that I have not to be speaking with you today. This is a tragic, unspeakable day for all people in the United States and around the world. We have suffered a loss that we cannot yet begin to comprehend or to understand. For me, it is a very personal tragedy. President Sheehan and Stephanie were my friends. I know that the world shares the grief that our nation bears, and we thank you for thinking of us and praying for us. Your support will sustain us through this dark, awful hour.

President Joshua Sheehan and First Lady Stephanie Sheehan were struck down today as the president accepted the Nobel Peace Prize in Norway, a prize that he so richly deserved. No words are sad enough to express our loss. A murderer's bullet has thrust upon me the awesome burden of the presidency. I am here to say that I need your help. I cannot bear this burden alone. I need the help of all Americans.

I also want to assure my fellow Americans that the government of the United States goes on. Through our grief, the transfer of power has taken place as provided by our Constitution. To the rest of the world, I say that while we have been shaken, we stand ready and committed to protect and defend ourselves against any enemy anywhere who would seek to take advantage of our loss.

In closing, I profoundly hope that the tragedy and horror of this day will somehow, in the passage of time, bind us together, making us one people. That is what President Sheehan would have wanted. That is what he dreamed of. And let us resolve that Joshua Sheehan neither lived, nor died, in vain. His vision and legacy will guide us. His goodness will inspire us. His memory, through the awful passage of time, will gladden our hearts. I promise to America and to the world that I will do my best to carry on the work that he began. That is all I can do. I ask for your help. And God's.

No sooner had President Anderson finished his address than the critics and trolls went to work. They lambasted the new president for stealing LBJ's words. How dare he! Never mind that President Anderson was sincere, there were important complaints to register and outrage to air. While the internet was abuzz about the speech, President Anderson, as his first official act as President of the United States, signed a proclamation that all American flags be flown at half-staff for thirty days. President Sheehan and Stephanie had not yet begun their journey home, but the work of government marched on.

Even as Air Force One, carrying the bodies of the president and first lady – but not Jackson Carter – was making its way across the North Atlantic en route to Joint Base Andrews, the Military District of Washington was beginning its planning for the state funeral, which it would present to President Anderson. It was the Military District's job to plan state funerals. There were binders full of instructions and protocols set out in minute detail, right down to the floral arrangements and flag placements. State funerals, with their solemnity and tradition, allow the country to collectively say goodbye and mourn together. While state funerals for presidents are the norm, and are expected, they are not mandatory. Richard Nixon refused a state funeral. On the other hand, Ronald Reagan's, painstakingly choreographed by Nancy Reagan, lasted for seven full days, playing out on both coasts.

The outline of a plan for Joshua Sheehan's state funeral began to take shape. The body would be arriving in the United States in the early hours of Thursday morning. It would be taken to Bethesda Naval Hospital for an autopsy, although that seemed incomprehensively unnecessary, and for preparation for burial.

"Should I meet Air Force One at Andrews?" President Anderson asked. Under different circumstances, the question wouldn't need to be asked. It was not a question of protocol or doing the right thing – of course, the president should be there – it was a question of safety. How could he trust the Secret Service to protect him? What if a plot went far deeper than simply Jackson Carter? What if the new president were next?

The first draft of the state funeral plan called for the president and first lady's remains to travel by motorcade to Washington National Cathedral for a service on Saturday. Speakers needed to be arranged. Seating was important, too. The cameras would mainly catch those in the coveted front rows. Invitations needed to be extended. Following the service, the bodies would be taken to the Lincoln Memorial, where they would be placed on a horse-drawn caisson for the procession to the United States Capitol, where President Sheehan would lie in state, possibly with Stephanie beside him. That was yet to be determined. President Anderson would have to make that decision. Either way, he would be criticized. On the way to the Capitol, the procession would stop outside of the White House and the curling rink.

No first lady ever lay in state, but no first lady and president ever died together, either. The Military District of Washington found no precedent or reason not to include Stephanie in their state funeral plans, and would propose that to President Anderson. Monday would be the burial, although the planners didn't know where. They were researching possibilities. Neither Joshua nor Stephanie were eligible for Arlington National Cemetery. Maine seemed like the most appropriate place.

The state funeral would never take place. After President Anderson finished his televised address, he opened the top drawer of the Resolute Desk. There was a sealed letter addressed, "To the President of the United States." That was him now, Anderson realized. Tentatively, he opened it.

Dear Mr. President:

In the event of my death during my presidency, it is my earnest wish that I not be afforded a state funeral. In the event of my passing, I am to be buried with as little public ceremony as possible in Oak Hill Cemetery in Bucksport, Maine, where Stephanie and I have purchased plots. Stephanie will be able to provide the details. I specifically request not to lie in state or in repose at any time or in any location. Joshua F. Sheehan

The letter was handwritten and dated Joshua's first day in office. It had been resting in the exact same place for nearly seven years. President Anderson didn't have to honor Joshua's request. He could have concluded that the American people and the world deserved the chance to say goodbye, to mourn and to grieve together. The people expected one. There was already rampant speculation about when the state funeral might be, who might attend, and who would be chosen to deliver the eulogy. Most of the speculation focused on Secretary of State Jill Mendoza, not Edward Todd Anderson. President Anderson directed the Military District of Washington to stop its planning and work on something different – getting the president and first lady home to Bucksport, Maine.

The one concession President Anderson made to the national desire for a public way of saying goodbye was the train ride. There was a lot of pressure on him to do something public. Anderson hated being pressured.

The two flag-draped caskets were loaded onto a funeral train at Union Station in Washington. In the darkness of Joshua's coffin, his hands were clasped together over his Nobel Peace Prize medal. It was Jill Mendoza and Sam Pelletier's suggestion that Joshua take it with him. Joshua and Stephanie were placed side-by-side to be easily viewable to mourners as the funeral train made its rumbling journey north. New, untinted, unscratched windows were installed on the president's train car. An honor guard stood silent, still sentry over the twin caskets.

To a dirge from the United States Marine Corps Band, the train pulled out of Union Station to begin its 430-mile journey to Boston. Traveling slowly to let the public see in as it passed, the funeral train took seventeen hours to reach Boston. People lined the tracks in daylight and in darkness. Many held signs. Pictures of curling stones and peace symbols were the most common.

As the train lumbered northward, Isaac Raven, still the Administrator of the General Services Administration, was meeting with President Anderson. The White House residence had to be prepared for the new president and first lady.

"We can have you moved in by tomorrow, sir," Raven began. Raven moved more slowly than he did seven years earlier, when he escorted Joshua on the tour of the White House grounds. He had a new knee, which was fine, and a new hip, which was less so. His shoulders stooped. He was shorter, diminished. "We just need to know how you would like things. Color scheme, drapes, linens, furniture, lighting." It felt blasphemous discussing such fripperies. "We can outfit the residence however you like." Raven had prepared his resignation letter, which he would submit as soon as the Andersons moved in. It was time. And he had a plane to catch.

It dawned on President Anderson that, despite his many years as a senator and vice president, he had never been invited to the residence. He had no idea what it looked like or how he wanted it outfitted. "I don't know, Isaac. Get ahold of the first lady. Ask her."

At South Station in Boston, Joshua and Stephanie were carried to a hearse, newly-emblazoned with the presidential seal. The frosted windows had been replaced with clear ones. Church bells in Boston chimed as the motorcade eased away from the station.

Joshua and Stephanie's final odyssey had 250 miles to go, up I-95 into New Hampshire, then Maine. It stopped in front of the Maine Turnpike sign reading, "*Welcome to Maine. The Way Life Should Be.*" People crowded onto overpasses, into buildings, anywhere they could get a glimpse. There would be three more stops before finally arriving at Oak Hill Cemetery. The first was in Augusta, in front of the Blaine House. The second was on Route 3 outside of the Belfast Curling Club, where a black mourning drape hung over the entrance. The last was in front of Joshua and Stephanie's home in Bucksport, where a fire burned in the fire pit. It was Sam's suggestion. At last, the procession wound its way up a stone drive into Oak Hill Cemetery.

There were just a dozen people gathered around the grave sites as sixteen uniformed pallbearers carried Joshua and Stephanie over frozen, uneven ground to their resting place. The mourners stood shivering on a stark, frigid Maine hillside. President Anderson had asked Joshua's long-time friend and chief of staff, Sam Pelletier, to extend the invitations. Sam knew Joshua far more intimately than Anderson did. A Marine bugler sounded *Taps*.

The president and first lady were there. Sam and Rose Pelletier. Secretary of State Jill Mendoza, of course, along with her daughters. Emily Carlson, Stephanie's friend from the Belfast Curling Club, who had been there when Stephanie and Joshua met. Isaac Raven, using a cane on the uneven ground. Elijah Turner, who would have been president now if Joshua had listened to Stephanie, and Sandra. Yu Song and Bao would have been there, but it was simply too dangerous. Jill Mendoza had called them personally to extend the invitation.

The sun was getting lower. The first star flickered. Each of the mourners held a small torch like the ones that illuminated the streets of Oslo four days earlier, warming and illuminating each anguished face. One-by-one, they made their way to the coffins, said what they needed to say, and placed a white poppy on each coffin. Slowly, in perfect unison, Joshua and Stephanie were lowered into the ground. When they came to rest, the mourners extinguished their torches.

It was December – the fourteenth, to be exact. The sky over Bucksport was clear and dark. It was a perfect night for viewing the Geminid meteor shower, which put on a dazzling show. The constellations were in place.

Chapter 22

The Letter

"I don't have any secrets I need kept anymore." – Frank Ocean, Channel Orange (2012)

Although it was immediately clear what had happened, there were consequential questions to answer, the most serious one being, "Why?" Encompassed within that single question were scores of others – Was anyone else involved? Why didn't anyone see this coming? Were the Secret Service's protection protocols flawed? How could this have been prevented? Did LeAnn Carter know? Who was at fault? *Someone had to be at fault.* The answers, of course, wouldn't undo anything.

Before the bodies of President Sheehan and Stephanie were back home in the United States, the investigators, led by the FBI, were combing through Jackson and LeAnn Carter's apartment in Virginia. They hauled away boxes of papers which would yield nothing, and a computer which would yield a little. A search warrant had been secured before Air Force One left the ground in Oslo. LeAnn Carter, now a widow and single mother, found herself at FBI headquarters in Washington, although she didn't recall exactly when or how she had gotten there.

LeAnn and Jackson were married for nearly ten years. Happily married. They met in Sunday School at the Open Bible Church in North Carolina when they were eleven years old. LeAnn thought that she knew everything that there was to know about Jackson. She did not. She hadn't seen the letter yet. Didn't know anything about it, she claimed.

The FBI investigation produced an enormous amount of data – all of Jackson Carter's personnel records, background checks, training records, transcribed interviews with everyone he had worked with, every text and phone call he had made, dozens of videos of the assassination. None of them offered any insight into why he had done it or whether it could have been prevented. The handwritten letter to LeAnn did.

Before leaving for Oslo, Jackson carefully composed and dated the letter. He was alone in his office at home, long after he and LeAnn had bathed Lucas and Emma and put them to bed. A single banker's lamp illuminated the desk as he wrote. His well-worn Bible was open to the eighth chapter of the Gospel of Luke. He spent a lot of time alone in his office recently. No, she didn't know what he did in there. Work, probably. Fantasy football, maybe.

Jackson doubted that LeAnn would find the letter before the FBI did. He knew that she would see it, though. He had intentionally placed it in his bottom desk drawer, where LeAnn never went, underneath his Award for Valor. It was where he kept his work, and there was no reason for her to go in there. He folded the letter into a plain white envelope, addressed simply to "LeAnn," and sealed it.

Jackson turned off the lamp, rose from his leather chair, and left his office, being careful to close the door quietly. He walked slowly past the master bedroom to the bedroom that Lucas and Emma shared. They were both asleep. Tomorrow morning at oh seven hundred, he would be leaving for Oslo.

Jackson stared down at Emma and gently placed his hand on her forehead. He offered a silent prayer, then leaned down and kissed her cheek. "Daddy loves you. I love you," he whispered to her. He turned to Lucas, placed his hand on Lucas's forehead, offered a prayer, and kissed him on the cheek.

"Take care of your sister and Mommy. Daddy loves you. I love you." Jackson straightened himself and walked to the door, pausing to look at his children one final time.

The letter began, "My Dearest LeAnn," and continued:

I love you. I didn't tell you that nearly enough, but I know that you know that it is true. I still love you. You brought me joy and happiness every single day. Someday, I know that we will be together again in Heaven. I will be waiting there for you. And when the time comes, for Lucas and Emma, too.

By now, you know what happened in Norway. I did it for you, LeAnn, and for Lucas and Emma. You each deserve to live in a country and world where Christ is King and all worship and exalt Him. Where His laws are our laws. Where leaders bow before Him and acknowledge His rule. Christ and God are being cast aside by America in favor of the atheists and the godless. Our country is casting the righteous out in favor of the wicked, the unholy, the blasphemers, the destroyers of all that is sacred and holy and good. Our Lord ordained me to stop them. He asked me to do His work. How could I say no? When we are called, we must obey. "And why call ye me, 'Lord, Lord,' and do not the things which I say?"

He had to be stopped, LeAnn. Before he destroyed everything we cherish and know in our hearts to be true. I had to do it for you and Lucas and Emma. I asked God to find another way, to take the cup away from me, to anoint someone else, but He told me that it had to be me. He chose me. "And we know that all things work together for good to them that love God, to them who are called according to His purpose." I faithfully obeyed His calling. Tell Lucas and Emma that I love them and am still looking after them. You were the last thing I thought about. All my love. Jackson

Chapter 23
Why?

"When the snows fall and the white winds blow, the lone wolf dies, but the pack survives." – Eddard Stark, Game of Thrones

"Mrs. Carter, I'd like to get some preliminary matters out of the way, if I may. I'm sorry to have to do this, ma'am, but I need to show you a picture." Senator Arnbuckle wasn't sorry in the least. It made for great theater. The picture was enlarged onto two-by-three posterboard. It showed Jackson Carter pulling the trigger. A staffer placed it on an easel beside the senator, strategically placed where the cameras would be sure to capture it. What more dramatic way to commence the hearing? The staffer who thought it up was due for a promotion.

"Can you confirm for the record that the man in the picture is your husband, Jackson Carter?"

"Yes, sir. That's Jackson," she answered, almost inaudibly. If the senator's intention was to rattle LeAnn, it worked.

"Mrs. Carter, we need for you to speak up so that everyone can hear you."

"Yes, sir. That's Jackson," she repeated, just slightly louder.

Congressional hearings, especially important, high-profile ones, the ones that are televised, are designed to accomplish three things. First, they should produce some tense, heated soundbites for the media to pick up or for the senator or representative to post to social media and fundraise off of. Second, they should find someone to blame, to scapegoat. Ideally, it should be someone from the other political party. Third, they should get to the truth, if need be.

Both the Senate and the House were frothing to investigate the assassination. The Senate, collectively convinced that it was comprised of more sober and distinguished members than the House, wanted the first crack at the most important witnesses. If every senator looks in the mirror and sees a president, every representative looks in the mirror and sees a senator. After contentious negotiations, the Senate and House agreed to form the *Joint Congressional Committee on the Assassination of President Joshua F. Sheehan.* The fighting for a seat on the committee was fierce. This was the time to call in favors.

LeAnn Carter seemed like the most obvious person to blame. It was her husband, after all, who did it. There must have been signs and warnings that Jackson was planning something, or acting strangely. LeAnn had to have noticed them and simply ignored them. Maybe she was even in on it. What a plum that would be for the senator who uncovered it. Congress grilled her for two straight days. Her husband had been dead for only a month. The testimony was staged in prime time.

The hearings were conducted in the Kennedy Caucus Room of the Russell Senate Office Building, the grand, ornate room where the *Watergate* hearings were held. The room was designed to hold 300 people. There were many more than that when LeAnn Carter entered with her attorney, one she could not possibly afford. For a moment, the room fell silent as she made her way to the witness table. No one had seen her since it happened. And now, here she was, the wife of a presidential assassin. The masses didn't know whether they should loathe her or pity her. LeAnn Carter was terrified. The largest group she had ever spoken in front of was her Sunday School class.

She was painfully thin, waifish, and pale. Until today, she had not been outside for weeks. Reporters camped in a twenty-four-hour-a-day vigil outside of her parents' home in North Carolina had seen no signs of her, although she was rumored to be living there. Her modest makeup did little to bring color to her face. Three dozen photographers sat in front of the witness table, their lenses trained on her, furiously clicking away, hoping for the perfect shot, the right angle, the perfect expression, of the assassin's wife that just might garner them a Pulitzer.

Her attorney poured her a glass of water, cupped his hand over LeAnn's microphone, and whispered something. She nodded. Everyone noticed her trembling hands as she took a sip. It took both hands to hold the glass. LeAnn Carter looked up at the bank of ominous-looking people towering before her. God, give me strength, she prayed. The chairman pounded his gavel three times, slowly, sharply, for maximum effect. LeAnn flinched at the first crack. The committee did not extend the courtesy of allowing her to make an opening statement. Why waste time listening to her read something her attorney wrote, anyway? She had identified the photo of Jackson pulling the trigger.

"Thank you, Mrs. Carter. Mrs. Carter, I'm from Arizona, where we don't believe in beating around the bush, so I'm going to get right down to it, if you don't mind." What was she going to do, say that yes, she did mind, would you please beat around the bush? "Mrs. Carter, were you aware that your husband planned to assassinate the President of the United States?" the senator asked.

"No, sir."

"Did your husband ever say anything bad or negative about the President of the United States?"

"No, sir."

"Did your husband ever say anything bad or negative about any of the president's policies?"

"No, sir."

"Did your husband ever say anything bad or negative to you about the CurTO treaty?"

"No, sir." LeAnn couldn't stop staring at the enlarged photograph of her husband. She summoned her courage. "Sir, the picture."

"Yes?"

"Could you take it down, please? I can't look at it."

"My apologies, Mrs. Carter." Senator Arnbuckle motioned to a staffer. He would have preferred to keep the picture up for the duration of his questioning.

"Now, did your husband ever say anything about the United States' attack on Israel pursuant to what's known as the CurTO treaty?"

"Jackson and I never talked about politics, sir." She forgot her attorney's advice to only answer the question, not elaborate.

"Mrs. Carter, that was not my question. Please listen carefully. My question is, did your husband ever say anything to you about the United States' attack on Israel under the CurTO treaty, yes or no, please?"

"I think that he said something once, right after it happened."

"What was it that your husband said?" The senator sensed that he was on the tail of something big.

"I don't remember exactly. Something like, 'I can't believe that he attacked the Holy Land.' Maybe he said 'we.'"

"Did he say 'he' or 'we?'"

"I'm not really sure."

"But he might have said 'he?'"

"Maybe. I just don't remember. I do remember that he said 'Holy Land.'"

"If he said 'he,' who would your husband have been referring to?" It was an unfair question, but one the senator hoped would yield the answer he was looking for. It did.

"President Sheehan, I suppose."

"Mrs. Carter, did you report this conversation to anyone at the Secret Service?"

"It wasn't a conversation."

"Let me rephrase the question. Did you report your husband's statement to anyone at the Secret Service?"

"No, sir."

"Anyone at the FBI?"

"No, sir."

"Anyone at all?"

"No, sir. I didn't have any reason . . ."

"Let me see if I have this correct, Mrs. Carter. You said that your husband was angry that . . ."

"I didn't say that he was angry . . ."

"Mrs. Carter, please allow me to finish my question. Your husband was angry, or upset, or agitated that President Sheehan had participated in the strike against Israel, the Holy Land. He had close, intimate access to the president on a daily basis, he carried a weapon and clearly knew how to use it, and yet you did not report your conversation to anyone?"

"I didn't say that he was angry or upset. He was . . . um, surprised, I guess you might call it. It wasn't even a conversation. It was just something he said once."

"Mrs. Carter, have you heard the phrase, 'If you see or hear something, say something?'"

"Yes, sir."

"And you never did say anything, did you? Thank you, Mrs. Carter. I yield back."

It was Senator Ashbee's turn. "Mrs. Carter, your husband was seriously wounded while on President Sheehan's Secret Service detail in Middletown, Ohio, is that correct?"

"Yes, sir."

"Could you describe his injuries for me, please?"

"He was stabbed in his right arm. Right up here," she motioned. "It took sixty-seven stitches. He almost bled to death."

"He received an Award for Valor, correct?"

"Yes, sir, he did. I was very proud of him."

"Did he fully recover – physically, I mean."

"It took several months."

"But he did recover physically?"

"Yes, sir."

"Well enough to return to the president's detail, unfortunately?"

"I don't know how to answer that."

"Your husband recovered well enough physically to return to the president's detail, is that correct?"

"Yes, sir."

"What about emotionally? Did he fully recover emotionally?"

"I'm not sure what you mean . . ."

"What I mean is, was he different after he was injured? Moody? Sullen? Withdrawn? I don't want to put words in your mouth. I just want to understand his mental state." Senator Ashbee hoped that LeAnn chose one of his carefully curated words.

"He was frustrated at how slow the recovery was. He wanted to get back to work."

"What about after he recovered? Were there any changes to his personality? His mood?"

"Not really. I mean, I guess he may have been a little quieter, more withdrawn. He had been through a lot."

"I don't want you to guess, Mrs. Carter. But you would say that he was more withdrawn, more aloof?"

"I guess . . . I mean yes, sir."

"You testified that you did not inform the Secret Service about your husband's negative comments about the president's attack on Israel . . ."

"I didn't say he made negative . . ."

"Mrs. Carter, please let me finish my question. You didn't report your husband's comments about Israel to anyone. Did you report your husband's sudden change in personality to anyone? The Secret Service or the FBI in particular?"

"His personality didn't change."

"What would you call it . . . let me see if I can find your exact words here . . . when someone becomes withdrawn, quieter, sullen, moody?" Those were not her exact words.

"Jackson was almost killed. He saved the president's life. I thought he just needed some time to get completely back to normal. Anyone would."

"Thank you, Mrs. Carter. I yield back." It was Senator Freeman's turn to join the fray. Part of the arrangements for the Joint Committee were that the senators got to ask questions first, so that the representatives didn't muck things up.

"Mrs. Carter, you testified that after your husband had recovered physically from his wounds, he was anxious to get back to work, correct?"

"Yes, sir."

"That he specifically wanted to get back to the president's protective detail, is that right?"

"Yes, sir. I begged him not to do it. I told him he had done his duty, that it was too dangerous."

"What was his response?"

"He said that that was where he was meant to be. That it was his calling."

"Did you find anything about that response unusual?"

"No, sir. I don't think I know what you mean."

"What I mean, Mrs. Carter, is that by your own testimony, your husband's personality changed after he was injured in Ohio, that he kept more to himself, shall we say. That he spent late nights alone at his computer, doing who knows what. That he had been critical of what President Sheehan had done to the Holy Land, and that he said that it was his destiny to return to the president's side. And yet none of that was the least bit concerning to you? You stood by and did absolutely nothing?"

"You're twisting my words. It wasn't . . ." LeAnn was crying.

"Your words and actions . . . inactions, more precisely, are very clear, Mrs. Carter. The record will reflect exactly what you have said. That your husband posed a grave and imminent threat to the President of the United States and that you did nothing to stop him. In my world, that's called being complicit. I yield back."

The other witness scheduled for a prime time filleting was the Director of the United States Secret Service. The director was under unrelenting public and political fire ever since the assassination. Senator Wayne opened the questioning. The Director knew what was in store. He would be the bug meeting the windshield.

"Good evening, Mr. Director. Thank you for coming in this evening." As if the director had any choice. He was under congressional subpoena.

"Good evening, Senator."

"Mr. Director, Jackson Carter was employed by the United States Secret Service, correct?"

"Yes, sir."

"For how long was he employed by the Secret Service?"

"Approximately nine years."

"Could you briefly tell us about Agent Carter's duties during those nine years?"

"Certainly. Immediately after his hiring, he was sent to the Federal Law Enforcement Training Center in Glynco for his initial training, where he excelled. His initial assignment was in our field office in Memphis, where he spent two years. He was then transferred to our field office in Chicago, where he remained for three additional years. After Chicago, he was assigned to Protective Services here in Washington. He initially worked on then-Vice President Anderson's detail for approximately one year and then on President Sheehan's detail."

"How long was Agent Carter on President Sheehan's detail?"

"Approximately three years, although he was sidelined for several months after he was wounded in Ohio."

"Let's focus on Agent Carter's initial hiring. Describe that process for this committee, please."

"Jackson Carter submitted a written application to the Department of Homeland Security. That application was accepted as meeting the basic age and educational requirements. An initial background check, including criminal history, was performed, which Agent Carter also passed. There was no juvenile or adult criminal history of any kind. A polygraph examination was administered, which revealed no evidence of deception, nor did a security interview. Finally, Agent Carter passed a drug screening and qualified for a Top Secret security clearance, as is required of all of our agents. At that point, he was hired and sent to Glynco for training."

"Let's talk about supervision and monitoring of your Special Agents, sir. How are they supervised and evaluated?"

"That is an ongoing process, Senator Wayne. After their initial three-month training, a report is filed with my office detailing their performance during training. In the case of Special Agent Carter, his performance evaluation was superior – the highest in his class. There were no areas of concern noted."

"Is there any ongoing assessment and evaluation process for Special Agents?"

"Yes, sir. Formal employee evaluations at the field office level are conducted by the Special Agent in Charge of the office. Those performance evaluations are completed annually. Areas of concern and areas for improvement are recorded and discussed with the employee. Again, in the case of Special Agent Carter, his performance reviews in Memphis and Chicago were uniformly outstanding, with no noted areas of concern."

"While Agent Carter was assigned to Protective Services, were performance evaluations conducted?"

"Yes, sir."

"Can you describe that process for the committee?"

"Yes. Once again, annual performance reviews are conducted. These reviews formally evaluate the agent's performance within Protective Services. Again, in the case of Special Agent Carter, his reviews were uniformly outstanding, with no noted areas of concern or for improvement."

"Was a performance review of Agent Carter performed after the incident in Ohio where he was injured?"

"Yes, sir. His annual review took place two months later, while he was out on medical."

"What were the findings of that review?"

"Once again, Agent Carter received an outstanding evaluation. His actions in Ohio were exemplary and wholly consistent with the Service's mission and protocols. It was also noted that Agent Carter was anxious to return to his duties on President Sheehan's detail."

"Did the Secret Service have any reservations about returning Agent Carter to the president's detail?"

"None whatsoever. Once Agent Carter had completed his physical rehabilitation and received medical clearance, we had no reservations."

"Let's talk about security clearances. Did Agent Carter have a security clearance?"

"Yes, sir. Agent Carter had a Top Secret security clearance throughout his entire tenure with the Secret Service."

"Did the Secret Service grant that Top Secret clearance?"

"No, sir. All security clearances for Secret Service personnel are granted by the Department of Homeland Security."

"When did Agent Carter receive his Top Secret clearance?"

"Upon his initial employment."

"For how long was that security clearance in effect?"

"Five years. Top Secret security clearances are valid for five years. It was then renewed for an additional five years."

"Which means that, if my math is correct, Agent Carter's renewed clearance was approximately four years old at the time of the assassination."

"Yes, sir. Approximately."

"Could you tell this committee what is entailed in being granted a Top Secret security clearance?"

"As I said, Senator, the Secret Service does not grant the clearances. That responsibility falls to Homeland Security. They could tell you about the process in more detail. I can tell you generally what the process looks like."

"Please."

"The background check process is extensive. Everyone being considered for a Top Secret clearance completes a questionnaire detailing their education, employment history, where they have lived or traveled, family relationships, financial information, foreign contacts, memberships. All of that information is verified. The subject also submits to a drug screening, interview, and polygraph examination. In some instances, family members or close personal contacts may also be interviewed. If all of that passes muster with Homeland Security, they then issue the clearance."

"After Agent Carter had his Top Secret clearance for five years, what happened next?"

"His clearance was renewed for an additional five years. That happened around the time he was leaving Chicago and joining Protective Services in Washington. The Secret Service was notified that his clearance had been renewed. His Top Secret clearance remained in effect until his death."

"And that renewal vetting took place, so that I'm perfectly clear on the time frame, four years before the assassination?"

"Yes, sir."

"Let me ask you one more question, sir." As if the Director could stop him. "After Agent Carter was wounded in Ohio, did you have any reason to be concerned about his future performance on President Sheehan's protective detail?"

"No, sir." *One more question* turned into several.

"Did you discuss with anyone Agent Carter's mental state after the incident in Ohio?"

"Other than Agent Carter himself, no."

"So you discussed Agent Carter's mental state with him?" Senator Wayne's pulse quickened, thinking that he may have struck gold.

"Not per se, no. I had several discussions with him during his recovery and shortly after his return to duty. I just wanted to see how he was doing." The senator's pulse returned to normal.

"And how was he doing?"

"He was disappointed in how slowly his recovery was progressing. He was anxious to get back to his detail. And he was a little more reserved, perhaps, than before the injury. Agent Carter was never terribly talkative even before Ohio. But he had been through a traumatic incident."

"Did you ever discuss with Agent Carter his thoughts or feelings about President Sheehan?"

"Absolutely not."

"Did Agent Carter ever express any thoughts or feelings about President Sheehan?"

"No, sir."

"One more thing, sir. Did you speak with LeAnn Carter after the incident in Ohio?"

"I have only spoken to Mrs. Carter one time, during the presentation of the Secretary's Award for Valor in the Oval Office. She was shy, didn't say much, but she was very, very proud of her husband."

"Thank you, Director. I yield back." Senator Wayne teed up Senator Crumley nicely.

"Good evening, Mr. Director," Senator Crumley began. Senator Crumley had been selected to lead the assault. "Let me begin by asking you this. Are you familiar with LeAnn Carter's testimony before this committee?"

"No, sir."

"You haven't even bothered to look at it?" The Senator's tone didn't bode well. The two men had a contentious history.

"No, sir. I've been working." Under different circumstances, the director's comment may have elicited a chuckle here and there.

"Well, then, since you haven't bothered, let me summarize it for you, if I may. Mrs. Carter testified to this committee, under oath, that her husband had been critical of President Sheehan's attack on Israel. She also testified that his emotional state changed after he was injured in Ohio. That he became quieter, withdrawn. You testified that you personally observed those personality changes. None of this was of any concern to you?"

"Mrs. Carter did not report anything concerning about her husband to the Secret Service. Neither did anyone else, I would add. All of our agents are mandated to report any concerning behaviors by another agent to their superiors. No one ever reported any concerns about Jackson Carter during his nine years of service. Nor did I say that there were 'personality changes' as you called them."

"Given your personal concerns about Agent Carter, did you . . ."

"Senator, I did not say that I had concerns about Agent Carter."

"Given your . . . what shall we call them . . . observations about Agent Carter, did you take any actions whatsoever to ascertain his fitness to return to the president's protective detail?"

"I saw no reason to, Senator."

"You saw no reason to." Senator Crumley let those words hang for a moment. "Let me ask you about a different topic. Did you or Homeland Security conduct any investigation or surveillance of Agent Carter's on-line activities? We know that he accessed what's called the 'dark web.'"

"We do not routinely monitor our agents' personal activities. There are privacy and legal issues at play. However, if there is credible information or concern about a specific agent's activities, we will make an inquiry. In the specific case of Agent Carter, we saw no reason." As soon as he said the words, his knew it was a mistake.

"You saw no reason. Isn't that your great failing here, sir, if I may put it bluntly? An agent who was critical of the president, whose personality had changed, who spent more time alone at night at his computer, who felt a 'special calling,' and yet the Secret Service did nothing. Nothing but return him to the president's side brandishing a gun and planning an assassination. This could have been prevented, sir, had a more vigilant man, a more observant man, a more competent man, a more responsible man, been in your position. I yield back."

The Director knew that his tenure was no longer viable. He also knew that someone had to take the fall. The Select Committee had decided, even before the hearings, that it would be him. He would go back to his office one final time, compose his one-sentence resignation letter, gather his belongings, and leave the Service after twenty-two years.

President Anderson did not afford the Director the dignity of a resignation. He had an election to consider and he needed to show strength and resolve. While watching the Director's testimony with his chief of staff, Anderson said, "I want him fired now. Before he runs to the press to announce that he's resigning. It has to be me who makes the decision, not him. Fire him now, before they take a break. And alert the media. I should have done this on day one."

A score of photographers engulfed the Director as he exited the Capitol and climbed into his limo. "To headquarters," he told the driver. The director's phone binged with a message from the president's chief of staff. *What a prick*, the director thought. "On second thought, just take me home, please."

The FBI's investigation was infinitely more productive than the congressional one. The Conclusion to the FBI's report read:

> *All available evidence points to the conclusion that United States Secret Service Special Agent Jackson Carter acted alone in the assassination of United States President Joshua F. Sheehan in Oslo, Norway. There is no credible evidence that anyone other than Jackson Carter was involved in the planning or execution of the assassination, nor is there any credible evidence that anyone knew in advance about the planned attack. The motivation behind the assassination, based on a letter forensically determined to have been written by Special Agent Carter, appears to have been a religious, cultural and/or social one specifically targeting President Sheehan.*

> *A forensic analysis of Special Agent Carter's home computer revealed that approximately four weeks after being wounded in Middletown, Ohio during an apparent assassination attempt on President Sheehan, Special Agent Carter began accessing materials advocating a Christian resistance to an increasingly secular society and government. LeAnn Carter testified that for many years, she and her husband participated jointly in web-based Bible study. That testimony was consistent with the forensic analysis of Special Agent Carter's computer and LeAnn Carter's*

iPad. LeAnn Carter further testified that she and her husband identified as evangelical Christians.

Interviews with more than eighty co-workers, administration officials, family, and friends revealed no information that Special Agent Carter was planning or considering an attack on the President of the United States. None of the individuals interviewed expressed concerns or reservations about Carter's mental fitness to serve, nor did they reveal any statements reflecting his personal beliefs about President Sheehan or any of his specific policies. Special Agent Carter maintained no social media accounts, nor did any electronic communications reveal such beliefs.

Forensic analysis further revealed that over the course of the ensuing months, Special Agent Carter continued to access materials advocating a Christian resistance to the secularization of the United States. Academic experts offered the opinion that the materials which Special Agent Carter was consuming became increasingly more divergent from traditional understandings of Christian teachings and theology over time.

In February, Special Agent Carter installed a specialized browser on his computer which enabled him to access the "dark web" with complete anonymity. Due to the encryption protocols utilized by this browser, it is not possible to know what, if any, specific material Special Agent Carter may, or may not, have accessed. The frequency of Special Agent Carter's utilization of this specialized browser increased over time, most notably after the announcement of the Nobel Peace Prize in October, two months before the assassination.

Scholars have testified that the dark web is a known source of materials advocating for a Christian uprising in the United States; for a national atonement; for armed resistance to government; for holy war; for the establishment of a Christian nation and a Christian Constitution; for an end to alliances and treaties with non-Christian nations and organizations such as the United Nations, the World Bank, the World Health Organization, and CurTO; and for execution of world leaders, globalists, atheists, and others perceived as heretics. Whether Special Agent Carter accessed any of those specific materials, and, if so, which ones, is neither known nor knowable with current technology.

There is no readily-apparent means by which the assassination of President Joshua Sheehan could have been foreseen or prevented. Interviews with dozens of Secret Service employees and Jackson Carter's co-workers revealed no concerning behaviors. Self-radicalization by an individual actor such as Special Agent Carter remains extremely difficult to identify, recognize, or prevent in advance of a radicalized person's actions in the absence of external indicators of such radicalization.

Buried within the report was one notable conclusion, which was disappointing to the *Joint Congressional Committee on the Assassination of President Joshua F. Sheehan.* "Based on extensive interviews with Special Agent Jackson Carter's wife, LeAnn, as well as on the contents of a handwritten letter to her composed shortly before Agent Carter left for Oslo, there is no credible evidence that LeAnn Carter knew anything about her husband's self-radicalization or planned assassination of President Sheehan in advance."

Chapter 24
Another Test

It must be that the increase [in lynchings] come of the inborn human instinct to imitate — that and man's commonest weakness, his aversion to being unpleasantly conspicuous, pointed at, shunned, as being on the unpopular side. Its other name is Moral Cowardice, and is the commanding feature of the make-up of 9,999 men in 10,000 . . . No revolt against a public infamy or oppression has ever been begun but by the one daring man in 10,000, the rest timidly waiting, and slowly and reluctantly joining, under the influence of that man . . . The abolitionists remember. Privately the public feeling was with them early, but each man was afraid to speak out until he got some hint that his neighbor was feeling privately as he privately felt himself . . .

Why does a crowd pretend to enjoy a lynching? Why does it lift no hand or voice in protest? Only because it would be unpopular to do it, I think; each man is afraid of his neighbor's disapproval — a thing which . . . is more dreaded than wounds and death. When there is to be a lynching the people hitch up and come miles to see it . . . Really to see it? No – they come only because they are afraid to stay at home, lest it be noticed and offensively commented upon." – *Mark Twain, The United States of Lyncherdom, 1901*

It was January. Edward Todd Anderson had been president for less than a month. He had barely had proper time to settle in, yet already he was being forced into making an important decision. The presidential primaries were approaching too quickly and plenty of other candidates had been campaigning and raising money for months. Should he run or not?

On the one hand, he was the incumbent and held that advantage. He was extremely well-qualified. He served as vice president for nearly seven years and now he was the President of the United States. He had fourteen distinguished years as a United States senator, too, and was the rightful heir to Joshua Sheehan's legacy. The sympathy factor certainly helped LBJ win after the Kennedy assassination. Most of the party elders would surely support him. He had been a loyal soldier for decades.

On the other hand – and there was always *on the other hand* with Anderson – there was not a lot of clamoring for him to jump into the race. For one thing, he was sixty-eight years old. But for the facts that President Sheehan had chosen him as vice president and that he had ascended to the presidency, there would be no great sentiment for Edward Todd Anderson to run for president.

By this time, other candidates had gobbled up the best campaign operatives and most of the biggest donors. Polls consistently showed that voters were lukewarm, to put it mildly, about him. Why hadn't he announced that he was running before the assassination? That would have made life simpler. He might have even gotten Joshua's endorsement, although that would have been a two-edged sword. Most of the other hopefuls would have backed off if he had only announced his candidacy then.

"What do you think I should do, Kim?" he asked his chief political strategist. Kim Forsythe had been with him since his Senate days and knew the routine. Anderson wanted poll numbers. Hard, reliable poll numbers. No decisions could be made without them.

"Well, sir, all of our polling indicates that if you were to announce your candidacy, you would probably win the nomination. No one in the current field has gotten much traction. None of them poll above twenty percent."

"What does 'probably' mean?" Anderson asked.

Kim knew that the president wanted a number, something concrete, so she fabricated one. "Sixty-five, seventy percent chance if you get in now." It was a reasonable guess.

"That isn't very high for an incumbent, is it?" Anderson asked.

"No, sir, but you would clearly have the advantage. You would be the clear frontrunner for the nomination."

"Why aren't my chances higher?"

"Israel, sir. The Israel strike continues to be very divisive. You are unavoidably saddled with that for the time being. If we can successfully manage that issue, you will win the nomination," Kim said.

"Can we? Manage it, I mean."

"Yes, sir. We are confident that we can."

"OK. Let me think it over. When do I need to have a decision?" Edward Todd Anderson hated deadlines, especially looming ones.

"Frankly, today would be best, sir," Kim said. She hoped that would coax an answer out of him within a week.

President Anderson would be challenged for the nomination by several candidates still furious about CurTOgate and the United States' participation in the assault on Israel. While all of those challengers acknowledged, to some degree, that CurTO had been successful in enforcing the global peace, and praised the response to North Korea, they nevertheless held fast that the action against Israel had been a horrific mistake, a betrayal. Other challengers sided with President Sheehan and supported the CurTO alliance. The anti-CurTO candidates missed, or consciously ignored the fact that it was precisely *because* of that action that CurTO continued to be successful.

Anderson's entry into the race cleared most of the primary field. The party machine and Anderson's narrow win in South Carolina convinced the candidates who were running as Sheehan legacy candidates to cede that lane to the president. To do otherwise would convey division and possibly cost the party the White House. The two candidates who were most critical of what the administration had done to Israel stayed in, which helped Anderson, splitting that voting bloc.

President Anderson tried his best to navigate a middle ground. It was where he was most at home. He knew that the public was divided and that his general election opponent would make the issue the focus of the campaign, and he was right. President Anderson didn't want a United States attack on a staunch and long-time ally to strip him of his presidency.

His pollsters and political operatives guided him through the issue. Every squishy word and muddy phrase was workshopped and poll-tested. Kim focus-grouped dozens of possible wording choices and positions. On the trail, Anderson praised President Sheehan's response to North Korea as "bold and necessary," he harbored "deep and serious concerns" about the strike against Israel, he made it known that he "was not consulted" about Israel in advance. He promised "sweeping changes" to the national security team. Things might have turned out "differently" had he been consulted in advance, he assured the voters. He managed to avoid saying *how* they might have been different or how he would have responded. His main objectives whenever he was asked about Israel were to answer the question as briefly and vaguely as possible and to change the subject to something else. Anything else.

The early polls indicated that the obfuscation and avoidance strategy was working. Edward Todd Anderson was ahead, slightly, throughout the campaign. The electorate didn't really care that much for him, but neither did they dislike him. They felt about him like they would feel about watered-down, unsweetened iced tea. Unoffensive, but uninspiring. If one word could describe his brief presidency, it would probably be "dull." "Boring," "flat," "lifeless," would do, as well.

Two weeks before the election, India launched an attack on Pakistan. It had been simmering for years and it finally boiled over in October. India was alarmed by the build-up of arms not far from the border. Tensions over a disputed territory within Pakistan, but long-coveted by India, erupted into an Indian attack. The border treaties which India and Pakistan had both certified in order to be admitted into CurTO unequivocally showed that the land belonged to Pakistan.

For the third time, CurTO was called upon to re-establish the peace. The secretaries of Defense and State, President Sheehan's holdover secretaries, consulted with the CurTO allies. President Anderson still hadn't gotten around to replacing the secretaries. The alliance was ready and willing to respond to India's aggression. The unpredictable tragedy of fate left the decision in the hands of President Edward Todd Anderson.

The Secretary of Defense briefed the president. "How do you want to proceed, sir?" the Secretary asked.

"Do we have assets in place?" the president asked.

"We do, sir," the Secretary assured him. "As do our allies in the region." President Anderson was paralyzed. The decision was all too binary. He was consumed by the political ramifications, by the election, by how history might judge him. He had watched President Sheehan's popularity nosedive after Israel. Anderson couldn't allow his to do the same. Not now. Not with an election in two weeks. The public response was unpredictable, uncertain.

The president's team offered conflicting advice, with most, particularly Secretary Jill Mendoza, advocating for honoring the CurTO treaty, and a few urging caution and restraint. Exercising caution appealed to the president. He felt the stares. It was all happening too fast. He needed time.

"Sir?" The Secretary of Defense asked. Every eye in the room was on the president.

"Tell them to stand down," President Anderson directed. "The United States will not be involved."

"Yes, sir," the Secretary of Defense replied.

Everyone in the room knew what the president's order meant. The CurTO alliance was dead.

Edward Todd Anderson didn't get to deliver an election-night victory speech. The election wasn't called until late the next morning. Anderson won, but barely. His polling and political instincts were proven right. There would be protests and charges and lawsuits over the outcome of the election, but the result stood. The pundits would debate for weeks why he won and whether his retreat from CurTO helped or hurt.

Jill Mendoza delivered her resignation as Secretary of State just an hour after President Anderson ordered the stand-down. President Anderson expected it and accepted it. "Thank you, madam Secretary" was all he said, barely looking up. He had his own people in mind and was finally ready to install them, anyway. People more focused on an American agenda, less dedicated to international entanglements and suspect alliances. That, he concluded, was what the American people wanted. Let's take care of ourselves, above all else. Jill Mendoza and CurTO didn't figure into his plans.

The last thing that Jill took in as she turned away from the president and the Resolute Desk was Joshua's curling stone, still atop the credenza. Did Anderson leave it there intentionally, or had he just not gotten around to moving it? The irony of Edward Todd Anderson behind the Resolute Desk struck her. The personality just didn't match the furniture.

Jill took her final walk down the corridor – it was starker and more antiseptic now than it had been during the past eight years – to the exit from the White House for the last time. A cold, wet wind slapped her face as she stepped outside. She lowered her head, unfurled her black umbrella, and dashed out to her awaiting limo.

"To the State Department, ma'am?"

"No. Take me home, please."

Jill needed to call her daughters. Baxter, old and tired and lonely, would be happy to have her home early.

Appendix

For readers who aren't intimately familiar with the sport of curling, a brief introduction to its origins and history, how it is played, the surface that it is played on, and the equipment that it is played with, may be helpful. Its spirit, too, is an integral part of the game. Curling's nickname – *The Roarin' Game* – comes from the sound of the forty-pound granite stones rumbling down a sheet of pebbled ice.

The first thing that you are likely to notice in watching curling is that almost everyone looks happy. Whether learning to curl for the first time or experienced curlers playing in a league or a bonspiel, curlers are smiling and laughing. Curling, above everything else, is fun. How could it not be – playing on a team, sliding stones down a 150-foot-long sheet of ice to a target that looks like a bullseye, guiding and listening to the clacking stones as they crash and carom into each other?

Curling is probably most familiar to people from being prominently featured on television every four years during the Winter Olympics. It is one of the most-watched events. To many, it is simply a curiosity. To others, though, it is mesmerizing.

Although the consensus is that the game originated in Scotland more than five centuries ago, there are still the occasional heated and emotional arguments claiming the Netherlands as its true home. Regardless, it was in Scotland where the game took root and flourished. A quick primer on the history of the game is in order.

The earliest *physical* evidence of curling being played comes from a curling stone inscribed with the date "1511," which was discovered when a pond in Dunblane, Scotland, was drained hundreds of years later. It is the oldest known curling stone still in existence, although it bears little resemblance to the stones that are used today. The "1511" curling stone resides at the Sterling Smith Art Gallery and Museum in Stirling, Scotland.

The earliest known *written* reference to curling also comes from Scotland and dates back nearly 500 years. In 1541, a notary named John McQuhin recorded a challenge made by John Sclater, a monk at Paisley Abbey outside of Glasgow, to Gavin Hamilton, the lay governor of Paisley Abbey. It seems that Gavin Hamilton was intensely disliked by nearly everyone, but because a monk could not possibly challenge a governor to a duel, the monk instead challenged him to a curling match. History does not record whether the challenge was accepted, or who won the match, if indeed it was contested, but the monk had made his point.

The first *artistic* depiction of curling comes from 1565, when Flemish artist Pieter Bruegel the Elder completed two paintings, *Winter Landscape with Ice Skaters and Bird Trap* and *The Hunters in the Snow*. Each painting depicts an outdoor curling scene. They represent the oldest known visual representations of curling. Only men are playing.

The first reference to curling in *literature* is found in a 1639 poem by Henry Adamson. Adamson wrote in *The Muses Threnodie*, that James Gall "was much given to pastime, as golf, archerie, curling; and Joviall companie." Scottish poet David Gray wrote of whisky-drinking curlers at the Luggie Water, a stream in Kirkintilloch. Of course, they were drinking whisky. They were curling and they were in Scotland.

The first formal curling society, or club, was apparently established in Kilsyth, Scotland in 1716. Only apparently, because, as with most matters related to curling, that honor is disputed by others claiming to have been the first, including curling societies in Kinross and Muthill. The Kilsyth Curling Club, at more than 300 years old, still exists today.

The earliest known written description of the game itself is found in Thomas Pennant's 1772 book, *A Tour in Scotland and Voyage to the Hebrides*. Two-and-a-half centuries later, the description ably and succinctly depicts the modern game:

> *Of the sports of these parts that of Curling is a favorite; and one unknown in England. It is an amusement of the winter, and played on the ice, by sliding from one mark to another great stones of forty to seventy pounds weight, of hemispherical form, with an iron or wooden handle at top. The object of the player is to lay his stone as near to the mark as possible, to guard that of his partner, which has been well laid before, or to strike off that of his antagonist.*

Poets have long celebrated the sport of curling, including Robert Burns, the legendary 18th century Scottish poet, in 1786's *Tam Samson's Elegy*:

> *When winter muffles up his cloak,*
> *And binds the mire like a rock;*
> *When to the loughs the Curlers flock,*
> *Wi' gleesome speed,*
> *Wha will they station at the cock?*
> *Tam Samson's dead!*

> *He was the king o' a' the Core,*
> *To guard, or draw, or wick a bore,*
> *Or up the rink like Jehu roar,*
> *In time o' need;*
> *But now he lags on Death's hog-score*
> *Tam Samson's dead!*

Curling, by the early 1800s, was professed to have definite medical benefits. Dr. Alexander Pennecuik wrote:

To Curle on the ice does greatly please;
Being a Manly Scottish Exercise,
It clears the Brains, stirs up the Native Heat,
And gives a gallant Appetite for Meat.

On July 25, 1838, the Grand Caledonian Curling Club, which would become the national governing body for the sport in Scotland, was founded at the Waterloo Hotel in Edinburgh. The Grand Caledonian Curling Club was formed to bring some sense of order to the chaos of each individual club playing by its own particular set of rules and with its own particular kinds of stones. It was granted a royal charter in 1843 by Queen Victoria, who became fascinated by the game after viewing a curling exhibition on the wooden floor of Scone Palace in Perth. The Queen even tried to throw a stone, but it proved "too heavy for her delicate arm." After the exhibition, Prince Albert was presented with "a splendid pair of Curling Stones, made of finest Ailsa Craig granite." Renamed the Royal Caledonian Curling Club after receiving a royal charter, the first formalized set of curling rules was adopted.

Around the time of the Royal Club's formation, stones made of Ailsa Craig granite were becoming increasingly popular, both in Scotland and Canada. Ailsa Craig is a small island ten miles to the west of the Scottish mainland, the remnant of a volcano which erupted sixty million years ago as Europe and North America pulled apart and Pangea was completing its disassemblage. When the volcano cooled, it left two kinds of granite. Varieties of granite which have never, to this day, been found anywhere else in the world other than on Ailsa Craig.

Blue hone granite is the rarer of the two, and holds the key to making the best curling stones in the world. Blue hone granite, because of its molecular structure and mineral composition, is completely impervious to water penetration. Water infiltrating the stone would repeatedly freeze and thaw during the stone's lifetime, causing it to weaken, crack, and ultimately fail. Blue hone granite, used for that part of the curling stone contacting the ice, eliminates that issue.

The bulk of an Ailsa Craig curling stone is made from the slightly more abundant common green granite, also found exclusively on Ailsa Craig. Common green granite is similar to blue hone granite, although slightly better suited to absorbing the non-stop collisions with other stones during the course of a game and a stone's useful lifetime. Because of these unique characteristics, Ailsa Craig curling stones may last upwards of forty or fifty years. Today, the only stones used in Olympic and other high-level competitions are Ailsa Craig stones, and they are manufactured exclusively by Andrew Kay & Co. Ltd. in Scotland.

Just as they have done with curling, poets have long celebrated Ailsa Craig, including John Keats in his poem, "To Ailsa Rock":

Hearken, thou craggy ocean pyramid!
Give answer from thy voice – the sea-fowl's screams!
When were thy shoulders mantled in huge streams?
When from the sun was thy broad forehead hid?
How long is't since the mighty Power bid
Thee heave to airy sleep from fathom dreams –
Sleep in the lap of thunder or sunbeams –
Or when gray clouds are thy cold coverlid?
Thou answerest not, for thou art dead asleep.
Thy life is but two dead eternities –
The last in air, the former in the deep!
First with the whales, last with the eagle skies!
Drown'd wast thou till an earthquake made thee steep,
Another cannot wake thy giant size!

Prior to 1838, there had been few serious attempts to unify or codify the rules of curling, although the Duddingston Curling Society had drawn up a set of regulations several years prior. Each club played by their own particular rules, and matches between different clubs required extensive negotiations over how the games would be played. With the formation of the Royal Caledonian Curling Club as a governing body, a uniform set of rules was finally adopted. With those rules now the standard, the modern sport of curling rapidly evolved and grew in popularity in Scotland and beyond.

One of those initial rules had, perhaps, the most significant effect on the game's development. Rule 9 required that "All Curling Stones shall be of a circular shape." Before the adoption of the rules, curlers played with any stones they pleased. One such stone was named "Whirlie," a large, triangular stone. Curlers loved naming their favorite stones. A man who played with Whirlie wrote this sad tale of playing with the stone. It reads like a love letter:

> *It was the first stone which the writer of this ever played with. It being our first attempt at curling, we were appointed to lead, which we happened to do in such a manner that Whirlie was uniformly laid on or near the Tee; to remove it from the position on which it had taken rest was no easy matter; because, should the stone which was destined to remove it strike any one of the angled corners, round went Whirlie, round and round, without ever shifting from its position. Stimulated with the success of our first attempt at curling, we went early next day on the field of action with Whirlie in our hand. But to our utter disappointment, dear fellows, a Curling Court was held upon him, and he was unanimously condemned to perpetual banishment. This, however, we could not stand. We got him mounted in a more modern and fashionable uniform, by rounding his more acute angles, and in this capacity we introduced him as a stranger on his ancient*

domain. A bad character and bad habits, however, have a mark put upon them, and are not easily surmounted. The rogue, in spite of our endeavours, was still seen in his new shape and in his habits likewise, for his roundabout way of going to work never forsook him, and again and again has he been banished from, and restored to the society of his fellows; until at last we had the galling mortification to hear his final doom decreed by the present Baronet that this favourite stone should be played with no more. Since then, the Ice, and all the curlers, except ourselves, who well knew him once, know him no more, and perhaps forever. But many are the lingering emotions and fond affection with which we have sought after him; nor will we desist from the search until we in our turn shall be consigned to oblivion.

Curling was introduced to North America, primarily to eastern Canada, by Scottish emigrants, in the eighteenth and nineteenth centuries. The first Canadian curling club was established in Montreal in 1807. During the 1800s, curling expanded across the entire breadth of Canada, where curlers sometimes played with "stones" made of iron, granite, or even wood.

It was not until the middle of the 1800s that women began curling in any significant numbers, although there are occasional references to them playing in historical accounts of curling's evolution. The first known representation of women playing the game is found in an 1859 watercolor painting from Scotland entitled *Eglinton Ladies 1859 Watercolour*. That painting was used for the cover of *The Shattered Curling Stone*, with the gracious permission of the Scottish Curling Trust.

I n order to understand modern curling, it is essential to understand both the surface on which it is played and the specialized equipment which it requires. Curling is played on a much different kind of ice surface than hockey or figure skating, both of which require smooth ice. Curling ice is a different beast. Curling is played on "pebbled" ice, which is created and maintained through a meticulous blend of art and science. While hockey and figure skating ice is smooth and renewed using a Zamboni, curling ice is a different animal altogether. First and foremost, curling ice must be completely level. A variation of one-eighth or one-quarter of an inch would make a curling sheet virtually unplayable in competition. The second notable feature is that a Zamboni is *never never ever* used on true curling ice. Curling ice also requires a very specific temperature, controlled by thousands of feet of piping or tubing an inch or two below the surface of the ice, through which a very cold brine or glycol is pumped.

Once a perfectly level sheet of ice at the proper temperature is laid down, the real, tedious process of making curling ice begins. "Pebbling" is what makes a curling stone travel as far as it does and enables it to curl, or turn, by reducing the area of the stone actually touching the ice and thus reducing friction. Ice technicians use warm, purified, deionized water with as few dissolved solids as possible to pebble the curling ice. Pebblers walk backwards down each sheet, with a tank of warm water on their backs, heated to around 120 degrees Fahrenheit, while waving an attached wand, similar to the aspergillum used by priests to sprinkle holy water. The wand disperses tiny droplets of warm water onto the ice. The droplets adhere to the ice and freeze almost instantly, creating tiny bumps on the ice. It may take several passes to apply sufficient pebble to the ice. The result is a sheet of ice which resembles the skin of an orange.

When the pebbling is complete, a scraper is pushed up and down the ice. The scraper is a large, expensive piece of machinery with what amounts to a four or five-foot wide razor blade attached to the bottom. As the scraper is pushed down the ice surface, it shaves off the top of the pebble so that the remaining pebble is of a uniform height, creating consistency in how a stone behaves as it travels down the ice. Uneven pebble would cause the curling stone to wobble and misbehave as it slides down the sheet. After the ice has been shaved, a soft, wide, sheepskin mop is pushed across the length of the sheets to remove the bits of ice which were shaved off by the scraper. At last, the ice is ready for play. The stones will glide across the top of the pebble.

Curlers use two kinds of specialized equipment unique to the game – curling shoes and brooms, which really aren't very similar to what are commonly thought of as brooms, although they once were. Curling shoes have a different sole on each shoe. When curlers push out of the hack to deliver a stone, which is essentially like a starting block in track, but embedded into the ice, they push off with their dominant leg. The shoe that is used to push out from the hack has a gripper on the sole, enabling the player to walk on the ice without slipping and to maintain the traction needed for sweeping. The grippers are made of a high-traction rubber, which provides the curler with stability when walking on the ice.

On the sole of the other shoe, which remains flat on the ice while delivering a stone, is a slider, usually made of Teflon. Teflon has an extremely low coefficient of friction, so that it can slide down the ice without slowing down the curler. Teflon on ice is an extremely slippery combination. Balancing on the slider foot, the player slides down the ice gripping the stone's handle to deliver it.

The broom, or "besom" in old Scotland, is a bit like a sponge mop, only dry. Attached to a handle made of lightweight fiberglass or carbon fiber is a brush often made of cordura nylon over foam, which is the part of the broom which actually touches the ice. By applying downward pressure on the broom and quickly sweeping (or "sooping" in old Scots vernacular) it back and forth in front of the sliding stone, the sweeper warms the ice, which reduces friction and allows the stone to travel farther and straighter. Through sweeping, players can guide the sliding stone to its desired location. Sweeping is the aerobic exercise part of the game, requiring more energy than delivering the stone. You might occasionally still hear some old-time skips yelling, "Soop, soop!" to the sweepers. Sweeping can add as much as eight or ten feet of distance to a shot if done properly. What a sweeper may never do is touch, or "burn," the stone with the broom.

Yet another bit of curling equipment, not often seen on the ice in modern play, is noted by the Reverend John Kerr in his 1890 *History of Curling*:

An indispensable equipment, according to a majority of curlers, is a flask . . . A flask is useful, but not indispensable. It is certainly dangerous to the feet if it affects the head . . . [E]very skip must take special care to keep this equipment in its proper place.

With the ice prepared, curling shoes on, broom in hand, and stones in place, the game can finally begin. Curling rules are fairly simple, although execution is quite complex, much like chess. In fact, curling is often referred to as "chess on ice." The ability to envision two or three shots ahead is critical to success at higher levels of competition and helpful at lower levels.

A curling match is generally scheduled for eight or ten ends, similar to innings in baseball. In a traditional match, each team consists of four players, teams alternating shots, although there is also mixed doubles curling, with two-person teams consisting of one man and one woman. Each player on a four-person team – lead, second, vice, and skip – takes two shots per end, meaning that a total of sixteen stones, eight per team, will be thrown by the two teams in each end.

The skip stands in the house, which consists of a twelve-foot wide circle, within which are smaller four-foot and eight-foot circles, as well as the button, or bulls-eye, which together comprise the scoring area. The skip directs the shooter and the sweepers as to what kind of shot to attempt and exactly where the skip wants the stone to come to rest.

The skip may want a shot to land in the house, but might also want the shooter to place a guard in front of a stone that is already there or to place a guard in anticipation of protecting a future stone placed in the house.

A guard protects the stone which is in the house from being "taken out" by an opponent's stone. The end continues with teams alternating shots, setting guards, knocking opponents' stones out of the house, and tapping their own stones closer to the button, trying ultimately to get the highest number of stones closest to the center of the house.

Players can control how their stones behave by gently turning the stone's handle either clockwise or counterclockwise upon release. A clockwise spin will make a stone curl from left to right, while a counterclockwise spin will make it curl from right to left. Whether or not that is the origin of the game's name is another matter of some dispute. The sound of the forty-pound stones rumbling down the ice, and they are noisy, gave curling its nickname of *The Roarin' Game*.

There are at least two competing theories as to how curling got its name. The one which is most often told is that the name derives from the way that shooters can make the stones turn, or curl, by turning the handle upon release. Another theory is that it derives from the Scottish word "curr," which describes a low, rumbling sound. The first theory makes for a better story, but the second may well be more accurate.

Once all sixteen stones have been played, the score for that end is tallied. Scoring begins with the stone that is closest to the button, or the center of the house. The stone need not be on the button, just closest to it. If a red-handled stone is closest to the button and a yellow-handled stone is the second closest, the red team gets one point. If a red stone is both the closest *and* second closest, red gets two points, and so on. In theory, therefore, one team could garner as many as eight points in an end, although that very, very rarely happens. A three or four point end is a significant score. With the score tallied, the process repeats itself for the next end.

Obviously, it is a big advantage to be taking the final shot in an end, which is known as having "the hammer." The hammer goes to the team which lost the previous end. Teams with the hammer would like to score two or three points in an end, while the team without the hammer would prefer to limit their opponent to one point, or even to "steal" a point for themselves when playing without the hammer.

That, in abbreviated form, is the history of the game, along with a description of the modern game. During the next Winter Olympics, you will be able to amaze your friends with what you know about the game. Now, you can begin *Negative Peace*.

About the Author

DAVID S. FLORIG lives in Ocean Park, Maine. He is a member of the Maine Writers and Publishers Alliance. Florig is past-president of the Pine Tree Curling Club in Portland, as well as a member of the Belfast Curling Club in Belfast, Maine. *The Stones of Ailsa Craig* was his debut novel and paid homage to Belfast, Maine; the glorious Maine coast; and the ancient Scottish sport of curling. Set in present-day Belfast, Maine and 1880s Scotland, the novel takes a sometimes dark look into one man's loss, loneliness, obsession, and quest for vengeance. Rich in curling and Maine history, *The Stones of Ailsa Craig* is a work of historical fiction and was named Best Historical Fiction of 2023 by *Indies Today.* It was also a 2023 Finalist for the *American Writing Awards.*

The Shattered Curling Stone, published in 2024, tells the allegorical story of Ailsa MacLaren, a Scottish girl who takes to the ice in the 1880s at age twelve to learn the game of curling from her father. Along the way, she encounters roadblocks and setbacks as she continues to grow and excel at "the manly Scottish exercise," including one particularly unexpected, dangerous, obstacle. *The Shattered Curling Stone* pays tribute to brave, fearless women who dare to go where they're told they shouldn't.

In 2023, Florig organized and led a group of ninety Maine authors as *Maine Authors for Lewiston,* who raised money to support victims and families of the tragic events in Lewiston on October 25th.

David grew up in South Jersey before retiring to Maine, where he lives with his wife, Nancy, and their rescue dog, Lily Munster. Adopted as an infant by Charles and Marjorie Florig for $130, he has seen just a single, black-and white picture of his birth mother.

For years, David practiced law in Pennsylvania and New Jersey. Following his legal career, he served as the Executive Director of two nonprofits - *Court Appointed Special Advocates of Burlington County* (New Jersey) and the *West Philadelphia Alliance for Children. WePAC* trained and deployed volunteers to open shuttered elementary school libraries in Philadelphia, and for his work on behalf of Philadelphia's children, he was honored as one of the inaugural *GameChangers* by KYW Newsradio in celebration of Black History Month.

David Florig can be reached at david@davidflorig.com or through his website at www.davidflorig.com.